,75

THE SECRET HOUR

FIREFLY BEACH

"A beautifully textured summertime read."
—*Publishers Weekly* (starred review)

"Rice does a masterful job of telling this powerful story
of love and reconciliation." —*Booklist*

SUMMER LIGHT

"Few . . . authors are able to portray the complex and
contradictory emotions that bind family members as
effortlessly as Rice. . . . This poignant tale of love, loss, and
reconciliation will have readers hitting the bookstores."
—*Publishers Weekly*

"Rice's fans will enjoy this well-spun yarn."
—*The Orlando Sentinel*

"The prolific Rice skillfully blends romance with magic."
—*Booklist*

DREAM COUNTRY

"A moving story of love and reunion . . . an absolute
joy to read . . . I finally put *Dream Country* down at two A.M.
and almost called in sick the next day to finish it."
—*The Denver Post*

"Superb . . . stunning." —*Houston Chronicle*

"Captivating . . . *Dream Country* will cast a spell
on readers." —*The Orlando Sentinel*

"A transcendent story about the power of hope and
family love . . . a compelling plot and nuanced character
portrayals contribute to the emotional impact. . . . Rice
creates believable dramatic tension." —*Publishers Weekly*

"Engaging . . . a taut thriller . . . Rice's descriptive gifts
are impressive." —*Minneapolis Star-Tribune*

"A story so real it will be deeply etched into the hearts of its readers . . . Rice once again delivers a wonderfully complex and full-bodied romance." —*Booklist*

"Highly readable . . . moving . . . a well-paced plot . . . Rice pulls off some clever surprises."
—*Pittsburgh Post-Gazette*

FOLLOW THE STARS HOME

"Addictive . . . irresistible." —*People*

"Involving, moving . . . stays with the reader long after the last page is turned." —*The Denver Post*

"Uplifting . . . The novel's theme—love's miraculous ability to heal—has the ingredients to warm readers' hearts."
—*Publishers Weekly*

"Rice has once again created a tender story of a new family unit, where love and loyalty are more important than biology and where learning to trust again opens the door to happiness." —*Library Journal*

"A moving romance that also illuminates the tangled resentments, ties and allegiances of family life . . . Rice spins a web of three families intertwined by affection and conflict. . . . [She] is a gifted storyteller with a keen sense of both the possibilities and contingencies of life."
—*Times Record*, Brunswick, ME

"Powerhouse author Luanne Rice returns with a novel guaranteed to wrench your emotional heartstrings. Deeply moving and rich with emotion, *Follow the Stars Home* is another of Ms. Rice's classics." —*Romantic Times*

"Beautiful, touching . . . Emotions run deep in this heartwarming tale. . . . This unforgettable journey will stay with you long after you've read the last chapter."
—*Rendezvous*

CLOUD NINE

HOME FIRES

Also by Luanne Rice

with Joseph Monninger

the

PERFECT
SUMMER

Luanne Rice

BANTAM BOOKS

THE PERFECT SUMMER
A Bantam Book

PUBLISHING HISTORY
Bantam mass market edition / August 2003
Bantam mass market reissue / July 2006

Published by Bantam Dell
A Division of Random House, Inc.
New York, New York

This is a work of fiction. Names, characters, places, and incidents either
are the product of the author's imagination or are used fictitiously.
Any resemblance to actual persons, living or dead, events,
or locales is entirely coincidental.

Bantam Books and the rooster colophon are registered trademarks of
Random House, Inc.

ISBN-13: 978-0-553-58404-2

Printed in the United States of America
Published simultaneously in Canada

www.bantamdell.com

OPM   20 19 18

To

Diana Atwood Johnson

with love

ACKNOWLEDGMENTS

Marguerite Mattison has the most beautiful garden in Connecticut, reflective of her kind, generous, loving spirit. No one could have a better friend and neighbor.

Donald Cleary: I'd ride the train to the ends of the earth for him.

I am grateful to Kevin J. Markey, Special Agent of the FBI, and John J. Markey, Retired Special Agent of the FBI. Their help in imagining an investigation of white-collar crime was invaluable; the mistakes and creative license are all my own.

Lynda Hunnicutt and Lynn Giroux, my trusted, wonderful bankers, gave me excellent insights into a very different sort of banker, and I thank them very much.

Thank you to my lifelong friend, Kim Dorfman, for everything.

The real "tis": Heather, Hannah, and Nora McNeil, Carol Kerr and Sister Leslie CHS . . . thank you for everything. *Faugh a ballagh!* Hiberian thanks and love also to Brother Luke Armour, O.C.S.O.

Love and thanks to Don, Marilyn, John, Dan, Emily, Nick, and Maggie Walsh. Dev Waldron (aka "Duke" of Duke and the Esoterics) really knows how to put together a house band and take it on the road.

The healing powers of Dr. Elizabeth Moreno are so strong, they reach all the way from Italy; *mille grazie*.

Gratitude to Colin McEnroe for all the poetry and ideas.

Love to Audrey and Bob Loggia.

Much appreciation to Domestic Violence Valley Shore Services, especially Susan Caruso, Mary Lou Cucinotta, Leah Tassone, Ellie Ford, and all the volunteers who make such important work possible.

Gratitude to Rob Peirce, Jackie, Nina, Betsy, Paula, Sandy, Leah and Leah, and Jolaine Johnson . . . and all the others, with love.

Thank you to McLean Hospital.

Susan Feaster has been endlessly helpful and supportive, and I thank her.

Love to Mia (Akuma) and the BDG: Ami (Tristin), Hanna (Releena), Kathryn (Akane), Tiffie (Tiffi), and Kungfu Panda...great friends on the road to great things (keep writing and drawing).

Much gratitude to Irwyn Applebaum, Nita Taublib, Tracy Devine, Micahlyn Whitt, Barb Burg, Susan Corcoran, Jaime Jennings, Betsy Hulsebosch, Molly Williams, Cynthia "Wendy" Lasky, Carolyn Schwartz, and everyone at Bantam Books; many thanks to Phyllis Mandel and everyone else at Westminster.

Last but most certainly not least, boundless love and thanks to William Twigg Crawford for a lifetime of summers, and for his support every second of the endless winter. Paul James: same thing. May the tides be propitious and the breezes fair, may the stripers always be running, may we continue this odyssey together. Always, forever.

In the depth of winter,
I finally learned that there was in
me an invincible summer.

—ALBERT CAMUS

I T WAS A PERFECT SUMMER DAY.

That was Bay McCabe's thought as she stood in her backyard, a basket of just-washed clothes at her feet, a late-afternoon sea breeze blowing off the Sound. The garden was spectacular this year: Old roses, hollyhocks, delphinium, day lilies, and Rosa rugosa were in bloom. Birds dipped into the water pooled in a rock cleft, and thick green stonecrop softened the contours of granite ledge.

Bay felt almost shocked with the beauty of it all, and she forced herself to put down the clothespins and pay attention. Life is made up of golden moments: She had learned that at her grandmother's knee.

Annie and Billy were at the beach with friends, and Peg was at Little League practice. It was a rare thing for Bay to have the house and yard to herself during the summer, and she intended to take advantage of every minute. She had called Sean at the bank, to remind him of his promise to pick up Peg from practice. Bay had met her best friend, Tara O'Toole, at the beach for a swim, and now she was going to hang the wash on the line and wait for everyone to come home for dinner.

Sunlight streamed down on her red hair and freckled arms. She wore shorts and a sleeveless white shirt, and she worked quickly, from years of watching her grandmother. Mary O'Neill had shown her how it was done: one wooden clothespin in her mouth, the other clipping sheets to the line. Sean teased that the neighbors would judge them, think he wasn't making enough money if his wife had to hang laundry out to dry.

He even wanted to hire a gardener. Never mind that digging in the dirt was one of her favorite things, that trying to outdo Tara in the competition—the only real one between them: to grow the tallest sunflowers and hollyhocks and most beautiful roses and prettiest pots of lemondrop marigolds—gave her reason to get up at dawn every morning.

Every morning, she went out to water the garden during the quiet hour before anyone else woke up, waving at Tara doing the same thing in her garden across the creek, then returning inside to make breakfast. All through the day, while her kids were out and about, she would return to the garden to nurture her plants—pruning, watering, feeding the roots. How could Sean not understand how important that was to her? How could he really think that Mary O'Neill's granddaughter would ever let her garden be cared for by a stranger?

Bay just laughed and kissed Sean, said he was too good to worry about what people thought about a little dirt under her fingernails or a few sheets flapping on the line. Her granny was from the old country, and Bay was a banker's wife, but she had learned the simple pleasures as a child and never forgotten them. When she had finished hanging the laundry, the bright clothes looked sharp against the blue sky: signal flags in a painting.

"Mom," Billy called, tearing around the corner of the white-shingled house. He had wet hair, sandy feet, and a wild look in his blue eyes that revealed his worry that something in life might happen without him. "What are we doing tonight? Are we going miniature golfing after dinner, like Dad said? Because if we are, can I ask Russell to come with us?"

"Sure, honey," Bay said, smiling at her eleven-year-old son. He had his father's golden coloring; even with sunblock, his skin turned honey brown and, to his sisters' chagrin, didn't freckle. "Where's Annie?"

"Right behind me," he said, glancing over his shoulder. "I think she's going to ask if she can invite someone, too. It's okay with me if she does."

"It is, is it?" Bay asked, suppressing a smile. She had noticed her son growing up this summer. He had grown two inches since last year. He would be tall, blond, and handsome, just like his dad. And his attitude toward his sister's friends had taken a radical shift from the teasing and tormenting of summers past.

Just then the phone rang inside the house, a high trill. Bay turned toward the door, but Billy was faster. "I'll get it," he called, again making her smile. Just last week Tara had said, "This is the summer your son gets socially activated. He's got an 'on' button that's going to be the bane of your existence. He's got his mother's eyes, and his father's personality . . . the girls had better watch out."

Annie must have entered the house through the front door, and answered the phone before her brother. She stood on the back steps in her blue tank suit—for once not covered by a towel or an oversized T-shirt, straight hair wet and drying reddish-gold in the sun, holding the portable phone out to her mother.

Bay gazed at her twelve-year-old daughter, knowing she felt awkward and stocky, feeling a flood of love in the same instant her attention was captured by the gutter overhead: just over the back porch, dangling by one bracket, damaged in an early spring nor'easter. Tonight, again, Bay would remind Sean to fix it or—of course—hire someone to do it. The thoughts passed in an instant. Bay blinked, and Annie was still there, holding the phone.

"Who's calling?" Bay asked.

"It's Peg," Annie said, frowning. "She's still at the field. Daddy didn't pick her up."

Bay took the phone. "Peg?" she said.

"Mommy, I thought you said Daddy was coming. I waited and waited, but he's not here. Did I do the wrong thing? Was I supposed to get a ride from Mrs. Jensen?"

"No, Peggy," Bay said, feeling a wave of frustration at Sean—how could he have forgotten their nine-year-old? "You didn't do anything wrong. Is someone with you? You're not alone at the park, are you?"

"Mr. Brown is here. He let me use his phone," Peg said, her voice starting to quiver. "He said he'd give me a ride, but I didn't want to leave in case Daddy came."

"Stay there, honey," Bay said, already reaching for her bag. "I'll come get you right now."

THE DRIVE TO THE LITTLE LEAGUE FIELD, ALONG SHORE Road and past the golf course, took nearly fifteen minutes. With late June came summer people, vacationing from all over, and the beach traffic was heavy. Bay looked at her watch and tried not to worry—although she didn't know Peg's coach very well, Sean seemed to like him. Wylie Brown owned a bait-and-tackle shop on the inlet, and Sean often stopped in to provision his boat for the fishing trips he took to Block Island and the canyon.

But where was Sean? How could he have forgotten? Bay had spoken with him herself; she had called the bank just three hours ago to remind him. He had had a loan committee meeting that afternoon, and he'd told her he would be finished in time to head down to the ball field to pick up their youngest. Bay had asked him to try to make time to pitch to her . . . Sean had sounded busy, distracted, but Bay knew how happy Peg would be, just as Bay used to be thrilled to play ball with *her* father.

Pulling into the dirt parking lot, Bay saw Peg and a sandy-haired man playing catch under a maple tree. At the sight of her mother's Volvo, Peg threw the ball to him and ran to the parking lot. She was small for her age, and streaked with dirt as if she'd slid into the plate.

"He's still not here," Peg said, green eyes glittering with disappointment. "He said he would be."

"Something must have come up at work," Bay said, feeling a pinch in her heart, the first in a long time. Was it starting again? Back during the troubles last winter, Tara had told her to quit making excuses for him. Bay hadn't taken the advice; she didn't want her kids to see their dad in a bad light.

"He said he'd pitch to me," Peg said, worry lines between her eyebrows as Bay motioned for her to climb into the back seat.

"I know, Peggy," Bay said, glancing back. "He was looking forward to it. Maybe you two can hit a few before dinner, when he gets home." Peg's coach started toward the car, but Bay felt too off balance to talk. So she just waved, calling "Thank you!" Then, quickly, she drove out of the lot, away from the shady field.

SEAN DIDN'T COME HOME FOR DINNER, AND HE DIDN'T call. They lived in an old farmhouse just off Shore Road, down a long driveway that took them through the marsh that marked the eastern edge of Hubbard's Point. Just across Eight Mile River—more of a tidal creek, really, a tributary of the Gill River—the Point was one of Black Hall's beach areas. Sean and Bay and Tara had been childhood friends there, and Tara had inherited her grandmother's small cottage. Bay could see it now, gleaming white across the golden marsh, the garden an impressionistic blur, spilling over with flowers of pink, peach, rose, violet, yellow, and bright blue.

Bay stood outside, cooking burgers on the grill. Billy had stepped in to pitch to Peg, and all three kids seemed happily oblivious. Their main concern was that Sean come home in time to take them to Pirate's Cove. Across the river, on a hillside that until last year had been covered with tall grass and meadow flowers, a new complex had been built: ice-cream stand, driving range, go-cart track, and an extravagant miniature golf course. Pirate flags, treasure chests, shark jaws, and wrecked galleons adorned the holes. Bay preferred the unspoiled landscape, but her kids loved the development.

Setting the picnic table, Bay called the kids to dinner. While they scrambled to fix their own burgers with pickles and ketchup, she went inside to use the phone. Sean's office answering machine picked up, and she decided against leaving another message. She dialed his cell phone, hearing his recorded voice for the fourth time in an hour: "Hi, this is Sean McCabe. I'm either at the bank or on the boat. Either way, I'll call you back as soon as I can."

"Sean, it's me," Bay said. "Don't you have your phone turned on?" She took a deep breath and held back what she really wanted to say: *Hey, buddy—what's the point of having a cell phone if you're not going to answer it? One of the kids could have an emergency. . . .*

Sean was a vice president at Shoreline Bank and Trust and had a huge clientele. Bay knew how busy he was. A small-town banker, he handled everything: commercial transactions, home equity loans, mortgages. Five years ago, during the stock market boom, he had pioneered a private banking division, catering specifically to the wealthiest residents of the area. The result had been a gold mine for Shoreline, and Sean had received huge bonuses based on the assets under his management.

He lived life with passion—a quality Bay had loved about him. She used to say there weren't enough hours in the day for Sean to do all the things he enjoyed. As much as Bay adored gardening, Sean loved fishing, the Red Sox, going to the Eagle Feather casino with his friends.

In recent years that passion had extended to other women. Even now, it shocked her—that she could know it and still stay with him. As a young woman, judging other marriages, she would have considered infidelity completely unforgivable: One strike and you're out. But marriage had turned out to be more complicated than that.

Some people belong to a landscape as much as the rocks and trees; Bay felt that way about Hubbard's Point. The salt water was in her blood; the beach roses and day lilies were in her heart. She felt as if she had sprung from the rocky soil, and that she had to be here, in order to exist. She had always known that she would marry a boy from the beach.

She and Sean had grown up at the beach together; they had the same memories and histories. While they hadn't been each other's first loves, they had turned out to be each other's true loves—hadn't they? They were so different—but they'd seemed to complement each other perfectly. Their love had seemed so right.

But Bay had learned that marriage wasn't easy questions about background and history. It was Sean needing more independence than she could understand, working later with every promotion, traveling more on business; it was Bay wondering why he was so late every night, calling his office and getting his voice mail, hearing his excuses and trying to believe them.

Bay had discovered in herself a huge capacity for compromise—and, to her growing distress, a realization that she had lied to herself for a long time. Sean's lies hurt—but the lies she had told herself had hurt much, much more. If staying together was good for the kids, she'd forgive him and stay together. But she had started admitting to herself that she had stopped loving him the way she once had.

Bay's own denial had ended the day her daughter began asking questions.

Last fall Annie had overheard a phone call her father made—picked up the receiver and heard him whispering to Lindsey Beale about a trip they had taken to Chicago. Lindsey was a young loan officer at the bank—very beautiful and glamorous, from a wealthy New England family, with an impressive education; Bay and the kids had met her at company picnics. They had had her for dinner to the house. Annie had thought they should fix her up with her math teacher.

The phone call had devastated Bay's daughter.

"It was a business trip, honey," Bay had said, holding

her, trying to keep it together for Annie's sake. "You know Daddy has to travel for the bank, and sometimes Lindsey goes with him. They work together."

"This was different," Annie had wept. "They were whispering."

Bay had felt the adrenaline, the fear, a funny feeling in her stomach. But she couldn't let Annie know, so she had just hugged her tighter. "Don't worry, Annie. I'm sure there's some explanation."

"Mommy, I don't want to tell you. Because you'll be mad at him...but I have to tell you. They were saying romantic things...Daddy wanted to kiss her again and again..."

"Oh, Annie," Bay had said, holding back her own anguish and rage at Sean—for betraying her, for leaving her no way to defend him to their daughter.

Annie had been heartbroken by what she'd overheard, but the other kids—younger, but with thicker skin—had been outraged when their sister told them. "Daddy, why do you talk to another woman in the night?" Pegeen had asked with steely eyes and an angry voice. "If you can't sleep, why don't you drink milk? Or read a book?"

Billy had been more direct: "Don't do it anymore, Dad. We need you more than she does."

Seeing the effect on her kids had awakened the warrior in Bay, and she had started to think that staying with Sean for the sake of the family might be worse for everyone. She thought of all the times—going back long before Lindsey—when she had stayed silent to keep the peace, keeping her doubts and fears to herself. They all came boiling back after that phone call.

"You've been so dishonest for so long—I don't know

when it started," she said, her voice breaking. "I don't even know you."

Sean had been shocked to think of Annie hearing him.

"What did she hear?" he had asked.

"Enough."

"Did you tell her—?"

"I told her you were probably talking about business. She didn't believe me. She said you were whispering."

"Oh, shit."

Bay had felt the kick in her stomach—he wasn't denying the accusation. He was just trying to do damage control. She'd cried softly, feeling their daughter's grief at losing the innocent belief that her parents still loved each other.

Sean had taken her hand, pressed it to his bowed forehead for a long moment, before raising his gaze to meet hers. "Bay, I'm sorry. I'm so sorry I hurt you and the kids. It's over, and it will never happen again. I swear to you. Everything is going to change," he'd said, his voice shaking.

"You've said that before," she had said, but something about his tone caught her attention and made her stare at him.

"This is different," he'd said.

"In what way?"

He paused, took a deep breath. "I've made a lot of mistakes. Big ones. Sometimes I look in the mirror, and I don't even know the guy looking back at me."

"I've thought that, too," she'd said, flooding with tears and bitter hurt. "I wonder what's happened to my husband."

"I swear, everything's going to change. You'll see—"

Bay tried not to be suspicious right now, but all Sean's

lies had changed her. She wasn't very trusting these days, and her mind went instantly to the worst. Where could he be? Sometimes he turned off his phone, stuck it in his pocket, and headed out on his boat.

But not on nights when he'd promised to take the kids miniature golfing.

And never, not even during the heat of his affairs, had he ever left one of the children waiting to be picked up.

Bay walked out to the garden. Usually this calmed her, to see the verbena and bee balm wafting in the sea breeze, to hear bees humming in the roses and honeysuckle. Although her breath was steady, her chest felt constricted, as if a weight had settled there. She looked at the driveway, magically willing Sean's Jeep to materialize. The sky was still bright blue; tomorrow would be the longest day of the year: the anniversary of the day he proposed to her.

As a kid, Sean had been irrepressible. He would be the one, among their friends, to try to swim across the Sound to Long Island, to catch blue crabs with his bare hands, to dive into the water from the railroad bridge, to shoot baskets till he made fifty in a row. With bright yellow hair and brighter green eyes, he crackled with electricity.

He had always worked, somehow making more money than the other kids. He'd bought himself a Boston Whaler with money from his busboy job—he always knew who to butter up, and just by filling one elderly rich woman's water glass ten times in one evening, he scored a seventy-five-dollar tip. A well-known, well-heeled drunk slipped him hundred-dollar bills from time to time, saying, "Use it for college."

He would, but first he would buy the boat. Then he would charge renters money for what he called "See Black Hall From the Water" tours. Twenty dollars per person. He had confided in Bay that lonely women whose husbands worked during the week would hire him. He said that nothing ever happened, but he knew that if he wanted more money, it was somehow *there*: offered in an unspoken way.

Bay had hated that story, and she had done her best to instantly repress her true feelings: It wasn't his fault, it was the women's. He was too young for them. Sean was irresistible—cute, funny, flattering, and ready for anything. He was a stick of dynamite with blond hair.

She was attracted to his energy and fire; all the girls were. Everyone at Hubbard's Point wanted to go out with him; town girls from Black Hall drove through the beach to see the house where he and his family spent the summers—a gray cottage just around the bend from the railroad tracks. Pretty, blond, tan, bikini-wearing, outgoing girls—the most popular girls, the cheerleaders, the class beauties.

But he loved Bay.

Even now, she couldn't quite believe how he had fixated on her. He would always put his towel near hers on the beach. When he went hand-over-hand down the rafters of the pavilion over the boardwalk, he always made sure she was watching. He would cannonball off the raft right in front of her, his body shooting through the water like a missile, coming up beside her and brushing her with his arms and legs as he swam past, making her heart thump and her skin tingle. She would always feel thrilled by his attention—and a little confused.

They seemed so opposite.

She was quiet and shy. When her high-school class voted her the queen of her junior prom, she had known it had to be a joke—she barely had the nerve to dance with her date, a boy as shy as she was, who said about ten words to her all night and never quite got the courage to kiss her good night. She was studious, in love with nature.

But they were beach kids; like so many other couples who had met at Hubbard's Point, they went to beach movies, kissed under the Milky Way, carved their initials into the tables at Foley's. Their history and the beach connection were too compelling to ignore. They were total opposites, yet bound by the sand and salt and pines of their beloved Point.

They were lifelong friends; they would grow old together, along with Tara, one big happy family, third-generation residents of Hubbard's Point.

Right after they had graduated from college, the longest day of the year: Sean had picked her up in his boat, seated her beside him at the wheel, opened the throttle wide as they sped out into the Sound. The light was bright and seemingly eternal. The minutes ticked on and on, the sun still high in the sky. They had made love in the bottom of the boat, waiting for darkness to fall. Far out in the Sound, almost into the ocean, the waves were huge. Bay had been frightened, but the danger had just excited Sean more.

"Don't look so scared," he had said, smoothing the hair back from her face.

"It feels as if we're going to capsize."

"What if we did? I'd swim home with you on my back."

Bay had shivered, loving that thought, but unable to chase the growing terror inside as the waves built and the wind picked up.

"Let's go home, Sean," she had said.

"Not till dark," he'd said. "And maybe not even then. Home is always there. Let's go somewhere we've never been—let's take the boat out to the Gulf Stream and turn off the engine and just drift wherever it takes us..."

She knew he was watching her for her reaction: He had such lively, devilish eyes. He loved to tease, but that night she felt he was almost serious, that he was testing her.

"Okay," she said, bravely. "Let's do it."

"That's what I like about you, Bay," he said. "We're going to go places together. Wild, amazing places. We're going to fly to the sun."

"How about the moon, Sean? Will you take me there, instead?" she asked. Someone else had promised her the moon once.

"Anyone can go to the moon," Sean had scoffed. "For me, it's the sun. The moon only reflects the sun's fire, has no heat of its own. I want fire in life, Bay. It's too bad one of us wasn't born rich, so we could do it right. Why couldn't you have a trust fund?"

He was joking, but he joked about that a lot.

"Because my ancestors were too busy not starving in the potato famine to get into the stock market," she said. "And so were yours."

His eyes had glinted with flashpoint anger, not wanting her reminding him of that. He opened his mouth, as if to admonish her, but changed his mind.

He had been lying on top of her, but he'd pushed up on his arms, to look around. The boat was pitching roughly, and the wind blew back his hair. Looking up, Bay had thought he looked like a wild sea sprite, and in that instant she'd known how different they really were. The realization had hit her hard, but she tore it down and buried it deep.

Sean had always wanted to be rich, and to go far away. Bay had always been happy with what she had, and she loved home more than anything.

Her heart falling, she wondered whether that explained what was happening now, tonight, one night shy of the longest day of this year, so many summers later. Sean was back to his old tricks, flying too close to the sun.

She turned back to the picnic table. Billy and Peg were there, digging into their burgers. But Annie's spot at the table was empty.

ANNIE MCCABE STOOD IN HER PARENTS' ROOM, RIGHT IN the middle of the blue-and-white rug, and knew that something was wrong. She felt it in her heart, where she always felt everything important. She'd known the minute Peg had called—by the look in her mother's eyes, the let-down crushed expression there so reminiscent of those terrible months last winter.

Walking slowly around the room, Annie's eyes lit on her father's bureau. She glanced at the framed photos there: of Mom, of Billy, Peg, and Annie, of her dad's old dog Lucky. He was a Boston bull, white with brown spots. Her dad had found Lucky in an alley in Hartford when he was twelve—Annie's age. He had adopted the abandoned dog, and his love was still so strong, Annie felt tears in her own eyes whenever her father talked about him.

Seeing Lucky's picture on her dad's bureau somehow made Annie feel better. His cuff links were there, too: gold ovals, with his monogram. He wore them with his tuxedo, when he and Mom had somewhere fancy to go, and sometimes with a special shirt when he had a big closing at the bank, or when one of his big private banking clients came in.

She looked in his closet. What did most girls her age care about their father's clothes? But Annie loved the way she could stand there, close her eyes, and imagine her father grabbing her in a big huge hug.

"My Annie-bear," he'd growl in her ear, rocking her

back and forth the way he had when she was little and her head only came to his waist. Now she was up to his shoulder, and sometimes he ended the hug with a whisper that she should cut down on her snacking.

She stood just inside his closet door, off balance with the memory, conjuring her father from his smell: wool from his suits, sweat from his days at the bank, machine oil from his boat, and bait from fishing. Her stomach hurt, thinking of where he might be. *Don't let him be with Lindsey. Don't let him be with her again. . . .*

"Annie, what are you doing?"

At the sound of her mother's voice, Annie opened her eyes. Before she could answer, the phone rang.

Sighing, her mother walked toward the bedside table. In that sigh, Annie thought she detected relief. Who would it be but her father, calling to say he was sorry to be late, sorry he'd missed picking up Peg, but that he'd be home in a jiffy to take them all to Pirate's Cove. Annie wanted to believe it herself, wanted to smile, but she couldn't yet.

Bay, unsettled at the sight of Annie standing half-inside Sean's closet, picked up the receiver, ready to keep her voice calm and not let Annie know how furious she was with Sean.

"Hello?" she said.

"Bay, it's Frank Allingham," came the deep voice.

"Hi, Frank," Bay said. Frank was an old friend of Sean's, their histories so interlocking, it was hard to remember where they'd started out: high school, college, business school, the boatyard, the bank.

"Bay, is Sean there?"

"No," she said, eyes on Annie. Her daughter had been avidly watching Bay's face, but the minute she realized it wasn't Sean on the phone, she turned back to the closet.

Now, as if she was searching for something, she was on her knees, going through her father's shoes.

"Do you know where I can get ahold of him?"

"I don't, Frank," Bay said, detecting uneasiness in his voice. "What's wrong?"

"Do you know...did he mention anything to you about where he was going today?"

"Yes—he said he had a loan committee meeting."

"So he knew..."

"What's wrong?" Bay said, hearing Annie gasp, watching her lunge deeper into Sean's closet. She started toward her daughter, began to reach down, to touch Annie's back, to pull her up and out of the closet, when Frank's words stopped her in her tracks.

"Nothing, probably," Frank said, and she could almost hear him wishing he hadn't called. "But, well, he wasn't there, Bay. We waited for him, and we have some important decisions pending, ten people waiting to hear if they get their mortgages. Mark is fit to be tied."

Mark Boland was the bank president—and the object of Sean's great resentment. Given his success with the new division, he had hoped to be tapped for the position, but the bank had brought Boland over from Anchor Trust.

"Is Sean okay? It's not like him to bail on a big meeting."

"No, it's not," Bay said.

"When he gets in, will you have him call me?" Frank asked.

"I will. Thanks for calling," Bay said.

But she'd already half-forgotten her promise. Annie turned to her, white-faced. Her mouth was open, her eyes confused, dark and almost bruised.

"What is it, Annie?"

"I can't tell if Daddy took his things. His suitcase is still here. But I don't see his boat shoes. He wouldn't need those, to go to his office. And he took something else..."

"Took what?"

But Annie just shook her head, tears running down her cheeks. "He said he'd never leave it behind no matter what happened. It's not here, Mommy. He took it. Daddy's gone!"

2

ANNIE RAN AROUND THE HOUSE, LOOKING IN closets and cupboards. Bay took a quick look outside, saw Peggy and Billy playing catch. She went into the den, where Sean had set up a home office. She glanced at the computer, and wondered what to do.

Should she call the police?

But what was there to call them about? Sean had taken his boat shoes on a workday, missed a meeting, failed to pick up Peg. The police would tell her he might be at the marina, might have gone fishing. Her heart was beating hard, as if she were just starting a race, picking up speed. Reaching out to pick up the phone, she realized her hand was shaking.

Was Sean with Lindsey, or someone else, right now?

When Sean had sworn that everything would change, she had thought he meant Lindsey, other women; but now, looking back as she tried to make sense of today, were there other secrets? She hadn't felt this pit in her stomach—the physical sense of the world tilting on its axis, making her feel like grabbing on to the nearest solid object—for months.

Annie came around the corner, tears on her cheeks.

"We have to call the police, Mom."

"Annie, I don't think—"

"No, we do. Something bad must have happened. He wouldn't have just left like this, unless someone was forcing him. It could be kidnappers."

"I don't think that's it, Annie."

"It has to be, Mom. What else could it be? He would never just leave on his own!"

"Annie, a lot of things might have come up..."

Annie let out a hiccup, half sob, and said, "You think he's with Lindsey, don't you?"

"I don't know," Bay said, reaching out for her daughter. Lying just made people confused and crazy and undermined any remaining solid ground. It was always better, Bay had learned, to tell the truth as much as she could. But with three children who loved and needed to look up to their father, she found it to be a very difficult balancing act.

But Annie stepped back, her eyes wide and wild. "I'll ride my bike down to the boat and see if he's there!"

"Annie, no—we'll drive down together."

But her daughter was already gone. Bay heard her bare feet flying across the floor, the screen door slam, and the whir of her bike tires.

Bay pushed back Sean's leather desk chair and sat down. Almost without thinking, she picked up the phone and dialed Tara's number. She stared out the picture window, across the wide green-gold marsh at Tara's white cottage. She saw Tara stand from where she was crouching in the herb garden, drop her trowel, and walk up the weathered steps.

"Hello?" Tara said after six rings.

"It's me."

"Hey, you forgot your sunscreen at the beach. I have it."

"Oh, good," Bay said. Just two syllables—"oh" "good"—and Tara knew.

"What's wrong?"

"Sunscreen's not the only thing I've misplaced today."

"Sean's gone somewhere? And that's a bad thing?"

"Oh, Tara," Bay said, unable to laugh. "He didn't pick Pegeen up, and Frank called me because he missed a bank meeting...Annie's beside herself. She's on her way down to his boat right now. I think she's hoping he's on a fishing trip he forgot to tell us about."

"Damn," Tara said. "That boy."

Bay didn't reply, rocking in the desk chair.

"I'm sorry, Bay," Tara said. "You know I've tried to hold my peace this last year. But I saw what you went through, and he is an asshole of such stupendously huge proportions, I can't even believe it. What a lack of grace."

"Can I tell you how much I HATE him right now? Stranding Pegeen at practice. Making Annie worry like this?"

"I'm on my way...I'll pick you up, and then we can go down and meet Annie at the boat."

Tara hung up, but Bay just sat there, holding the phone. The Irish Sisterhood; Tara had coined the name years ago, to celebrate their friendship—closer than best friends, almost like the sisters neither of them had. Many people at Hubbard's Point thought Bay and Tara *were* sisters, and they never bothered setting anyone straight. They were united by their hearts, humor, and Irish roots; they both loved Yeats and U2, and they both swore they'd always, no matter how settled they might look from the outside, live passionate lives.

Tara was almost defined by her singleness. She had really fallen in love only twice—with an artist and an artistic "type," both of whom she had wanted to be much more brilliant than they actually were. Both men had proposed, but at the last minute she had veered away.

Bay knew it had something to do with having an alcoholic father—unable in the end to stand up to the strength of the women in the family. Tara had learned to trust herself more than any relationship. Bay felt tender and protective toward her best friend, understanding that her toughness was more an act than anything.

Tara had dropped out of UConn after two years, despite her sparkling intelligence, her stellar grades.

"I think I'm born to be self-employed," she had told Bay on the phone, calling her at Connecticut College even before she told her own parents. "I don't even like showing up for classes in my major—imagine what fun I'd have in corporate America."

"What will you do?"

"I'm going to go skiing in Vermont for the winter— someone in my dorm has an aunt who runs a B-and-B near Mad River Glen, and she says I can have a job as a chambermaid."

"Tara, making beds?" Bay asked, her mind boggled by the idea of her bright, vibrant friend scrubbing floors, pushing a vacuum.

"I think it will be good," Tara said. "I'll be able to whip through all the rooms before lunch, ski all afternoon."

"Tara, I don't want you to make a mistake. You're so smart, you have so much going for you—"

"I like the idea of having time to think," Tara said. "Cleaning is mindless—I'll be able to just open my mind and figure out what I really want to do with my life."

Tara had taken that winter job, and that summer she

had returned to Hubbard's Point. Her parents had told her that if she was going leave college for good, she'd have to support herself, so she had tacked up signs at the beach and Foley's: "Sand on the floors? In the beds? Come home to a clean house! Call Tara."

Her mother had cringed, but the phone had started ringing and never stopped. Tara had never had less than a full roster of clients. She had never stopped working, and she'd never gone back to college. She still liked making her own hours, having the freedom to think.

Pushing back the desk chair, Bay glanced across the room at her wedding picture. Tara was right beside Bay, smiling with joy. And Bay and Sean looked so happy— smiling, holding hands, eyes sparkling with love for each other. What had her dreams been that day? Bay could hardly remember, but over the years she had gradually come to the terrible conclusion that they were far, far different from her husband's.

Now she had to tell the other kids she was going out with Tara, would be back soon. Stepping away from the desk, something caught her eye. The fax machine's red light was blinking, the message "out of paper" subtle in the small screen.

Bay hesitated. Tara was coming, they had to catch up with Annie . . .

Something made her stop in the room's wide doorway. She turned and walked back to the machine. The red light blinked only when the machine had received a fax but had no paper on which to print it. Bay reached into the drawer, took out a handful of printer paper, and inserted it into the slot.

Instantly, the machine began to print.

Bay read the page as it came out. It bore the letterhead of a boatbuilding firm in New London. Handwritten, it bore yesterday's date at the top and a series of measurements at the bottom. The handwriting was familiar, but Bay didn't know anyone who built boats. She read:

> *Dear Sean,*
>   *Thanks for stopping by again. Check these specifications—are they what you have in mind? I've added two more inches of beam, for stability. Come by the boatyard anytime, or give me a call at the office.*
>   *Dan Connolly*

Bay was so shocked, she let out a small sound. This was an estimate of some sort: The bottom line was two thousand dollars, but she hardly noticed. Dan Connolly. She hadn't spoken of him in years, hadn't seen his handwriting since she was in high school. But she thought of him every time she walked down the boardwalk, every time she saw a crescent moon.

Other than Tara, the only person Bay had ever really been able to talk to had been Danny Connolly, the summer she was fifteen. He was a recent college graduate, working as a carpenter that season at the Point, and he was brilliant about the things he loved: engineering, wood, marine architecture. Bay had hovered around him for hours, helping him build the new boardwalk, in love with his gentle intelligence. And Danny never shooed her away, took time to answer her endless questions, to let her share in all the things he did.

"If you were just three years older," Tara had said, "this would really be interesting."

"Eighteen?" Bay asked.

"Yep," Tara said. "Maybe he'll wait for you. I'll bet he thinks about it."

"Right, Tara."

"If he didn't," Tara smiled, "he wouldn't let you hang around all day. He could work twice as fast without you there. He likes you, Bay. Face it!"

Somehow that idea had been too excitingly scary to really take seriously.

Sean was so different. He would race by, waving from his Boston Whaler as he gunned the engine and sent up rooster tails of white water. He'd ride his dirt bike on the beach, breaking all the rules, and Danny would shake his head.

"He's out of control," he said. "You know what he's doing, don't you?"

"Just playing with his toys," Bay said.

"No, he's patrolling, to make sure I don't get too close to you."

"You're twenty-two!" Bay said, hearing Tara's words, blushing with wild delight to imagine such a thing could really occur to him.

"I know, and you know that we're just friends, but boyfriends don't think that way."

"He's not my boyfriend!"

"He will be, if he has anything to say about it. But you take your time, Galway Bay."

And Danny had turned out to be right. Long after his summer job was over, and he left the beach for good, Bay and Sean stayed on. She turned sixteen; Sean had kissed her on the boardwalk Danny had built the year before. She missed the quiet carpenter, with his Irish poetry and steady vision, his way of observing everything and then talking it over with her. Sean was too busy living life— moving fast, grabbing for every second of pleasure—to waste much time discussing it. Holding Sean, her lips had found his neck, and for ten seconds she thought of Danny, wishing it could be him instead, wishing Tara's prediction had come true and he could have waited for her to grow up. She remembered him pointing at the thin, sickle moon, telling her that he'd make it into a swing just for her.

And she had told him that he could make anything.

New London—a salty old maritime center, a Navy town, just ten miles east, but somehow the other side of the world from Black Hall. Was it possible that Danny had been there this whole time?

Just then Bay heard Tara's car in the driveway. She placed the fax on the desk and hurried to tell the kids she'd be right back.

ANNIE KNEW ALL THE BEST ROUTES TO HER DAD'S BOAT. Right now, she took the most direct route, straight through the center of town.

She passed the white church, the yellow art gallery, the mansion that had come across Long Island Sound on a barge one hundred years ago, crossing the main road and just missing having her rear tire clipped by a speeding pickup truck, finally turning down the dirt road that led into the marina. Annie knew how close the truck had come, but she didn't care. She couldn't let herself feel anything—not yet.

Her bike skidded to a stop by the boat works. She leaned it against the big red barn, then ran down dock one. This was the nicest marina in the area, and most of the boats were, actually, yachts. Big, beautiful sailboats. Although Annie herself wished for a graceful sailboat, or maybe a rowing boat, her dad was strictly a power-boat man.

"A powerboat gets me where I want to go," he'd say to

her. "No waiting for the wind or the tides or anything else. I just fire her up, and we're off and running."

"I know, Daddy," Annie would say, watching white sails on the horizon, peaceful and romantic and somehow so much lovelier and more comforting than the loud throb of diesel engines. Tara called them "stinkpots." "But sailboats are so pretty."

"Who needs a pretty boat when I have you?" he would ask, hugging her. "You're all the pretty I need."

Annie ached, to remember him saying that. Her feet pounded down the dock, past all the big Hinckleys and Herreshoffs and Aldens. Now, at the end, she turned left, onto the T part of the dock, and almost instantly she began to smile.

Relief came flooding in. There, gently rocking against the dock, was her father's boat. The large sports fisher, *Aldebaran*, gleamed in the sunlight. The chrome was polished, the hull's graceful sheer curved and caught the light.

Grinning now, Annie padded barefoot down the dock. She half expected to hear Jimmy Buffett, her father's favorite, singing on the stereo. Maybe her dad had just needed a day off from work. He had come down here to the *Aldebaran* for a little rest and relaxation. Stepping over the lifeline onto the deck, she tiptoed over to the porthole.

Sometimes, during the past year, he had kept Annie's special present here on the boat, and she almost expected to see it now: a small model boat she had made him for Christmas two years ago, carved from balsa wood, painted dark green: a rowing dory instead of a motor boat. He'd said he'd always keep it with him. But it wasn't there . . .

As she moved around to the cockpit, she saw that the hatch appeared to be locked tight; she could see the closed silver padlock. That meant her father wasn't here now—but still, she wasn't really panicked. Annie knew the combination: 3–5–6–2. She could go below and check things out.

But as she started to turn the lock's dial with her thumb, she realized that it felt wet and oily. Looking at her hand, she saw blood.

And it wasn't just on her hand, on the lock: It was on the teak framing the companionway. Right there, on the corner, as if someone had really cracked his head going down into the cabin—a thick smear of red blood.

Annie wanted to believe it was from a fish.

Her dad had gone out, caught some bluefish. Or stripers. Or even a shark.

He was always bringing fish on board, and where there were fish, there was blood. Gutting, cleaning, rinsing fish ... such a messy job.

But Annie's eyes filled with tears, and she somehow knew that this blood hadn't come from a fish. Her father was the neatest boater on earth. He kept a hose coiled on the dock, and he carefully washed his boat down after each trip.

"Annie!"

At the sound of her name, Annie wheeled around. Her mother was walking down the dock with Tara, but at the sight of Annie's face, her mother began to run. Annie was crying so hard now, she couldn't even see her mother anymore, but she heard the hollow thud of her footsteps on the long dock, and then she felt the boat rock and lurch as her mother leapt on board and wrapped Annie in her arms.

"Something awful's happened to him," Annie wept. "He's hurt, Mom, or something worse ... he was here, but he isn't now, and he's hurt ..."

3

THE POLICE ARRIVED LESS THAN TEN MINUTES AFTER
Bay called, three cars pulling into the boatyard within
seconds of each other. Bay tried to keep her arm around
Annie, but her daughter yanked away, too agitated to
stand still. She walked down the dock, waving so the officers would see.

"Must be a slow crime day," Tara said. "So many po-
licemen for such a little bit of fish blood."

"I hope that's all it is."

"Really? I'd completely understand if you felt otherwise," Tara began, trying to lighten the mood; but at Bay's
expression, she stopped.

"Look at Annie—she's beside herself. What if he's
badly hurt somewhere?"

When the police officers approached, Annie ran over
to stand by her mother's side. Bay spoke carefully, trying
to stay calm as she gave them the facts she knew: that
Sean had missed a bank meeting, she and Annie had

come to the boat looking for him, and they had found blood on the doorway.

"Which boat is his?" asked Officer Perry, a tall young man with short dark hair and a kind smile for Annie.

"This one," Annie said, pointing and running over to the *Aldebaran*.

"Nice fishing boat." Officer Dayton nodded.

Bay said nothing, watching the police officers step aboard. Her stomach churned; Tara took her hand and squeezed it. They watched the officers look closely at the blood, walk slowly around the deck, gazing up at the sky and over the side into the water. Annie stood on the dock, not taking her eyes off them.

"Why are they looking in the water?" Annie asked suddenly, turning toward her mother.

"I think they have to look everywhere for clues," Bay replied, reaching for her.

"Just clues?"

"Yes, honey."

The furrow between Annie's brows deepened, and Bay's heart slammed her rib cage. She would never forgive Sean for this moment, as their daughter watched the police scanning the water for his body. And with that thought, Bay's own skin turned ice cold, terrified for her husband.

One of the officers used his handheld radio to make a call, while Officer Perry asked Bay if she had the boat's combination, so they could make sure Sean, or someone else, wasn't lying hurt inside.

"The hatch has to be locked from the outside," she said. "He can't be in there."

"Still, just in case."

Bay hesitated.

She wasn't sure why, exactly. The longer she waited,

the more she realized that she was afraid of what they would find inside—Sean lying hurt, or worse, and all the things he was keeping from her.

"Three-five-six-two," Annie blurted out.

"Okay?" Officer Perry asked, looking for Bay's permission to enter. She nodded.

He opened the hatch door and disappeared below, into the boat. Officer Dayton followed. Bay watched. Tires crunched on gravel; she turned to look, seeing a dark sedan park by the police cars. Two men, both dressed in suits, got out, and the other two uniformed officers walked over.

"Looks like the big brass," Tara said.

"They'll find Daddy, right?" Annie asked.

"You bet your boots they will," Tara said, hugging her. "My grandfather was a policeman, and I can always pick out the best investigators. Those two are excellent—I can tell."

Leaving her daughter in the hands of her best friend, Bay climbed on board her husband's boat. She had to see for herself; if he was down there, she wanted to be there, too. Grabbing the chrome handle at the top of the ladder, she eased herself down below, into the cabin.

The officers didn't see her right away. They were huddled together over something up forward, talking in low voices. The cabin had been closed up, and it smelled musty and sweet. The boat rocked gently against the dock, making an irregular muffled bumping sound as the fenders absorbed the hull's impact.

Bay's heart thudded inside her chest. She thought, tears springing to her eyes, of the family's most recent time aboard: a fishing trip out to the Race, going after stripers with live eels. Billy had caught the biggest fish, Pegeen had caught the most. They had sped right past the spot where, on the summer solstice so long ago, Sean had told her he wanted to fly to the sun.

Now, her mouth dry, she turned toward the aft cabin.

The bunk itself was mussed—the blue-and-white striped pillow was bunched up, the coverlet wrinkled as if someone had recently lain upon it. Oddly, seeing that, her heart began to slow down. Had Sean been down here making love with someone when he should have been picking up Peg? Her panic decreased, numbness taking its place, washing her skin and all her nerves with soft grief.

About to leave the cabin, out of the corner of her eye, she noticed an open folder of papers on top of the chest of drawers. Some appeared to be account statements—of clients at the bank. A tally sheet, like the kind the kids used at miniature golf to keep score, was marked "X,Y,Z." In the margin, he had doodled a panel truck, or a delivery van, in heavy black ink; written on the side and surrounded with dark swirls were the words "the girl" and "help," and the name "Ed."

What girl? Annie? Pegeen? Bay? Somehow Bay didn't think so. She stared at Sean's drawing. He had always had the nervous habit of doodling while he talked on the phone, trying to concentrate. Years ago Bay had teased that she was going to collect his drawings and put them in a book—he was a master of cross-hatching and caricature—or take them to a psychologist for interpretation.

What could a truck and "the girl" mean? Some kind of male Mack-truck logic, eighteen-wheel velocity and desire for Lindsey? Or someone new? Her heart broke to think of it. Hands shaking, she scanned through the rest of the folder.

A sheet of white-lined paper caught her eye. It couldn't be . . . She picked it up, and felt shocked—for the second time that day—by a ghost from the past. A letter, in her own handwriting, written so long ago ...

She must have exclaimed out loud, because suddenly the police officers knew she was there. They heard her, and hurried through the main salon to the aft cabin.

"Ma'am, you can't be down here," Officer Perry said, his voice much sterner than before.

"But it's my—our—boat," she said, trying to smile.

"I'm sorry," he said firmly. "Right now it's a possible crime scene. Please go back onto the dock and wait there."

Bay froze, shocked by his words. Stuffing the letter into the back pocket of her shorts, she followed him to the companion ladder and saw what she had somehow missed upon boarding earlier: a crooked trail of red splotches.

Small red spots leading to or from the hatch opening toward the bow. And there, at the forward end of the settee where on that last voyage the kids had eaten dinner— the swordfish Sean had grilled for them on deck—was a blue blanket now stained purple and black.

Only it wasn't purple or black at all, Bay realized as she climbed up to the deck, her heart in her throat: It was red blood, and a lot of it.

As she stepped out of the cabin, into the fresh air, she caught sight of Annie and Tara, their grave faces confirming that everything was wrong and they knew it, too, that somehow, during the course of this brilliant, blessed, bright blue day, their lives had all been shaken like a snow globe, turned upside down.

WHILE ANNIE STOOD THERE, A STRANGE THING HAPPENED: She left her body. Not like those people on TV, who died on the operating table or in a car accident and rose above the scene, watching their doctors and families with new, wise insights.

No, when Annie left her body, she flew far from the dock, into the past. She flew into her childhood, when her father would walk her to school. He would hold her hand, sing a little song to her when they got to the crosswalk:

> "Stop, look, and listen, before you cross the street.
> Use your eyes, use your ears, before you use
>   your feet . . ."

He had kept her safe, taught her how to do it on her own. Those were her favorite times with her father, when the other kids were home with her mom, when he wasn't too busy with work, fishing, or friends—and before she had gained weight and disappointed him. Annie had felt the full force of his love on those walks to school; when he had turned away, to leave her on the wide granite steps, she had felt as if the sun was setting, as if his great warmth had been removed.

Now her mother and Tara spoke in soft voices. Police officers hurried around the dock; their car radios squawked in the parking lot. People didn't pay the same attention to kids as they did to other adults, so the two men in dark suits spoke to the uniformed officers as if Annie wasn't there.

"Investigation," she heard them say. "Internal . . . at the bank . . . the Feds . . ."

"Mommy, what are 'the Feds'?" Annie asked, running over.

"It means the Federal government," her mother said, putting her arms around Annie, rocking her so soothingly that Annie could almost think everything was going to be fine, that the whole Federal government was going to come to look for her father. Annie just held her mother and smelled her wonderful Mom-smell of sunscreen, lemon cologne, and salt water.

But then Tara whispered to her mom, "It means the FBI," and her mother gasped, and Annie pulled away.

Before, everyone had been friendly, but now they were brusque and cold, and Annie understood that her father—somehow, a mistake, a nightmare—had become a suspect in something. A new car drove up, and two people got out carrying large cases. Tara said, "Forensics team," and Annie's mother said, "This can't be happening."

To Annie, it wasn't. Her body was air. The breeze moved through her, cooling her bones. Her bare feet, rooted on the dock's wide planking, hardly felt the summer heat. Her skin felt singed, as if it had been ripped away and her insides were leaking into the sky. Her mother reached for her, but Annie couldn't be held.

"Annie?" her mother said, arms reaching out.

Annie knew that her mother was trying to comfort her, and that she probably needed a hug back, but Annie couldn't let herself give it right now. She was Air-Girl. She had left her body entirely—just like a periwinkle crawls out of its shell.

And now, time traveler that she had become, she flew forward into the future. She closed her eyes, to block out every sight.

She thought of her life, of her father holding her hand all through it. "What's your favorite song, Annie?" he asked her sometimes. "Because we'll have them play it the day I walk you down the aisle. Forget Mendelssohn . . . whatever you want."

But Annie veered away from her wedding day—boys

didn't like her, anyway—and dreamed of her sports banquet instead. She had been to them before, for her brother and her best friend's sister, and now her throat choked up to imagine herself at the big table, flanked by her parents. They would be eating…prime rib, her father's favorite.

Annie would be thin. She wouldn't have eaten so much, exercised so little. She would have tried out for teams, made the cuts, taken their school all the way to the state championships. And she would be so thin and pretty…

The principal would call her name. Annie would push back her chair and, standing tall, so her father wouldn't criticize her posture, walk among the tables to the stage. People would be cheering. The other parents would be smiling at her father, giving him thumbs-ups for her excellence in—Annie cast about, searching her mind for the perfect sport—field hockey!

Or soccer. Or lacrosse. Or crew. Or basketball…

The sport was less important than the applause Annie would receive as she accepted the certificate and trophy, as the whole crowd of parents, children, and especially her father stood in an ovation, as Annie ran down from the stage, straight into her father's arms.

"Mrs. McCabe?"

The officer's voice interrupted Annie's reverie.

"Yes?" her mother said.

"We're going to clear this area right now. Why don't you go home? Someone will contact you very soon."

"What were those officers saying about 'the Feds'?" her mother asked, pointing.

"You'll be contacted very soon."

"Please tell me now," her mother said, her voice shaking. "I have three children. They're all so worried about their father. Please tell me what to tell them."

"Soon, Mrs. McCabe. As soon as we have any real information."

Her mother stood her ground, as if she was making up her mind about whether to insist on knowing more now, whether to demand to speak to someone higher up. Annie had seen her be bold and insistent when she needed to.

But right now, Annie saw the way her mother looked from the man to Annie...Staring into Annie's eyes seemed to make up her mother's mind. Their eyes met, and her mother smiled. Annie watched the fight go right out of her.

"Let's go home, honey," her mother said.

Annie nodded, unable to speak.

Her mother gathered Annie into her arms as if she were a very small child instead of a twelve-year-old soon-to-be-recognized sports star. And Annie didn't even mind. She squished against her mother's body, not wanting even an inch of space between them, as they walked with Tara back down the dock, away from the boats and the police and into their car.

BILLY WATCHED FOR A CAR TO PULL INTO THE DRIVEWAY: his mother's, his father's, he almost didn't care whose. He wasn't too worried about his dad, even though he knew everyone else was. His dad was probably working late. He had made a promise a while back—to never mess around with that weird lady again—and Billy believed him.

But even if he wasn't messing around, he'd kind of screwed up. Billy hated to think that. Pegeen was really upset about not going to mini golf. She'd been looking forward to it all day, and she was only nine—nine-year-olds took things like this really hard.

He looked over at her, sulking at the picnic table. She was this wiry little kid, no bigger than a string bean. A beetle was climbing up the leg of the table. She was crooked over to one side, her head upside down, watching the beetle—and talking to it. That was the best part. Billy moved closer to listen.

"He promised, he really did. I was going to get the green ball today. Pirate's Cove lets you pick your own golf ball, and they come in all colors, and I usually pick bright blue, but today I felt like green. He must have forgotten. I wouldn't forget if it was me, if he was waiting for me. Beetles are pretty. Why's your shell so shiny?"

"Hey," Billy said.

"What?" Pegeen said, not looking up.

"Who're you talking to?"

"No one."

"Oh. You sure you're not talking to that bug?"

"I don't talk to *bugs*. When's Mommy getting home?"

"Soon."

Peggy's head was still upside down. Billy could just imagine all the blood in her body rushing to her brain and knew that certain older-sibling measures were necessary here. Annie had showed him how to do it countless times, so he gently put his hand on Peggy's shoulder and eased her up.

"Hey," he said. "Sit up straight."

"I was just watching that beetle, not *talking* to it."

"Watch it with your head up."

"I wanted to go golfing," she said, her eyes glittering.

"We'll still get to go. Just not today, probably."

"That sucks."

"Big time."

"Is Daddy with that lady again?"

"Nah," Billy said.

"How do you know?"

"He promised he wouldn't."

Peggy nodded. That was good enough for her. Or maybe, like Billy, she just chose to believe the best of their dad—it was called "the benefit of the doubt."

"You going to sit here all day?" Billy asked.

"Yeah," Peggy said. "I'm going to sit here at this picnic table watching this beetle with the shiny shell all day." Her mouth wiggled; he got a smile out of her.

"Then you'll miss your ups."

"Huh?"

"I'll pitch to you. Go on, get the bat. Let's see you hit one out of the park."

"It's the *yard*, Billy. Duh!"

"Yuck, yuck, I forgot—good thing I got you to remind me!"

AT HOME, ALL WAS QUIET. THE SUN WAS GOING DOWN, BUT there was still plenty of light. Billy and Peg were playing baseball in the side yard; they came running over to the car the minute she drove in. Everyone gathered together, a little tribal pod, asking a million questions.

Billy and Pegeen: "Have you seen Daddy? What's going on?"

Annie, back to them, "He didn't come home? He wasn't here at all?"

And Bay, pierced to the heart by her kids, by the family she and Sean had created, "Will you guys just keep playing, while I try to find out some answers? Just keep looking after each other . . . Peggy, I know . . . can you wait till tomorrow for mini golf? We'll go tomorrow . . ."

Billy and Peggy said they would keep playing, watching for their father. Annie wanted to come inside. While Bay went into the kitchen, Tara followed Annie into the den. She could hear them in there.

"Okay, darling," Tara said in a brogue borrowed from her Irish grandmother. "We're going to play beauty parlor. I'm going to give you a pedicure now, all right? I've chosen this lovely shade for you . . . 'Tickled Pink.' Is that to your liking now, darling?"

"Oh, Tara . . . I don't want to play."

"Nonsense, darling. Sit still. Give me your tootsies, that's a girl. Sit back and relax, and I'll tell you about my last trip to the beautician. It was a facial-gone-bad. The steam was a tad too hot, and it left me looking like my grandmother with rosacea. Truly, not the look I'd been seeking. Ever had one of those?"

"I've never had a facial," Annie said, the tiniest bit of laughter in her voice.

"Oh, darling. Perhaps once the toes are done, I'll administer a mask of egg whites and beer. Not that you need it, with skin like that. Did anyone tell you you've the complexion of a wild Irish rose? No? Well, just sit back and let me be the first . . ."

Tara's words and pretend accent almost made Bay smile. Her friend had such a generous way about her, enfolding those she loved with boundless kindness and humor, always knowing just what to do to help.

Hoping that Annie was okay for the moment, Bay steeled herself. She headed out of the kitchen, down the hall, up the stairs, into her bedroom. She looked around, as if she had never entered the room before, and then she closed the door behind her.

White curtains lifted in the gentle breeze blowing through open windows. The children's voices came up from the yard, but Bay hardly heard. She walked across the floor—polished wood covered by old hooked rugs, made by her own grandmother—to the bed. Everything on it was white: sheets, pillowcases, and summer-weight quilt. It was one of her favorite luxuries, an all-white bed. It always looked so clean and fresh, so ready to bestow sweet dreams.

Now, sitting on the edge, she reached into her pocket and pulled out the letter she had found on the boat. Her hands, to her surprise, were shaking. Her eyes scanned the page. Although she had written this to Danny Connolly twenty-five years ago, her own handwriting looked the same as it did today.

This copy had never been sent. She had written it as a draft, then copied it over on better stationery. She had been fifteen at the time; she had had long, long strawberry-blond hair and as much of a summer tan as she ever got, and she had ridden her bike everywhere. She had worn her bathing suit with just a T-shirt over it, without a trace of self-consciousness.

She had been so in love.

Had she known that was what it was? Even now, she wasn't sure. The first stirrings of love are mysterious to the girls feeling them. Heart beating too fast, a sense of standing on the edge of the world, hands that won't stay still . . .

Danny had been everything to her. To him, she was a summer kid, someone who bothered him while he did his job, building the new boardwalk. There were other jobs, too—painting and reroofing the parking lot guard shack, repairing the latticework at Foley's store—but the main thing was the new boardwalk.

While Sean had tried to talk her into swimming to the Wickland Light, or diving off the trestle over Eight Mile

River, or joining the flotilla of boats out to Orient Point, Bay had stayed by Danny's side, handing him nails and learning how to swing a hammer.

Bay remembered thinking that he could build anything. He had worn khaki shorts and a faded beach T-shirt. She remembered his brown hair glinting in the sun. He had a Red Sox hat, but rarely wore it.

One morning, just before he started work, the baseball hat had been resting on the hood of his car, and she had stared at it, and as if he could read her mind, he had grinned and placed it on her head. His fingers had brushed her hair, just slightly, and she had felt weak and strong all at once and wished he would touch her hair again.

Daniel Connolly. Danny. His name had always been magic to her. She stared at the name now and thought about that summer so long ago—she could almost see him. Before he'd gone away at the end of the summer, he'd made her a swing out of the crescent moon—a sea-silvered arc of driftwood.

They had written to each other all through that next winter; Bay turned sixteen and began to date Sean. Danny took a trip to Europe. Their correspondence dwindled off, and he didn't come back the next summer, and as Bay's life took off, she lost touch with him.

Now, holding her letter, she wondered why Sean had taken it. What was the fax about; why had Sean contacted him? Could it even be the same Dan Connolly? Bay hadn't been aware that Sean remembered his existence—or if he did, why he would care. It had all been so long ago.

She stood and walked to the end of the bed. An antique chest rested at the foot. She used it to store blankets, but at one time, it had been her hope chest. Such an old-fashioned concept, she thought now. Her grandmother had given it to her upon graduation from high school. It had belonged to her great-grandmother, had come over on the boat from Ireland. Some of the first things Bay had packed inside had been her and Dan's letters.

After twenty-five years, marriage to Sean, and three children, she could hardly believe she still had them, but lifting the lid and pushing aside the blankets and old baby clothes, there they were: a stack of letters nearly an inch thick, held together by a frayed rubber band. Looking more carefully at the paper she'd found on the boat, she realized it was a photocopy and noticed what she had only glanced at before—notations in Sean's own handwriting: *Eliza Day Boat Builders, New London CT.*

Bewildered, Bay closed her eyes. She knew she had only a few minutes, before Annie or the other kids came in and wanted to know what was going on. They were frantic about their father, and Bay needed to have something to tell them.

Her palms were clammy, her heart racing too fast, her mind swirling with disbelief that today could be happening. What did any of this mean? It felt like someone else's nightmare. Holding the letter, staring at it, she wondered what her husband could have been thinking.

He had been jealous of Danny Connolly, way back in the day. Despite the differences in their ages, despite Dan treating her like a little sister, Sean was sharp enough to spot a rival. He had wondered how Bay could prefer hanging around a half-built boardwalk to waterskiing in the Sound. And Sean, with all his fire, could never understand the quiet incandescence of the poetic, Irish carpenter.

Bay cast her mind back to the folder in which she had found the letter. She could see the bold drawing of the van, the swirled-out doodles of "the girl." Sean was at it again; that's all she could think of. He was obsessing about someone new.

She didn't know what else it could be; she couldn't imagine. After all these years together, she knew less than ever about how her husband's mind worked.

4

TARA HELD ANNIE'S FOOT CUPPED IN HER LEFT HAND, painted her toenails pink with the other. The girl's foot was as big as a woman's now, but holding it in her hand, Tara was transported back in time, to when Annie was a baby and Tara—her godmother—would play "this little piggy" and make her laugh and would wish to someday have a daughter of her own.

"Darling, you get the prize," Tara said now.

Annie didn't reply. She was almost oblivious to the pedicure, attention riveted on the stairs. No sounds issued from up there. Bay was frighteningly silent, causing Tara's own anxiety level to kick up a notch.

"Don't you want to know what prize?" Tara prodded.

"What prize?" Annie asked.

"For the best beach feet. A-one beach girl beach feet. These calluses rival anything your mother and I had at your age. Close encounters with barnacles, crabbing on the rocks, scalded by hot tar—you are the real deal."

"Thanks," Annie said, not even slightly smiling. "What's she doing up there? Why aren't we looking for Dad?"

Tara took a deep, steady breath, concentrating as she applied a dab of shell-pink polish to Annie's baby toe—as if there was nothing more pressing in this world than getting the lacquer on right.

"Well, we are. Or, by that I mean, your mother is on top of it. She's in constant contact with the police, as you know, and I'm sure she's talking to your father's friends, asking where he might have gone. You know your father..." Tara said, and then stopped herself, because she was veering into dangerous territory.

"What do you mean, 'know' him?" Annie asked, picking up on it.

"Oh, I mean, he's such a fun-lover. Always up for an adventure, right?" Tara asked mildly. Like philandering, breaking your mother's heart, running out on his family, blowing the money for your tuition at the casinos...

"You mean, fishing? And camping?"

"Exactly," Tara said.

"But what about all that blood?" Annie asked.

"Darling, I know," Tara said. She stroked Annie's foot gently, staring into her godchild's worried eyes. There was nothing she could say to explain the blood. If only she could be blithe, like her own mother, and come up with reassuring but slightly askew pearls of wisdom...or, as her mother used to say, "pears of wisdom."

"Stop, Tara," Annie said, staring at her toes. "I can't just sit here, letting you give me a pedicure. I should be out looking for him—"

"No, you should stay right here, Annie," Tara said. "It's getting dark out, and you can't just go—"

"No, I have to," Annie said, almost apologetically, getting up from the wicker couch, hobbling toward the door with her toes arched skyward. "He might need me!"

"Annie, it's getting dark," Tara called after her, but Annie walked out of the room, out of the house. She opened the back door, and the smell of sweet tidal decay blew in on the summer breeze. The sky was still light, the trees luminous; they were still in longest-day-of-the-year territory.

Time to call in the mother. Tara walked upstairs and stood before Bay's closed door. She knocked once, and then walked in. Her best friend sat on the end of the bed, staring into her open hope chest, holding a bunch of letters in her hands. Tara sat beside her, slid her arm around her shoulders.

"Your daughter is on a mission."

"She's gone out to find Sean."

"Of course. With seven toes painted pink. I suppose it will make her feel better, to be doing something, but it'll be dark soon."

"Okay, let's go get her," Bay said, standing up.

"What have you got there?"

"Danny Connolly."

"What?" Tara asked, shocked by the old name.

Tara sensed that the letters were somehow holding Bay together.

"I kept our old letters," Bay said. "And I found one of them on Sean's boat today."

"You're kidding—what would he be doing with it?"

"I have no idea, but I also found a fax from Danny. Seems Sean got in touch with him, about having a boat built. I guess Danny's become a boatbuilder."

"That works." Tara nodded. "That makes sense."

"It all seems so far-fetched, Sean going to Danny for anything. With all the troubles in our marriage, what good does he think can come from dredging up that part of the past?"

"I'd say Sean isn't thinking clearly," Tara said. "Because he sure doesn't come up looking good next to Dan Connolly—at least the Danny we all knew. That Danny would hate him for what he's put you through. Are you going to call him?"

"I thought about it just now," Bay said. "But I don't think so. I don't feel like dropping out of the blue after all these years and saying, 'Oh, I hear my husband wants to buy a boat from you, and by the way—he's disappeared.'"

She took a long breath, as if to continue, when the front door knocker sounded downstairs. Without a word, she dropped the letters on the bed, and Tara glanced down to look. Dan Connolly—the cutest guy ever to swing a hammer within the summer realm of Hubbard's Point.

Now, there was a man who could have gotten to Bay's soul. Not like Sean McCabe, who'd only managed to break her heart.

IT WAS DUSK OUT, AND FIREFLIES HAD BEGUN TO BLINK IN the rosebushes as Bay opened the door. Billy and Pegeen had come inside, and she scanned for Annie even as she saw Mark Boland standing on the bottom step. Very tall, he wore a dark blue suit, a red tie, and gold-rimmed glasses. Bay tried to smile in greeting, but as she noticed his stern expression—and the even sterner looks on the faces of the two dark-suited strangers flanking him and several others behind them, and as she saw Officers Perry and Dayton climb out of their squad cars at the end of the driveway—her heart fell and her smile followed.

"Hi, Mark," she said.

"Bay, we need to find Sean," he said.

"I know—we're all worried," she said.

"Worried doesn't begin to cover it," Mark said.

"I'm Special Agent Joe Holmes," one of the other men said, stepping forward to shake Bay's hand and look her in the eye as if she and he were the only ones there. "I'm with the FBI. This is my colleague, Andrew Crane."

"The FBI?" Bay asked, and thought of what Annie had overheard and asked about earlier: *the Feds*.

"If you can tell us where he is, Bay," Mark said, his face bright red and beads of sweat thick along the border of his receding black hair. "He—"

"This is a search warrant," Joe Holmes said, handing Bay a piece of paper. She glanced at it as several men walked up the front steps, around her and Tara, into her house.

"Let me see that," Tara said, taking the paper from her hand as Bay looked down and saw "...data, records, documents, materials..." typed in.

Bay caught the annoyance in Joe Holmes's eye as Tara took charge.

"And you are?" he asked.

"I'm Mrs. McCabe's *consiglière*," Tara said, eyes glinting dangerously. "Just so you know."

Special Agents Holmes and Crane and the others brushed past them. Bay could hear their footsteps on her floors, hear them spreading out through the rooms of her house. She rushed into the kitchen. "Kids!" she called, feeling panicked. "Come here!"

Billy and Pegeen came running down the hall, looking up at their mother.

"Billy, honey," Bay said, patting her pockets for money. Her hands were shaking so hard, she almost couldn't get them to work. She pulled out a ten-dollar bill and handed it to him. "Is the Good Humor truck at the beach? Will you go buy your sister an ice cream?" After-dinner Good Humors were one of the great Hubbard's Point treats, but right now both kids were rooted to the kitchen.

"What's wrong, Mom?" Billy asked.

"Mom, there are police cars," Peggy whispered, staring with wide eyes out the window.

"I know, Peggy," Bay said, holding her close. "Try not to worry, okay? Everything will be fine. Now, will you go with your brother down to the beach?"

"Is it Daddy? Is something wrong with Daddy?" Peggy asked in a reedy voice.

"Everyone is looking for him," Bay said. "We'll find him really soon. Billy?"

Her son nodded reluctantly, and she had to hold back from kissing him. He took the money and grabbed his sister's arm. "C'mon, Peggy."

"I don't want to—"

"Will you keep an eye out for your other sister, too?" Bay asked. "Annie went out a little while ago. I don't want her to be out after it really gets dark. Okay?"

"It's almost dark now," Peggy said.

"Stay close to your brother. Just down to the beach, to the Good Humor truck, okay? I'll come get you in a little while."

The kids left the house. What should have been a treat must have felt like exile; Bay watched them walk down the sidewalk, making sure they couldn't hear her, before she wheeled to face Mark Boland.

"The FBI?" Bay asked, totally shocked. "You called the FBI because of the blood on the boat?"

"No," Mark said, looking very sorry.

Bay blinked, feeling surreal. "Why are they here, Mark? What's going on?"

"They're investigating Sean, and have been. I received subpoenas last week, for bank records..."

"What are they saying he did?" Bay asked.

"Embezzled money," Mark said.

Bay felt Tara's arm around her. She shook her head. "Not Sean. He wouldn't do that."

"Did he ever mention the Cayman Islands?" Mark asked. "Or Belize? Costa Rica?"

"Only as a place to dive," Bay said. "And to go sports fishing... He dreamed of taking the *Aldebaran* down to Belize with the kids... take everyone out of school and go after black marlin..."

"Because that's where we think he moved the money. He could have used wire transfers to deposit funds into accounts there and in the Caymans—we're looking into a shell company, the misuse of a trust account..."

"The *Aldebaran*?" Agent Holmes asked, coming into the kitchen with a sheaf of papers in his hand.

"Yes—the bright red star in the constellation Taurus, the bull. It's the name of his boat."

"Mrs. McCabe," Special Agent Holmes said, "we've typed the blood on the boat, chances are looking good it's your husband's. Type AB negative is uncommon."

"Oh, God," Bay said, suddenly feeling weak, picturing that blood-soaked blanket.

"If it's his, and we think it probably is, he lost a lot of blood. He would have needed medical attention..."

"Did you check the hospitals?" Tara asked, supporting Bay. Her voice sounded strong and steady, almost a challenge to the agent.

"Of course, Ms.—"

"O'Toole," Tara said.

"Well, Ms. O'Toole, we've checked all the local hospitals and emergency clinics. We've found no sign of him, at all."

"People don't vanish into thin air," Tara said. "My grandfather was a policeman, and he always said that."

"Your grandfather was right," the agent said, his brown eyes warm but unyielding as he looked from Tara to Bay and back, locking on Tara's. "People don't vanish. But people with head wounds like Mr. McCabe's are in serious trouble."

"How do you know it's a head wound?" Bay asked.

"Because we found hair and blood on the corner of a table," Special Agent Holmes said. "Someone hit that table with great force—more than if he just lost his balance. We believe it was Sean, and he was fighting with someone, that they pushed or punched him hard."

"Sean wasn't a fighter," Mark Boland said, looking pale, from the corner of the room. He pushed the hair back from his forehead, looking at Bay. "He was so easygoing."

"*Is* easygoing," Bay corrected him sharply.

If only Mark knew how much Sean had hated him, when he had first come over to Shoreline from Anchor Trust to take the presidency Sean had expected for himself.

"Could he have amnesia?" Tara asked the agent. "If he hit his head?"

"Anything is possible," Holmes said. "But this story is going to hit the media tonight, and people will recognize him and contact us. Or call you, Mrs. McCabe. If they haven't already. Have you talked to your husband? Or has anyone seen him?"

"No," Bay said quietly, still struck by Mark's use of the past tense. He thought—they all thought—that Sean was long gone. And Bay knew her husband was anything but easygoing. He was fiery, edgy, wildly enthusiastic about everything he loved, and very outspoken about the things he hated. Didn't Mark know that? Sean had been a championship basketball player in high school and college. And he still played hard at everything he did. It was part of who he was. And Sean had often invited Mark aboard the *Aldebaran* for shark fishing tournaments off Montauk and the Vineyard, as well as to gambling outings to the casino. And golf matches at the club. How many different faces did Sean wear for people? For her?

Bay remembered the bank's Christmas party at the yacht club last year. Raw from everything with Lindsey, Bay hadn't even wanted to go. She had wanted to stay home, hiding from everyone's prying eyes. But Sean had wrapped her in his arms, rocked her back and forth, asked her to change her mind.

"You're the one I love," he'd said, looking straight into her eyes. "I doubt anyone even knows what happened, but if they do, let's show them what we're made of, Bay. Please? People will talk if you stay home. They keep score about things like this—who shows up and who doesn't. Mark and Alise have their perfect marriage—"

"Who cares, Sean? It's not what people at the bank think—it's what we have between us."

"I want it to be better between us; I want to be a better man," Sean said, his eyes so intense that he caught Bay's attention; she could almost believe he meant it. "I want to stop—"

"Stop what?" Bay asked.

Sean had paused, bowing his head, touching his eyes. Bay had tensed up, wondering whether he was about to confess something new about Lindsey—or another woman. Now, thinking back, she wondered whether he had been about to tell her about something else.

They had gone to the Christmas party at the yacht club. Mark and Alise had greeted them warmly, with hugs and kisses. Lindsey had done the right thing and stayed across the big open room. Frank Allingham had kissed Bay's cheek and made her promise to dance with him. Mark had grabbed Sean, pulled him aside for a moment of bank business... thinking back, Bay remembered that Mark had been concerned about one of Sean's private banking clients.

"My husband is always working," Alise had said, smiling wryly. "Even at the Christmas party, he can't just let Sean have a good time."

Bay remembered being mesmerized by how radiant Alise looked, as if she didn't have a worry in the world. Glowing skin, perfect pageboy hair, diamond earrings, eyes gazing adoringly at her husband. They didn't have kids, and they ran in fancier social circles than the Mc-Cabes. Lindsey, Fiona Mills, Frank Allingham—they all looked like perfect people from another world.

Bay had felt like a wraith, burning with humiliation, just to be in the same room as Lindsey. And she hadn't missed Alise's subtle dig about Mark's seniority. But in spite of all that, she had drawn herself up tall, taken a deep breath, and smiled right back at Alise.

"My husband never minds taking care of bank business," Bay said lightly. "You know he'd do anything for his clients, Alise."

Now, with the police and FBI swarming through her house, she cringed at the memory. And she thought of Sean's words: *"I want to stop."*

Stop what?

"Mrs. McCabe," Special Agent Holmes said. "When

you hear from Sean, or if someone calls to tell you they've seen him, I want you to contact me."

Bay just stared at him, frozen by memories.

"Bay *always* does the right thing, Mr. Holmes," Tara said, drawing herself up, tossing her black hair back from her tan face. She was black Irish, all fire and nerve. "You can count on that."

5

THIRTEEN DAYS PASSED.

And in thirteen days, nearly half of one precious summer month, so much happened, and so much didn't. The local press was filled with stories about Sean's alleged embezzlement and disappearance. News trucks from New Haven and Hartford parked outside the McCabes' house. Bay tried to protect the kids from all of it, but it started to feel as if they were living in a fishbowl. One reporter called to Pegeen as she came out the front door, and she started to cry and ran back inside.

"How do they know our names?" Peggy cried. "Why are they here? Where's Daddy?"

"The police are still looking for him," Bay said. "They'll find him, honey."

"But they're looking for him because they say he's bad," Peggy wept. "He's not, Mommy. Tell them he's not!"

"I will, Peggy." Bay held and soothed her, boiling inside. When Peggy had calmed down, Bay kissed her forehead, then walked to the door. She took a deep breath, then went down the steps. Flashes snapped, and hand-held video cameras were shoved in her face. Her red hair was a mess, her shirt and shorts wrinkled and salty.

"Mrs. McCabe, what do you think—"

"Where is your husband?"

"What do you say about the allegations that—"

"The bank trustees blame—"

Bay took a deep shuddering breath. The reporters, thinking she was about to reply, fell silent. She looked slowly around the crowd, saw all the microphones, cleared her throat.

"Leave my children alone," she said quietly, with passion and menace in her heart.

A moment of shocked silence, and then the questions began again. "The bank . . . your husband . . . serious head wound . . . his whereabouts . . . the accounts . . . the allegations . . ."

Bay had said all she needed to say. Without another word, she walked back inside her house and closed the door behind her. She called Billy and Peggy downstairs; Annie had gone to Tara's. Her two younger children faced her with fear and trepidation in their eyes.

"What did you say to them, Mom?" Billy asked.

"I told them to leave us alone."

"Didn't you tell them Daddy is *good*? I thought you were going to tell them that he's *good*! They can't keep saying such terrible things about him," Peg said, the words spilling out. "Everyone has the wrong idea. We have to tell everyone the truth about him!"

"Yeah," Billy said. "Peggy's right about that. We have to tell everyone what a great guy Dad is. I'm sick of those jerks writing lies about him! I'm gonna go outside and tell them the real story!"

"No," Bay said. "I don't want you to do that, Billy. Do you hear me?"

Billy's jaw was set tight, his eyes full of fight. He was stubborn, just like his father. Bay wouldn't look away.

"Do you hear me?"

Billy nodded, but his face stayed tense.

"From now on, until the reporters leave, I want you to use the back door. Cut through the yard to the marsh, and go to the beach that way. Okay? No one's going to follow you through the mud. Don't talk to any of them. We want to give your father a chance to explain all this."

"Is he coming home?" Billy asked.

Bay's heart thudded. "I hope so, Billy."

"What if bad people hit him over the head and threw him overboard?" Peggy asked.

"I swear, I'll kill anyone who hurt Dad," Billy said.

"Me, too," Peg said.

"Don't talk like that," Bay said gently, looking into their troubled eyes. "Your father tripped and hit his head on the table. The police told us that. Remember?"

"Yeah, he has amnesia," Billy said, sounding more confident. "He's getting medical help somewhere and can't remember his name."

Peggy's face twisted in agony. "If he doesn't remember his own *name*, how will he remember *us*? How will he know how to come *home*?"

"He'll remember," Bay said, trying to stay steady and not let Peggy see her own anguish or rage—or her growing conviction that Sean remembered everything and had run away in spite of it.

Billy seemed to enjoy the idea of eluding the press, so he gathered together his and Peggy's beach things and took her out the back door. Bay watched them cross the yard, begin to walk along the marsh's soggy bank toward the beach. She saw them wave at their sister and Tara across the creek, in Tara's garden. Annie had been sleeping only fitfully, crying to think of her father somewhere alone in the world, with only her small green boat to keep him company.

Staring at her kids, aching as she thought of their pain, Bay went upstairs to lie down.

Her husband had very probably had a serious head injury, and no one knew where he was. He seemed to have fallen off the earth. Had he left them, run away because of the crimes he was accused of committing? Or were the kids' and her worst fears true—was he dead?

She cried into her pillow, and although she hated Sean for what he was putting them through, she didn't want to wash his pillowcase, because it smelled so much like him. Hearing a knock at the door, she ignored it. But it didn't stop, so she dried her eyes and walked downstairs.

It was Joe Holmes, with the reporters fanning out behind him. Bay stared through the screen door.

"Hi, Mr. Holmes," she said.

"Call me Joe," he said. "How are you?" When she didn't reply, he reddened slightly. "I'm sorry—stupid question," he said, and she suddenly felt self-conscious about the circles under her eyes, the fact she had lost ten pounds.

"Come in," she said, opening the screen door.

"Are your kids here?" he asked.

Bay blinked and shook her head. Looking out the window, she could see Annie and Tara watering Tara's garden. A silver stream arched from the hose, sparkling in the sun. Bay's throat felt parched and dry. She hadn't set foot in her own garden for thirteen days, since Sean had disappeared. Joe followed her gaze, and they were silent for a moment.

"We thought we would have found Sean by now," Joe said finally.

Bay nodded, grasping her upper arms, as if holding herself together.

"Why HAVEN'T you?" she burst out. "You said he was badly hurt—wouldn't he have needed medical help?"

"Definitely," Joe said. "We've checked every hospital in three states. We've called doctors, clinics..."

"Who else was on the boat with him?" she asked. "Couldn't they help find him?"

"Whoever was there knew enough to wipe their prints away. There are other things...Can we talk?"

Bay nodded, and he followed her into the kitchen and sat down at a stool at the breakfast bar. A stuffed and mounted bull shark hung above. Sean had hooked it last summer, on a trip to Montauk Point. Bay had objected to a dead creature hanging in her kitchen, but Sean had won out.

"Do you love your husband?" Joe asked.

"Yes," Bay answered without hesitation.

"Are you sure?"

He stared at her, as if he could read her mind and know whether she was lying or not. Unsure herself, Bay just stared back at him and raised her chin, and repeated, "Yes."

She had learned how to stand up for her family—at all costs—from her own mother, and from Tara's.

"Then I hope that what I have to say won't devastate you," Joe said.

"It won't," Bay said steadily. But inside, she was shaking.

"You probably know, I specialize in major bank embezzlement."

"I don't know that, Joe. All I know is that you're with the FBI."

"Fair enough. Well, I'm with the New Haven division. When a major crime comes in, they assign people who specialize in certain types of crime. I'm major—"

"Bank embezzlement," Bay said, the words strange to her ears.

Joe nodded.

"One thing I know, have learned, is that normally the vice presidents of a bank don't find it easy to embezzle, because they don't handle money. If there's theft, it's more common to look to the tellers. Or, sometimes, the executives enlist the branch managers to help. Or, another alternative, other executives. Bank insiders."

Bay's mouth was dry. Out the window, she could see her garden. It was horrible, really. In such a short time, she had gone from feeling so blessed, so overflowing with blessings, from having bowers of roses, peonies, black-eyed Susans, sweet peas, delphinium bloom as if by magic, to having the garden of her life, of her family, wilt and turn brown before her very eyes.

She blinked, listening.

"More commonly, vice presidents use their influence ... lending money to fictitious corporations they've set up ... or making 'bad' loans they know won't be paid back ... collecting kickbacks ... they use their authority ..."

"Sean couldn't do that," Bay said. "He has a whole bank board to answer to. Trustees, other executives ..."

"People know him, trust him," Joe continued. He wore a pin-striped suit and navy tie with small white dots; she saw him run a finger around his neck and noticed a film of sweat on his forehead. They didn't have air-conditioning; they didn't need it, with the sea breeze. Summers were spent in shorts and bathing suits. No one wore jackets and ties for long in this house. Every night Sean would walk in, peel off his coat before he got through the kitchen.

"Exactly. They trust him," she said, watching Joe sweat.

"He goes to the loan committee meeting, puts his stamp of approval on a questionable loan; the others might wonder, but they let it pass. They say, 'Hey, if it's good enough for Sean . . .' They might suspect something, but if he says it's okay, they do it. They say nothing. Or, and we've just about ruled this out, he had help from one of them."

"Are you saying there was a bad loan?"

Joe nodded slowly. "Yes, there was. Six months ago."

Bay felt shocked. "And you're just investigating now? Besides, what makes you think Sean did anything wrong? If someone defaulted, it was their fault, not his . . ."

"The thing fell apart when the FDIC did its internal audit. A high percentage of questionable loans from Shoreline—too many obvious corners being cut. They called us in."

Us, Bay thought: the FBI. She thought of that movie, *The Untouchables*, of how the FBI caught Al Capone through an accounting glitch. Was she really having this conversation about her husband?

"There were three different companies 'on the bubble' with loans approved by Sean. No payments made . . . and we saw what the FDIC knew right away—that the institution shouldn't have made these loans."

"So, Sean made a mistake."

"That's unclear."

"Can't you give him the benefit of the doubt?" Bay asked, her voice a cry. "What about the other officers? Isn't it just as much their fault?"

He gave her a look of pity. Those officers hadn't disappeared, hadn't abandoned their families. Bay dug her fingernails into her palms as she stared at Sean's picture on the bookshelf and tried to stay calm.

"In Connecticut, police departments and the FBI have close contact with security officers at banks. Once a month, bank security hosts law enforcement agencies and we all discuss things."

"What things?" Bay asked, although Sean had spoken to her of those conferences. "Baby, we're keeping the bank safe for our money and everyone else's," he would say.

"Just procedures, ways of staying ahead of problems. By law, when the bank is aware of wrongdoing, they have to file a report with the FBI. An SAR—Suspicious Activity Report."

"Wouldn't Sean have known?" Bay said, tension building in her head and chest.

"In this case, it was filed by a young woman named Fiona Mills. She took it on herself—perhaps she wasn't sure who to trust, or who the investigation would lead to."

Fiona—one of Sean's colleagues. Another upper-class young woman, a lot like Lindsey. Bay wondered whether Fiona had also caught Sean's eye.

Now she glanced at an old picture of herself and Sean, stuck to the refrigerator door with a ladybug magnet. Annie had found it, put it there—possibly to remind her parents of happier times. They had been so young, just out of school. She had been so happy, in love, willing to believe anything he told her, willing to overlook his recklessness. Thoughts swirling, she had to look away.

"We were following up on the criminal referral form for this loan situation when we came across some improprieties in the audit . . . several cash deposits of nine thousand nine hundred dollars each, and two money orders."

"Regarding the loan?" Bay asked, confused, feeling unreasonable resentment for Sean's colleague Fiona.

"No," Joe said. "It's still possible that the loans were no more than bad judgment on Sean's part. We haven't finished investigating."

Joe Holmes sat very still, watching her carefully with steady brown eyes.

"What else?" she asked. "Is there something else?"

"Before," Joe said. "When I asked you about the loans, you said that Sean 'couldn't' get away with them, because of an overseeing bank board. You didn't say he 'wouldn't' do it... There's a difference."

Bay's lip trembled, but she refused to let him see. Her gaze traveled to the sink, the family's mugs lined up on a shelf between the windows.

"The money orders and cash deposits," Joe said, "were the tip-offs."

"To what?" Bay asked.

"The fact that Sean was diverting money from his private banking clients. He started off small—a hundred dollars a day at first, then two hundred. He thought no one would notice, and why would they? These were good-sized accounts, with continuous dividends coming in. He'd take money from one account, park it in a trust. Later, he would write a money order or take out cash. He'd take a walk at lunch, head down to his boat, deposit his new money in an account he set up down at Anchor Trust."

"He'd never bank at Anchor. They were the competition," Bay said, her eyes burning as she watched Joe slide some forms across the counter. She knew before she even looked that Sean's name was on the accounts... and his signature.

"His clients trusted him one hundred percent," Joe

said. "First he'd funnel their funds into a trust at Shoreline, and from there, using the money orders, to an account at Anchor, where he had check-writing ability to spend it at will."

"No," Bay said, shaking her head. Were her kids going to have to hear this? It couldn't be true; it would kill Annie. "He would never want to hurt people like that."

"Most people don't," Joe said. "They don't even think of themselves as criminals. They have a need—right now. Something that they have an absolute need for."

"We have enough money," Bay said. "We're comfortable."

"In his mind, he probably wasn't even stealing—at first. 'I'll just help myself to a hundred dollars, and put it back Tuesday. Use it over the weekend.'"

"No...we have plenty..." Wasn't that always Sean's argument for Bay to stay home? The times she had wanted to go back to school, back to work? He would tell her they were comfortable...they had plenty...he didn't want the neighbors to think they needed money.

"Then Tuesday would come, and no one questioned... so he just kept going. The amounts increased. A thousand, five thousand. Nine thousand nine hundred. See, he knew that any cash transaction over ten thousand requires a CTR—Cash Transaction Report. He tried to fly under the radar, but Fiona noticed. He chose high-asset clients to steal from; perhaps he thought they wouldn't miss it. They didn't. None of the clients even noticed. He had a need—it was just a need that kept him going."

"No!" Bay said. What kind of need? The mortgage, vacations, two cars, three kids, the boat...an affair? Why would he risk everything they had to steal from the bank?

"It mounted up, over time," Joe said.

"Months?"

"We're investigating that now. The amounts increased dramatically about eleven months ago."

A need. Just a need.

"By law," Joe said, "anyone who handles money in a financial institution—tellers, branch managers—has to take a two-consecutive-week vacation. Financial advisors and trust officers just handle paper, so they're exempt."

Bay understood the rationale. Sean had explained it to her. Any financial misdeeds would come to light within two weeks.

"But these thirteen days since Sean's disappearance have revealed quite a bit. He didn't cover his tracks."

"Something terrible must have happened to him," Bay whispered, her throat as dry as the stalks outside. She thought of the blood on the *Aldebaran*. The blackness of all that blood on the blanket. "A reason he can't come home. What if he's..."

"You're afraid he's dead," Joe said.

Bay held herself, nodding.

"His body hasn't been found," Joe said. "If it were winter, with a lot of snow and ice, that would make more sense. But it's summer. Excuse my insensitivity, but bodies don't stay hidden in hot weather. We think he found medical help somewhere, and that he's hiding." He slid a paper toward her, the account statement from Anchor Trust.

Bay glanced down the debit side of the page. There had been one hundred and seventy-five thousand dollars in the account fourteen days ago. As of thirteen days ago, the balance read "zero."

"Our family accounts are at Shoreline," she said shakily. The first thing she had done, after absorbing the idea that Sean was missing, had been to check the status of their bank accounts.

Joe Holmes removed a second sheet of paper from his folder. He hesitated, then handed it to her. "Twenty-seven thousand dollars," he said. "Checking, savings, money market."

"That's plenty," she said, echoing her husband. She had expected there to be more.

"No stocks, bonds, other investments?"

"The market has been volatile. Sean takes a lot of risks, investing. We've had some big losses. But he's saving for college—three kids."

"And he likes his boat, and he likes the casino, and he likes..."

Bay lifted her eyes, to see whether he would say "other women."

But he didn't. The FBI agent looked tired, hot, sorry about everything, as if he wished this day would end and he could just go home. Did he have kids, a wife? He wasn't wearing a ring.... The sea breeze had stopped blowing. The air in the house was very still, and Bay suddenly felt as if she could dry up and turn to dust.

"Where do you think he is, Bay?" he asked.

She just sat very still, staring at the two account statements. She had done the math herself, over and over during the past days. With mortgage payments and insurance premiums and taxes, with feeding the kids and paying for electric, heat when the cold weather came, with paying the minimum on the credit cards, they had about five months before the savings would run out.

How long would that hundred and seventy-five thousand dollars last Sean, and where had he taken it?

"When someone violates a trust," Joe said, "it's heartbreaking. All checks and balances go by the wayside."

Was he talking about people at the bank? Or about her and the kids? Bay wondered.

"Who is 'Ed'?" he asked.

Bay just frowned and shook her head. "I can't think of anyone."

"I'm going to ask you something else," Joe said. "What do you think the words 'the girl' mean to Sean?"

The girl. The words sounded familiar, and Bay remembered the folder on Sean's boat. He's talking about that note Sean doodled, Bay thought, her pulse beginning to race as she remembered the drawing of the delivery van and the name Ed.

"I don't know," Bay said, aware that he was watching her carefully, not knowing why. "Something to do with one of our daughters?"

"I don't think so," Joe said.

He thinks "the girl" is about another woman, and he's probably right, Bay thought, feeling her shoulders fold forward with shame. A small breeze again stirred the sheer white curtains at the picture window. Upon it were carried the salty scents of sea and marsh, the fresh tang of sea lavender and beach roses. Bay heard Tara and Annie's voices carrying across the marsh and felt Tara watching over her.

"You might think of something," Joe said, gently sliding the papers back into their folder. "Something that will help us find him."

Find whom? she wanted to ask. Who was she supposed to help Joe Holmes find? She didn't know this Sean Mc-Cabe at all. What was worse, she didn't know herself. Somewhere during her marriage she must have made a deal with herself to stop paying attention, to start looking the other way. To shut down.

Because how could any of this have happened without her knowing?

"If I knew anything," she said very quietly, so he wouldn't be able to see the panic flooding through her, "I would tell you."

AS JOE HOLMES BACKED OUT OF BAY MCCABE'S DRIVEWAY, he saw her friend Tara O'Toole watching him from her house across the marsh—the *consiglière*. Her eyes were dark blue, her gaze so penetrating even at this distance, he felt a shiver go down his spine—Bay had a true friend. Joe had the feeling Tara was barely holding herself back from sprinting across the tide flats to confront him herself.

He'd like to tell Tara that this was one of the parts of the job he hated most—questioning fine, innocent people about their spouses' criminal activity. The look in Bay's eyes was enough to make him think about taking the next month off. Hitting some golf resort in Tucson, somewhere far from here, where all he had to do was tee off and work on his game.

His father had worked for the Bureau, and he'd been the one who first taught Joe that golf went far toward easing the stress of the job. Joe had grown up thinking his dad was the coolest hero, a spy just like James Bond only bigger and stronger and without an English accent, and there had never been a chance that Joe wouldn't follow in his footsteps.

Maynard Holmes had wound up head of the New Haven division. They had lived in a big blue house on Main Street in Crandell, between the store and the library. While other fathers went off to be schoolteachers, bankers, lawyers, mechanics, Joe knew his father was heading off to catch bad guys.

"How do you know who's bad?" Joe asked his father once.

"Not by how the person looks," his father had said. "Never judge anyone by their appearance, Joe. Or the car they drive, or the house they live in, or even by the words they say. Judge people by their actions. That's how you know whether they're bad or good."

Joe had always remembered that. He thought of his father's lessons every day, working for the Bureau. He wished his father was still alive; he would really like to discuss the McCabe case with him. But that was the least of it. Joe missed both of his parents. His mother had died of a stroke two years ago; his father hadn't lasted six months after that.

That's the kind of love Joe wished he had. But, investigating white-collar crime, he saw so many liars and the broken hearts they left behind, he wasn't sure love like his parents' existed anymore. He viewed most of the people he met with the same intense suspicion he had seen in Tara O'Toole's eyes just ten minutes ago.

Passing through town, Joe's next stop was Shoreline Bank, to question Fiona Mills. The receptionist waved him back to her office, and he walked in. She had striking blue eyes and chestnut hair held back by a sterling silver headband; she wore a simple, expensive pin-striped suit.

"I have a few questions," he said.

"I have a very full plate today, Mr. Holmes," she said, gesturing at her desk. "With Sean gone . . . and with the mess he left behind . . . Of course I want to do everything I can to help you, but I don't have much time right now."

"I know," Joe said, thinking of how different her dark blue eyes were from Tara O'Toole's. He swallowed, settling down. "Thank you for cooperating. We're just going over the latest details, trying to get to the bottom of everything. First of all, is there someone named Ed who works here?"

"Edwin Taylor, in the trust department," she said. "And Eduardo Valenti, a summer intern from New York. His parents live in the area."

Joe made notes, then looked up. "Can you tell me a little about yourself, and what you know about Sean McCabe?"

Fiona had arrived at Shoreline Bank about five years ago, and everything had seemed great. The bank was a terrific place to work, she had liked her colleagues, everyone had seemed to get along and worked together to keep the bank growing.

"Sean is always very competitive," she said. "We're about the same level, came up for vice president at the same time. He made no bones about wanting the promotion, and he courted the president and board . . . I knew we'd both eventually get it, which we did, but Sean really seemed to sweat it."

"Is that his personality?"

"Very much so. He likes contests, prizes. One year he was in charge of tellers, and he was always setting up competitions. In one, I remember, the person who opened the most new accounts got a weekend in Newport—things like that. He loves having the biggest boat, the newest car."

The opposite of Bay, Joe thought, taking notes.

"Did you ever think he was embezzling from clients?"

"Not back then," she said. "Never. It started after the presidency thing—"

"When Shoreline brought Mark Boland over from another bank?"

"Yes. Anchor. I have to admit, I was upset, too. Both Sean and I were hoping for the job. I think either one of us would have been great at it. But they brought in Boland instead."

"And Sean's behavior changed after that?"

Fiona nodded. "Yes, he was furious. He was really un-cooperative at first—unwilling to share numbers, discuss loans. He'd miss meetings, going out on his boat every chance he got. I actually grabbed him after work one day, told him to pull it together—for his family's sake, if not his own."

"He was on the way to getting fired?"

Fiona nodded. "I think he was heading in that direction."

"And then what?"

"Well, a few bad loans—I suspected something, but I didn't want to say. Sean began seeing one of the loan offi-cers, Lindsey Beale—very openly, brazenly. I know Bay and like her, and I thought he was acting like an ass. He began taking Lindsey to the casino, and she'd come in the next day and talk about it."

"Indiscreet."

"Very. Lindsey would talk about Sean blowing lots of money, and suddenly he started having some bad loans, and I began getting a bad feeling."

"Did you talk to him?"

"Yes. He told me it was nothing. At first . . . but then he started avoiding me. Any time I wanted to discuss some-thing, he'd tell me to leave him a voice mail, send him an e-mail. Eventually, I brought it up to Mark."

"Really?"

"Yes. He was very upset. He liked Sean—everyone did. And I think Mark is sensitive enough to know that Sean hated losing out to him. They had a history of some sort—high school sports. And they played golf, I think.

Sean was the kind of guy who, if he played golf against you, wanted to play for your watch, your cuff links."

"And money?"

Fiona shook her head. "Not so much. I think it was an heirloom thing; Sean came from a working-class family, and he really liked the trappings of growing up WASP. So many New England bankers have that sort of upbringing..."

Joe nodded. He had read the file. Fiona had gone to New York with Sean on a bank seminar, three years ago; records obtained from the Hotel Gregory indicated that they had shared a room. They had the job in common, but Joe suspected that it had been her boarding-school poise that had attracted him most. Fiona had grown up in Providence, summered in Newport. Her family was listed in the Social Register. She had attended the Madeira School and Middlebury College, with an advanced degree from Columbia Business School.

She was very cool right now, staring at Joe. In spite of the air-conditioning, a trickle of sweat ran down between his shoulder blades. He found himself wondering whether she could be "the girl."

The police had found a folder full of bank statements and account ledgers on Sean's boat. Joe had analyzed them, realized that they represented many of the people Sean had stolen from. What confused him was the way Sean had written "the girl" over and over—Joe had examined many criminals' doodles, and he could generally make sense of the emotions inside at the time of the drawings.

He had seen the way a check forger had written "Paris," and the way a murderer had doodled "Mary Ann," and the way a smuggler had written "South Beach" with a certain lightness, with the criminal's dreams present in the word.

Not "the girl." Joe had noticed the thick black letters, the heavily scored border: as if the real girl, whoever she might be, had been weighing on Sean's mind.

"Did Sean ever talk to you about his work, about the bank?"

"Naturally," she said. "We're colleagues."

"Did he ever hint at what he was doing about the embezzlement?"

"Of course not," she said. "I had no idea...I find it hard to believe now. His clients loved him. And he talked about them as if he cared. He cared about everyone."

Joe nodded. That wasn't inconsistent with other white-collar criminals; they were so invested in lying to everyone, they also lied to themselves.

"Can you tell me who he seemed closest to? Here at the bank?"

"Frank Allingham. And I've seen him having drinks with the bank's attorney, Ralph Benjamin."

"What about Mark Boland? Did they ever get past their feud?"

"No. In fact, Mark was the one who told me to file that criminal report. I thought he should do it himself—at first I'd hoped he could handle it in-house..."

"But of course that would be against regulations," Joe said slowly. "Once you'd blown the whistle, Mark was required by law to call the FBI."

"What would we do without banking regulations?" Fiona asked, shaking her head. "Sean might not have gotten hurt."

"Excuse me?"

"Banged his head, I mean," she said. "Whatever happened on that boat."

"Why do you say that?"

"Because he went so crazy after he was passed over for

Mark's job. If only he could have had more time, to pull himself together. He must have gotten wind of the investigation, gotten scared. I think he'd started drinking a little—maybe even doing some drugs."

"Why do you say that?"

"Sean likes to party," Fiona said. "Surely I'm not the first one to tell you this."

"No," Joe said. "You're not. I'm getting the feeling he was pretty wild. Was there anyone in particular you can think of that he called 'the girl'?"

Fiona frowned and seemed at a loss.

Just then Mark Boland stuck his head into the office. He looked uptight and harried, but he threw Joe a wide smile. "How's it going, Agent Holmes?" he asked, shaking his hand. "Is there anything I can add to whatever Fiona's helping you with?"

"He was just asking who Sean called 'the girl'."

"He calls his daughters 'the girls,' I think. Sometimes he includes Bay in that. As in 'The girls and Billy are waiting for me at home,'" Boland said. "Do you have a wife, Mr. Holmes?"

"No, I don't."

"Well, my wife might kill me for saying it, but there's no time limit on calling your wife a girl. Maybe Sean meant Bay. On the other hand, with Sean it could just as easily mean a whole different thing."

"I'm getting the picture," Joe said.

"Well, I'll leave Fiona to answer the rest of your questions. I have a conference call with the IRS and our lawyer right now. Excuse me."

Joe thanked him, then turned back to Fiona Mills. She had given him plenty of her time, and it was time for him to get going. "Is there anything else you'd like to add?" he asked.

Fiona shrugged. "Sometimes I think Sean was just completely bowled over by all the money he oversaw."

Joe watched as she clasped her hands, touched the edge of her desk thoughtfully. "Sean's from a working-class family. We're not very close, but we did—take a few business trips together. We'd talk on the way, or having drinks at the hotel. I take it that they never had much money—Oh, they were comfortable in a middle-class way. But real money—that came much later, after Sean became a banker. He felt left out of so many things growing up."

"Like what?"

"Well, like the country club. He caddied for the members. And the yacht club; he worked as a deckhand for people like my father and uncles, who owned their own yachts. I think I represent something to him, that he's wanted all his life: to belong."

"Belong to what?" Joe asked. Didn't he belong to a great family—Bay, the kids?

"You know, Mr. Holmes," she said. "You're just being obtuse. I mean belong to 'the club.' To be in instead of out. To have doors open for you. Some of us grew up taking that for granted. Sean didn't."

"I see, Ms. Mills. Thank you very much for your time." As he stood to leave, he noticed a glass case filled with trophies—for horse shows, regattas, tennis matches. "Are those yours?"

"Yes," she said. "My father rather values athleticism."

"The competitive spirit is alive and well here at Shoreline Bank," he said, noticing an empty spot on a middle shelf, with dust around the shiny circle of a round base. "What was there?"

"Odd you should ask," she said, her eyes clouding over.

"I'm missing a silver bowl. Nothing terribly important—something I won for a jumping event several years ago."

Joe nodded, thanking Fiona for her time. Passing from her office through the bank, he was aware of all the bank personnel discretely watching him.

Everyone except Mark Boland. He was on the phone, back to the door, jabbing the air with his finger. Seemed like a pretty competitive guy himself, Joe thought, walking to his car.

AFTER WATCHING JOE HOLMES DRIVE AWAY, TARA GAVE BAY half an hour alone, while she and Annie picked a huge bouquet. Then they waded across the creek and cut through the backyard. The news vultures called from the driveway, and Annie's shoulders went up to her ears. When they were safely inside, Tara instructed her goddaughter to arrange the tangled flowers in a tall vase, and she climbed the stairs and found Bay curled up on her bed.

"It's too nice a day out for you to be in here," Tara said. "In spite of all the idiots parked in front of your house."

Bay's face stayed in the pillow.

Tara sat down on the edge of the bed, put her hand on Bay's shoulder. It felt far too thin, almost frail, as if this ordeal was literally taking everything out of her.

"Bay? I saw Joe Holmes over here."

No words, just quiet crying.

"Bay?"

"It's awful, Tara," Bay said finally. "It's so much worse than we thought. Sean really did it—embezzled money, planned it all out, used his clients. Stole money, parked money—it's bad."

"He's sure?"

"Yes. He has lots of evidence. He showed me a lot of it. Including our accounts..."

"Bay, no—he didn't take money from you..."

Bay nodded, starting to sob. She clutched the pillow-case, and Tara could see that it was already soaking wet with tears. She felt such overwhelming fury at Sean she could barely keep her voice steady.

"How bad is it?"

"I don't know yet, Tara," Bay said. "I can't even think. It's all just hitting me: He's a criminal. My husband! What kind of an idiot was I to not know? What'll I tell the kids? Every day there's something new and horrible. They're all just hanging on, praying that their father's okay."

"I know. The whole time Annie was over, she couldn't take her eyes off your house. As though he was going to show up any second."

"Waiting for him to come home—when he's probably going to jail!"

"No wonder he's hiding somewhere."

Bay rolled onto her back, looked up at Tara with swollen, red eyes. "What are we going to do?" she asked.

"You're going to stay strong," Tara said firmly. "We'll get through this together."

"Thanks for being here," Bay said. "I don't know what the kids or I would do without you."

Tara just shook her head—such a thing wasn't even worth saying. Bay had enfolded Tara into her family, into the warmth of her life, just as if she was a sister. The depth of her love was without bounds, and she couldn't bear to hear Bay thank her.

"Just know how wonderful you are," Tara said, leaning over to hug Bay, to look straight into her eyes. "And how wrong he is."

The best friends locked gazes, and Bay nodded.

"And go see that boatbuilder," Tara said.

"That what?"

"Danny Connolly," Tara said.

"Why?" Bay asked, her eyes clouded with confusion and pain.

Tara swallowed, holding back what she really thought: that maybe the one decent thing Sean had done this whole horrific year was to open this door for Bay. But she didn't say that. Instead, she conjured up Joe Holmes and her grandfather and made herself feel and sound like an investigator on the case.

"Because you're in a mystery right now," she said steadily, "and Daniel Connolly is one of the clues."

6

As days went by without any new developments, the news trucks began to travel to other stories, leaving the McCabes alone. Joe Holmes took note as he drove by, and he was relieved. He also took note of Tara O'Toole sitting on the front steps, reading to the youngest McCabe child, Pegeen. He saw her watch him like a mother eagle, sharp-eyed and ready to use her talons if necessary.

He had checked her grandfather out. Since she'd mentioned the law-enforcement connection, he'd been curious. So he'd looked up all the O'Tooles he could find. The most prominent one in Connecticut had been Seamus O'Toole, Captain of Detectives, in Eastport. The particulars seemed right—his wife was named Eileen, and they had retired to their summerhouse in the Hubbard's Point section of Black Hall.

Captain O'Toole had been known in the department for his tough crackdown on drugs, in the early days of an epidemic that had seen neighborhoods turned into war zones. He had become known for brash raids on dealers in the West End, leading his officers into warehouses filled with drugs just off boats, in Long Island Sound, hidden in trucks speeding up the northeast corridor of I-95.

His record was full of gun battles, important arrests, personal injuries, being shot three times. Medals for valor and bravery, for his prowess as a pistol shot. The file also included the story of how Captain O'Toole had been the first on the scene of a head-on traffic fatality: One of the drivers had been drunk. He had died instantly, as had the woman in the other car. His name was Dermot O'Toole. He was the captain's son.

And Tara's father.

Joe nodded at Tara as he drove by. She nodded gravely back. Two products of law-enforcement families, he thought. She'd probably want nothing to do with another officer—not that he'd ever get the chance to find out. She was too close to this investigation.

Pulling into the parking lot at Shoreline Bank, he shook her from his mind and went inside. He had seen Eduardo Valenti yesterday, a dark-haired college kid spending his summer as a teller. His contact with Sean McCabe had been minimal. He had told Joe about an outing on the *Aldebaran* with a few other people who worked at the bank, and times when McCabe would stop by his desk to ask how things were going. Eduardo hadn't liked Sean.

"I found him to be slick and superficial."

"That's quite a comment to make about your boss," Joe said, smiling and amused at the kid's haughtiness.

"My parents raised me to recognize sincerity," Eduardo said. "I didn't see it in Mr. McCabe."

Eduardo Valenti came from a very wealthy Castilian

family, formal and dignified, and he was always called
"Eduardo"—never "Ed."

Joe didn't see any red flags there. He then asked for Edwin Taylor, and the receptionist told him he'd be back
from vacation the next day.

And now she said he was in. Joe said a quick hello to
Mark Boland and Frank Allingham, then walked across
the lobby and was greeted by a man, about thirty-five,
with a high forehead, glasses, and a perplexed expression
in his eyes.

"I'm sorry I wasn't in yesterday when you came," Edwin Taylor said, shaking Joe's hand. "I just got back from
Scotland, and I'm in total shock. I can't believe what
they're saying about Sean. Is it true?"

"From what we've been able to gather," Joe said. "Why
don't you tell me what you know about Sean and his
banking practices?"

Edwin Taylor ran through basically the same story Joe
had heard from every other Shoreline employee. Sean
was a charming, witty guy with a great work ethic and a
need to succeed. He had been upset about Mark Boland's
appointment to the presidency; like others, Taylor had
thought Sean had had a shot at the position.

"What are you called, Mr. Taylor?" Joe asked. Although he had already asked other employees, he wanted
to hear it directly from him.

"Excuse me?"

"Is your nickname Ed?"

"No, 'Trip,'" he said. "I'm the third. My dad is called
Ed. Why?"

"Does your father live nearby? Does he bank here at
Shoreline?"

"Yes, to both," Trip Taylor said. "He lives in Hawthorne,
and yes, he banks here."

"Is he one of Sean McCabe's clients? Or does he work directly with you?"

"Actually, I asked Sean to take care of him," Taylor said. "Sean's very good at what he does. He did a great job, getting the private banking division up and running. Besides, my dad's a friend of Augusta Renwick's, one of Shoreline's biggest clients, and she's always singing Sean's praises."

"I'm going to need to talk to your dad," Joe said grimly, picturing Sean's strange drawings and doodles, remembering the name Edwin Taylor, Jr., from the account ledger Joe had found on Sean's boat.

ELIZA DAY BOAT BUILDERS WAS LOCATED IN A LARGE SHED at the far end of the New London Shipyard. The shipyard did major marine business, including hauling and servicing the ferries that plied Long Island Sound between New London and Orient Point, providing dockage for large yachts and commercial fishing vessels, and serving as home port for the wild-card, dark-horse, and long-shot America's Cup challenger built by Paul James and skippered by Twigg Crawford.

The boatbuilders were a different story. This was a small operation. The shed was large and airy, about the size of a cow barn. With both doors open, the sea wind gusted through, blowing sawdust and feathers all over the place. The feathers were from all the swallows that nested in the rafters. The sawdust was from all the wooden boats built or restored by Dan Connolly, owner. Charlotte Day Connolly had been the backer.

Bent over an old hull, Dan pried back a section of veneer sheathing to see what was underneath. This was a delicate operation, but he had to find out whether the original planks had been planed back enough for the sheathing to lie flush with the ballast.

"Shit," he said, as the veneer broke off in his hand.

"Nice, Dad," came a voice from above.

"You really need to get out more," Dan said.

"Trying to get rid of me?"

"That'd be the general idea."

"You shouldn't swear at the boats."

"I wasn't. I was swearing at myself."

"Yeah, sure."

"Seriously," Dan said, looking up and over his shoulder to peer into the murky darkness. All he could see were shadows, beams, and two very white legs dangling down. "How did you get here?"

"I flew."

"That's a bunch of bullshit, and we both know it. How did you get here?"

"I climbed on the back of a sea hawk and said, 'I'm Eliza Day, take me to my boathouse.' And the sea hawk obliged and just came straight across the harbor..."

"You rode in my truck again, didn't you?" Dan asked, straightening up as he smacked his hand down on the now-broken hull. "You hid under the tarp and let me drive you right down the highway; the back gate's been broken all summer, goddamn it, you could have slid straight into traffic, for Christ's—"

"Don't take the name of the Lord in vain," came the voice, sounding dangerous now.

"And don't tell your father what he can and can't say," Dan said, voice rising, walking over to the ladder to the loft. "First I can't swear in my own shop, now I can't take the name—"

"Of the Lord in vain," she said beatifically.

"Get down here right now," he said, tanned hands on the rough ladder. "Don't make me go up there after you."

"Or what? Or what? You're going to beat me? Beat your child? Maybe I should just scream for help now. Mr. Crawford will hear me and come rescue me. Maybe they'll take me away from you. You have no idea how to take care of a motherless child."

"Eliza, shut up."

"And NOW you tell me to shut up," she said, her voice rising to a squeak. Were the tears real or fake? Dan had lost the ability to tell. He was at the end of his rope—an excellent cliché, if ever he'd heard one. He thought of boats he'd seen at the end of their ropes—boats in hurricanes, nor'easters, spring tides, ebb tides—violently bucking and straining to break free.

"I didn't mean it," he said slowly, carefully. "I didn't mean it."

"Which part? The part where you told me to shut up? Or the part where you threatened to beat me?"

"Eliza, I never did, and you know it. I just meant, don't make me come up there to get you. It's too hot, okay? Take it easy on your old dad. Come on down, and I'll take you to the Dutch for a burger."

"The Dutch is a bar," Eliza said.

"True," Dan said, craving a beer. He never drank during the day when Charlie was alive, and he hardly ever did now, but the desire to check out was strong: He wanted out of the fury and sorrow he almost always felt, and the shame he was trying to bury, and there was nothing like a visit to Dutch's Tavern to help it all along.

"Mom wouldn't want you taking me to a *saloon*."

"Mom liked Peter and Martha so much, I think she'd let it slide," Dan said, thinking of the Dutch's owners.

The place was a classic New London hole-in-the-wall, hidden on a side street in an old building with a tin ceiling and scarred wooden tables reputed to have once accommodated Eugene O'Neill. "And you like them, too."

"Yeah," Eliza had to agree. "I do."

"So what're you bellyaching for? Come on down and we'll go to lunch."

Gripping the ladder, he watched a swallow circle the shed twice before flying out the open door. The white legs just dangled, crossed daintily at the ankles.

"Eliza?"

"Will you make me go home after lunch? Because I don't want to."

Dan exhaled, grimacing so she couldn't see and counting to ten. He knew this was a test. He could lie, and they'd be on their way to lunch. Or he could equivocate, and work out the details later. "We'll see."

"Forget it," she said, pulling her legs up into the darkness so he couldn't see them at all. "Here's the deal, Dad. I stay. That's that. That's all there is to it. This is MY business, and don't you forget it."

"Oh, yeah? This is a boatbuilding business, in case you didn't know. Who's the one who builds the boats around here?"

"Who's the one who's named 'Eliza Day' after her great-grandmother with all the MONEY?" screeched the voice.

Just then, Dan heard footsteps on the old plank floor. He looked up and saw someone silhouetted in the light of the doorway, framed by the midday summer sun like some otherworldly figure in the opening credits of one of those quack-religious TV shows Eliza watched.

"Can I help you?" he asked.

"You've come a long way since the boardwalk," said a voice that seemed piercingly familiar. "We both have."

BAY STOOD IN THE DOORWAY, STARING AT DAN CONNOLLY. She would have known him anywhere. He looked exactly the same as he had twenty-five years ago, but, somehow, very different. He smiled at her, lines around his mouth and eyes scored deep in his tan face. His eyes were blue, the color of his faded jeans, and wary, as if he'd seen too many things he didn't want to see. Lean and strong, he looked like a man who had spent his life building things.

As he came toward her, Bay felt her stomach dip. Their eyes met and held.

"It's really you," she said, almost unable to believe her eyes.

"Bay?" he asked, taking one hand, then grabbing for the other, and then, because how could a reunion between them be otherwise, pulled her toward him in a hug. She hung on to him, completely lost in the smell of sawdust and machine oil, and then pushed back to look up into his eyes.

"I'd forgotten how tall you were," she said.

"Why would you remember?" he asked, laughing.

She smiled. If he only knew how she had adored him, how she had reflexively compared all others, Sean included, to him for years.

"The last time I saw you," he said, "you were fifteen years old."

"About to turn sixteen," she said.

"Galway," he said, using her old nickname.

"Galway Bay..." She laughed, remembering.

"How have you been, Bay? How has life treated you?"

She smiled, but her face felt frozen, her insides locked up. "I've had a wonderful life," she said. Would he notice the past tense?

"Good. I'm glad," he said.

"How about you, Dan?"

His smile washed away; his face tightened, especially around the eyes. She waited, wondering what would come next. Suddenly he looked like she felt: shell-shocked by life. A week ago, Bay wouldn't have been able to see it, to recognize someone suffering like this. But now she could.

"My life's been..." he began.

Just then something came flying down from up above. Shielding her head, Bay ducked and tried to see. Light coming in the big open doors couldn't illuminate the vast darkness above the shed's rafters, but Bay thought she saw two beacon-white legs dangling from one of the beams. Another projectile came whizzing past. Bay crouched down and picked it up: a paper airplane.

"Eliza," Dan said sternly.

"His life's been ruined," came a voice from above. "By me. That's what he was going to say."

"No, I wasn't," Dan said. "Don't put words into my mouth."

"That's one of the stupidest clichés around," the voice said. "How can someone put words into someone else's mouth?"

"How old are you?" Bay called up.

Silence.

"She's twelve," Dan said.

"Eliza can talk, you know," said Eliza.

"Is Eliza Day Boat Builders named after you?" Bay asked, squinting into the dark loft.

"Officially, no. It's named after my grandmother. But

since I'm named after her, yes. That would be the general idea."

"Why don't you come down here, Eliza?" Dan asked. "I want you to meet an old friend."

Bay heard some rustling above, watched as the girl walked gracefully the length of one rafter, as if it were a balance beam, and then climbed down a rough ladder at the end of the shed. She was tall and thin, like her father, but—unlike him—with translucent pale skin, and a wreath of curly blond hair. Her coloring must have come from her mother.

"Eliza, this is my friend, Bay Clarke—"

"Bay McCabe," she corrected him, watching for a reaction. Dan smiled.

"You married Sean," he said.

"I couldn't wait forever," she joked, because it was *such* a joke—he had broken her young heart without even having a clue.

"WAIT?" Eliza asked. "You mean for my FATHER?"

Bay's heart tugged, thinking of Annie and her proprietary attitude toward Sean. Children cherished the illusion that their parents had never loved anyone but each other. She smiled reassuringly.

"Your father was way out of my league, Eliza," she said. "I was just a kid—not much older than you. He was the man who fixed everything at the beach. I looked up to him, that's all. He taught me to fix things."

Eliza nodded, satisfied. She was very pale, as if she never went out in the sun. Even now, standing on the first floor of the big shed, she backed into the shadows, to keep from standing in the summer sunlight pouring through the open doors.

Now Bay handed her the small paper airplane she had picked up. "You must have some of your father's talent," she said. "For making things. This is a really good airplane."

"It's a dove," Eliza said, holding it in her hands. "A white-winged dove."

"Well, it's beautiful," Bay said, feeling emotion pouring off the child. Bay felt it herself. She had come here on terrible business, and she didn't even know what to ask. It felt more comfortable to tune in to this little girl, who was so unlike Annie in almost every way—height, weight, pallor, outspokenness—yet like her in heart; Bay could read this girl's pain the way she could her own daughter.

"It reminds me of my mother; the way she is now," Eliza said, still staring at what Bay now realized was an origami bird. The girl tilted her head, to look up at her father. Following her gaze, Bay was shocked by the expression on Dan's face.

It was hard and cold. His jaw was set, as if he was holding a barrage of feelings inside—and they weren't good, and they weren't simple. He was staring at his daughter as if the sight of her caused him agony.

Eliza registered his expression, too. Her eyes flickered, and as if with acceptance she blinked and looked away.

"Maybe I will go home, Dad," Eliza said.

"Let me talk to Bay for a minute," he said, "and then I'll drive you." The icy stare was gone; his voice was warm and loving. But Bay knew what she had seen, and she leaned just slightly closer to Eliza.

"I'd be happy to give you a ride," she said. "On my way home…"

"You live in Hubbard's Point," Dan said, over Eliza's pointed silence.

"Yes—you know?" she asked, her heart flipping over at the confirmation of Sean's having been here.

He nodded. "Is the boardwalk still there?"

"Don't tell me you haven't brought your wife and Eliza down to the beach!" Bay said. "Showed them all the things you built—a hurricane washed away the old foot-bridge, but we replaced it, and almost everything else is still there."

"Dad builds things to last," Eliza said. The statement was proud, but she said it quietly, as if there was some-thing dark beneath it. "Too bad people aren't made that way."

"People?" Bay asked.

"I'm going to wait in your truck, Dad," Eliza said, as if Bay hadn't just spoken, and as if she hadn't offered to give her a ride. "Tell her about Mom."

"I'll be right out," Dan said.

Now, as he turned to face Bay, she saw worry in his eyes. She had his fax with her and she wanted to ask him to explain it, but she couldn't speak just yet. She knew very well those furrows around his eyes, the worry that showed itself in lines on a person's face. She probably had quite a few going herself.

"Thanks for the offer," Dan said. "But I need to talk to her. You can probably tell, she's got a lot going on. Her mother died last year."

"Your wife? I'm sorry!" Bay exclaimed.

"Thank you," he said simply, almost brusquely. "Any-way, we live out of the way for you. The opposite direc-tion, in fact—in Mystic. Near my parents' old house."

"You've lived in the area this whole time, and I didn't know," Bay said.

"It's strange. Whenever I drive past the Black Hall exit on Ninety-five, I think about the beach, wonder whether you and some of the others are still there."

"You must have known, though," she said, taking the fax from her pocket and handing it to him. "You've been in touch with my husband."

"I know," he said, pulling a pair of reading glasses from his breast pocket. His dark brown hair was streaked with gray. So much time had passed, Bay thought. No one was the same anymore. "I couldn't believe when he came to see me."

"Why did he?" she asked.

"He wants me to build him a boat," Danny said, tapping the fax.

"I see that," Bay said. "But why? Why you?"

Danny's eyes glimmered for a second. "I wondered the same thing. But after we got through the pleasantries, and I asked about you, he got straight to business. His visit was all about boats."

"Have the—I was wondering—have the police or the," she paused, because it was still so unbelievable to her, "FBI...contacted you?"

"No," he said, taking off his glasses. "I'm sorry for what you're going through, I've seen the news."

She nodded with as much dignity as possible. "Thank you," she said.

"I just barely remember Sean from the beach—really only in context with you," Dan said.

She took a deep breath, trying to settle down.

Dan's building was filled with works-in-progress. Bay recognized finished but unpainted dories and skiffs, all made of wood, as well as a twenty-foot sailboat under construction. There were gracefully curved ribs, fine cedar planks, sheets of plywood, lengths of oak.

"Are you still particular about wood, Bay?" he asked, watching as she leaned over to touch a smooth-grained board. "That's okoume plywood, and that's luan. For a catboat on order from a guy in Maine. I'll finish it off with white oak and mahogany, and she'll be a pretty boat."

"I like the way it smells," she said, closing her eyes.

"Are you still in love with the moon?" he asked quietly.

"Yes, I am," she said. "Especially the crescent moon..."

He nodded. That summer she had kept a moon watch, reporting to him each day on the phases of the moon. "Everyone always thinks the full moon is so romantic," she used to say, "but I think it's so bright and obvious! I love the crescent moon, just a mysterious little sliver there in the sky..."

"Since the beach hasn't given me a budget to pay you for all your help," Dan had joked, "I'll have to give you the crescent moon. I'll make something out of it for you."

"You think you can make anything," she said. "I dare you to make something from the moon!"

And he had. He had found a weathered sickle of a driftwood log washed up on the beach after a storm, smooth and silver as moonlight, and he had made it into a swing, for her alone.

"Is it still there?" he asked, letting her know he was thinking the same thing. Was he remembering her surprise and delight, how he had pushed her on the swing that first time? She could see the spot: a sunny clearing deep in the woods, off the path to Little Beach. The swing's ropes had looked like vines, and no one but Bay knew how to find it.

"No," she said, looking into his blue eyes. "The ropes rotted years ago. I took my oldest daughter over when she was little, to show it to her. The seat is still there. I keep expecting it to turn back into the moon, to just disappear into the sky."

He stood still, leaning against one of the boats, arms folded across his chest.

"You have more serious things on your mind," he said, "than an old swing in the woods."

"I do," she said.

"I wish I could help you more," he said. As he spoke he began to walk, through the shed—dust golden in the hot sunlight slanting through the open doors—to a small office toward the back. Bay followed him inside, watched him begin to rummage through a stack of papers on the top of an old desk.

"That's beautiful," she said, noticing the carving in the dark wood: fish, shells, sea monsters, and mermaids.

"It belonged to my wife's grandfather," Dan said. "And it was carved by my grandfather. Long story..."

"Is that her? Your wife?" Bay asked, spotting a framed photo of Eliza and a lovely woman with light hair and pale skin, both wearing straw hats with long blue ribbons.

"Yes," Dan said. "That's my Charlie..."

Bay's heart broke at the way he said it: *my Charlie*. With so much love and sorrow, leaving absolutely no doubt about the way he had felt about her. Now, staring at the photo, his eyes were narrowed and tight, as if the pain of her loss, of never seeing her again, was hitting him again. Bay wondered how she had died, but knew it wasn't the time to ask. She considered her own horrible mixed feelings about Sean and wished she had nothing but love for him, nothing but regret for the missed chances, for the wonderful times they had shared.

"You must miss her," Bay said awkwardly.

"Yes," he said, still frowning as he continued looking through invoices on the old carved desk. "We both do."

Bay couldn't stop looking at his wife's picture—she

had such striking eyes, such an open gaze. Had Dan taken the picture? Bay recognized the background—the carousel at Watch Hill—a favorite spot of all the little girls of southern New England. Annie and Pegeen adored it, as had their mother and Tara before them.

Her gaze wandered the rest of the room. Big windows overlooked the Thames River. Electric Boat was on the other side, one submarine at the dock. Ferries passed— the high-speed hovercraft heading out as the Cross Sound boat came in from Long Island. Small sailboats tacked, their white sails and hulls gleaming.

"I know I have his order somewhere," he said. "He was very specific, if only I can find it..."

"My husband isn't really a wooden boat person. That's why I'm surprised he came to you," she said, noticing his drafting table, drawings of rowing boats spread over its surface. Now she glanced at his bookshelves, books on Herreshoffs and Concordias beside the collected letters of E. B. White and a stack of old maritime magazines. "Did he say anything about letters?" Bay asked abruptly. "The ones we wrote to each other?"

"You and I?" Dan asked, glancing up. "No, he didn't. God, those were a long long time ago..."

And I saved them all, Bay thought. Was that crazy? She glanced at the picture of Charlie again and felt embarrassed. What had she been holding on to, all these years? If her own marriage had ever been really happy, wouldn't she have thrown them out? Clearly Dan had found the real love of his life in Charlie... Bay's gaze swept across the desk, and settled again on Dan. He was older, more rugged than she had remembered, weathered by life and love. But he was still her first love, and she still felt a thrill just to see him.

"I'm getting closer," he said. "Up to June now... hang on."

"Take your time," she said, exhausted by the storm of emotions. She arched her back, walked over to the window to look out at the river, tripping over a tool belt lying on the floor.

Reaching out to steady herself, she stumbled into the bookshelf and cried out with surprise.

"What is this doing here?" she asked, reaching forward with a trembling hand for the object on the top shelf.

Dan's eyes widened, and he flushed slightly.

"It's my daughter's," Bay explained, her eyes filling with tears as she lifted down the small green dory. "Annie made it for her father."

"She did a great job," Dan said. "The details are excellent—the joinery, and the fairing..."

"He promised her he would keep it with him always."

"I think he meant to," Dan said, finding the invoice. "This is the order form for a twelve-foot rowing dory. He just left her boat for me, so I'd know what to build."

"But why would he want a dory?" Bay asked, looking into Dan's clear blue eyes. "Sean's taste in boats is so different..."

"He wanted it for your daughter."

"Annie?" she asked, her heart thudding.

Dan nodded. "Yes. It was going to be for her. I haven't started it. I'd put the whole thing aside, after I read about Sean in the paper. But he was adamant about it—he said he wanted it for Annie. And that he wanted me to build it myself—not to give it to my assistants to help with. He showed me the model on that first visit—and finally dropped it off for me to work with, just a couple of weeks ago. Should I go ahead and keep working?"

"You'd better hold off for a while," Bay said, thinking of the money, feeling confused about it all.

Just then, the truck horn sounded from out in the yard. "DAAAAADDDD!" came Eliza's voice. Dan gave Bay a look of apology, and she managed to say something about kids being kids. She shook his hand across the ornate desk, and without asking or explaining, tucked Annie's boat under her arm and walked out to the parking lot at Dan's side.

She climbed into her car, set Annie's boat on the seat beside her. Inserting the key in the ignition, she started up the Volvo and rolled down the windows. Salt air blew through the car with boatyard smells of epoxy, varnish, and fish. She couldn't wait to get back home, to the beach.

But as Dan and Eliza pulled out, in a big green truck with "ELIZA DAY BOAT BUILDERS" painted in small gold letters on the doors, Bay again reached for Annie's boat.

It felt so fine, so light. Bay remembered how she and Annie had bought the balsa wood together, how Annie had soaked it to get it to bend...how they had had to hold the boards together with tiny clamps and elastic bands, to wait for the glue to dry.

Holding it together...

Sean's secret-keeping was as powerful as ever. Bay sensed that somehow Annie's boat and Sean's visit to Dan—and his dropping off Annie's model—could shed light on his disappearance: on why he had pulled one of Bay's old letters to Danny Connolly from the hope chest, on all the mysteries of his last weeks at home.

She remembered how hard her daughter had worked, to make her father a wonderful present he'd never forget. Annie cried herself to sleep every night, thinking of Sean alone somewhere, hiding from his family and the bank and the law, with nothing but her little green boat to keep him company.

"Sean, how could you?" Bay said out loud, as she held the boat in her hands and imagined what Annie would say when she saw it, when she understood that her father hadn't taken it with him after all.

7

PRETTY UGLY," BILLY SAID, STANDING BESIDE ANNIE. IT was like summer going backward instead of forward, from the full-bloom beauty of late June into a brown, dry, wilting farewell to the flowers, almost as if they had never really even been alive at all. "We used to have the best yard, now we have the worst yard."

"It's not Mommy's fault," Peggy said. "She's busy looking for Daddy."

"I never said it was Mom's fault," Billy said patiently. "Will you please consider opening your ears?"

"They are open!" Peg said. "What's wrong with you? You're supposed to be taking care of me today, and I was supposed to go to Little League practice, but Mommy's not home yet, and you won't pitch to me, and I hate you!"

"When you say 'hate' you really mean 'love,' so you love me," Billy said.

"You wish," Peg said.

"Roses are red, violets are blue, dirt is stupid, and Pegeen is, too."

"Dirt's not stupid. It's smart. That's why roots can't wait to get down in it. That's why earthworms think it's like the best palace in the world. Dirt rules."

"Well, if dirt rules, then I guess we have the greatest garden at the beach, because all we got is dirt and dead flowers," Billy said, grabbing the ball out of Peg's hand. "Come on, I'll pitch to you. You can practice sliding face-first into the DIRT. Just so you can't grow up and tell one of those rotten TV reporters you had a neglected child-hood. At least you won't be able to blame your brother."

"Yeah, I'll find a way," Peg said, scooting ahead, into the backyard where she'd left her glove and the bat.

All of this occurred within thirty seconds, with Annie standing perfectly still in the midst of it, as if she wasn't even there. As if she was some sort of rotund lawn orna-ment, to go with the brown flowers, watching her brother and sister tear after each other in a form of mad, familial, therapeutic batting practice.

If only Annie liked playing ball; she just knew she'd be a happier person. She was always envious of how Billy and Pegeen seemed to get over things so much faster than she did, whacking the ball and sliding into home plate and generally working all their frustrations out through physical activity: just like what her father used to tell her she should do.

"You'd be happier and healthier, Annie-bear, and all your problems would go away," he'd say, "if you'd just get some exercise." By "healthier," of course, he had meant "thinner," but the boat of thinness had long since sailed for this summer.

Looking across the marsh, she saw Tara's little white house and bright yard, shining like a garden of jewels.

Pale pink foxgloves waved in the breeze, azure morning glories climbed the trellis. Maybe Annie could help bring their yard back...

Just as she was crouching down in an attempt to discern the flowers from the weeds, her mother's car pulled into the driveway. Annie looked up and waved. Her mother looked so pretty and thin; she wore khaki shorts and a faded blue shirt, and her arms and legs were tanned and freckled.

"Hi, sweetheart," her mother said, walking over. She held a paper bag tightly in her arms, as if something precious was inside.

"Hi, Mom. Where were you?"

"I had some errands to run. Will you come inside for a minute?"

Annie nodded, but first she brushed the dry leaves with her hand. "The poor garden," she said. "I think it needs some help."

"I know, Annie. It does. I've really let it get away from me these last couple of weeks. I'm sorry."

"You don't have to be," Annie said quickly, hugging her mother, then stepping back. "I didn't mean it that way."

Her mother took a deep breath, trying to smile. The sun was coming through the kitchen window, turning her hair into a tangle of copper.

"Oh, sweetheart," her mother said, stroking her hair. She stared at Annie with a worried smile, as if she was trying to read Annie's mind.

"What's wrong, Mom?"

"Annie..." her mother said, still trying to smile, as she put an arm around Annie's shoulders and walked her into the house. Annie's heart began to beat harder. She had been so worried about her father—did her mother have news about him? No, it couldn't be that. Her mother wouldn't be smiling at all. Or else, if it was good news, she'd be jumping up and down for joy.

"Tell me, Mom. What is it?"

"Sit down, Annie," her mother said quietly, putting her hand on Annie's arm. "I want to talk to you about something. Where are the other kids?"

Yikes, Annie thought. Not good. Never a good thing when one of her parents wanted to single her out, separate her from the herd. Very bad, very bad. She had the deep sibling sense that there was safety in numbers—that any message delivered to the whole family, as hard as it might be to swallow, was one thing. But being talked to solo meant nothing but trouble.

"They're playing baseball," Annie said reluctantly, edging toward the door. "Maybe they want me to play... I should..."

"Annie," her mother said, smiling. "We both know..."

Annie shrugged and smiled, knowing her mother was on her wavelength about not liking sports, especially anything involving a ball. Her father, on the other hand, had tried to get her to play every chance she got, telling her stories about his own glory days in school.

Her mother's face was very serious, her blue eyes focused on Annie's with concern and love. "Sweetheart, there's something I want to tell you, and show you..."

"Show me?" Annie asked, her voice reedy and thin.

Her mother nodded, and with that, Annie did sit down, at the breakfast bar. Her blood was going *ba-boom, ba-boom,* like a whole battalion marching into her throat. The bag was sitting on the counter in front of her mother, and Annie suddenly felt very afraid.

"What's in there, Mom?" she asked.

"Annie, darling," her mother began.

"Show me, Mom," Annie said, feeling as if her skin

would unzip and she'd fly out like a ghost. She grabbed the bag from her mother's hands, and began to tear the paper away. Before she had gotten half of it off, she saw: "My boat!" she cried out.

"Annie, I know you've liked thinking of your dad having it with him..."

"I made this for him," Annie cried, cradling her little green boat in her arms, rocking it back and forth as if it was a baby in need of great comfort and love. "This was for Daddy. He said he'd never go anywhere without it—it was keeping him company! It's all he had!"

"Oh, Annie," her mother said, rushing around to hold her. "I knew you'd be upset. I wouldn't have even shown it to you, honey. But your father left it behind for a good reason, a very loving reason."

"No," Annie sobbed. "He wouldn't have."

"Annie, he wanted to have a rowboat built—"

"This was his rowboat," she cried. "The only one that mattered. I made it for him. He would never have left it behind."

"He showed it to the boatbuilder, and he even went back to check that he was copying it properly," her mother said.

"He's gone forever," Annie said, feeling waves of cold sweep through her body. It was as if a cold front—the Alberta Clipper—had rushed down from Canada, to chill her skin and blood, to freeze the marrow in her bones.

"No, Annie. This doesn't mean—"

The telephone rang. Annie vaguely sensed her mother crossing the room to answer it.

"Hello?" her mother said.

Annie held the boat against her body, remembering how she had felt making it. Her mother had helped her—driving her to the hobby shop, picking out the balsa wood. Annie had lovingly soaked each piece, getting it to bend in the graceful lines of the pretty dory in the classic boat magazine. She had put in little seats and oarlocks. She had carved oars. When the glue was dry, she had painted it dark green—the color of pine trees. And she had lettered the name of the boat on the transom, in gold paint:

ANNIE

"So you don't forget who to row home to," she had told her father when she'd given him the boat.

"I love it, Annie," he had said, wrapping her in his arms and pulling her close.

"I made it for you," she'd said. "Every bit. Mom only helped a little."

"It's the nicest present I've ever gotten."

"Because you love boats?" she'd asked, her heart swelling.

"No, because you made it for me," he'd said, still hugging her with one arm, holding the boat out for both of them to admire with the other. "No one's ever made me anything this wonderful before. I love it."

"Really?"

"Really," he'd said, the arm squeezing Annie a little tighter, making her feel happier than she'd ever felt. "I'll tell you how much I love it. I will never let it out of my sight. That's a promise. Wherever I go, this boat goes..."

And he had kept his promise. He had taken the boat to his office for a few months, but then they had done some renovation at the bank and he'd brought it home. It had been on his bureau, but then summer came, and he put it into a bag; Annie assumed he had taken it back to his office, or down to the *Aldebaran*.

Annie held the model, thinking of how much her father had loved it. Warmth flooded through her and gave her comfort as her mother turned to look at her and Annie saw the whiteness of her face. The near-blue color of the skin around her lips, as if she was in shock. The way she moved her hand—so slowly, almost fumbling—up to her cheek, trying to touch her own face but seeming almost unable to find it. The roundness of her eyes. Her almond-shaped blue eyes, shocked into a different shape.

As her mother hung up the phone, Annie curved her body around the boat. If she couldn't protect her father, she could at least shield the boat.

"Sweetheart," her mother said, touching Annie's shoulder with a trembling hand.

"I already know," Annie whispered, so softly only her boat could hear.

"I have bad news," her mother said.

"I already know," Annie whispered, more softly than before.

8

THE FUNERAL TOOK PLACE ON WEDNESDAY MORNING
at the same small white chapel where Sean and Bay had
been married, where all the children had been baptized,
where Tara and Bay had made their first communion together. Sitting in the second row, Tara looked at the
back of her best friend's head and remembered back to
first grade, when they had both worn white dresses and
veils with silver crowns.

The kids seemed to be holding up. They were so well
behaved, dressed in their best summer clothes, much more
dignified than Tara had been at her own father's funeral.
She had been eleven, Billy's age, and he had died in a car
crash. He had been drunk, and he had smashed head-on
into a station wagon, killing the woman driving. Tara had
dreaded the funeral—how would she get through it?

With Bay, of course. Bay had helped her put on her
black dress, held her trembling hand. Now they were
here again, to bury Sean.

How was it possible that that tall, athletic, fast-talking, life-loving man could be lying in that gleaming wooden box? Tara stared at it, wishing she could shake him one last time.

The end had come so differently from the way anyone had expected. So...the word drifted into Tara's mind: softly. Everyone had thought Sean was a fugitive on the run, fleeing the jurisdiction with his loot. While the truth was, he had died alone just three miles from home, in his car, at the bottom of the Gill River. He had bled from the gash in his head, according to the police. Whatever had happened on his boat had caused him to lose so much blood, he had lost control of his car.

Sitting there, Tara ran her gaze over Bay and the children. They were all so quiet and composed, following along with the songbook, they might be at any Sunday Mass. Billy was the first to cry out loud, to show any outward signs of grief.

Now, as if it were catching, Pegeen began to cry. She tried to hold in the sobs, but they overtook her, and for half a minute she keened without being able to hold the sounds inside. Annie put her arm around her, weeping softly herself.

"But I want Daddy back!" Peg wept.

Tara concentrated all her energy on Bay. *Just get through this*, was the message she sent. *You can do it. You are strong. You're their mother, and they need every bit of you right now.* Tara's eyes bored into the back of her friend's head, sending her all the strength she could muster.

The priest went through the motions of Mass, saying the right things: "Sean McCabe, cherished husband of Bairbre..." he stumbled over Bay's name, Gaelic for Barbara, "beloved father of Anne, William, and Pegeen,

taken too soon...the mysteries of the human spirit...
unknown reasons of the heart..."

"What's he talking about?" Billy asked out loud.

"Dad," Peg replied.

"But he's not *saying* anything," Billy sobbed. "I don't
even know what he *means*."

Then it was Annie's turn to go to the lectern and recite her father's favorite poem. Tara held her breath,
watching Annie make her way through the pew, past her
mother, down the aisle, to the front of the church. She
wore a navy blue skirt and pale pink shirt, her add-a-pearl
necklace, and the small forget-me-not earrings her father
had given her when she'd had her ears pierced. Her posture was hunched, her shoulder blades drawn forward, as
if she had invisible wings and could enclose herself from
behind. In spite of or because of that, her movements
were filled with grace.

Annie cleared her throat. She had memorized the
poem, Frost's "Stopping by Woods on a Snowy Evening."
Without any paper to refer to, she recited the haunting
words of the timeless poem.

Annie never took her eyes off her father. For Tara was
sure that, as her goddaughter gazed down, she was seeing
not a wood box but Sean himself. Seeing the father she
loved so much, in winter, the icy blue air and frozen
marsh all around.

Tara reached over the back of the pew, and Bay
squeezed her hand. They were sisters, after all. Not bound
by blood, but by love. They had adopted each other early
in life, a lifelong commitment without any ritual, without any symbols but the breeze blowing off the Sound,
the roses growing in their gardens.

Tara's chest felt heavy. Scanning the church, she'd
seen a host of friends filling the pews. Hubbard's Point's

Les Dames de la Roche—Winnie Hubbard, Annabelle McCray, Hecate Frost—were there with Sixtus Larkin; Zeb and Rumer Mayhew with the recently eloped Quinn and Michael Mayhew; Sam and Dana Trevor with Quinn's sister Allie . . . People from the beach, the bank, and town.

Some of Sean's clients had come: May and Martin Cartier, Ben Atkin from Silver Bay Auto, and Augusta Renwick—who was also one of Tara's housecleaning clients. She caught Tara's eye and gave her a dignified nod. Way in the back, seated in the last pew, was a face from the past: Dan Connolly. Tara would have recognized him anywhere. Hubbard's Point had a way of gathering everyone together, even the ones who had left long ago.

And new people, as well. Tara glimpsed Joe Holmes, standing by the back door. Her spine stiffened, wondering why he had come—couldn't he leave Bay and the family alone, let them get through the funeral?

But when Joe caught her eye, he held her gaze in a strange look of recognition, as if he understood her role in Bay's life and was sending her strength to help Bay get through this day. The look was fierce yet kind. Tara realized then that his being here was beyond duty—the kind of thing her grandfather would have done. Attending the funeral of a criminal in his precinct, just to support the family left behind.

Tara nodded back, and with that thought bowed her head. A sob ripped out of her chest as she thought of her grandfather, and as she realized that Sean's family would never see Sean again.

At the end, the priest extended the customary invitation for everyone to gather at the family's home, but very few people actually showed up. Bay stood at the door, greeting friends, trying to soothe the kids who couldn't understand why no one was coming.

"Is it because it's such a nice beach day?" Peggy asked. "They'd rather go swimming than come here?"

"Or is it," Billy said hotly, "that they're scorning us because of everything at the bank and Dad being in the papers and all?"

Both kids looked up at Bay, wanting her to dispute Billy's statement. She knew he was right, but she'd never tell her kids that. "Daddy's friends love him," she said. "And so do we. We're here, aren't we?"

"I'm his friend," Tara said, nodding. "And I love him."

"But there aren't many people here," Peggy said doubtfully. "Not as many as at Granny's funeral."

"Well, Granny was very old," Bay said steadily, speaking of her mother, who had died at eighty-one. She wished her children could have remembered their great-grandmother, too. "She lived for so long, and everyone knew her..."

"Everyone knew Daddy, too," Peggy said. "He was their banker."

"Yeah. It SUCKS that he was their banker, and they can only think of the bad things about him," Billy said. "Because there were good things, too. Lots more good things than bad. Right?"

"Right," Bay said.

"Right," Tara agreed.

"Dad is, was, will always BE, a great guy, and everyone should KNOW that."

"Well, maybe we should have something to eat," Tara said, pointing toward the table. They had ordered salads and small sandwiches from Foley's. "To keep up our strength."

"I'm not hungry," Peg said.

"No, I lost my APPETITE because of idiots who don't know the real Sean McCabe," Billy said.

"He's got the old Irish fighting spirit," Bay said to Tara as Billy stormed away. "Even when there's nothing to fight about."

"When you're Irish," Tara said, "there's *always* something to fight about." Bay ached, because she knew Billy was hurting for his father's sake. She thought of Sean, of how competitive he had always been. Tears filled her eyes, to think that her son was right, that people were thinking badly of Sean right now. In so many ways, all Sean had really ever wanted was to be liked.

Mark and Alise Boland walked in, and came straight over.

No matter how composed Bay tried to seem, she struggled to hold back tears as Alise gave her a hug.

"You're so strong," Alise said, patting her back. "To see you in church, you and your kids...Your daughter did such a good job, reciting the poem."

"We're so sorry he's gone, Bay," Mark said.

"Thank you," Bay said.

"We can't believe it," Alise said. "Any of it..."

"I know," Bay said, her voice breaking. How could she do this, talk about her husband's death with the president of his bank? They were such an attractive couple, Mark tall and athletic, Alise small and chic. She owned a decorating business, and had an impeccable sense of style. Bay and Sean had never spent much time with them. They didn't have kids, so there wasn't the usual socializing at soccer and baseball, but Alise had always seemed friendly and dynamic—Bay often thought she would like to get to know her better.

Now their presence made her feel so ashamed of what

Sean had done, while all she wanted, today, was to mourn his loss.

"If there's anything we can do," Mark said gently.

"Anything," Alise said, her expression worried, pained, somehow letting Bay know she really meant it.

Bay nodded as they walked away. Tara stood by, watching from across the kitchen. She was making a pot of coffee, but at the sight of Bay dissolving in tears, she hurried over.

"That was nice of them." Bay shuddered. "Considering what Sean did at the bank."

"They don't blame you for that," Tara said. "No one does."

"Why did he do it?" Bay asked. "I can't understand."

"It's not the Sean we know," Tara said, holding her.

Bay closed her eyes, weeping silently into Tara's shoulder. She couldn't believe any of it. Sean would never pitch another ball to the kids, shoot free throws down at the basketball court, never take them on another boat ride. He had been so wildly alive, and now he was gone. It seemed impossible that life could just go on, that the kids would grow up without him knowing them. She couldn't believe she would never see him again. She would never hear his voice . . .

When she pulled back to dry her eyes, she saw Dan and Eliza Connolly entering the room.

"Thank you for coming," she said, immeasurably touched as they came forward.

"We're so sorry, Bay," Dan said.

"I know what you're going through," Eliza said. She was wearing all black: a long-sleeved ballet top, ankle-length black tube skirt, onyx necklace. Bay saw lavender crescents in the pale skin beneath her eyes, and she recognized someone else who couldn't sleep.

"You do," Bay said, meeting her eyes, drawn to take her hands. They felt cold and so thin; Bay wanted to hold them, warm them up, and Eliza seemed to want that, too.

"It's terrible for your kids," Eliza said.

"Oh, it is," Bay said, her voice breaking.

Eliza's gaze slid around the kitchen, as if looking for something, taking everything in: the photos and drawings and reminder lists held to the refrigerator door by magnets, the collection of balls and bats by the side door, the tall green bottle filled with change, the oak table with Bay's mother's blue willow sugar bowl and cobalt blue glass salt and pepper shakers.

"Annie," Eliza said. "Anne. I saw her name in the paper. In the obituary. And I heard her read the poem. She's my age."

"Yes, she is," Bay said, feeling something come together even as Eliza slid her hands away. "Would you like to meet her?"

Eliza nodded. "Yes," she said.

"I'll take you to her room," Bay said.

"You don't have to," Eliza said, glancing around the kitchen—right past her father, who seemed to be watching her intently—at some of the other people standing around, speaking in quiet voices. "I can go myself."

"It's just upstairs," Bay said. "The second door on the left."

ELIZA WALKED THROUGH THE FAMILY'S HOUSE.

She had never been here before, but she knew everything she needed to know about the people who lived here. They were the new lost souls.

In one instant, in the blink of their father's eye, their lives had changed forever. She took in the polished wood floors, the bright hooked rugs, the sports trophies on bookshelves, the watercolors on the wall of serene shoreline scenes: lighthouses, beaches, boats, breakwaters.

She wondered whether the family had ever before looked at the pretty pictures and thought of those girls who had been murdered last year and left in the breakwaters, of boats that sank, of beaches washed away by hurricanes.

Her heart hurt, because she knew that those were the things they would think of now...

When she got to Annie's door on the left, she stopped and stood very still. The upstairs hallway was cool and dark. Light came from an open door down the hall, but Eliza stood in shadow. Like a detective, ear against the heavy door, she used all her senses and instantly felt Annie's presence inside—she could feel the grief coming through.

She considered coming back later, but something told her that now was the time, and so she knocked.

"Annie?" she asked, as a girl opened the door.

She was large, and her eyes were—as in a children's story—as wide as saucers. She wore the clothes Eliza had seen her wearing in church: a blue skirt and pale pink shirt.

"Yes?" Annie asked. Confusion ruled her eyes.

"Um, I'm Eliza Connolly."

"Oh."

Eliza took a breath. She saw Annie looking her up and down. They were fun-house-mirror images of each other: one a little heavy, one much too thin. Almost by instinct, Eliza found herself curling her left hand around her scarred right wrist. Her heart was beating fast. She took a step forward, stumbling on her own feet.

Annie caught her, arms coming around her in an

almost-hug. Crashing into the soft body, Eliza felt tears burn into her eyes.

"Are you okay?" Annie asked.

Eliza tried to nod, but a huge sob was rattling her chest.

"You're not, are you?" Annie asked.

Eliza shook her head very slowly from side to side. She felt as if she was going to faint.

"Do you want some water?" Annie asked, leading Eliza to the side of her bed, gently easing her down. "Or are you hungry?"

"I haven't had anything to eat in two and a half days," Eliza said.

"Oh, my God," Annie said. "Why?"

Eliza stared into her huge blue eyes and felt the pain in her chest dissolve in slow, hot tears. She licked her lips, wishing the room would stop spinning, wished her feet could touch the ground. Her gaze was caught by a small, obviously homemade boat model over Annie's bed. She focused on it, and it brought her back to earth.

"Because I'm so sad for you," Eliza said.

"So sad you can't eat?" Annie asked, and Eliza knew it was the opposite for her.

"Yes."

"But why?"

"For your family. My father knows your mother, and he showed me the obituary...I'm so, so sorry about your father."

"Does your mother know us, too?" Annie asked.

Eliza closed her eyes. This was the hard part, the awful part. That question could not be answered—at least not now. It didn't really have to be, though. This was the moment when Annie would begin to know that they were different, they were alone in this world together, they were lost souls...

"My mother is dead," Eliza said. "That's why I had to meet you."

"Because my father is..."

Eliza nodded, not making Annie say that word that was still so new, so terrible, so unwanted. *Dead.*

"The poem you recited was beautiful," Eliza said.

"It was my father's favorite."

"My mother had a favorite poem, too," Eliza said. "About Paul Revere."

"Will you say a little of it to me?" Annie asked.

Eliza nodded. She took a deep breath, and as she began to recite, she calmed down.

> " 'Hang a lantern aloft in the belfry arch,
>   Of the North Church tower as a signal light—
>   One, if by land, and two, if by sea,
>   And I on the opposite shore will be ...' "

"I love that poem," Annie said. "The part about the signal."

"I do, too," Eliza said, glowing at the immediate, intimate connection.

"You have to eat something," Annie whispered, reaching into a bedside drawer, pulling out a candy bar. She offered it to Eliza as if it were a gift. Eliza stared down at the blue square and shook her head.

"But you'll waste away," Annie said, touching the back of Eliza's wrist.

Eliza stared down at her long sleeves and with the X-ray vision of a girl whose father hated her, whose mother was a ghost, saw a spiderweb of scars spelling out the real truth of the matter, the truth that Annie couldn't possibly know, and understood that she couldn't tell this grieving girl that wasting away was, in fact, the point.

"I'm fine," Eliza said, handing her back the candy bar.

"No," Annie said, blushing. Girls who ate a lot always pretended they weren't hungry. Eliza knew, so she was patient.

Annie blinked, plump tears filling her eyes again. Eliza followed her gaze, saw her staring at the little green boat that had been sitting in her father's office for the past couple of weeks. Somehow Eliza understood that that boat was the most important object in Annie's universe at that moment.

"I like that little boat," Eliza whispered.

"It reminds me of my father," Annie said, starting to cry. "I made it for him."

"Then I bet he loved it a lot," Eliza whispered, holding Annie's hand. "I bet he loved it more than anything."

DAN AND BAY STOOD TOGETHER IN THE KITCHEN, SUR-rounded by people he half-recognized from the summer he had worked at Hubbard's Point. It felt strange, to be back after so many years, and he had to ask himself why he'd come. The beach had given him a summer job—his last before starting his business. He had grown up fifteen miles east, near Mystic—across the Thames River and a world away; he had settled there again, when he and Charlie got married. Perhaps he had subconsciously avoided coming here all this time...People helping themselves to coffee or iced tea at the counter glanced over at him with curiosity.

"They're wondering where they know you from," Bay said.

"The boardwalk, about a hundred years ago," he said. "The one you helped me build."

He watched her try to smile. She couldn't, quite. She had changed, even in the days since her visit to his yard. Her eyes looked bruised, guarded. He remembered the bright young girl who had hung around him at the beach that year so long ago, who had taught him to love the moon, and felt a rush of sorrow.

Back then she had been unlike anyone else, and he thought that was still the same today. She had such a warm, comfortable way about her—her gray eyes were sad but still bright, her hair streaked by the sun and salt. Her house was filled with love—mementos of her family and the beach. He looked around and saw baskets of seashells and beach heather, a few basketball and baseball trophies on a shelf, smooth stones painted by the kids, driftwood scoured by the waves. He glanced down— couldn't stop himself. She had always gone barefoot, even on rainy days, and he half-expected to see her barefoot now.

"What is it?" she asked.

"Oh, nothing," he said, feeling self-conscious.

"You didn't have to come," she said.

"I know."

"But I'm glad you did." Her gaze drifted to the staircase, where Eliza had gone up in search of Annie. "I wonder how they're doing up there."

"Eliza wanted to meet Annie," he said.

"That's so sweet of her," Bay said. "Really unusual for a girl her age, to be outgoing in that way."

"Eliza's nothing if not unusual," Dan said.

"It must be awfully hard, without her mother," Bay said.

"Hard for both of us," Dan said.

"I can't imagine what lies ahead..." Bay said.

Dan thought of Charlie, of how the world had gone so dark for so long when she'd died—very few people, even those closest to him, knew the depths of what he felt. And no one, with the possible exception of his daughter, knew why. He knew a little of what Bay had to face—having lost a spouse she at *best* had mixed feelings for—and he wished he could protect her from it.

"I know," Dan began carefully, "that I can't begin to say what might help, what I might be able to do to help, but..."

She blinked, dully, as if he was speaking a foreign language.

"What I mean is, no one can fill his shoes," Dan said, thinking of Charlie, of the huge hole torn in the sky by her death.

Still, Bay didn't respond. But he saw her eyes fill; she'd been crying when he first arrived.

"He's your husband, I know," Dan said, reaching for Bay's hand as she clenched her fists, her face a knot of anguish. "Bay, I've been there—let me help you."

"You haven't been here," she said, tears pouring down her cheeks.

"I lost my wife—"

"But you loved her," she said, choking on the words. "You loved Charlie so much... it's in your voice, it's all in your face... you loved her... adored her... but I..."

Dan stared into her red-rimmed eyes, swimming in tears. Still, in spite of the heat pouring off her skin, in spite of the fury in her face, he would have taken her hands, but she wouldn't let him—they were fists, all knuckles.

"But I hate Sean," she said, the words bursting forth. She looked toward the stairs up which Eliza had gone, to-

ward Annie's room. "I hate him! For what he's done to
our kids and..."

Dan's eyes widened in shock and understanding. But
then he nodded, hardly able to breathe, taking a step
closer. And...she had said. She unclenched her fists,
hugged her own arms as if the room had suddenly turned
cold, as if she could keep herself warm.

"And to me," she whispered, the fight going out of her,
the rage in her eyes turning to pure grief. "We grew up together, and I *tried* to love him all this time, but..."

"But what, Bay?"

"I didn't know him at all," she whispered, sobbing in
such wrenching sorrow, private anguish, that Dan could
only stand very near, very still, not touching her at all,
not saying one word.

9

A HEAT WAVE SETTLED IN, AND THE NEXT DAYS were oppressively hot, with the sun a ball of fire in the thick, white sky. Bay tried to gather the kids close, help them get through every day. Tara helped her remember and plan things they had always loved—picnics in the shade, beach time, trips to Paradise Ice Cream.

Bay went through the motions, doing the best she could—if she fell apart, the kids would be more terrified than they already were.

Every morning, she and the two younger kids would go to the beach, lay down their blanket, dive into the water. Billy and Pegeen would race out to the raft, as if frantic activity could block reality. Annie wouldn't come to the beach at all; she wanted to sleep late, and then she'd get up and stay inside to read. Bay was consumed with worry for her, and tried to keep an eye on her without seeming to hover.

Frank Allingham stopped by with casseroles made by

his wife. Mark Boland had called twice, to see if Bay needed any help, and Alise called, too. They were trying to be friendly, but the sound of their voices cut her badly. Their efforts reminded her of what Sean had done.

On Tuesday morning, the doorbell rang. Bay answered it in her beach clothes: bathing suit, big old shirt. And it was Joe Holmes, dressed as always in what seemed to be the FBI uniform of a dark suit, dark tie.

"Bay, may I come in?"

"All right," she said, opening the door wider. She felt vulnerable, only half dressed, but she didn't want to take time to change: She wanted this over and him out of her house quickly. She led him into the living room, and he sat down in Sean's chair. Her stomach froze.

"I'm sorry to intrude like this. But our investigation has turned up some more things I want you to know."

She waited, her skin tingling, unable to speak.

"We've been going over the scene where your husband's car went off the road. We've measured the skid marks, the turning radius . . . and they don't add up to an accident. We think Sean was murdered."

"No . . . Why? I don't understand. *Murdered* . . ." she whispered, in shock, shattered by the word.

"We don't know for sure," the agent said. His eyes were soft, and she swore they were filled with compassion, as if he really cared about her feelings. Her eyes stung. How could she ask her kids to face this? And how could she herself face it? There seemed to be one shock after another.

"What makes you think that it's possible?" she asked when she could speak. "You said he'd gotten hurt on the boat, that he'd lost a lot of blood . . ."

"That's true, he did," Joe said quietly. "But even so, why didn't he pull off sooner? Why didn't he call for help? Accidents like this don't usually happen on a quiet country road with a well-maintained car. Did Sean take drugs?"

"No, never. Why?"

"We found cocaine in his system."

"Sean NEVER used cocaine," Bay said. "He was really straight—he was so against drugs. He was—wild in other ways, but not drugs."

"Maybe he changed his position on that."

Bay lowered her head. He had changed his position on so many things—why not drugs? But her gut told her he hadn't. "Could it have killed him?" she asked.

"It could have impaired him so as to make his driving unsafe, especially with the blood loss. And he may not have been alone."

"What do you mean?"

"He may have had someone in the car with him."

"When he went off the road? When he died?" Bay asked. "Who?"

"That's really all I can say right now," Joe said. "The investigation is ongoing; I'm very sorry for it all. For you and your children."

"Oh, Sean," Bay gasped, bowing her head.

"The press will get hold of the story, I'm sure, by the end of the day," the agent said. "I just wanted you to know first."

She couldn't even thank him for that; she didn't stand when he left. She just sat very still, listening to his car drive away, staring at the stairs that led up to her children's rooms.

She thought of how happy she and Sean had been the day they'd bought this house. It was at the beach, near Tara, near all their best summer memories. Her vision blurred with tears, with fresh grief for Sean and the realization that he was gone forever, a feeling of heaven splitting apart. Although her marriage had been far, far from perfect, it had been her dearest, wildest hope that they could make it better.

She walked up the stairs and down the hall. It seemed very important to be very quiet right now. As if to counterbalance the violence that had been done to Sean, she knew she needed to tread very lightly, speak very softly to his children. Walking into Annie's room, she asked, "Can you come out here?" and Annie got off her bed without a word.

The same to Billy, who wanted to know, "What was HE doing here?"

"Mr. Holmes? I'll tell you in a minute. Come into Peggy's room for a minute."

She moved slowly, as if through water. Her voice was thick with tears even before she began to speak. The children sat on Peggy's bed, looking up at her with bruised eyes. Every time Joe Holmes visited their house, their world fell apart a little more.

"It's about Daddy," Bay said.

They all just stared. She had already told them the worst thing possible: that he was dead. She could see in their eyes that they were past shock, into a new realm. She wanted just to clutch them to her, take them back to their babyhoods, start everything over.

"What is it?" Billy asked. "What did the FBI guy want?"

Bay looked into the eyes of her three children, so guarded and hurt, and she couldn't bring herself to tell them.

"Let me sit with you," she said, squeezing between Annie and Peggy on the bed. She reached around Peggy to hold Billy's hand. Her heart was beating so fast, she thought the force would knock her over. She heard Peg starting to whimper, and she hadn't even said a word.

"It's about Daddy," she said, and the word sounded so sweet, and she could hear each one of them saying it to Sean, and she could see the delight in his eyes—how happy it had made him. Her eyes filled, and she didn't think she could go on.

"Tell us, Mom," Annie pleaded. "Don't make us wait."

"It's upsetting," she said, feeling their tension. "I'm going to tell you, and you'll have to be very brave. We all will. Okay?"

They all nodded.

"Annie, Billy, Peggy. Mr. Holmes said, that is, he thinks that Daddy was, probably...murdered."

"Murdered." Peggy tried the word out, scarcely audibly.

"No," Billy said. "Not Daddy."

"Why would someone do that?" Annie asked. "They wouldn't. No one could do that to him."

"It happens on TV," Peggy said, starting to cry. "It does, all the time. So why *not* Daddy?"

"This isn't TV," Billy said. "This is our *dad*."

"It wouldn't be fair for someone to just *do* that," Peg wept. "If his car just went off the road, that's one thing. But for another person to *do* that to him, I can't stand it."

"I can't stand any of it," Annie said, her hands tightly clenched on her lap.

"I don't believe he's even gone," Billy said, breaking on the words. He began to sob, rubbing his eyes with fists. "He can't be—he's so great and *real*. How can he just suddenly be gone? He's supposed to be here, with us."

"No one should be able to just take him away from us," Peggy cried.

"We're a family," Annie said. "And he's our father."

"I hate what they're saying about him," Billy said.

"And this will just make it worse. I want him to be here to defend himself."

Bay sat among her children, dry-eyed now, holding them close. She felt the same way they did—that Sean had been too strong and real to just suddenly be gone. She couldn't respond to Billy. Maybe Sean couldn't defend himself, because he had done everything that people were saying.

This was her family's first lesson in death, and it seared their hearts, cauterized their veins. Bay knew it was like being in the car with Sean, that whoever had killed him was killing a part of them, too. And that realization helped her summon a resolve stronger than any she had ever felt.

"We're going to get through this," she said.

"How?" Peggy wailed.

"Together," Bay said. "We have each other."

"But not Daddy," Billy said. "We don't have him anymore."

"That's not true," Bay said. "You do have him. You have his love."

"What do you mean? He's gone. You just said he was *murdered*."

"Love never dies," Bay said. "Your father loved you too much for that to happen. I promise you, he still loves you. I promise." She said it so ferociously, the children all sat up a little straighter, staring at her with wide eyes. "I promise," she said again.

"If you promise," Annie said very quietly, "then I believe you."

Bay hugged each of her children. Violence had come to their home. She would be gentle, and she would fill their home with love.

Annie's words did that for Bay. *If you promise, then I believe you.*

BY THE NEXT DAY, WEDNESDAY, IT WAS THE NEW TALK OF the beach. Sean's accident might have been murder. Had *probably* been murder. And he'd been using cocaine. He might have had help, stealing from the bank. With all of the executives already exonerated, the authorities were still, according to the paper, interviewing tellers. *Young female tellers* went the whispers up and down the beach.

Or it might have been someone from outside the bank, someone who wanted Sean to commit the crime: One sidebar story talked about a wife in Dallas who had gotten her banker husband to pilfer accounts so she could buy her own oil well.

Sitting in her beach chair, Bay glanced around at her neighbors, wondering which of them thought she had egged him on. She took the morning paper from her straw basket. Trying to pretend that her husband wasn't the front-page story, she struggled to keep her hands steady as she began reading the classifieds, looking for a job.

Tara came down to join them, and together the two friends walked on the hard sand below the high tide line. Their footsteps made shallow impressions, and they walked slowly, with the lifelong habit of staring downward for treasures: shells, sea glass, lost diamond rings. The summer they were six, they had heard a woman cry out: Her engagement ring had slipped off while she was coming out of the water. They had never, in all these years, really stopped looking for it.

"How are you doing?" Tara asked.

"Great," Bay said in a tone she knew her best friend would instantly translate into "really rotten."

"I figured," Tara said.

"I thought you might," Bay said. "Frank Allingham called again. He was just trying to be nice, but I feel too horrible to talk to him . . . I'm looking for a job."

"Finding anything?"

"Not yet," Bay said. "I don't know enough about computers, and everyone seems to want someone who knows Windows and Excel . . ."

"Computer illiteracy is highly underrated in our society today," Tara soothed. "But I get by, and so will you. What else?"

"Have you heard people talking?" Bay asked, her gaze snapping up. She wore a straw sun hat and had to peer beneath the rim to see Tara's face.

Tara shook her head. "No one is going to bad-mouth Sean to me."

"I'll bad-mouth Sean to you," Bay said. "I just lost my husband, he was probably murdered, but I'm so angry, Tara. You can't believe it. If I had him here in front of me . . ." Bay shook her head, as if to banish the violence of her thoughts. "I started adding up the mortgage, the insurance, the utilities, expenses to keep us all going . . . I'm worried we'll have to sell the house."

"Never," Tara said. "I'll die myself before I let that happen."

"Oh, Tara. Thanks. How could he do this? What was he thinking? Unless I get a job right away . . . and one that pays me enough money . . ." Her dark heart was throbbing, she swooned with the possibilities of loss, when there had already been so much.

"You'll find something. Keep reading the ads, and I'll ask around. You're so good at so many things."

She had always liked working hard, the more strenuous the better.

"I told Dan Connolly I hated Sean," she said.

"It's okay for you to hate him right now," Tara said. "It would be impossible for you not to. Are you going to have Dan build the dory for Annie?"

"I don't see how."

"The money?"

She nodded. "Summer's almost over. We're going to need every cent we have to last till I get a job. I'd pawn my engagement ring to pay for the dory, but it wouldn't do any good sitting in the yard till next summer anyway..." Bay said, trailing off. Every part of her hurt to think of how happy Annie would have been if her father had been able to follow through on having a boat built for her.

She glanced at the sandy rise, bristling with silvergreen beach grass, the thicket of bayberry and gorse, the craggy cliff, the narrow path leading under the fallen tree. She knew that if she followed the path, she would eventually come to the turnoff leading into the thick woods...She could almost picture the clearing, the spot where Danny had hung the swing.

And now she looked behind her, toward the boardwalk. *He builds things that last*, his daughter had said. And how true that was. The boardwalk—a hundred or more thick planks nailed in line, weathered pewter by storms, battered by the high tides and fierce waves of nor'easters—was a testament to his enduring work. An image of Dan from long ago shimmered in the summer heat: tall, lean, tan, grinning.

The man who builds things that last.

A boat for Annie, Bay thought.

But for what? What good would it do, what happiness could it bring a daughter whose father had arranged for a wooden boat, a classic dory, to be built—even, say, from the strongest, hardest wood? What good would it do, considering that he had just vanished from their lives?

Just like that?

"Did you see the part in the paper about Augusta Renwick?" Tara asked.

Bay cringed, recalling the story. The FBI had been interviewing all of Sean's clients and discovered that a large percentage of his ill-gotten gains had come from Renwick accounts—money left to Augusta by her late husband, the famous artist Hugh Renwick.

"It could be worse," Tara said gently. "It could have been someone who'd really miss the fifty thousand or so. He probably singled her out because she has so much."

"Has she said anything?"

"Not yet. I clean her house tomorrow."

"Tell me everything she says. Promise?"

"I promise," Tara said, sounding worried.

They walked in silence, picking up shells. Bay put hers in the pocket of her shirt. It was one of Sean's castoffs, a blue oxford with fraying collar and cuffs. She had always snagged his softest old shirts to wear over her bathing suit; while playing at the beach with the kids, his kids, his shirt would remind her of him, working hard for them at the bank.

Working hard, stealing, and getting murdered...

She happened to glance back, over her shoulder, the way they had come. There, walking along the boardwalk, never taking his eyes off her, was a man in a dark shirt. His khakis were freshly pressed, his sneakers were brand-new, and his sunglasses were too cool. But it was the shirt that really gave him away.

Someone should tell the FBI that no real beachgoer would wear such a dark shirt on a day as hot as this. It would soak up the sun, bake the person wearing it. Watching the man watching her, Bay almost felt sorry for him.

ANNIE LAY ON HER BED, CLOTHES STICKING TO HER BODY. She felt like a big, wilting flower, with her T-shirt sticking to her skin, her hair clinging damply to her head. Even with the windows wide open, today's sea breeze was in the high nineties.

Murdered. Maybe.

Her mom and Tara had taken the other kids to the beach. They had invited Annie, as they always did: "Hey, Annie, let's go take a dunk together . . . get wet and cool off . . . a quick swim . . ."

Annie launched herself off the bed and padded barefoot down the dark hallway, down the stairs, to the kitchen.

Daddy—murdered? It was impossible . . .

Opening the freezer door, she let a blast of icy air chill her sweaty skin.

As shocking as murder, drugs . . . cocaine! Daddy couldn't, wouldn't have taken cocaine . . . he always told Annie that drugs were bad, that they would wreck her brain, would keep her from being a good athlete, keep her from destroying her opponent on the basketball court. But he had also told her never to steal. And they were saying he stole, too.

Shaking the thoughts away, Annie stared into the freezer, at all the choices. A whole stack of Lean Cuisine—thank you, Mom, for buying these just for me. A pint of lemon sorbet, another of low-fat vanilla yogurt. And there, way in back, was a half gallon of Paradise peach ice cream, bought to go with the blueberry pie her mother was going to make later.

Don't think "murder." Maybe it wasn't, maybe it was still

an accident—and maybe it wasn't cocaine. It couldn't be.
Annie reached for the ice cream just as the phone rang.

Annie paused. She clutched the plastic tub of peach
ice cream, hesitating between impulse and duty. Leaving
the ice cream just inside the freezer, she held the door
open with her extended arm and leaned over to get the
telephone.

"Hello?" she said.

"I can't believe I found your number. Believe me, it
wasn't easy, in spite of the fact that calling wasn't my idea
in the first place. It's not that you're unlisted, because you
ARE listed, but it's because a) I spelled your last name
wrong, and b) I got the name of your town wrong."

"Who is this?" Annie asked, even as she felt a thrill
under her skin, because of course she knew who it was—
Eliza—and because the call wasn't the coach calling for
Billy or Pegeen, or the bank or a lawyer or anyone calling
for her mother—it was all for Annie.

"Um, I'll give you three guesses, but if you don't get it
on the first try, I'll be really upset."

"Eliza?"

Annie heard her laugh with satisfaction. "Good job.
SO, first I looked up 'MacCabe' instead of 'McCabe,' and
then I asked for Silver Bay instead of Black Hall...but I
finally found you! Are you okay?"

"Um..." Annie began. Her eyes strayed to the freezer
door. With most people, she wouldn't even consider
telling the truth. But something made her edge toward
wanting to tell Eliza: *I think my father was murdered, and
I'm about to stuff my face with a half gallon of peach ice
cream,* she could say, and she had the feeling Eliza would
understand. But instead, she said, "I guess."

"I don't think you are. I know what they've been saying about your dad."

"You do?"

"Yes. You don't have to talk to me about it, but I know how hard it is. I do."

A silence fell over the phone line.

"I'm sorry," Eliza whispered. "It's so soon for you."

"I miss him," Annie said, her eyes tearing up. "I miss him so much, if he was here, I'd even want to shoot baskets with him. And I hate shooting baskets..."

"When you feel better... after more time has passed," Eliza began.

Annie nearly hung up; she didn't want to hear that she'd EVER feel better; that the pain of missing her father would ever dull. But the instant trust she had felt with Eliza carried her through the moment, and she just kept breathing, listening for what would come next.

"When you feel better," Eliza continued, "you'll be able to think of him where he is now."

"Where he is now?" Annie asked dully, thinking of the cemetery, the stone with his name carved into it: Sean Thomas McCabe, and then the dates of his birth and death, and then the line from the poem Annie had read in church: *Promises to keep...*

"Yes," Eliza said. "It's somewhere so wonderful..."

"I wish that were true," Annie said, more tears stinging her eyes.

"Oh, but it is!" Eliza said. "I know it for sure!"

"How?"

Now it was Eliza's turn to be silent. She breathed in and out, and Annie could hear the rhythm and catch, as if Eliza's lips were on the phone. Annie closed her eyes, breathing along with Eliza.

"I'll tell you next time I see you," Eliza whispered.

"But when—"

"When will that be? That is the question. If we lived closer, I'd ride my bike over. Do you have a boat?"

"My dad does—did—why?"

"Because Mystic is on the water and your house is on the water..." She giggled. "We could commute."

Annie laughed, thinking of the two of them zooming up and down Long Island Sound to see each other. "Do you have a boat?" she asked.

"You'd *think* I would," Eliza said. "Considering that my dad's a boatbuilder, and his company is named after me...I mean, my grandmother...but we have the same name...it's a long story."

"And I want to hear it."

"And you could, if one of us had a BOAT! I could tell you that story, and I could tell you about our other parents..."

Annie cringed again, but just slightly less than before; as if she was getting used to, ever so gradually, during this very conversation with Eliza, the idea of her father being gone. The word *murder* wasn't running through her head quite so furiously.

"We are going to see each other soon," Eliza said. "One way or another. We'll get my father to drive me over. Or your mother to drive you here."

"Yeah!" Annie said, feeling almost excited.

"I'll obsess about it!"

"Obsess?"

"That's a word I picked up in the bin. It means 'think about constantly.'"

"Oh," Annie said, not quite getting "bin," but getting "think about constantly." She thought about her father, and the way her family used to be. She thought about her little boat, how he was supposed to have it with him always.

Eliza must have kept listening, even though the only sound audible was Annie swallowing and swallowing, all those tears running down her throat. Annie was crying, as all the things she thought about constantly filled her head, all the love she felt for her family and how much it hurt. It made her feel just a little better, though, holding the receiver, holding it tight against her ear, feeling it wet and slippery with her tears, knowing Eliza was still listening, that even in the broken silence, Eliza was *there*.

10

THEY WERE BLUEBERRY PICKING, TO GET BERRIES FOR the pie. Fields of blue and green shimmering in the heat. Netting over one whole acre, to keep the deer away. Bay, Tara, Billy, and Pegeen filling their baskets—the only family at the farm today, the hottest day of the summer so far—the hills of northern Black Hall hazy in the distance, softened by humidity, a picture. Looking around, Bay calmed down.

"When you look at that," Tara said, "you can really see why the artists came here. Why they all came to Black Hall from New York..."

Bay shielded her eyes, gazing at the scene.

"I think that when I'm on the beach," she said. "When I look at the coastline, all the rocks and beaches, the marshes... we both love the beach, but you love the land a little more... We're true to our names."

Bay and Tara... sea and earth.

"Let's become painters," Tara said. "Let's become artists."

"Oh, Tara," Bay said. The idea exhausted her. She watched her two youngest children move through the wide field like little ghosts, like small zombies, with none of the spark and verve of previous berry-picking jaunts. A family of deer grazed in the shadows along a stone wall to the east, and the kids didn't even notice.

"I want to become an artist instead of just dating them. They all smell like linseed oil, and honestly, I think I have a much more vivid view of life than any of them. My love life rots. At least I have a great career." She laughed. "Cleaning the best houses in Black Hall."

"That's why you get so much beach time," Bay said. "You get to make your own hours."

"Damn right," Tara said. "If only I had that special someone to slather with sunscreen. Besides you, of course. I want to meet someone strong and amazing. The male equivalent of you."

Bay laughed.

"I'm serious," Tara said. "I want someone to hold hands with, and go to concerts with, and step out onto the porch to look at the stars with . . . but when an actual man is involved, I can't quite see spending the rest of my life with him."

"I can understand that," Bay said softly, crouching by a small bush, reaching beneath the lowest branches for a cache of berries.

"But you did it," Tara said, kneeling beside her. "You took the risk, fell in love . . . you had three great kids."

"I know," Bay said. "But Sean and I didn't have any-thing real. What you're describing? Wanting to hold hands and dance? I look at my marriage and wonder where that went, if it was ever there at all."

"Do you think it was?"

"I don't know," she said. "I think I wanted it to be so badly, I convinced myself it was there. Right now, I hear about the investigation, the things Sean was doing that I knew nothing about, and I want to jump off a cliff. What does it say about me—about our marriage—that the biggest part of his life was a secret from me?"

"He was an idiot," Tara said. "For doing that."

"I don't even know how to go on from here," Bay said.

"That's why you should be an artist. Both of us—we could use all our Irish passion, channel it into our art."

"I don't have much passion right now," Bay said, still hunched down, glancing up at Tara looking tall and powerful, backlit by the hazy sun. Bay's body ached so much, she couldn't move; she felt as if she'd been in that car with Sean, had spent all those days crushed by the weight of seawater, had had her fingers and face picked at by crabs and fish.

"Yes, you do," Tara said quietly. "You live and breathe passion . . ."

"I'm just a suburban mom," Bay said. "That's all."

"But you do it with all your heart."

Bay didn't reply, but Tara's words sank in. Worried sick about her children, especially Annie, she was determined to get them through this, do what she could to find their way back to normal, to show them joy again.

They filled their baskets, paid the woman at the stand, drove back to the shore. Pulling into the driveway, Bay's first thoughts were for Annie. Was Bay wrong to let her— so quiet and withdrawn—have her way these days, to not make her join the family, to let her stay in her room?

But as soon as they walked into the kitchen, Annie met them at the door.

"Mom, I'm going to need a ride," Annie said. "Not today, but soon—okay?"

"Where to?" Bay asked, surprised and happy.

"Mystic."

"You don't have any friends in *Mystic*," Billy said. "You don't even want to hang out with your friends at Hubbard's Point."

"Yeah," Peg said, sounding injured. "You don't even want to hang out with me."

"Who do you want to visit?" Bay asked.

"Eliza."

"Eliza Connolly? You only met her that one time…" Bay said.

"But she called me, Mom," Annie said, her eyes shining. "While you were at the beach. She wants me to come over. She tracked me down."

Seeing her daughter's smile, the long-hidden light in her eyes, Bay felt her heart vise.

"She could have just asked her father how to find you," Tara said. "Considering how well he knows his way back to Hubbard's Point."

Bay felt herself blush.

"Mom?" Annie asked.

"Sure," Bay said. "You can have a ride. Just tell me when."

Smiling across the room at her daughter, she glanced out the side window. There, in a dark car across the street, were two men. She hadn't seen them before, but she knew who they were. They were watching her house. Did they think Sean had given her the money to hide, to keep? Perhaps she should show them her dwindling bank account, the help-wanted ads she had circled that morning. The car windows were up, the air-conditioning running. The men looked as if they might sit there all day.

Just then the phone rang; relieved to be distracted from the men in the car, Bay answered it.

"Hello?"

"Bay, this is Dan Connolly."

"How are you?"

"I'm okay ... but something happened. And I have to see you."

"See me? Can't you tell me on the phone, because—"

"No," he interrupted. "It has to be in person. Are you free tomorrow afternoon? Around two?"

"Yes, I can be," Bay said. "Would you like to come here?"

"We can't talk at your house ... I don't want your kids to hear."

"Foley's store, then," Bay said, turning her back to the group, suddenly aware they were all paying close attention. Sean's death had left the family in a state of high alert. "Do you remember it? Come under the train trestle, and go straight—"

"I remember it," he said. "I'll see you there tomorrow."

"Fine," Bay said, feeling off balance as she hung up the phone and glanced out the window again at the sentinels across the street.

THE HEAT WAVE CONTINUED, WITH THE NEXT DAY DAWN-ing every bit as hot and muggy as the several that had preceded it.

Augusta Renwick lived in salty, artistic grandeur on a cliff overlooking the sea, just a few miles west along the coast from Hubbard's Point. The white house had wide porches with white wicker furniture covered with faded striped cushions. Pots of pink geraniums were everywhere. That was the extent of Augusta's gardening: pink geraniums bought at Kelly's. They had the best quality.

But today, walking across her veranda in search of a sea breeze, Augusta was most displeased with her flowers. To call them "wilted" would be to give them a rather generous compliment. The poor dears were, in truth, quite dead.

"You're drooping," Augusta said pejoratively, leaning on her silver-topped black hawthorn walking stick. She sighed. She had come to appreciate and champion the infirm, even among the plant world. Ever since her former son-in-law, the vile and incarcerated Simon, had coshed her on the noggin while attacking her daughter Skye, leaving Augusta's right side weakened, she had needed to walk with a cane. The upside to this—and, Augusta believed, there was *always* an upside—was heightened compassion for all living things.

With the exception of bad men.

Augusta had no kind feelings for men, or women for that matter, who harmed others. Simon had been just one horrible exemplar of what evil a person can wreak, but he was by no means the only such villain.

Casting another baleful look at her dead potted geraniums, she limped through the screen door into the relative cool of her wide front hallway. A ceiling fan helped out from above. Hugh, her adored and dead husband, had loved Somerset Maugham and Noel Coward; had, in fact, named the house "Firefly Hill" after Coward's great estate in Jamaica. Augusta supposed that Noel had allowed ceiling fans to help out the sea breeze there, too.

Hugh had been a painter on the scale of Hassam and

Metcalf, as good as America had to offer. He had lived the life of an artist, wild and unbridled. Collectors had instantly recognized his greatness, and Hugh had been one of those rare artists who became rich during his own lifetime. Wise investments and savvy financial advisors had enabled the Renwick wealth to grow into a fortune.

One of those advisors had been Sean McCabe.

Augusta continued through the great hall, across the living room, past portraits Hugh had done of all three of her daughters, into a small study at the west end of the house. No morning sun came in the tall windows. The room was cozy, made for winter evenings by the fire. Books lined every wall.

Listening carefully for Tara, the cleaning lady, Augusta leaned out the room's doorway. There she was, upstairs—Augusta still had keen hearing, and she could make out the bump of Tara's dust mop against the back stair risers. Dusting her way down, Tara wouldn't walk through the door to this room for at least ten minutes.

Augusta went to the poetry-drama bookcase. Each of the study's four walls had books organized by subject. The largest, by far, contained art books, including twenty or so biographies and picture books of Hugh and his work, and another fifty volumes pertaining more generally to the Black Hall art colony and the artists who had filled its ranks.

Another wall bore history and science books—field guides to the birds, sky, shells, and fish found around Black Hall, as well as more complicated and dense works on the geology and geophysics of the eastern seaboard.

But it was to poetry and drama that Augusta now turned. She adored the erudite; she worshiped the poetic. She reached for her much-thumbed and oft-read copy of the Bard, third shelf up, flush against the right side of the shelf. As Augusta removed the book, a mechanism clicked, and the shelf swung outward to reveal a secret safe.

Hurrying, knowing that Tara would soon reach the room for its weekly cleaning, Augusta spun the dial. The combination was simple, unforgettable: the months and days of each of her daughters' birthdays.

Once into the safe, Augusta pushed aside a sack of gold doubloons and a small case of Burmese rubies her treasure-hunter son-in-law had given her for safekeeping; a sheaf of bearer bonds, a stack of cash, vintage Harry Winston bracelets and necklaces of platinum, diamonds, and sapphires. The Vuarnet emerald earrings.

Augusta sought one single piece of paper. Correspondence from her bank, received that very month. Hurriedly removing it, then slamming shut the safe, Augusta returned Shakespeare to his rightly spot, then settled herself at the desk. Long white hair pulled back from her face, she reached for her calculator, and, staring with fierce concentration at the paper, began to add things up.

TARA WHIPPED THROUGH THE RENWICK MANSE. SHE HAD just one other house to clean that day, a working artist's small cottage on the banks of the Ibis River. Cake, compared to Firefly Hill. The main thing was, she wanted to get back to Hubbard's Point as soon as she could. Bay was meeting with Dan Connolly at two, and Tara wanted to be there—half to give moral support, half because she was dying of curiosity.

Doing the downstairs with her dust mop and damp cloth, she had saved the study for last. She always did. It was her favorite room in the whole house, snug and inviting, filled with books and family photos. Wheeling around the corner, she was startled to come upon Augusta Renwick sitting at the big mahogany desk.

"Oh, Mrs. Renwick!" she exclaimed. "I thought you were outside, on the porch."

"No, Tara," the matriarch said, staring at a paper on the desk. "I'm too worried to be outside."

"I'm sorry. Should I do this room later?"

Augusta pushed the paper aside, looking up at Tara over tortoiseshell half-glasses. "You knew him very well. Didn't you?"

"Who?" Tara asked, her stomach flipping.

"Sean McCabe. Let's not be coy with each other. He's the one who recommended you to me. I needed a cleaning lady, he told me his wife's best friend had a house-cleaning business, I hired you."

"Yes, I knew him very well," Tara said, staring Augusta right in the eye.

"Tell me about him," Augusta said, gesturing at the cracked leather chair across the desk. Tara took a breath. She was on thin ice right now; she wanted to be loyal to Bay, yet she didn't want to be rude to her employer. Eyeing Augusta, she carefully sat down on the edge of the seat.

"He was a good friend," Tara said. "A very good friend. We grew up together, summering at Hubbard's Point."

"The Irish Riviera," Augusta said.

Tara smiled politely. The WASPs called Hubbard's Point "the Irish Riviera of Connecticut." Her grandmother had always told her it was because they were jealous.

"Go on," Augusta prompted. "Tell me more about Sean."

"Well, he went to St. Thomas Aquinas High School

in New Britain, then Boston College. He played varsity basketball both places; he had an MBA from UConn. He married a girl from the beach. Then he became a banker at Shoreline Bank and Trust."

Augusta waved her hand impatiently. "I could get that from his resume," she said. "Those things don't interest me." She tapped the paper on the desk, running her fingernail down the page. "*This* interests me."

"What is it?" Tara asked.

"My bank balance. For one small account. I had almost forgotten about it. Sean encouraged me to set it up years ago. He had some CDs for sale at a favorable rate. I remember that he called me one snowy morning, in his infectious way—you know how he could be."

Tara nodded. She knew so well; she could almost hear him: "Hello, Augusta, top of the morning to you! How's the snowy scene out your window? As beautiful as it is here in town? I'll bet your husband could do a great painting of it..."

"Sean had a talent for knowing people," Tara said. "And liking them."

"Liking them enough to steal from them?" Augusta asked sharply.

"No one can understand that," Tara said.

"Did the family need money?" Augusta asked. "One of the children, perhaps? For school? Or were there health problems?"

"The children are fine. Everyone is healthy," Tara said evenly.

"The wife, then? Did she wish for a grander lifestyle? Was—is—she very demanding?"

Tara stared at the old woman. She took in Augusta's black pearls, worth more than most of the houses in this wealthy seaside town. The white hair had once been black, perhaps as dark as Tara's own; she could tell by Augusta's stately eyebrows, arched over violet eyes. Tara was just the cleaning lady, and Augusta was the grand dame, but Tara stared her down.

"Bay isn't demanding," Tara said, picturing her friend, barefooted, wind blowing her red hair, clothespins in her mouth as she hung out the wash.

"Surely something must have compelled him to do what he did," Augusta said.

"You're right. We just don't know what it is."

"Another woman?" Augusta asked. "Is that it?"

Tara sat still, expressionless, knowing there was no way on earth she would ever say one word about that.

"Loyalty is to be admired," Augusta said, squinting at Tara. "It is a fine quality."

"Thank you."

"I had expected it of Sean."

We all did, Tara thought.

"What will his wife do now? Does she work?"

"She works very hard," Tara said. "Raising their kids."

"How many are there?"

"Three."

"Just like our family," Augusta said, softening, sounding suddenly wistful. "Three children without a father. My girls lost their father too young as well."

"For what it's worth, Mrs. Renwick," Tara said. "I'm very sorry for what Sean did to you. Would you feel more comfortable if I quit? I'd understand completely if you did, considering that he recommended me to you."

"God, no," Augusta said, sounding aghast. "Tara, I need you more than ever. Although the amount of money he took was small, the damage he did to me is large. I loathe being taken advantage of. I am old, Tara, and society utterly discounts and disrespects the old. They patronize us, and they think we're too dotty to notice we've been fleeced."

"You're anything but dotty, Mrs. Renwick." Tara smiled. "You're one of the sharpest people I've ever met."

"I'd like to think you're right," Augusta said, drawing herself up haughtily. "And I had thought Sean felt the same way. That is why this is so devastating. My trust in humanity is shattered. It's happened before; wealthy old women are particularly vulnerable. Remember that when you're elderly and the fruits of your work have multiplied—You do save your money, don't you?"

"Yes," Tara said. "My mother taught me to be frugal. My biggest expense is my garden—"

"Your garden?"

"Yes," Tara said. "My pride and joy. I buy too many plants...and I can't resist soft leather gardening gloves, and copper watering cans, and the newest, sharpest trowels..."

"Ah, the Irish are superb with flowers and soil. Hugh used to have a gardener from Wicklow. That was back in the days when Firefly Hill was a showplace. He wanted beautiful gardens to paint. Now all I have are the old herb garden out back and all those dry brown geraniums. I have a black thumb."

"Water, water, water." Tara smiled, thinking of Bay. "That's the only secret."

Augusta thumped her black thorn stick on the floor, then flexed her weakened right hand. "Can't drag a hose around the way I used to. Or lug a watering can. And my daughters are all busy with their own lives—*trop occupé,* as Caroline would say, now that she lives in France, to help their old mother water her garden—and also, come to think of it, a bit too far away."

"I could do it for you," Tara said, suddenly getting an idea. "Or..."

"Or what?"

"You could hire a gardener."

11

JUST BEFORE TWO, BAY PULLED HER OLD BIKE OUT OF the garage. Shoved into a corner with Sean's golf clubs and basketball, it was covered with spiderwebs, and she dusted it off.

Riding past the men in their dark car, she felt like a gangster in a movie, taunting the law. They pulled out and followed her down the road, but she took a shortcut through the green marsh, over a series of narrow planks laid down in the mud by her son to facilitate bike-riding and blue-crabbing—a trail no Ford LTD would dare to follow.

Focusing on the ground, she kept her bike tires on the boards. One false move, and she'd fall into the marshy, decomposing, black mud. Her body was tense, not knowing what to expect when she saw Danny. What did he have to tell her, and how would she feel? She had already exposed too much of herself to him, and she wished she could take it back.

Then out of the swamp, up the hidden Mute Swan Road, a road so isolated most Hubbard's Point residents didn't even know it was there, past the house where the Hubbard's Point winter security guard lived, the blue lights atop his green car camouflaged in the shadow of the woods all around.

Finally onto the main road and into the sandy parking lot of Foley's store—a green barnlike structure, the beach's general store. Bay glanced at the cars, saw Danny's truck. Her pulse kicked; after all these years, she still felt the ancient excitement at seeing him. She climbed off her bike, and then, conscious of the presence of police in her life, parked it out of sight, beneath the store's wide porch.

Walking into the big, airy store, she saw the three aisles were empty—too hot to shop—but she found Danny in back, sitting at a table. Spotting her instantly, he stood up to wave and pull out her chair. As she sat down, she ran her hand, as always, over the scarred table-top. Generations of Hubbard's Point kids had carved their initials into the wood: SP+DM, ML+EE, ZM+RL, AE+PC. There, off to the side, were Bay and Sean's: BC+SM.

"A long time ago," Bay said as she caught Dan watching her, a serious expression in his blue eyes.

"I know what you mean," he said, relaxing into a smile that overtook his face. "Thanks for coming."

She nodded, smiling back. Danny Connolly had always had the nicest, warmest smile, one of the things she had liked about him most. Looking at him now, she remembered why: It was one of the truest smiles in the world; it touched every part of his face. When Allie Grayson—a beach girl, in her first summer job—walked over, they both ordered lemonade.

"So, what did you want to tell me?" she asked.

The smile went away. "I've been getting a lot of phone calls. Hang-ups, you know? At first I thought it was a wrong number. Or someone trying to send a fax but getting my phone line instead. But finally I picked up, and the person at the other end asked if I had spoken to Sean McCabe, if I had seen him. For about half a second, I thought it was you."

"Me?"

"It was a woman," he said.

"Really?"

"Yes. I knew it wasn't you, of course, but I couldn't figure out who else could know Sean had been to see me. And what difference it could make."

"What did she sound like?" Bay asked.

"Careful," Dan said. "She sounded very cautious, as if she wanted to make sure she didn't say too much."

"Do you have caller ID?"

Dan smiled again, and shook his head. "No. I'm not big on electronics. Eliza keeps telling me to enter the modern age—maybe it's the wooden boat mentality. I don't like things that take the mystery out of life."

Bay shrugged, perplexed. "I have no idea who it could be. Did you call the police?"

He paused. Allie delivered the lemonades, and he waited for her to walk away. He traced the moisture on the glass with his finger. Then he looked up, holding Bay's gaze with his own. "No," he said. "I didn't, because of you."

"Me? What do you mean?"

He squinted slightly, then smiled. "Because try as I might, I can't stop feeling protective toward you."

"Thank you," she said. "I could use a little of that."

"I'm glad you see it that way. I know you're all grown

up now, a great mom, super competent...It's just," he said, trying to keep his expression neutral, but his smile taking over, "It's just that in my mind you're still that skinny kid who kept getting underfoot while I was trying to build the boardwalk."

"I wasn't a kid! I was fifteen."

"Well, Galway, maybe you're right," he said, and in that moment, memories came flooding back in a rush. He had called her his deputy; he'd given her his tool belt to wear so she could hand him nails as he'd made his way down the boardwalk, hammering in the boards. He had called her Galway Bay, or just "Galway," for the famous bay in Ireland, in a mock-gruff way, so teasing and cute that she'd tingled every time she'd heard it—as she did now.

"I was a good assistant," she protested. "That board-walk wouldn't have lasted this long if I hadn't done such a fine job helping you out."

"You weren't too bad," he said sternly. "For a rank amateur."

"Handing you the nails?"

"And swinging the hammer. If I remember correctly, you were pretty good."

"That's right," she said, smiling. "You taught me. To this day, when I hang a picture, I shorten up on the hammer and keep my eye on the nail—like hitting a baseball ... don't think about it ... very Zen—and I never bang my thumb. After I learned the hard way ..."

"When you hit it, and I had to spend the whole day with you getting stitches at the clinic," he said, grinning. "I worried that I hadn't done a good job of teaching you."

"But you had, and I remember still. When the kids were little, at batting practice," she said, "I used to think of you telling me to shorten up, let the hammer find the nail, to not think about it . . . and I'd tell the kids to choke up on the bat, to let the bat find the ball. It used to drive Sean . . ." She paused, falling silent as she looked down at her knees.

"Why did it drive him crazy?" Dan asked.

"Because he didn't understand it," she said. "He had such an immediate approach to things. He'd tell the kids to whack the ball, to hit the hell out of it, to send it to the sun."

"It upsets you to think about that?"

"Thinking of Sean upsets me," she said. She glanced up. "And not because of what I said to you the other day, after his funeral. I didn't mean that, you know. I don't hate my husband."

"I didn't think you did, Bay."

"It's just complicated. I'm angry with him. For what he did, and for dying. Leaving the kids. Lying to me."

"I know," Dan said. "I was angry with Charlie for the same things."

Bay nodded, although she felt surprised to hear him saying he'd felt angry at Charlie for anything. Had she lied to him? Or was he just referring to the hole a person's death left in their family's lives?

"Since we're speaking about Sean," she said. "There's something I've been meaning to talk to you about. You know our letters?"

"Sure, Galway. The ones you sent me nonstop the winter after that summer of the boardwalk."

"You sent a few back, as I recall," Bay said.

"Only because I didn't want you to forget the basics . . . and to let you know I was still paying attention to the moon." He grinned again, as if relenting. "But, that I did, didn't I? Sent a few back . . ."

"So long ago," Bay said, feeling embarrassed because

she didn't want him to get the wrong idea. "I saved them."

Surprise flashed across his eyes; of course he would have thrown hers away years ago.

"I save everything," she explained. "I have a whole chest full of old letters, pictures, yearbooks...locks of the kids' hair..."

"So, you're saying I shouldn't think I'm too special. Don't worry about that—I don't. You probably wanted to preserve my ramblings about rare woods, the properties of mahogany versus teak—right?"

"Something like that," she said, glad to be joking, but suddenly unable to laugh about it.

"What, then? What is it?"

"They really were buried in that chest; I haven't looked at them in years. But I found one on Sean's boat."

"You left it there?" he asked, looking confused.

"No. Sean must have. I hadn't even known he knew about them. And I can't really imagine why he'd care. Or if he did care, why he didn't talk to me about it. It seems as if he just dug them out, and decided to track you down on his own."

"Well, I'm sure Sean just decided he wanted a boat for your daughter. And he knew that's what I do, build boats."

"But there must be lots of other boatbuilders around," Bay said. "With all the harbors and marinas on the shoreline..."

Dan didn't say anything, but in the three-second silence Bay sensed that he was uncomfortable, talking about this.

"You're the best, aren't you?" she asked, wondering if he was just being modest.

"I don't know," he said.

"That's why Sean went to you," Bay said. "Because he always had to have the best of everything."

"The man had great taste in some things, obviously," Dan said. "But he didn't know wooden boats. Now that you're asking me about it, I did wonder what was driving him. There's such a difference between people who like plastic—big glossy powerboats—and people who like wood."

"Yes, I know," Bay said quietly. To her, wooden boats were like the moon: subtle, cool, and reflective. While powerboats were huge suns, blasting everyone with too much heat and light. But she held back from saying that to Dan.

"So, when he showed up at the shop, I couldn't really figure him out. He asked a lot of questions, he was ready to pay what I charge, but he wasn't—" He paused, searching for the right word. "Passionate. People who buy wooden boats are pretty in love with the whole thing."

"What was Sean?"

Dan took a long drink of his lemonade, as if he wanted to postpone for as long as possible answering that question. "I don't know," he said, looking away. "Maybe he just didn't like that we'd written each other letters."

"He might have teased me about you long ago, but I don't think he ever felt threatened," Bay said. "About me with anyone..." Her eyes filled, thinking of how it had been the other way around.

"I'm sorry," Dan said. "Did I say something wrong?"

Bay shook her head, getting herself under control. She didn't need to tell Danny Connolly her woes, confide in him about her marriage problems.

"The letter has been bothering me," she said. "I haven't told the police about it."

"Why would you?" he asked, frowning slightly.

"Because I found it in a folder on Sean's boat. I know they've been looking into everything that was in that folder—account statements, some scribbles Sean left behind. I've been wondering what the letter was doing there."

"Okay, then why don't you show it to them?"

"Because it's private," she said. "It's *all* so private, and I don't like having strangers look through my life this way. I don't want them knowing us—and now, what's even the point? Sean's gone."

"Don't you want to know why he did what he did?"

"I'm not sure I do," she said. "I just want to get my family back to normal."

"I want that for you, too, Bay. I'll help however I can."

"Annie likes Eliza," Bay said. "A lot. She wants me to drive her over to Mystic so they can get together. And we'd like for Eliza to come to our house, too."

"Well, I'm sure she'd love it," he said. "Do you have a day in mind?"

"We'll have to have them check their schedules." Bay smiled. "Wouldn't want to make assumptions, but how about Saturday?"

"Good. But about the other thing—the woman who called?"

"I guess the police will have to know," she said. "I'm so sorry that knowing Sean means involving you in an investigation."

Looking across the table, she saw him react to her words: He flinched, as if he hadn't quite thought of it that way. His eyes clouded over, troubled. She waited for him to say something, but he didn't. The seconds ticked by.

"Danny?" she asked.

"Just what you said before, about things being private.

It's weird, thinking of calling the police, or having them call me."

Bay closed her eyes. She wished the police would just disappear from their lives. "I know," she said. "At least you're not part of the main investigation. Tell them whatever you think you should, about the call. And I'll probably tell them about the letter, too."

"Okay," he said. "I'm glad I know that."

Opening her eyes, she took a sip of lemonade. "Why do I feel like we're coconspirators?"

"Just like the old days. When the beach board of governors wanted green shutters on the guardhouse and I made them blue, because blue was your favorite color."

"You did that," she said, trying to smile. "I'd forgotten. You used to bring me here for lemonade sometimes… you said it was to thank me, for doing half your job."

"I didn't want you to think I was getting away cheap. And besides, they did have the best lemonade here. They still do," he said, draining his glass. "What makes it so different?"

Foley's lemonade was famous, made with fresh lemons and two secret ingredients. No one but the Foley family—not even the summer kids who worked here every season—knew what they were. Back when they were teenagers, Tara had had Allie's job, and she swore she wouldn't quit till she'd divined the potion. "Fresh mint!" she'd announce after work. Or, "Lime peel!" or "Cayenne!" But no matter how they tried, no one in Hubbard's Point had ever been able to replicate the taste outside the store.

"No one knows," she said.

"Not even you, Galway?" he asked. "After all your summers here?"

She gazed at him, thinking of how fast those summers

had sped by. His face was weathered, his hair graying at the temples, but his blue eyes still seemed so lively, so ready to smile.

"Not even me," she said.

"Old Mr. Foley tried to hire me to sand these tables," Dan said. "He wanted me to come in with a belt sander and take the wood right down to the grain. Get rid of all the carvings..."

"The kids would have just carved them again," Bay said.

"I think he knew that," Dan said.

"Beach tradition...such a simple thing," Bay said, tracing Sean's deeply scored initials with her fingertips.

"Well, I wish making life good for you was still as simple, Bay McCabe," he said, "as painting the shutters blue. Or taking you here for lemonade."

She couldn't really say anything after that. She drank the rest of her drink, and then just sat there at the scarred old table, holding the cool, empty glass in her hands and waiting for the lump in her throat to go away.

12

JOE HOLMES SAT IN HIS OFFICE, THE TEMPORARY SATEL-
lite office of the FBI tucked in between East Shore Coffee Roasters and Andy's Used Records in a strip mall, or
what passed for a strip mall here in Black Hall, Connecticut. This town was classy, with a capital C. Their
idea of commercialism was allowing the coffee shop to
fly a flag with their logo—"ESCR" printed on a steaming
mug—on a pole jutting out from the storefront. Joe liked
the coffee, he liked Andy and his used records, but right
now he had to concentrate.

He had thrown his jacket over the back of his chair, and
now he loosened his tie and rolled up his white shirt-
sleeves, running down the list of things he knew so far, and
what he still had to learn before he could close out the
case. He really wanted to take the detail off Bay McCabe,
but he couldn't quite yet. Andy Crane was doing background even now interviewing neighbors. And for what?

To learn that Bay had a secret; deeply hidden penchant for diamonds and platinum? Joe stared at Sean's file.

Sean McCabe. Ruthless criminal or hapless idiot? Unfortunately, like most of the people—"perps" was actually too edgy a word for these guys—Joe investigated, he was both. While the air conditioner hummed, he looked through the file. Sean's corporate portrait beamed out at him: neatly combed sandy hair, green eyes, huge smile, blue suit, and red tie. The picture said, "I went to school with you; we can shoot hoops together; our wives shop at the same A&P."

The nine-by-twelve color picture had joined the gallery hanging in the bank foyer to convince the customers that their money was safe.

Except it wasn't.

Most small-town bankers were fine, honest, upstanding individuals who wouldn't dream of stealing. They earned their clients' trust by hard work, impeccable management, wise investments, good community relations. They had degrees from fine colleges and had every bit as much financial acumen as their counterparts on Wall Street.

Working in small banks suited their temperaments better. They weren't so high-flying, so likely to take risks. If the rewards weren't as heady and extreme, they were more steady and consistent. Instead of penthouse apartments with airplane views and late city hours, local bankers had big houses on expansive lots and generally made it home every night in time to play with the kids before dinner.

Joe had investigated scammers all over, had logged time in New York and Boston, going after major-league hotshots who hid their money in Switzerland or Buenos Aires. The public could better handle thinking of some savoir-faire sophisticate skating off with the clients' money than Mr. Regular, the next-door neighbor who coached their kids in Little League.

Sean was an especially tough case. Everyone had loved him. Joe was getting it everywhere he went: "I've known Sean his whole life—he couldn't have done this." "He has the nicest wife in the world. There's no way." "We went fishing together!" "We went golfing together!" "I saw him play basketball in the state championship!" "We saw him at church on Sundays..."

The sense of betrayal among the townspeople was great, exceeded only—if possible—by their denial. Joe got this all the time in these cases; an unwillingness, or inability, to believe that this nice guy everyone trusted could have stolen their money. Getting victims to testify was very often a bitch. Augusta Renwick was the exception, Joe thought, and he smiled to remember her phone call earlier that day, saying she wished crooks had three lives so she could repeat the pleasure she would feel sitting on the witness stand and making her disgust at Sean McCabe part of the record.

Still, she was the exception, not the rule. Most of the other victims still wanted to believe there was an explanation, or that the crime really hadn't happened at all— that the money had simply been shifted around in an accounting error. *But it ain't coming back,* Joe's mentor would always say.

In Sean's case, some of it had. Of the hundred seventy-five thousand dollars that had disappeared with Sean, one hundred thousand had been found hidden in the driver's door panel.

Joe pored through the evidence, trying to determine whether Sean had acted alone. He examined the folder found on the *Aldebaran*. Why were these accounts high-lighted? Were these the only customers Sean had stolen from? And why the vehemence with which Sean had written in the margins? Who was Ed, and what had he done to get his name underlined and circled so many times?

Visiting Shoreline Bank's main office, Joe was frequently welcomed by Mark Boland, the president, himself. Mark had made all documents available, and he had told his staff to be open and forthcoming.

Boland was worried about the bank's reputation, anxious for Joe to wrap up his investigation.

"No one had any idea," Boland said, sitting in his big leather swivel chair, across the desk from Joe. "We all loved Sean. Everyone did."

"Did you and he personally get along?"

"Yes. We went through a phase, a couple of years ago, where I got the job he wanted and came over from An-chor, but we made it past that. We both love sports, played all through school and college; he put me up for member-ship at the yacht club...my nephew plays baseball with Billy, and we'd always sit together in the stands. I never saw this coming. Never." Boland raked his hair back with one hand; his eyes were filled with pain. "If he had needed money—anything—he could have come to me."

"Did he seem especially close to anyone else here?"

"Frank Allingham," Mark said.

Joe had already known that, but they'd taken the op-portunity to call Allingham into the office. Frank was a short, bald man, affable and easygoing. He had been the one to call Bay that first day, tell her that Sean had missed the meeting.

"And did you have any idea of what Sean was doing? Did he seem troubled? Unfocused? Especially secretive?"

"No to everything."

"Drugs. Did you know he used cocaine?"

Mark Boland shook his head vehemently no. Allingham hesitated.

"Did you?" Joe pressed.

"Once, driving home from Eagle Feather, Sean asked me if I'd ever used cocaine. I said no, and he said—"

"Go ahead, Mr. Allingham."

"He said it was a great high. That it made him feel like he could fly. And..." The man had a deep summer tan, but he blushed from his neck to the shiny top of his bald head. "And he said it made sex amazing."

"Did he use any that night?"

Frank shook his head. "Not in front of me. I don't see why he would have needed it. Sean was always so energetic, so full of himself—he was always riding a thermal. He didn't need cocaine to fly."

"If I'd known about drug use," Mark Boland said, "I'd have fired him. We have drug testing for employees—Sean administered it! Besides, he was an athlete, going way back."

"He liked risks," Joe said. "He probably enjoyed coke while others had to worry about getting caught."

"Well, you know..." Mark began, reddening. Joe could feel the man's tension, but he just sat back and waited. "You know how you've been asking about 'the girl'?"

"Yes," Joe said.

"I know what Sean meant by that." Mark cast a glance over at Frank. "You do, too, don't you, Frank?"

"Jesus, yes," Frank said, shaking his head. "I don't want to say—because it will hurt Bay."

"That's why we've both stayed quiet," Mark said. "Please don't take this the wrong way—Shoreline Bank doesn't want to do anything to impede the investigation in any way. The decision to hold this back was mine alone."

"And mine," Frank said.

"'The girl,'" Mark said, speaking methodically, holding a pen between the index fingers of both hands, as if he was too embarrassed to look up, "referred to 'the girl of the moment.' Sean's next conquest."

"His what?"

"Sean's libido was world-class," Frank said. "This guy treated women like an Olympic sport. To Sean, meeting a new woman, asking her out, was all a big game. He never even pretended it was love. To him it was just a score."

"Really," Joe said.

Mark nodded. "He even did it here at the bank. I won't go into details, but it came to my attention that he was crossing the line with one of our female executives. I told him he was leaving himself—and the bank—wide open for a sexual harassment suit. I told him to stop. And he said, 'Mark, I'm just chasing the girl. That's all.'"

"Was he referring to someone in particular?"

"No," Frank said, glancing from Mark to Joe. "I've heard him say it, too. About strangers. At the casino—'the girl.' At the dock—'the girl.' The whole thing..." Frank trailed off. "I never understood it. A guy with a nice family like that..."

That was the part that got under Joe's skin, too. He wasn't supposed to care, but he couldn't help himself. What kind of moron had a wife like Bay and left her alone, while he ran, chanced messing everything up with cocaine and other women? And what father of daughters would speak so cavalierly about girls? It was so crummy, it almost didn't ring true, even for Sean.

Most recently, Joe Holmes's focus had become a safety-deposit box.

Box 463 in the Silver Bay branch of Anchor Trust Company. Joe might never have stumbled upon it if, while questioning Ralph "Red" Benjamin, the bank's lawyer hadn't casually mentioned Sean's spare tire while Joe was interviewing him.

"So, was the car badly wrecked?" Mr. Benjamin had asked.

"Badly enough to kill McCabe."

"Is the crash what killed him? There was talk about murder."

"There still is."

"You don't think he drove off the road on purpose?" Benjamin asked. "He knew you were closing in on him, and he wanted out?"

"It wasn't on purpose," Joe said simply, picturing the deep gash in Sean's head, the scarlet edges and white bone. The injury alone, untreated, would have killed him; he would have bled out, which he ultimately did.

But there were other signs of murder as well; the tire patterns that argued against an accident; Sean's toxicology screen which had revealed the cocaine, and evidence of a passenger: the door ajar, a perfume bottle that had held cocaine, suggesting the presence of a woman, a pair of latex gloves caught in reeds along the shore.

"Why are the divers still down in that creek?" Red Benjamin had asked. "I went by this morning, and the trucks are still there; I saw the red-and-white flag, bobbing on the float..."

"It's a murder investigation," Joe had said. He wasn't about to tell the lawyer they were searching for McCabe's cell phone. Everyone Joe had talked to said Sean never went anywhere without it, but it hadn't been in the car.

Strong currents beneath the bridge might have swept it away; the divers were dredging the marsh's silted bottom.

"Huh," Benjamin had said, and he shook his head and gave Joe a wry smile. "Thought they might be looking into Sean's spare tire."

"Why would they do that?"

Benjamin shrugged, still half smiling. He was about McCabe's age, early forties, with a receding hairline and a serious paunch. Joe was a little older, but he stayed in shape with ass-kicking workouts.

"No one's told you?" Benjamin asked, surprised. "Shit, I should have held out and gone looking myself . . ."

"The car is no longer in the water," Joe said, his interest piqued, watching the lawyer's reaction.

"I wouldn't think so. Well. It's just that Sean used to stuff his valuables, including casino winnings, back in the wheel well. Guess he thought it was safer back there."

"Valuables?" Joe asked.

"Yeah. When he had them. Neither one of us had much luck at the casino. Sean used to talk about going to Vegas or Monte Carlo, but that was just talk. He said his wife would like Monte Carlo."

"He said that, did he?" Joe asked, deadpan; it was one of the first comments he'd heard McCabe had made that took Bay into consideration at all.

"Yes. He said she'd like to see the flowers on the Cote d'Azur. She's a sweet girl; likes nature. Simple things." The lawyer's expression revealed that he agreed with Sean, and that he didn't consider simple things to be worth much. Joe couldn't understand his own reaction, which was to want to shove the lawyer's smug smile down his throat.

"Anyway," Benjamin continued. "That's where he

would have kept his winnings—in the spare tire. Look, I have to get to court. If there's nothing else..."

Joe had let him go. He'd called the forensics lab at the State Police facility in Meriden and gotten Louie Dobbin on the phone. Louie had, of course, checked the spare tire wheel well. He had examined the jack. There was no cash, no casino chips. Joe sent him back to check again, just in case. And although there was still no cash, no chips, Louie found what he had missed the first time:

A key.

Wedged into the tire jack, as if it were part of the machinery, between the crank and the handle, there was a small safety-deposit key. The code stamped into the metal was that of Anchor Trust, Silver Bay branch. So, Joe had gotten a court order. He had gone to the bank, a fine institution overlooking the town green, the railroad tracks, and Silver Bay itself with the red-and-white stack and reactor of the Mayflower Power Plant inhabiting the western headland.

The key had fit box 463.

And inside that box were three things:

An antique silver cup, engraved and stamped with the silversmith's mark.

A sheaf of three letters, dated over twenty years ago, from Daniel Connolly to Bay.

A scrap of yellow paper, torn from the yellow pages of a phone book, with two letters and seven digits written in almost calligraphic handwriting: CD9275482.

Joe knew the sign of a numbered account the way he knew his own name. Sean McCabe had a secret bank account—offshore somewhere. The Bahamas, the Caymans, Costa Rica, Zurich, Geneva...

Was it possible that Bay knew anything about it?

Joe would bet anything she didn't. When he'd asked

her, flat-out, what she knew about Sean's financial life, she had looked him right in the eye and given him straight answers. Joe had believed her. He knew that practiced liars could fool anyone, even him, but somehow he didn't think Bay was like that. Those freckles, the way she constantly looked out the window at the agents' car parked in front, her stern eyes, hating Joe for dragging her kids through the mud: marks of an innocent woman.

Joe wasn't sure how, but he knew he was going to solve this case and give her some answers. He knew that Tara O'Toole would expect nothing less. So would his dad, for that matter. Joe wanted Bay and her kids to get through this without losing anything more. They had already lost their family pride and dignity; they had lost their husband and father. Joe had seen their savings account, and he knew their mortgage, and that they were probably going to lose their house.

Sean had thought to hide his own winnings amid a spare tire and tire iron, but he hadn't managed to take care of his own family—to provide the security of knowing they'd have a roof over their heads.

Joe might not have a wife or kids of his own, but one thing he knew for sure: If he did, he'd do it right. He'd learn from the idiots he had investigated over the years—the family men who had put their families last—and do the opposite in every way.

But he was forty-seven. Unlike Ralph Benjamin, attorney-at-law, and Frank Allingham, bank executive, he had all his hair. He was in FBI fighting trim. But he was a little too old to be starting out as a husband and father. And with that, he wondered whether Tara had ever been married. He wondered what it would feel like to go home to her, be met at the door with those fierce blue eyes and that sexy smile.

Stick to crime solving, Holmes, he told himself. Catch the bad guys. That's what you do, so keep doing it.

But right now it was time to knock off for the day, so he'd lock the silver cup and photocopied letters and scrap of yellow paper in the bureau's satellite office safe, stop thinking about the great husband he might have made someone, and head next door to see what Andy had in the way of old Dylan.

THE EVENING WAS STILL AND COOL, BUT THE DAY'S EXtreme heat continued to rise from the dry earth, blue stones, and rosebushes. Everyone had eaten—grilled chicken and sliced tomatoes from Tara's garden. Billy and Pegeen were at the beach movie; Annie was in the TV room with the sound turned low but the blue light reflecting off the walls.

"Come on, Annie," Bay said quietly. "Come on outside with me and Tara. We're going to watch for shooting stars."

"I don't want to," Annie said, looking up. "Do I have to?"

Bay smiled. "No. But we'd like you to."

"I know. I'm okay, Mom. Eliza said she might call. I want to wait by the phone."

"We'll hear it outside."

"I know, but—"

"Don't worry," Bay said, smiling and kissing her. "I get it."

She remembered back to when she and Tara had been twelve. They had been the most important things in each other's world. Now, heading into the kitchen, Bay found that Tara had finished the dishes, had gone outside to wait. Bay could see her, sitting on a chaise longue, barefoot, gazing at the milky sky, filled with haze and stars. And she went out to join her.

"HEAR THAT?" TARA ASKED, SETTING THE SCENE, THE IN-stant Bay walked outside from talking to Annie.

"Crickets?" Bay asked, because her yard abutted the marsh where spiky green grass grew thick and tall, and it was a haven for crickets.

"No, a whippoorwill. Listen."

They both waited, silent, until the night bird called again—distant, across the water. Bay raised her eyebrows in acknowledgment.

"It's a good omen," Tara said.

"Do you think so?"

"I know so."

"Hmm," Bay said. She fell silent again, and Tara wondered whether she was thinking about her meeting with Danny Connolly.

Grabbing Bay's arm, she gave a tug and hauled her out of the chaise longue. "Come on," she said. "We have to get you back in training!"

"Training?"

Without replying, Tara walked around the side of Bay's house. The hose was coiled, like a dry green snake, behind a wilting rose of Sharon bush. Turning the spigot—a brass sea horse Tara had bought her for Christmas several years ago—she handed the nozzle to Bay.

"Water," she commanded.

"Oh, it's too late," Bay said. "It's too late for this summer. I'll be lucky if anything comes back next year."

"We'll have none of that, my fine lassie," Tara said. "Water your garden. That's an order. I should have gotten on your case weeks ago, but there's no time like the present. Of course, I'll still have the best garden in eastern Connecticut, but I hate to win it in a walk."

With that, Bay grabbed the hose. It hissed as the silver stream of water hit the old roses, beach roses, lavender, delphinium, larkspur, snapdragons, cosmos, alyssum, sweet peas, black-eyed Susies, salvia, beach heather, and wild mint.

"I can't believe I let this happen," Bay said.

"You're doing it now."

"I wonder how long it will be my garden," Bay said. "I wonder whether we'll even own it next year."

"That's what I want to talk to you about," Tara said. "I found a job for you."

"You're kidding!" Bay said, nearly spraying Tara with the hose.

"I'm not ... and it's so perfect, you're going to be incensed you didn't think of it yourself. You're—going—to—be," she said, pacing the words for maximum effect, "a—GARDENER!"

Bay didn't speak right away. But when she did, the words were wreathed in a grin. "That's too perfect," she said.

"Isn't it? It hit me like a ton of bricks: No one does it better, except maybe me. You've got the green thumb, you've got the shabby straw hat, you're maniacal about sunscreen, but what's more, you've got your granny's talent for the soil."

Bay's smile was fragile, shimmering. "Remember? She always said that flowers were incidental; if we loved the earth, we couldn't help but bring forth beautiful things."

"She loved me for my name," Tara said, lifting her eyes and looking up across the beach toward the Point. "Irish for 'rocky hill.' Just like that ledge up there, and she said,

'If you can grow flowers here, you can grow them any-where.' She said that you and I were sea and earth . . ."

"Bay and Tara," Bay said.

"I want you to do something you love," Tara said, aching. When Bay hurt, so did Tara.

"My kids lost their father this summer," Bay said, look-ing around the yard. "And I lost my husband. Gardening just seemed so trivial."

"I don't see it that way," Tara said quietly. "I think life is supposed to be beautiful. We're supposed to try to make it that way . . . Sad, terrible things happen, but it's up to us to plant flowers. To bring forth the beauty."

Bay trained the hose on the grass. It was so dry and brown, each blade was a hard, brittle stick. Tara's bare feet longed for a walk in the cool, soft sand. Instead, she stepped right into the stream of water.

"About your career," Tara said. "I even have your first client lined up."

"Who?"

"Augusta Renwick."

"You're kidding."

"She's lovely, Bay."

"My husband stole money from her!"

"She doesn't hold that against *you*."

"You talked about it? I knew she'd bring it up to you. What did she say?"

"Well, she's Augusta. She's exactly how I want to be when I get to be her age—tough, regal, and entirely self-supporting. I mean, I know she inherited millions from Hugh, but still—they're *her* millions now."

"And? What did she say?"

"Well. She's pissed. Very, very pissed. At *Sean*. But she needs you to work in her garden."

"Great—a mercy job. No way, Tara. You couldn't

think I'd be able to work for Mrs. Renwick after what Sean did—to have to look her in the eye..."

"Darling, hate to break it to you, but there'll be no looking her in the eye. There'll be kneeling in the dirt, toiling in the hay, wrestling with the thorns of a thousand roses... You won't even see her."

"Come on," Bay said. "She's the kind of woman who would oversee every single thing that happens on her property. She'd probably tell me how to prune her roses."

"Not a chance. This woman sets foot outside only to admire the sunsets her husband once painted, and only to play with her grandchildren when they come over. She has geraniums even browner than yours. I'm serious."

"You asked her about hiring me?"

"Yes," Tara said.

"Really? And she didn't object?"

"Au contraire. See, you have to know Augusta. There's nothing she likes better in life than 'rising above' everything and everyone else. What she said was, 'When can my new gardener start?'"

"And you replied?"

"Right away. Tomorrow, if possible. And she was madly enthusiastic... to have her new gardener get started," Tara said.

"Wow," Bay said. "I can hardly believe it... but you know? It feels right. I'm not sure how or why, but it does. Maybe I can help make up to her for what Sean did. The only thing is, the kids will hate not having me here all the time."

"Don't kid yourself. They'll be overjoyed."

"What if they start getting in trouble? After everything that's happened... that's how it starts. Peggy's only nine—"

"And they'll feel so much better if you can't keep up

payments on the house? The other kids'll babysit for her. And you know I'm always available. I can adjust my schedule to help."

Bay stood still, staring at the silver water arching onto the lawn.

"Okay . . . if you're sure she wants me."

"Shake on it," Tara said, and the two friends reached across the now soggy grass to clasp hands.

13

BAY WISHED SHE COULD HAVE PROTECTED HER KIDS
forever, or at least a few more years: given them the security of thinking they were safe, that they would always
be taken care of, that their parents, their home would always be there.

She told them each individually that she had decided
to start working; she took Billy for a ride in the car, Annie for a walk on the beach, and Peggy for a stroll to the
Point. Each child reacted differently. Annie was excited
for her, especially about the gardening, and she promised
she would help look after the two younger kids. Billy was
worried that if she worked for someone else, their garden
would continue to deteriorate. She assured him she'd
make sure that didn't happen, especially if he'd consider
helping out with the yard work.

"I could do that," he said. "Can I drive the ride-on
mower?"

"When you're twelve," Bay said. "That's what your father and I decided."

"You and Dad talked about it?" Billy asked.

"Yes," Bay said. "He said he knew you'd be a good driver."

"I thought he'd teach me," Billy said, staring out the car window. "When I was little, he used to let me sit on his lap and steer. So I always thought he'd teach me."

"He thought that, too, Billy," Bay said, swallowing hard at the thought of all those moments the kids would miss with their father; and that he would miss with them. She reached across the seat to grab her son's hand, and to her shock, he grabbed hers first.

Pegeen was uncharacteristically silent on their walk, as darkness came to Hubbard's Point, and the air felt the first chill of summer's end. Bay explained that she would be starting to work next week, that Annie and Billy would be helping Tara fill in by looking after Peggy after school on days when Bay would be working. She waited for a question or two, but Peggy just walked in silence. So Bay found herself talking about Firefly Hill, the Renwick's great house on the promontory overlooking Wickland Ledge Light.

"Mrs. Renwick wants me to get her garden back into shape," Bay said. "It used to be beautiful, years ago, and her husband did lots of famous paintings of it. Some of them are in museums. I'll take you to the Wadsworth Atheneum in Hartford, to see one he did of his three daughters sitting on a garden bench."

"Did you see red leaves?" Peggy asked as they passed from the circle of a yellow streetlight into the darkness. "On that tree back there?"

"No, honey," Bay said, looking down at the top of her head.

"I did," Peggy said. "I wish we didn't have to start school. Fall's almost here. I want it to stay summer."

"Maybe we'll go to New York for Christmas vacation," Bay said, taking Peggy's small hand, excited by the prospect of making her own money and finding their way into the future. "There's a painting at the Metropolitan Museum of Art called 'Girl in a White Dress.' Would you like to do that, honey? We could see the tree at Rockefeller Center, and go to *The Nutcracker* . . ."

"I just want summer to last," Peggy said. "I don't like those red leaves."

Bay was to begin as Augusta Renwick's gardener the next week, but Pegeen got badly stung by a red jellyfish and was so upset that Bay postponed her first day of work. She began to wonder whether that had been Peg's plan.

Kissing Pegeen, she returned to the kitchen. Annie jumped up from the table when she entered.

"Mom, can I use the phone to call Eliza? I want to make plans for Saturday."

"Eliza," Billy said. "Is she the one who came to our house after Dad's thing all in black, with scars all over her arms?"

"The 'thing,'" Annie said, "was his funeral. So of course she wore black."

"Yeah, well, what about the scars? We learned about girls like her in health," Billy said. "She's a cutter."

Bay's stomach dropped. She looked at Annie, who was blinking slowly, as if she had never heard the word, as if it was a foreign language.

"Annie, is that true?" Bay asked.

"No," Annie said.

"How would you know?" Billy burst out angrily, close to crying. "You think she's going to just tell you? 'Oh, and by the way, I like to slice my skin with razor blades'? She does—everyone saw."

"Even if she does that," Annie said, skin growing paler, eyes flooding with tears, "I care about her. And she cares about me. So be careful, Billy. She's my friend. And I'm going to her house on Saturday. Right, Mom?"

Bay took a deep breath. The two children had unconsciously gone to stand behind their father's empty seat at the table, where Sean would never sit again.

"That's the plan," she said, calmly.

"So, can I call her?"

"Yes, honey," Bay said, knowing that she would call Danny to subtly follow up on Billy's words. But right now, she could see that her own kids were on edge, tense with all the changes: Summer was about to end, school was about to start, she was about to go to work. "But first," she said, "listen to me."

"What?" Annie asked.

"Yeah," Billy asked. "What?"

"I think you're amazing," Bay said.

Both kids stood still, looking slightly confused, waiting for her to say more. She almost couldn't go on, but she made herself. "I don't know how we're doing this," she said.

"Doing what?" Annie asked.

"Getting through this summer," Bay said. "It's been so hard, and you've all been through so much."

"Losing Daddy," Annie whispered.

"The worst thing that ever happened," Billy said.

"Yes," Bay said. "It is. It's been terrible. And so has the rest of it: the newspapers, and the TV, and all the stories..."

"People talking on the beach," Billy said.

"Being worried about money," Annie said.

"You having to go to work," Billy added.

"No," Annie said. "That part's good—she gets to be a gardener."

"Will we get to keep our house?" Billy asked.

Annie watched, seeming to hold her breath.

"We'll keep it," Bay said, "I promise."

"We can all get jobs," Billy offered. "To help."

"I'm so proud of you," Bay said. "I know your father would be, too." The kids tried to smile, but the memory still felt too raw. Bay hugged them both, and while Annie went off to call Eliza, Billy ran outside to turn the sprinkler on the garden.

Bay felt almost like a schoolgirl right now, preparing for the first day of school. Her kids were more ready for September than she was. Peggy's jellyfish sting had given her a few days' reprieve—partly because of its severity, but even more because her youngest had been so quiet since hearing the news about Bay's job.

Bay went into Peggy's room. It was swathed in darkness; of the three kids, Peggy was the only one who liked heavy curtains. She seemed to crave sleep as a restorative cocoon, blocking out the moon at night, the rising sun, to grab every last moment of dreamtime before launching herself full-blast into the light of day.

"Peg?" Bay asked softly, sitting on the edge of the bed, wiping her eyes.

"Hi, Mom."

"I'm glad you're still awake, honey. How's the sting?"

"Better. Not so itchy. What is it?"

"I want to ask you something. Just . . . how do you feel about my going to work?"

"Did you see the geese flying in a V this afternoon?" Peggy asked. "They're starting their fall migration, aren't they? I don't want them to, Mom. I want summer to last this year."

"Peggy..."

"And the leaves are turning. I don't want them to. I want them to stay green..."

Bay took a breath, gently pushed the hair back from Peggy's eyes.

"Honey," she said. "Never mind the leaves for now. Or the geese. Will you tell me what you think about my going to work?"

Pegeen, lying on her back in bed, stared up at her mother. She shrugged. Their eyes met and glinted, and in the darkness, Bay could see the hard glitter of tears. She reached for her youngest daughter's hand. Above her bed was a poster for a Connecticut College production of *Playboy of the Western World*. Bay had studied Synge in college, and she had played Pegeen in her senior play.

"I don't want you to," Peggy whispered.

"You don't?" Bay asked, her heart sinking.

Peg shook her head. "I like it when you're home. You've *always* been home. I used to feel sorry for the kids whose mothers weren't there after school..."

"Peggy, I won't be working all the time. Just doing some gardening for Mrs. Renwick. You know where she lives, right? In that big house on the cliff...you know, I told you about her husband, the famous artist, and the paintings he did of their garden...I want to make it just as beautiful as—"

"You'll be working for a rich lady," Peggy said, her throat thick with tears, "and I thought we were..."

"You thought we were rich?"

Peggy nodded. "Daddy was a banker..."

Bay sat very still, just holding Peggy's hand. She thought of their nice house, their two cars, Sean's big boat, all the kids' bikes and games and toys. What did any of them matter? "We're rich in lots of ways," Bay said. "The ways that matter."

"Then why do you have to work?"

"Because riches don't always pay the freight," Bay said.

"I still wish you didn't have to go to work. I *hate* that you have to."

"I know. I know you do. But it's doing something I love—gardening. How lucky can I be?"

"It doesn't seem lucky at all," Peggy said, breaking down. "It seems awful. As awful as anything! Almost as bad as the leaves turning red!"

"Oh, Peggy," Bay said, holding her. "You love fall. It used to be your favorite season. Why does it upset you so much this year?"

"Because of Daddy," Peggy sobbed, clutching Bay's neck. "Because I don't want to leave him behind in summer. I want to have him with me all through the year, but I can't. He's never going to see fall leaves again, Mommy—never! I want this summer to last forever!"

Bay held Peggy, rocking her back and forth as they both cried. Bay felt her little girl's hot tears on her own skin, and she thought she would burst with new grief. Every day there was a little less sadness in one place and a little more in another. She thought of the year to come, of all the "nexts" that Sean would miss—and that their children would miss about him.

When Peggy was limp from crying, Bay kissed her and slid her onto the pillow. She sat with her a little longer, until her breathing grew steady and calm. But when Bay went back to the kitchen, she found Annie upset. She reported that she hadn't been able to speak with Eliza—her dad had answered and said that something came up, that they would have to reschedule Saturday. Eliza had to "go out of state."

"What does that mean, Mom?" Annie asked.

"I'm not sure," Bay said. "Maybe she went to visit someone or something."

"She could have called me," Annie said, her lower lip quivering.

"I'm sure she will when she gets back," Bay said, giving her a hug.

"If she even remembers," Annie said into Bay's shoulder.

"Oh, she will, honey. I know she will."

They stood in the middle of the kitchen, crickets chirping outside, Bay rocking her. She thought of Dan, wondered what had really happened, wondered whether he was as constantly worried about his child as Bay was about all of hers. Maybe she should call, after the kids fell asleep, to make sure Eliza was all right.

Later, at ten o'clock, the house was finally all hers. Out on the back porch, she thought of Danny again. But it seemed too late to phone. She didn't know what might be happening with Eliza, and she didn't want to bother him. Time had changed everything, and she no longer felt free to just show up in his life when he least expected it.

She thought back to the summer she was fifteen, when she had first met Danny Connolly. What a perfect summer that had been. Love had come along, without her even asking for it. It had just been in the air, calling her down to the boardwalk every day. She had never felt so close to anyone; she hadn't wanted to let a minute go by without him.

And she thought of how silly and fleeting it could seem—a young girl's first crush. Against the backdrop of summer and the Point, the boardwalk and the blue sky, she had fallen in love for the first time. But now, twenty-five summers later, Bay was beginning to see that those feelings had been real and lasting, had spoken to something deep and true in herself. And she was seeing, now, that those feelings had colored all her actions since.

She had to admit, and it wasn't easy, that she had held Sean up for comparison all along. All these years, she had kept waiting for him to grow up to be like Danny. She had waited for him to outgrow his wildness, to finish sowing his wild oats.

Last winter, when he had looked her straight in the eye and promised he would change, she had wanted to believe there was a chance. But too much damage had been done; whatever promise he had been trying to make, he had been unable to keep. And even if he had, Bay suspected that her heart had been too broken for too long to ever really open up to Sean again.

"Our kids," she whispered up at the sky, just in case Sean was listening, "love you way more than you deserve."

By the light of a kerosene lantern, she tried to start reading her grandmother's yellowed and brittle *Gardens by the Sea*, one of the books she had brought over from *her* grandmother's house in Ireland. If she was going to start a new career, she was going to do it right. She would resurrect dead grass, restore vine-tangled borders, prune out-of-control rosebushes, make Black Hall gardens more beautiful than ever.

And amid all that beauty and new life, everyone would forget the things her husband had done.

But her kids would never forget. And they would never stop wondering why he had done them. And they would never stop loving him. And they might never, like Peggy, stop wishing that the year would stop right where it was: that the flowers would stay in bloom and the leaves wouldn't change and the snow wouldn't fall.

Because every day that passed took them farther away from their father, from the sound of his voice and the touch of his hand. And because no matter what Sean McCabe may have done to his customers, and to his wife, he was still the light of his children's eyes.

14

"DAD, ARE YOU THERE?"

"I'm here, Eliza."

"I didn't mean it—I swear I didn't."

"Okay. Just keep being honest with your doctor."

"I hate my doctor. He's an atheist."

"But he's a very good physician. That's what counts."

"You expect me to trust a man who doesn't believe in God?"

"First of all, I doubt very much that Dr. Reiss has discussed his religious beliefs with you. Second of all, regardless of what he believes, he's the best there is, and I want you to keep being open and honest with him," Dan said, although what he wanted to say was "*start* being open and honest with him..."

"Great," Eliza said, starting to cry. "You're calling your own daughter a liar. First a murderer, then a liar."

"I have never, NEVER called you a murderer."

"But you THINK it."

Dan tensed his jaw and resumed planing the plank of teak supported between two sawhorses. As economical as he tried to make his movements, to keep them as quiet as possible, Eliza heard. "You are working, aren't you?"

"I'm in my shop, yes."

"Your only daughter calls you practically from DEATH'S DOOR, and you're happily building someone a pretty little sailboat. How WONDERFUL for them, so they'll have a Daniel Connolly original, to go tra-la-la-ing in, sailing, sailing, fucking sailing into the goddamn sunset with—"

"Eliza."

"The goddamn FUCKING sunset."

"That's enough. You're not even supposed to be talking on the phone. Now go back to group and let the doctors take care of you."

"I want to come home."

"You will. As soon as you're ready."

"Right NOW, Dad. Today!"

"You can't come home today. I couldn't legally get you out today, even if I thought it was a good idea."

"I'm supposed to see Annie tomorrow!"

"She knows you're not available."

"You didn't TELL her!" she wailed.

"No, of course not. I said you were away for a short time."

"GREAT, Dad. Just as I get a friend, a real friend, you have to tell her I'm locked up..."

"Eliza, pull yourself together. I did not say you were locked up."

"Well, of course she'll figure it out! She'd know the only reason I wouldn't see her would be if wild horses dragged me away or a shark ate me or I was locked up!"

"Maybe she's not as...lyrical as you are. Maybe she just thinks you're visiting your grandmother."

"We are soul sisters, Dad," Eliza said. "I know she knows the truth."

"Well, if you're really soul sisters, she'd probably know the truth whether I screwed up and said the wrong thing or not," Dan said. The scary thing was, Eliza's logic was starting to make sense to him.

"The minute I get out, I'm seeing her."

"Fine."

"Don't patronize me, Dad. Just because I'm in here," she growled.

"Never."

"Hey, I learned a new grounding technique. Want to hear?" she asked, her voice and mood changing completely, suddenly sounding like his sweet little girl instead of the reincarnation of Bela Lugosi.

"Sure. What is it?"

"Frozen oranges. You stick an orange in the freezer, and when you feel yourself going off, you take it in your hands. It feels so cold and solid...and it smells wonderful. Will you put an orange in the freezer for me? For when I come home?"

"Of course, sweetheart."

Now she was silent, and so was Dan, but the line fairly shook with the emotion between them.

"I'm sorry I did it," she whispered.

"I wish you hadn't," he said. "I wish you could have talked to me instead."

"I just keep thinking I'd be better off dead. You wouldn't have to look at me and know that Mom died because of me."

Dan squeezed his eyes shut. His heart lurched as he thought of Charlie's death, of Eliza keening for hours afterward. That single night—with his anguish and horror—was the reason for all his daughter's problems now, had caused all her scars, inside and out. He was certain of it. He should have done a much better job of just loving his suddenly motherless child.

So he was very careful now, knowing he held Eliza's life in the palm of his hand, as he held back his own tears and cleared his throat.

"You're so wrong," he lied. "I never look at you that way."

"Promise, Dad?" she wept.

"Oh, I promise, Eliza. My sweet girl—I promise. Just talk to your doctor, and get well, and come home."

"Will you send me another phone card, Dad?" she cried. "Or bring me one when you visit?"

"I will, Eliza. Now go back to group."

"Okay. Bye, Dad. Call me!"

"Soon," he said. "I'll call you soon."

When they hung up, he put all his strength into planing the board. Teak was so hard and true. The grain was fine. He kept at it, feeling one hand on the steel plane, one on the smooth teak as curls of wood fell at his feet. That's what he loved about his work—it was so solid, and it was so satisfying to see the results: a smooth board, a well-joined boat.

If only life could be that way.

Back when he had been working on the boardwalk at Hubbard's Point, he had had such young ideas about love. He and Charlie had fallen in love the next year, after he'd returned from a trip to Ireland; shortly after that he had proposed to her. In some ways she was the opposite of Bay—cool, reserved, with a mysterious unhappiness that Dan had, at first, considered a romantic challenge: He would make her the happiest woman alive.

And they had gotten married, in the church on the green in Stonington, where he'd sworn to love her for the rest of his life. And he'd done his best. . . .

They had tried to have a baby for twelve years, and had just about given up when Eliza came along. Dan had been bowled over with love for his daughter. He still found it hard to fathom this: Eliza not only cemented him and Charlie as a family, but she was proof of miracles right here on earth.

"She's ours," Charlie had said once, within the circle of Dan's arms, while Eliza slept in her crib.

"No, she's *us*," Dan had corrected—and she was. The tiny girl, a very distinct person in her own right, had her father's eyes and chin, her mother's nose and cheeks. Looking at her was like seeing a miracle come to life: Dan—who made graceful, amazing boats out of white cedar planking and silicon-bronze screws—was a total hack amateur creator when it came to this league. Eliza's presence in the world bonded her parents together as nothing else could.

Until the night of the accident.

Dan couldn't deny that, in some sense, Eliza was right. When he looked at her, he still saw her mother—and all the hopes that had died the night of her accident. Dan had never stopped believing it was his job to make her happy, his remote, elusive Charlie. That last year of her life, Charlie had seemed to come more alive, gotten more interested in things—and Dan had hoped she would finally feel that sense of joy he'd always wanted to give her but had never felt she truly shared.

Now Dan knew he had lost the chance to have a happy wife, a close marriage. He'd seen the life they'd been building all those years come crashing down. He could never blame Eliza for it—he never would. But she reminded him of what had happened; and sometimes, when he looked in her eyes, he saw hints of her mother's unhappiness, and he almost couldn't stand it.

Dan had already lost his wife and his sense of hope and, for what it was worth, security: his little unit of love and family. Now he felt on the verge of losing even more. He felt he was on the brink of losing his daughter.

As he tried to persuade the steam-bent frames into shape aft, he felt all the muscles in his back and shoulders strain and burn, and he suddenly thought of another parent in pain: Bay McCabe.

This summer was ending soon, and she had the fall and winter to look forward to. Her kids' first Thanksgiving and Christmas without their dad. He hoped the Mc-Cabe children wouldn't shatter the way Eliza had. As Dan leaned harder into the curved frame, he was glad for the work and wished Bay would have something to distract her from the worries he knew she had, and the ones he knew were coming. Dan had some new fears of his own: That anonymous call, asking for Sean McCabe, meant that someone knew something. It had to be a warning, but of what?

Even though it was still August, and the shed was thick with sawdust and summer's damp heat, Dan felt a shiver go through his bones as if it were the dead of December. He thought of the moon, of how much Bay loved it. Would it comfort her now? He hoped she'd look out her window tonight and know that he was there for her.

And later that night, unable to sleep, with his daughter miles away in the hospital, Dan pulled himself out of bed. He went to the window, to look. There it was, angling overhead, the white moon—not quite full, but getting there.

"An obvious moon," Bay would have said to him years

ago. "I like the crescent moon better, just resting on top of the sunset..."

But it was all they had that night, so Dan found himself getting into his truck. It was after two in the morning as he drove west. The almost-full moon lit his way, weaving a path of silver on the water he glimpsed from the highway. New London spread out beneath the Gold Star Bridge. He caught sight of his boatyard, just a few piers south of the railroad station, the boats' masts glistening in the mysterious light.

When he got to the Hubbard's Point exit, he turned off and wound down the Shore Road. The countryside was dark and quiet, all the trees blocking the moonlight. He felt strange, excited, as if he had a mission and he needed to accomplish it before moonset.

Under the train trestle, right toward the marsh, he drove through the sleeping community. The small cottages were all dark, their beach toys stacked on the porches until the morning.

He parked in the sandy parking lot, walked past the boat basin to stand on the boardwalk. From here he had the best view anyone could have of the moon: Tilting westward in the sky, just above the big rock behind the raft, it spread its white light like a blanket on the waves.

Could Bay see it from her window?

He wanted her to...

Staring across the marsh, he saw her house. Sean had bragged about it, of course. The big white farmhouse had been separate from the beach at one time; the farmer who owned it had used the salt flats to graze his sheep. Dan was glad that Bay owned such a great Hubbard's Point landmark. He would have killed Sean himself if he'd known that his recklessness would put Bay and the children's house in jeopardy.

The moon was hazy around the edges: from summer's humidity, and from the fact that it was a few days shy of being really full.

"Obvious"...what a potent word. Too bad Dan had never thought more about it, paid more attention to the obvious things in life. He had always been more drawn to the subtle mysteries.

As he watched Bay's house, he saw a light upstairs go on. His heart sped up. He wished she would look out her window, see the moon, walk down to the boardwalk to see it on the water. The boardwalk they had built together.

Dan wanted to talk to her. He wanted to tell her the whole story. Even more, he longed to be with a woman with whom he'd built something. Right now his chest was aching so hard, his heart hurting so badly...He really wanted to talk to Bay, to enjoy her gentle presence in his life again. To have her remind him to look up at the sky.

It was as obvious as the almost-full moon, over the big rock.

ON THE LAST TUESDAY BEFORE LABOR DAY, WHEN TARA went to work at Mrs. Renwick's, Bay accompanied her. She wore her garden clothes: chinos, a long-sleeved blue chambray shirt, white socks, green plastic clogs. And she brought her ratty old straw hat, soft deerskin gloves with a four-inch gauntlet to protect her arms from thorns, and her old Girl Scout canteen filled with ice water.

"You're the only holdout I know, still putting tap water in that thing."

"I'm not going to spend a dollar on bottled water," Bay said, staring at the Renwick manse as if it were a haunted castle. "That's the whole reason I'm doing this—because we need the money."

"Can you imagine what we'd have said, back when we were kids, if someone ever told us that we'd be paying someone a buck for water? What a bunch of suckers we all are," Tara said.

"That's for sure," Bay said, yawning because she hadn't slept well the last few nights. The moon had been shining through her windows, trying to pull her down to the beach.

The two friends stood outside Augusta's house, right by the kitchen door. Most of the windows were open, and white curtains were blowing around on the cross-ventilation of a breeze coming off the sea. Bay glanced up, thought she saw a shadow pass the window.

"Is Augusta in there?" Bay asked.

"Probably," Tara said. "But she's pretty reclusive. She asked me to get you started."

"Well, you tell her that next summer she's going to have the most beautiful flowers on the coastline. Just look at those bushes! Black Beauty roses, hydrangeas, lilies, anemones..."

"Go to it," Tara said. "I've got to get the house done early today. There's an opening at the Black Hall Art Academy tonight, and I want to arrive at six sharp, to have my pick of the single artists. For whatever that's worth."

"Leave when you're done—I'll walk home," Bay said, smiling and waving Tara away.

She went into the garden shed, locating clippers, shears, shovels, rakes, and trowels. Cobwebs filled the space, but the walls were covered with fantastic, whimsical drawings by Hugh Renwick. Charmed, Bay spent a few minutes regarding the sketches he'd done of his wife in her sunhat, his daughters building sand castles and dancing with mermen, a sky filled with starfish, and a flying dog with a bone in his smiling mouth and a ribbon reading "Homer" around his neck.

Then she filled her arms with garden tools and went outside.

For four straight hours she walked the property, familiarizing herself with the land, starting in on some of the most tangled hedges and beds. Her grandmother had taught her to never be afraid of pruning.

"Right down to the ground with those blue star bushes," Granny Clarke had said in her Wicklow brogue.

"But I can't," Bay would protest. "It will kill them!"

"No, darling...the new growth brings the flowers. Chop away...that's a girl..."

And so Bay did that now, ruthlessly cutting and hacking away dead growth, snipping pennybright bushes straight down to the leaf nodes. Leaving a trail of small and large piles of sticks and brown leaves, like a series of bonfires waiting to be ignited, she made her way through the yard. Only when the air began to cool and the shadows lengthen did she realize that it was almost the dinner hour; time to get home to her kids.

"I see that you believe in annihilation," came the stern, throaty voice.

Peering over one especially large heap of vegetation, Bay came face-to-face with her employer.

"Oh, Mrs. Renwick," Bay said, pulling off her garden gloves, reaching across the brambles to shake her hand.

"So. You are my new gardener."

"Yes," Bay said, smiling. "Don't be alarmed—I know it looks as if I've cut a lot, but I promise it will all grow back."

"I'm particularly concerned," Mrs. Renwick said,

drawing out the word with her extremely patrician accent, making it sound like con*suhhhh*ned, "with all of those sticks that were once my husband's prize blue star bushes."

"And they will be again," Bay assured her. "They've been choked by ivy and bittersweet, almost strangled; so now I've cut off all the dead wood, and all the vines... They'll focus their energy during the winter, and come back strong next summer."

"I certainly," or *suhhhh*tainly, "hope so," Mrs. Renwick said darkly, "for Tara's sake."

"Tara?"

"She's your friend, isn't she? She recommended you."

"I know. Thank you for giving me this chance."

Mrs. Renwick stood tall, white tendrils of hair blowing in the wind, the legendary black pearls she wore everywhere, even to the A&P, at her throat. But she looked perplexed. "Why would you say that? Tara assured me that you are the best there is."

"Well, she might be a little biased. I am her best friend."

"So she said."

Bay tried to smile. "You came to my husband's funeral," she said.

"We haven't formally been introduced, Barbara," the older woman said. "I, as you obviously know, am Augusta Renwick."

Barbara? Bay thought. No one called her that; it wasn't even her name.

"It's actually 'Bairbre,' but my friends call me 'Bay.'"

"Bay," Mrs. Renwick said. "I always thought that was such an unusual nickname, when your husband would speak of you."

"Sean spoke of me?" As the sun began to tilt downward toward the horizon, Bay felt herself getting paler by the moment.

"Yes, he did," Mrs. Renwick said, her voice thin. "He sensed that I would be amenable to hearing about his wife and three children. I have three children myself."

"I know," Bay said.

"Sean always knew what to draw on, in order to get what he wanted. He realized that we had three children in common, so he very often talked about his. Yours."

"He loved them," Bay said.

The wind picked up, and Bay felt the chill as she noticed the look in her employer's eyes. The conversation felt very tense, and suddenly Bay had the sinking feeling that Tara had talked them both into a situation that was all wrong.

"So much," Mrs. Renwick said, "that he disgraced them the way he did?"

Bay felt her face turning white, her hands shaking as she twisted her leather gloves.

"He stole from me," Mrs. Renwick said.

"I know. I'm so sorry."

"I hate being taken advantage of," Mrs. Renwick said, suddenly seeming very old and fragile. "I trusted him! I trusted your husband!"

"I'm so sorry," Bay said again, reaching for her hand as Mrs. Renwick stumbled backward, steadying herself on a thornbush, pricking her hand.

Bay gasped, feeling suddenly frantic, realizing that this was a disaster, gathering up the tools. "I'll put these away, Mrs. Renwick," she said. "It's getting late, so I have to get home and feed my kids, but as soon as I do, I'll come back and rake up these piles of brambles—"

"It will be dark!"

"That's okay. I'll come back to do it tonight, so you won't have to see me tomorrow," Bay said, stepping on the head of a rake and whacking herself in the forehead. She was in a panic, upset with herself for thinking this job ever could have worked out.

"Now, look what you've done," Augusta said, sounding outraged. "You've gone and hurt yourself. This isn't going to turn into a lawsuit, is it? Because I'm telling you right now, if you think I'm going to let one more McCabe cheat me..."

"No, Mrs. Renwick," Bay said, her forehead throbbing and the bone above her right eyebrow starting to swell. "I would never, in a million—"

"That's what I would have said about your husband!" Mrs. Renwick said, her voice rising. "I trusted him! That's what devastates me—I *liked* Sean very much!"

Bay tried to block out the voice, gathering the tools together, dropping the shears, picking them up, slicing the palm of her right hand. So Mrs. Renwick wouldn't see, she slapped her hand into the pocket of her pants.

"And now, to have YOU on my property, butchering my Hugh's blue stars and hurting yourself, why, it's too much! It's too much!"

Bay's hand was bleeding, stars dancing in her vision, tears blurring her eyes. But as she looked across the pile of vines and dead wood, she saw the old woman bury her face in elegant hands—gnarled with age, but still with long, slim fingers pressed into her eyes—and begin to sob.

"Oh, Mrs. Renwick," Bay said, coming around the heap of vegetation. Not knowing what to do, not wanting to increase the woman's distress and needing to escape herself, Bay just stood there.

"I trusted him...and I cared about him very much," Augusta wept. "I saw you at the funeral...we are both mothers...Tara loves you very much...Oh, I wanted to help you. I did."

"You don't have to help me, Mrs. Renwick. I'm just so sorry for the pain we've caused you," Bay said, starting to cry herself, moved by the old woman's acute suffering. Again, she remembered words her grandmother had once said to her: "Always look kindly on the old, Bairbre... Because they have loved people so much longer than you have, they have so very much more to lose..."

"When I think of your children," Augusta said, unable to look up, "I can't bear it. I simply can't abide the thought of what they must be going through..."

"They're fine," Bay said. "They'll be fine. They're my worry, not yours. Please, just forget I was here. I'll leave now..."

And feeling dizzy with grief and pain, she began to walk.

15

B LACK HALL ART ACADEMY.

Twilight.

White wine flowing like white wine. Artists and people who wanted to meet or be artists buzzing, the art incidental to the conversation. The cognoscenti somewhere else because the word was out that Dana Underhill was giving a private gallery talk wherever that somewhere else was. New York, maybe. Tara tan and clad in a red sarong, eyeing the crowd.

The evening was a bust, manwise, the opening a deadly bore, until into the midst of all the paunchy artists and skinny art students, everyone wishing they were Hugh Renwick—or could at least paint like he could— walked a true man. Arms like iron, a chest that wouldn't quit, blue eyes that could melt rock: Dan Connolly.

Tara saw him enter the gallery from the parking lot side, thinking he really did look awfully fine, if awkward, in his blue blazer. The exhibit was a sculpture show:

"Found Objects and Maritime Media"—work that incorporated things found in boatyards.

"Way back in the day when you were reroofing the Hubbard's Point guardhouse, did you ever think that you could wire a barnacle-encrusted plank to a chipped propeller and get famous as an artist?" Tara asked, sidling up to him.

"No, and I still don't." Dan grinned. "But I told Eddie Wilson I'd come see the work he did with the old stem apron and hood ends I gave him . . . and I have to admit, I thought maybe you and Bay might be here."

"Really!"

"Yep."

"Well, she's not here, but why don't I give her a call and see if I can tempt her to come? It was her first day at a new job, and I bet she'd enjoy the diversion. Meanwhile, do you see your friend's work?"

Dan accepted a glass of wine from a tray being passed by a young art student, and pointed at a chipped and peeling sculpture that incorporated the worst of an old boat's stern with the worst of an older boat's bow.

"The American Impressionists would roll in their graves if they could see what Black Hall has come to," Tara said, rummaging through her bag for her cell phone.

"Really? I think it's pretty cool," Dan said, drinking his wine. "I wasn't expecting to like it, but I do."

"Oh," Tara said, her eyes widening as she saw who was coming.

"Bay!" Dan said, sounding as happy as a teenager in love one moment, looking as worried as a bystander at a disaster the next. "What happened?"

Bay walked into the gallery and over to them, her face streaked with dirt and her red hair filled with twigs and leaves, her forehead bruised and swelling. But the truly frightening thing was the streak of blood soaking through her right pants pocket.

"Tara," Bay said, breathless.

"Honey, what happened?" Tara asked, her heart beating very fast, alarmed by Bay's pallor, by the high pitch of her voice.

"I saw your car here. Will you drive me home?"

"Oh, Bay, what happened?" Tara asked, realizing that she was about to pass out—putting her arm around her and leading her to a chair.

"She saw me from the window and thought I was desecrating her husband's blue star bushes. She's lost so much trust this summer already…" Bay's voice trailed off, and she bowed her head. "It was a huge mistake for me to be there, Tara."

"I hoped it would be good for both of you," Tara said.

"It was a train wreck."

"What happened to your hand?" Dan asked, touching her elbow. Her right hand was still shoved in her pocket.

"I cut it," Bay said, seeming to see him for the first time.

"Let me see," Dan said, frowning with worry.

"I have to get home to the kids," Bay said. "Tara, will you drive me?"

"Let's go," Tara said, helping her out of the chair. "Bay, you know I only did it because I love you, and because you needed a job, and Augusta needed a gardener…It was like one of those moments, when the elements come together so perfectly, you just know you'll get struck by lightning if you ignore them."

"I know that's what you thought," Bay whispered.

"Bay!" Dan cried, as she turned slightly, took a few graceful steps away from Tara toward one of the sculptures, weaved like a reed in the breeze, and fainted straight into his arms.

WHEN BAY CAME TO, SHE WAS LYING ON AN EXAM TABLE AT the Coastwise Clinic. Two men were peering down into her face: a man in green scrubs, and Dan.

"What happened?" she asked.

"You passed out," Dan said.

"My kids . . ."

"Tara went home to feed them dinner."

She realized that he was holding her left hand, and that her right hand was stiff and aching. A clear plastic bag filled with fluid hung on a pole above her head; a tube ran into her arm. Hospital sounds of beeping machines and police radios were muffled, on the other side of a curtain.

"Good, you're awake," said the man in green scrubs. "I'll get the doctor." He left the cubicle, leaving Bay and Dan alone.

"I shouldn't have gone to the gallery," Bay said, turning her head, so her cheek was pressed flat against the table's cool surface. "But I saw her car, and I wasn't sure I could make it home."

"You couldn't have," Dan said, squeezing her good hand. "Tara was very glad you stopped. Kicking herself for sending you to Mrs. Renwick, though. She's still the same as ever—irrepressible. Damn the torpedoes, full speed ahead, but with a heart of gold. I'm glad you two are still best friends. She knows she put you in a bad situation, though . . . the last thing she said was that she hopes you'll forgive her."

"She knows I will," Bay said. Then, as the seconds ticked by, "How did I get here?"

"I drove you. Tara wanted to call nine-one-one, but I didn't want to wait for the ambulance to arrive."

"How did I get to your car?"

"I carried you. To my truck. Now that they've got you stabilized, you're going to need stitches in your hand. I think they want a plastic surgeon to take a look; you cut it pretty deeply."

"I know," she said. In spite of the pain medication they'd given her, her palm felt white-hot, as if she was holding molten iron.

"And you've got a shiner and a bump the size of an egg on your head. What happened, did Mrs. Renwick beat you up?"

Bay shook her head, which felt very foggy. "I stepped on a rake and grabbed a sharp pair of shears."

"Very graceful, Galway," Dan said.

"That's really a nice thing to say," Bay said, trying to keep her words straight. "You have a world-class bedside manner, you know? I remember when I hit my thumb with that hammer."

"I remember that. You lost your nail."

"But not right away," Bay said slowly, the memory washing through her. "At first, it just hurt like crazy—I'd split the skin along the side, and you had to take me to the clinic—here—for stitches."

"That's how I knew how to find the place tonight," Dan said, still holding her hand. "From all the times I've had to drop what I was doing and drive you to the emergency room."

"One other time," she corrected him.

"Well, if you want to be *exact*," he said.

"And you were so very helpful that time, too. Telling me I'd lose my thumbnail and that when it grew back it would probably be 'misshapen and grotesque.'"

Dan lifted her left hand, bringing his face close to it, examining her thumbnail. "Looks like I was wrong. It's very pretty."

"It was my right thumb," Bay said.

She drew her right arm out from beneath the sheet, wincing as she did. Her hand throbbed in spite of the shot, and every movement made it worse. But she held her thumb for Dan to see.

"Ah," he said, as if he were a doctor and knew what he was seeing.

"What?" Bay asked, light-headed with pain, medication, and emotion.

"I'm assessing the situation, young lady," he said.

"I didn't know you were a doctor."

"Twelve years as a father gives a man certain expertise," Dan said, "in the realm of medical care."

"Eliza," Bay said, remembering the mysterious message, that she had gone away. "How is Eliza?"

"You're my patient right now—let's not get off track, here."

"Well, tell me, then. Were you right all those years ago, when you told me my nail would be 'misshapen and grotesque'?"

"You certainly have a mind like a steel trap," he said. "To remember the exact phrase I used."

"When you're a fifteen-year-old girl and you read *Seventeen* and all the models have perfect, oval nails, the words 'misshapen and grotesque' carry quite a lot of weight."

"I'm so sorry, Bay," Dan said, holding her mangled right hand, staring into her eyes. "I was wrong about what would happen to your thumbnail. Most apprentice boardwalk-builders who smash their thumbs end up with nails misshapen—well, you know. But not you."

16

I T WAS A WEEK LATER, JUST AS SCHOOL WAS STARTING
and summer ending—not the calendar summer with its
final segue into the autumnal equinox, but the real summer, the summer of the beach and crabbing and Good
Humors and endless free time—when Annie finally got
together with Eliza. Dan had driven her over to Black
Hall so the girls could spend the day together.

Eliza was paler than ever.

That was the first thing Annie saw. The second thing
was that she was also, impossibly, even skinnier. And the
third thing was that she had fine scars, like the almost invisible tentacles of jellyfish, crisscrossing her forearms
and the backs of her hands and the calves of her legs.
Some scars were old and white and others were fresh and
red. Billy was right: Eliza was a cutter.

"So, where were you?" Annie asked as the two girls
walked down the sandy road toward the beach. Not to
actually *go* to the beach, of course. They both hated the

sun, and kept to the shade. But just for something to do, to get away from parental observation.

"Your mom's hand is still bandaged," Eliza said, as if she hadn't heard.

"Yes, she cut it."

"I know. My dad told me. He drove her to the clinic."

"Just like he did when they were young and she got hurt helping him build the boardwalk."

"He's a regular freaking knight in shining armor." Eliza chuckled. "Is the boardwalk he built still here? I want to see it."

"Where were you?" Annie asked again.

"My dad likes your mom," Eliza said bluntly, once more dodging the question.

"She likes him, too. She loves her old friends."

"But what if they really like each other? What if they end up falling in love with each other? What if we end up being stepsisters? You don't want to move out of your house and I don't want to move out of my house, so we'll all end up fighting and hating each other."

"You're crazy," Annie said, laughing. "They're just friends. That's all."

"Bingo! You got it right!" Eliza said.

"That they're just friends?"

"No, that I'm crazy. That's where I was—in the bin."

" 'The bin'?"

"The loony bin. The nuthouse," Eliza said in a loud voice, even though they were passing people in their yards. She might just as easily be saying she'd been at school, at camp, on vacation. Annie swallowed hard, looking at Eliza to see if she was kidding. She wore a long slinky black dress with an artificial flower pinned to the bodice, and a floppy yellow hat.

"You're joking," Annie said.

"Nope. I was at Banquo Hospital in Delmont, Massachusetts. My alma mater. I kind of have D.I.D. and P.T.S.D. and I've been there ... a few times."

"Why?" Annie asked.

"Because ... sometimes I can't keep myself safe," Eliza said.

Annie scrunched up her face. Now, that sounded crazy. How hard could it be, to keep herself "safe"?

"What do you mean?" Annie asked, but she found her eyes moving to the scars on Eliza's arms.

"Don't you ever do it?" Eliza asked, her eyes shining. "Hurt yourself?"

"On purpose? Why would I do that?"

"To let the real pain out!" Eliza said. "You know, you have so much inside ... like I do ... doesn't the pressure ever build up so much you have to let it out?"

"By hurting myself?"

"Sticking yourself with pins, writing on your skin with a razor blade?" Eliza asked, as if it was the most normal, sensible solution in the world. "Putting your finger in a candle flame?" At that, she showed Annie the tip of her right index finger: dark and thickly callused, as if it had been passed through fire over and over.

"Eliza, you ARE weird," Annie said.

"Actually, everyone else is," Eliza said, shrugging huffily and walking ahead, a straight pencil line of a girl, so thin she could almost be taken for the shadow of a bare branch. When she turned around, she was grinning, as if she had something really great to say and couldn't keep it in another minute. She cupped the flower pinned to her chest.

"I love this," she said. "It was my mother's. And she got it from *her* mother. Isn't it beautiful and old-fashioned?"

"It is," Annie agreed.

"No one wears flowers pinned to their dresses any-more, right? Isn't it original, for someone our age?"

"Very."

"They wouldn't let me have it at the hospital. Because of the pin," Eliza said. "No sharps."

"Sharps?"

"Pins, needles and thread, even the silver spiral on spiral-bound notebooks. No razors in the shower—all the girls there have the hairiest legs you've ever seen."

"Gross!" Annie said.

"I know. The first thing I did when I got home was say 'Dad, you're getting me an electric shaver, or I'm out of here on the next tide.'"

"Did he get it for you?" Annie asked, bending slightly and lifting Eliza's long skirt, to view her smooth legs. "Looks like he did."

"Yeah. I love my dad," Eliza said. "Even if he hates me."

"There is no way he hates you."

"You don't have the whole story yet," Eliza said. "We might be best-friends-to-be, but we have a few secrets from each other still. Can't rush these things. I learned that in the bin, where we're all like drowning people in a lifeboat together, clinging to each other and best-friends-for-life . . . until we walk out the door and never see each other again. 'Write me, call me, I'll never forget you!' But we do forget . . . Hey, is that my father's boardwalk?"

"Yes, it is," Annie said.

Together they walked up the steps—in silence, with reverence—as if they were making a pilgrimage. To Notre Dame, Mecca, the Taj Mahal, St. Patrick's Cathedral: a sacred, holy place, the boardwalk at Hubbard's Point.

"Just imagine," Eliza said, crouching down to brush

the boards with her fingertips, "how long it must have taken my father to build this."

"With my mom helping him," Annie said.

With tiny steps, making sure her toes touched each and every board, Eliza began to walk the length of the span. As boardwalks went, Annie knew that this one wasn't very long. Just about fifty yards from end to end, with a blue-roofed pavilion in its center, to shade people from the sun.

On one side, the boardwalk gave onto the beach itself, the white strand easing down into the sea. On the other side, the boardwalk was lined with benches backed by a chest-high white fence designed to keep people from pitching into the boat basin, about fifteen feet below.

"What was here before my dad built the boardwalk?" Eliza asked.

"Well, there was always a boardwalk," Annie said. "I think he actually replaced an old one that washed away in a hurricane."

"Do you have a boat in there?" Eliza asked, still taking mincingly small steps as she gestured at the boat basin.

"No," Annie said. "I wish I did. My dad's boat was too big to fit in there; he kept it at the marina in town. But my dad was going to hire your dad to build me a boat," Annie said.

"I know. He told me."

"I wish it had happened," Annie said.

"There aren't many rowboats in there now," Eliza said, checking out the boats.

"No," Annie said. "It's pretty funny, actually. My mom said that when she was young, it was totally tidal—filled with water at high tide, but dry at low. The boats were all small and wooden, with a few Boston Whalers. There was an island in the middle, where the swans could build their nest..." Annie looked at the ugly corrugated steel forming the basin itself, recalling her mother's description of graceful stone walls. "A lot of the new people at the beach call this 'the yacht basin' now."

"New people," Eliza said. "I'm guessing you and your family are 'the old people.'"

"Yep. Been here forever. That's why I wish we had a little boat to go in the boat basin," she said sadly. "Because it would be so right..."

"And you could row me around."

"Yes," Annie said, smiling. "I could row you around."

The two girls stared at the basin's still surface, as if they could both imagine the rowboat, as if they were already rocking on the water. Annie could feel the gentle motion, she could hear the peaceful waves.

"It's nice here," Eliza said, looking around at the pretty cottages, at the boardwalk along the white beach.

"People fall in love here," Annie said. "That's what everyone says. The air is filled with magic, or something."

"I don't want to fall in love," Eliza said. "Ever. It leads to pain."

"Well, there are lots of different kinds of love," Annie said. "And it's all here at Hubbard's Point. A lot of these cottages are owned by different family members. Sisters, brothers, parents, grandparents, kids...and they all come back, year after year, to be together."

"Really?" Eliza asked wistfully.

"Yep. People at the Point call them their 'beloveds.' It doesn't matter whether you're married, or even related—you can love anyone. My mother's best friend, Tara—you met her—lives right across the creek from us. They've been best friends since they were young."

"Our age?"

"Even younger," Annie said. "And their grandmothers

were best friends, too—they met on the boat from Ireland. My mother said they grabbed onto each other's hands and never let go."

With that, she felt Eliza grab hold of her hand, look into her eyes. "Like that?" Eliza asked.

"Yes," Annie said, nodding. "I think so."

"Do you think best friends can last forever? Through anything?"

Annie thought back to the mess Tara had made with her mother and Mrs. Renwick, one of the people her father had stolen from. The whole thing had sort of blown up.

And her mother had been so humiliated, she had managed to bang her head and cut her hand while trying to get away without making Mrs. Renwick even more upset. Although her mother could have been really mad at Tara for it, she just kind of laughed and said she'd figure out a way to get her back, after she strangled her.

"Yes," Annie said. "I do."

"Then, if I never let go of your hand," Eliza said, "do you think we can be like the beloved grandmothers? And have little white houses together here at Hubbard's Point?"

"The beloved grannies," Annie said, smiling at the thought. "I think we could!"

"And in a hundred years," Eliza said, "our granddaughters will be standing right here in this same spot, talking about rowboats and imagining how their families got here. And it will be from this very second—where we decided to be best friends."

"Forever," Annie said.

"Forever," Eliza said. And with that, another generation of Hubbard's Point beloveds was born.

17

M OM, WHAT'S D.I.D?" ANNIE ASKED JUST BEFORE
she was leaving for school the next Monday.

"That's how you spell 'did,'" Billy called from the
breakfast table. "As in, 'Did you know I really really don't
want to go to school?'"

Annie ignored him with such impressive equanimity
that Bay had to smile.

"Seriously, Mom. What do the letters D-I-D stand for?"

"I'm not sure, honey."

"Then, what's P.T.S.D.?"

"I think that's 'post-traumatic stress disorder,'" Bay
said. "People who've been through trauma sometimes
suffer from it."

"Like Vietnam vets," Billy said. "I saw it in the movies.
Why? You know someone who's been to war?"

"Not that kind of war," Annie said softly. "I wonder
what D.I.D. is, though. I'm going to look it up at the
school library."

"It's great to hear you wanting to learn something new," Bay said, knowing that the questions had to do with Eliza.

Annie's eyes met her mother's. "She's my best friend," Annie said. "I want to know everything about her."

Bay hugged her just as the bus pulled up outside and the phone rang. Kissing all three kids good-bye, she answered the phone, pulling it with her as she waved at them from the door.

"Hello?"

"Hey, Bay."

"Dan! Hi," she said, Annie's questions fresh in her mind.

"Last time I checked, your hand was healing nicely. You were almost ready to grab a hammer again."

Bay smiled. "Almost," she said, flexing her palm, looking down at the bandage. "How are you?"

"I'm great. Listen, I'm almost finished restoring an old catboat, and I wondered whether you'd like to come out for a sail."

"A sail?" Bay asked.

"The sea trial," he laughed. "Where I make sure she's seaworthy. You know, I figured it would remind you of walking the boardwalk for the first time, checking to make sure all the boards were secure."

"Sure," Bay said, looking out the kitchen door at the black car driving past. Joe Holmes had taken the surveillance off her family, but she was pretty sure he still patrolled once in a while. What other unmarked black car with two guys in suits would go sliding through Hubbard's Point?

"When would you like to go?" Dan asked.

"Well, I need to make some job search calls today," she said, "and if I get something, I'll have to start right away..."

"Keeping that in mind, what about trying for Saturday?" Dan asked. "The weather's supposed to be mild, and maybe we'll have some better wind than today. Late afternoon? Five or so?"

"Sounds good," Bay said. "See you then."

She held on to the phone, glancing down at the classifieds covering her kitchen table. Across the marsh Tara's house gleamed in the sunlight, her hollyhocks and morning glories waving in the breeze. Bay dialed the number.

"Hi," Bay said.

"Hi. I saw the bus. Are they off?"

"Yep—it's just me and the classifieds. Though Danny just called to ask me to go sailing."

"Really? That's great, Bay. The classifieds, though... I'm sorry."

"It's not your fault."

"But I feel it is," Tara said. "I should have known better. It's just that I know you separately, you and Augusta, and I love and adore you, and like and respect her, and her gardens need help, and I know that Sean hurt you both, and I just thought—"

"I know. Please, Tara—don't," Bay said quickly, to stop the apology, and because she still couldn't stand thinking about how distraught Mrs. Renwick had been.

"See? You're still upset," Tara said. "I knew it."

"I guess I am, a little," Bay said. "But not at you. You were trying to help. Anyway, I'm going to get busy. Maybe I'll try some of the garden centers and see if they're looking for help. Being a gardener was your idea—I have you to thank for that."

"Thanks for nothing, after what happened," Tara said. "I'm going to make it up to you. I swear, I am. With God as my witness..."

"Tara, it's okay," Bay said. "Stop, okay? I'll see you later."

She hung up and looked out the window. There was Tara standing in *her* kitchen window. They raised hands in a small wave. How often they had reached out to each other like this over the years...

Bay thought of the time their two grannies, both about eighty, had decided to take a trip back to Ireland. They were widows by then, and they hadn't set foot on Irish soil since they'd first come to America. Bay and Tara were sixteen; they had just gotten their driver's licenses. Tara's mother had told her she could drive their grandmothers to the airport limo in New Haven—but when they got there, all it took was one look between the girls to know they were taking them all the way to New York.

Bay remembered Tara driving to Bridgeport, then switching so Bay could drive the rest of the way. She recalled the thrill and tension of driving into the morass of New York traffic.

Relying solely on Tara's navigation and map-reading—through the Bronx, over the Whitestone Bridge, onto the truck-and-yellow-taxi-studded Van Wyck Expressway—Bay managed to get them to the Aer Lingus terminal at JFK airport. And Bay and Tara had stood at the International Departures concourse, waving at their two grandmothers, holding hands as they walked onto the ramp to their plane.

She had been grounded for coming home four hours later than planned and for the next week she had waved through the window as Tara—whose mother was less strict than Bay's—walked or rode her bike past the cottage every chance she got.

And Bay remembered waving to Tara from the podium at her college graduation, from the back of Sean's motorcycle, the summer he had a BMW, from the altar at each of her children's christenings, and, embarrassed, from the deck of the *Aldebaran*, the first time he brought it over to Hubbard's Point, to moor off the beach so everyone would see.

Life had a way of gaining meaning when she could share it with Tara. Mulling over the details of their days, observations and overheard bits of conversation, turning their hearts inside out.

Their friendship was old and burnished; Bay couldn't imagine anything that would breech it. She and Tara were the Irish Sisterhood, heirs to their grandmothers.

What good was a sisterhood without sisters?

TARA HUNG UP THE PHONE.

No matter what Bay said, Tara was determined to make it up to her.

Hopping on her bike, Tara rode through beach roads. She stopped along the way, picking a bouquet of asters, goldenrod, and Queen Anne's lace, wildflowers to hand to Bay along with a poem she had spent a few sleepless nights composing.

The poem was short in length, full in meaning, punchy yet lyrical, heartfelt to the very tips of her toes.

She'd been browsing in Andy's Used Records yesterday, looking for a way to say with music the sentiments she had so far been too upset to articulate to Bay's face. But she had run smack into Joe Holmes at the "British Invasion" rack and had attempted to slink out of the aisle like a criminal on the FBI's top ten wanted list.

"Miss O'Toole?" he had called after her, dropping his *Let it Bleed* on the floor in a suave crime-fighting move.

Tara tried to ignore him, but he followed her into the

parking lot. Evading the FBI in a town as small as Black Hall was guaranteed to be a losing proposition, so she turned to face him.

"Why are you still here?" she asked.

"Oh, tying up loose ends."

"Well. I certainly wish you'd tie them up and solve this case."

His eyes widened, and Tara couldn't believe she'd said that. He was very cute, in a geeky, federal agent sort of way—short brown hair, worry lines around his eyes, a bulge under his jacket that had to be a Glock 9, or something of that nature.

"I'm sorry for being rude," she said. "But my friend has had about as much as she can take."

"I know. And I'm very sorry about that. But I'm sure you can appreciate the fact that I have a case to investigate, and I still have lots of unanswered questions."

"Well, have you talked to the women Sean was seeing? I believe the most recent one was Lindsey Beale, a banker who lives in Westerly, I think," Tara said, wanting to be helpful, but also hoping to remind him that Sean's bad behavior had taken him east of Black Hall, and enjoying the idea of Lindsey's sharing in some of Bay's current misery. Maybe he should concentrate his efforts in Rhode Island. . . .

"Generally I ask the questions," Agent Holmes said, half-smiling. "But yes. I have."

"Humph. Good," Tara said, finding herself uncomfortably diverted by the agent's crooked half-smile. Sort of an Elvis-y thing, half lust and half evil. Or maybe half lust-and-evil together, and the other half sarcasm. Tara wasn't sure. She was very good at flirting, but when she really liked someone, she sometimes found herself groping for words.

"Miss O'Toole," he said. "I know we took up a lot of your time at the beginning of this investigation, but a few things have come to light, and I was wondering . . ."

"Whether you could interrogate me again? Go ahead. Ask away."

Agent Holmes flinched slightly. Once again, she had knocked the man off balance. Had he been planning to haul her into the FBI office? She checked her watch. Even though she had nowhere pressing to go, she didn't want him to think that she was a woman without a destination.

"Fine," he said. And then he'd asked her a series of questions about offshore bank accounts, a safety-deposit box, and a silver cup. Tara listened, not really able to offer anything helpful.

"Sorry," she said. "The kids had silver baby cups . . . they used to drink their juice from them sometimes. Bay's mother gave them each one when they were born. And Sean had a bunch of trophy-type cups, from basketball seasons gone by . . ."

"This cup is very old," he said. "More like a goblet, no handles . . . would you take a look at it? It's in the office."

"Sure," Tara said.

Agent Holmes led her across the parking lot, toward a curtained storefront between the record store and coffee shop. Tara's pulse increased—not only because she was about to enter an FBI office, but because Agent Holmes had a really terrific, playful, and coconspiratorial smile. He almost made her think he *needed* her to solve this case. "I wish you could tell me why he did it," Agent Holmes said, reaching into his pocket for his keys.

"Why Sean did it?" Tara asked. "I wish you could tell me the same thing."

"Were there signs?"

"We ask ourselves that," Tara said, staring east, toward the beach. Even here in town, the air smelled like salt. "Did we ever know him at all?"

"You knew him a long time," he said. "Hard for a con man to fool everyone his whole life."

"Well, maybe it wasn't his whole life. But do people really . . . go bad?" Tara asked. "Like just out of the blue?"

"Depends on how you define 'bad,'" the agent said, unlocking the door. Tara followed him inside and was surprised to see the place looking like a small, one-man insurance agency: fax machine, copier, computer, phone, piles of papers, McDonald's wrappers in the trash.

"What do you mean?" Tara asked, breathing in his aftershave—spicy, with hints of lemon and cinnamon—as he leaned across her to hit the overhead lights.

"Well, the FBI has a fairly broad definition of 'bad.' But the average person's definition is even broader. When a man starts cheating on his wife, for example; it might be morally wrong, therefore 'bad,' but not necessarily criminal."

"So, you're asking me when Sean started misbehaving?" Tara asked. "Or when he became a criminal? And does one lead to the other?"

"Hard to say," the agent said. "Sometimes, but not always."

"Well, Sean was always wild. A basketball star and powerboat guy who loved to drink beer and party. She was such a classic good girl, and opposites attract. Right?"

"Seems that way," Joe said, making Tara blush.

"Well, anyway, it was one thing when we were kids. But it was another when he started running around, going to the casino."

"Was that a change in behavior—going to the casino, I mean?"

"The casinos weren't always here. When we were growing up, eastern Connecticut was a bucolic little haven. Seaports on the shoreline, farms and cows inland. Lots of stone walls. But suddenly it's become Vegas in the Nutmeg State. I don't think anyone who grew up here saw it coming."

"Did Sean get into going right away?"

"No—in fact, he used to gripe that the casinos would make it harder for him to get to his boat. The traffic would be worse, and he'd be stuck inching along on I-Ninety-five. He'd say that that part of the state was depressed, that his bank was always foreclosing on homes and farms out that way. And it was immoral, for the casinos to even exist—taking money from out-of-work people who couldn't even afford to feed their families."

"But he started eventually . . ."

"Yes. A lot of people who stayed away at first—boycotting them, in effect—were curious. Sean took Bay to see a show there, his first time. Carly Simon, a few years ago. I went with them, with a date, and we all stayed to gamble. It was a novelty, but I never wanted to do it again."

"How about Bay?"

"She liked it even less than I did. It depressed her, seeing so many old people dropping quarters into slot machines. She thought they were running through their retirement, coin by coin." Tara smiled at Bay's words. "I remember her pointing to this little old lady, perched on a stool, with her arm through the handle of a coin basket as she pulled the handle over and over. There was a whole *row* of ladies like that, and they looked as if they *lived* there: personalized coin baskets, visors to cut the glare . . . 'Can you imagine our grandmothers here?' Bay asked me, 'instead of doing what they did? Instead of telling stories and teaching us how to garden, they could have taught us how to gamble.'"

"Did she disapprove of Sean going there?"

"When he started going a lot . . . and lying about it."

"So, that contributed to their rift."

"Wouldn't it contribute to a rift with *your* wife?" Tara asked. "If every time she left the house she hightailed it out to be with someone else?"

The agent turned red. He really did—Tara saw the heat in his neck and cheeks. He wasn't wearing a wedding ring. Of course, she wasn't either. She felt a shiver go down her back as he tilted his head and gave her that sexy half-smile again.

"Can you tell me when it started?" he asked. "Can you relate it, at all, to the time he was passed over for the bank presidency?"

Tara thought back. "It seems funny you'd mention that, but it *was* shortly after he lost that job. I remember he bought his new boat and started gambling, and Bay became more and more upset and worried. She thought he was having a really expensive midlife crisis. But I think he just let himself get corrupted."

"Corrupted," Agent Holmes said. "That sounds like a very New England word."

"Don't forget," Tara said. "We're in a state that was founded by Puritans. Thomas Hooker."

"Was Sean ever puritanical?"

"No," Tara said, laughing. "He was always fun, ready to have a good time, from the time we were kids. The big jerk."

"You're very close to his wife?"

"Very," Tara said, feeling another twinge about Bay. She decided to change the subject. "So, will you show me your gun?"

"My gun?"

"Yes. What is it?"

"It's a ten-millimeter," he answered, smiling. "You ask some interesting questions yourself, Miss O'Toole. You think like a cop."

"I come from a long line of cops," she said. "My grandfather was the captain of detectives in Eastford. He was the number-one pistol shot in America, back in the forties."

"I know," he said.

"You do?" she asked, shocked.

"Um, yes. Seamus O'Toole. You mentioned that your grandfather was an officer, and during the course of my investigation, I happened to look him up."

"Agent Holmes," Tara said, smiling and raising an eyebrow.

"So. Your grandfather was the number-one pistol shot . . ."

"Yes," Tara said. "I inherited his guns. But I didn't want them in the house, with Bay's kids coming over, so I donated them to the State Library. They have a big collection of Colt firearms."

"That's impressive," he said. "So, Miss O'Toole . . ."

"Call me Tara," she said.

"Okay," he said. "Call me Joe."

"Wow. I'm on a first-name basis with the G," she said.

"Yes," he said. "As I am with Captain Seamus O'Toole's granddaughter. Let me get the cup. Maybe you can help me figure out where McCabe got it. He had it in his safety-deposit box at Anchor Trust . . ."

But just then his cell phone rang. It was important, and Tara had to go.

He had said he would call her to reschedule, but so far he hadn't. Just as well, she thought, riding down the beach road. All she needed was to fall in love with the FBI agent trying to dig up dirt on Sean.

And Joe Holmes was definitely material for falling in love. He seemed strong, as if he really knew who he was, Tara thought, wheeling up Bay's driveway on her bike. Her heart began racing as she knocked at the back door. Usually she just walked in and called out, "I'm home!"

Bay came to the door wearing an old white beach shirt, cutoff jeans, and half-glasses. The bump on her head had gone down, leaving a yellowish bruise.

"We just hung up!" Bay said, smiling.

"Somehow, that little phone call couldn't say enough."

"Tara—stop. You've apologized too much already. I mean it, okay?"

Tara looked past Bay, into her kitchen, and saw all the kids' pictures, the basket of shells she and Bay had picked up on their beach walks, the piece of driftwood they had found that looked like a monkey. She thought the lump in her throat would choke her, but she just shook her head and said, "No. Not okay. These are yours with a poem," Tara said, handing the flowers to Bay.

"They're beautiful," Bay said.

And then, clasping her hands, the way the nuns had taught her to do while reciting, Tara went for it:

> "Wildflowers
> So rare,
> To show you
> I care.
> You are gold,
> I'm brass,
> You should kick
> My ass

But you know
I'm your friend.
I'll love you
Till the end."

Bay stood there holding the wildflowers, her chin quivering and eyes flooding, but her face wreathed in an unambiguous smile. She opened her arms to grab Tara into a great hug.

Relief washed over Tara like a wild wave—the storm surge that comes later, after the sun is out and the sea seems calm. She clutched Bay as hard as she could.

"Oh, Bay," she said. "I'm so sorry for being an idiot, a really big stupid idiot."

"Tara!" Bay said, pushing her slightly away, sounding very stern.

"What?"

"Love means never having to say you're a big stupid idiot."

Tara grinned. "No?"

"No. Come in and drink coffee with me, okay?"

"Till we get the caffeine jitters?"

"Yes, exactly. French roast."

The telephone rang before the coffee could be poured. Tara was assembling mugs and silver spoons and glancing at the want ads spread across the table while Bay answered the phone.

"Yes..." Bay said. "I'm sorry...I didn't think that... Please, no, don't apologize...honestly, I understand... no, but...you're sure...well, actually, she's with me now...we can be there in fifteen minutes."

Bay hung up and turned to regard Tara with amused eyes.

"Command performance," she said.

"What?" Tara asked. "Someone heard about my poem already and wants me to go on *Star Search*?"

"Something like that," Bay said. "Augusta Renwick wants to see us. Together. At her house, in fifteen minutes."

"Gulp," Tara said.

18

AUGUSTA RENWICK PACED HER HOUSE. SHE TOOK a tour of every room and communed with her husband through some of his paintings. Not all of them "spoke" to her, but several did. His portraits of their daughters, for example. When Augusta viewed Hugh's paintings of Caroline, Clea, and Skye, she could feel his love for their children pouring through.

"It's not enough, Hugh," she said, standing before the large painting of the three girls at the piano, "that I have bungled so disastrously with my—our—own children. Now I have been a clod with someone else's."

Gravel crunched under tires in the driveway.

"Here they are, my darling," Augusta said, checking herself in the hall mirror: white hair, beige cashmere shawl over black cashmere ensemble, black pearls, the Vuarnet emeralds in her ears. Augusta so rarely wore them, but today she needed all the magic she could get.

Knock-knock—a rather bold approach to the satyr's-head door knocker. Augusta always judged callers by the force or timidity of their knocks, and this person had true brass in their knuckles. Marvelously dauntless.

"*Entrée*," Augusta said, finding Bay and Tara standing on the wide porch.

The two women walked in, dressed endearingly like hillbillies—cutoff jeans and flowing old shirts, Tara's tied around her middle.

"Hello, Tara, hello, Bay," Augusta said.

"Hi, Mrs. Renwick," they both said.

"Call me Augusta. Let's step in here, shall we?" She led them through the living room, past Hugh's great painting of the Renwick Barn, past the shelves of Renwick silver, including the empty spot... What had she done with that cup? She adored drinking Florizars from it...

Once in the study, Augusta gestured for her guests to take seats. They chose—as Augusta's own daughters might—to sit side by side on the sofa. Tara looked a bit apprehensive, as if she feared repercussion for her part in the drama.

"Relax, Tara," Augusta said. "I've made peace with the situation and your part in it. Which was, honestly, quite kind and well-meaning."

"Mrs. Renwick—"

"Augusta," she reminded her. "After all these years you've worked for me, my asking you to call me by my first name should tell you something. I don't often do that... but I did it with your husband, Bay."

"With Sean?"

"Yes." At the sight of Bay's face, which fell at the mention of her husband's name, Augusta related completely and brimmed with compassion. "Please, don't think that

I have brought you here to berate you for your husband's sins. I have quite another purpose in mind."

Both women gazed at her mutely.

"First of all, I would like you to resume working as my gardener. I toured the property during the days after you did your work—and thank you for coming back to pick up the piles of cuttings, by the way. That couldn't have been easy, with your injured hand." Bay looked surprised, but Augusta continued. "Therefore, I want you both to continue in my employ. Is that clear, and agreeable?"

"It is," Bay said. "Thank you."

"Thank you, Augusta," Tara said. "I'm very sorry—"

Augusta halted her with a stop-sign hand. "Enough! I loathe apologies that go on for days. It is over, do you hear me? I have daughters about your ages. Although you are all pushing, if not well into, middle age, you will all always be girls to me. I know the lengths my girls would go to, to help their sisters. You did nothing less."

"We are sisters," Tara explained. "In spirit."

"How I longed for sisters, when I was a child," Augusta said. "I never had any...only a series of doomed, fated pets...but that is another story. Anyway, back to the reason I've called you here today."

"To talk about the garden?" Bay asked.

"No, dear," Augusta said, leaning forward. "To talk about you."

"Me?"

"Yes. And what we are going through."

"You mean, what Sean did?"

"Yes. I'd like to share with you a few of my impressions. Perhaps they will help you."

"Go ahead," Bay said, but Augusta saw her shut down—subtly but completely. People became concretized as life went on, just for their own protection.

They wore invisible snail shells that got harder with every heartbreak.

"Your husband was a charmer. He was handsome and bright and witty, and he was very good with my money, and he had the gift of being able to make me feel beautiful and young. Well, maybe not young. But not so old."

"That sounds like Sean," Bay said.

"Believe me, I knew Sean well—because he was exactly like my husband, Hugh Renwick."

That surprised them—Augusta could see she had Bay's full attention now. What could a small-town banker have in common with a giant of American art?

"Everyone adored Hugh. Men wanted to be him, and women wanted to sleep with him. Sadly—for me—he didn't resist their charms—women's, that is—as much as the girls and I would have liked him to."

"I'm sorry," Bay said.

"Thank you. As I am for you. But the main thing they had in common was competition. I understand about Sean having been passed over for Mark Boland. That would have driven Hugh mad."

"Yes, Sean was furious."

"Who can blame him? He was a highly valued executive, and then out of the clear blue, the board goes outside and brings in Mark Boland from Anchor Trust. How devastating to the male ego."

"I knew he was upset by it," Bay said, sounding tight; Augusta felt the defenses coming back up. "But I still can't imagine him starting to steal, just to get back at the bank—"

"I knew a jewel thief once," Augusta said. "At Villefranche-sur-Mer. He would come around with the other artists once in a while, and I asked him why he did it. Why he stole."

"Why did he?" Bay asked, her eyes sad and hollow.

"He told me he loved the game," Augusta said. "He had women and expensive tastes, and he needed to finance his chaotic life. He was constantly upping the ante and increasing the excitement."

"Sean loved excitement," Tara agreed, eyes on Bay.

"Perhaps we'll never know exactly why he turned to stealing; perhaps he wanted to make Mark Boland look bad. Which isn't so hard to do; Boland's a cold fish. But obsequious. I see exactly what he's doing as he butters me up."

"Are you sure you want me to work for you?" Bay asked, with tremendous dignity. "I'd understand if you didn't. The investigation isn't over yet. The FBI is still in town."

"Of course they are, darling," Augusta said. "This is bank business. If Sean had merely come in here and stolen cash and paintings, the case would be closed. But Sean was a banker—and I believe he didn't act alone. I have an instinct for these things."

"Have they said anything? Do they suspect someone else?"

"They never say anything. But I was on the bank's board for many years, so I have my sources."

"That FBI agent, Joe Holmes," Tara said, with a telltale blush, "was questioning me the other day."

"He is a dish," Augusta said. "With a very high IQ."

"You like him?" Bay asked. "I find him very hard to take."

Tara shrugged and flushed more deeply, but Augusta could see right through her.

"Life is amazing," Augusta said, gripping the arms of her chair and staring daggers at the two younger women. Did they know how wonderful they were, how short life was, how it would be over in the blink of an eye? "Passion," she said mournfully.

Bay opened her eyes, extraordinary blue eyes filled with such love and sorrow that Augusta longed to hug her as she would her own daughters.

Augusta gazed at her. "I think perhaps this is why I reacted so strongly to you that day. I know what you are going through. I know what you have suffered. When I look at the portraits my husband did of me, I am forced to see that they lack passion."

"Passion?"

Augusta nodded. "His love for the children was such a tremendous force, it's there for all to see in their paintings. Wild, unbridled love! But in the pictures he did of me—gentility, elegance, grace, propriety . . . but no passion."

"I'm so sorry . . ."

"I'm not," Augusta said. "Any longer. It caused me anguish . . ." she paused, because the word was so inadequate, ". . . years ago. But I'm over that now."

"You stayed together," Bay said, obviously thinking of herself and Sean.

"We did. Our marriage was passionless and estranged. I could have, and perhaps should have, divorced him a hundred times over. But I didn't."

"I should have, too," Bay said.

"You're linked by your children," Augusta said. "Let that be enough. Take all that passion he should have felt for you—that Hugh should have felt for me—and channel it into your life. If you fall in love again, make sure it is with a man who is wildly in love with you. Do you understand me? You couldn't bear it, knowing what you now know, to be with someone who feels less than insanely passionate for you."

"I'll never fall in love again," Bay said.

"But IF you do."

"I won't."

"But promise me—IF you do."

"All right, Augusta. If I do," Bay said, as if mollifying an old woman. Augusta didn't care; she'd done her good deed, exacted her promise. She gazed upon Bay McCabe and knew that something wonderful was out there for her.

"And you'll come back and make my garden as beautiful as Giverny?"

"Yes. Thank you." Bay smiled.

"And *you'll* come back and make my house sparkle and dance?" Augusta asked Tara.

"I will."

"And help me find my missing chalice? I can't imagine where I put it. Florizars just don't taste the same in anything else."

"I'll find it," Tara said. "Remember when you misplaced one of the Vuarnet emeralds, and I found it in the toe of your marabou mule?"

"Darling, you have a divine memory. And here it is, on my ear. Thank you. Thank you both. Bay, we'll work out the tedious financial details when you come again. Now, leave me be, so I can resume discussing important matters with the father of my children!"

"Thank you, Augusta," the two friends said.

"You're so welcome, children," Augusta said.

And then, rising, she kissed their cheeks twice each, the way she had learned how to do so very long ago, when she and Hugh had lived in Paris, in the Sixth, when they had still been young, when they had gotten drunk with Picasso, when they had fed each other sugar cubes dipped in Armagnac at the cafés of St.-Germaindes-Prés, when they had made love on the quays along the Seine.

When anything less than a life of passion would have seemed a tragedy.

THAT SATURDAY EVENING, BAY WENT SAILING.

Danny called to tell her the air and water were still warm enough, the breeze steady enough, to make it a perfect day to try out the new catboat. Tara had taken all the kids, including Eliza, to the movies and Paradise Ice Cream.

Bay was bundled up in jeans and a fisherman's sweater, her hand thickly bandaged, and she felt like no help at all, sitting in the stern while he made everything ready. Then he raised the sails, they caught the wind, and the boat sailed straight away from his boatyard dock, into New London Harbor.

He sat beside her, hand on the tiller, as the pretty boat made her way down the Thames River to the Sound. Their backs were straight, their arms not quite touching as the boat rounded Ledge Light, the imposing square brick lighthouse that guarded the mouth of the river.

As the wind picked up, he kept the sail trimmed, and they heeled over, exhilarated with speed and freedom. Bay felt the wind in her hair, salt spray in her eyes. She was able to breathe out here, and for the first time in months, she realized she wasn't looking over her shoulder to see who was watching.

"Thank you," she said.

"For what?"

"For this. For helping me get away."

"Get away from real life for a little while," he agreed, and she knew he understood.

She glanced at him sideways, not wanting him to see her watching. He still looked so sensitive, as if he was more a part of nature and the sea than the rat race of modern life. His skin was tan and weathered, with deep lines around his eyes and mouth—squinting into the sun, working outside.

"Do you have a lot of starfish on your dock at the boat-yard?" she asked.

"Quite a few. Why?"

She smiled, remembering when he had repaired the beach raft and found all the starfish clinging to the wooden underside; he threw them back into the water, to save them, before continuing the job on dry land.

"You told me that starfish fell from the sky, to make their homes in the sea," she said.

"I did?"

"Yes. And that narwhals are really unicorns."

"Wow. I was pretty poetic that summer."

"And—this was my favorite—that the reason whales breach, heave their huge bodies out of the ocean, with such amazing force and effort, is that they were created to pull the moon…like great, primeval draft horses, harnessed to the moon, pulling it from one phase to the next…"

"Around and around the earth," Dan said, his eyes softening as if with moon glow, looking down at Bay as she sat beside him.

"Do you remember telling me those things?"

"I do," he said.

"Did you really believe them? Or did you just make them up for me?"

"I think maybe knowing you," Dan said, pausing as the catboat sailed gently over the waves, or as if he had a lump in his throat, "made me believe them."

"How?" she asked, cradling her injured hand in her good one.

He didn't reply for a while. It was almost dusk, and the sky met the sea at the wide, pink horizon. Bay scanned the sky for the moon, as if she might see it roving the sky, hitched to a team of whales.

"Building things is very practical," he said. "You taught me to look for magic."

"Really?"

"More than anyone before or since."

She bowed her head over her bandaged hand and thought of the police and FBI agents and rumors and, especially, Annie and Billy and Peggy, hurt and always worried now, waiting for her back at home.

"I wish I had looked for more of it in my own life," she said.

"The old Bay would have said it's there whether you look for it or not," he said.

Just then, they bounced over a wave, and slid together on the seat. Bay decided to stay there and not move away.

"Who is that old Bay?" she whispered.

"She's here right now," he whispered back, taking one hand off the tiller, to slide around her shoulders.

It felt right. They were riding the tide together. Having rounded Ledge Light, Danny shouldered back into the harbor. They had a following sea now, so he let out the sheet, sailing downwind, the great sail catching every bit of sunset light.

It reflected onto their faces. Dan's face had a rosy glow, and Bay could see it reflected on her white bandage and fisherman's sweater. She thought of the moon, icy silver with the sun's light, being pulled by pale gray whales.

The old Bay... She swallowed hard, feeling her way toward the idea that she might have herself back. The summer had been so hurtful, and she was only beginning to let herself feel how damaging the years of lies had been, the years of living in the harsh glare of a blazing sun.

When she tilted her head back, from within the crook of Danny's arm, to thank him again for the sail, she saw him gazing down at her.

The look in his eyes took her breath away.

It was full of so many things: old love, new worry, something secret she couldn't put into words. It was like looking into the face of the moon, from a million miles away, and it made her think of what Augusta had said the other day: *"You couldn't bear it, knowing what you now know, to be with someone who feels less than insanely passionate for you."* Bay trembled now, because she saw passion in Danny's face, and she felt it in her own heart.

And as they drew closer to the dock, just before it was time to drop the sail, he said, "Okay, Galway. I've been waiting years for this. Since I already gave you the crescent moon once, I had to work overtime for this one."

He pointed, and she looked northeast.

Rising over Groton, behind the industrial buildings and submarines, over the Gold Star Bridge, a huge, shimmering, soft orange disc of a September full moon, ready to light the night.

"Is that too obvious?" Dan whispered into her ear.

Bay gasped, tears in her eyes. "Don't tell me you planned it," she said.

"All I did was look at the almanac," he said. "And make sure I got us away from the dock on time."

"Dan," she started to say, but caught herself. Her voice broke. She couldn't speak, but what she would have said out loud and was saying to herself was, "Sean never did this for me."

In all their years together, he had never even seemed to know how much she loved the moon.

Insanely passionate, Augusta had said, and Bay had thought it was an impossible state of mind. Until right now.

19

DAN CUT TWO PIECES OF HALF-INCH PLYWOOD, THE
grain of each oriented parallel to the sheer line for
beauty and strength. Carefully, he spread epoxy on the
surfaces for a sure hold. He beveled the edges along the
centerline, so the finished piece would show a crown.
This was going to be one special dinghy; he wanted
every detail to be perfect.

He had a pencil behind his ear, which he used to make
notations on paper or the wood itself. His white face
mask had slipped down, and he let it hang around his
neck. He wore jeans and a sweatshirt; September had
come in on fresh breezes, cool and clear.

Every minute reminded him of sailing with Bay. Con-
flicting emotions swirled through him, and working
helped to push them away. His feelings for Bay were so
strong, but he came with a lot of baggage these days—
how could he embark on a new relationship after everything with Charlie? And considering the way Sean—her

husband—was involved? As the day went on, he worked up a sweat driving himself crazy thinking about it all, stripping down to an old Springsteen T-shirt.

"The Convention Center, Asbury Park, with the Big Man on bagpipes," came the voice from the door.

"Excuse me?"

"Rehearsing for the *Rising* tour," the voice said, "Clarence Clemons played bagpipes on 'Into the Fire.' Did you catch that?"

"No," Dan said, glancing down at his shirt. "I saw the show at the Garden. There was a rumor, must've drifted up from the Jersey Shore, about Clarence and the bagpipes, but he didn't play them in New York."

"Too bad. It was haunting," the visitor said.

"I can imagine. The concert I saw was amazing."

"Must have been something, to hear that music in New York City."

"Yes, it was," Dan said. "Can I help you?"

"I'm Joe Holmes, with the FBI. Got a call from the local police, saying you have information about the Sean McCabe case."

"Oh, right." Dan put down his tools and straightened up, wiping his hands on his jeans. "Sean McCabe wanted to commission a boat from me. He showed up here a few weeks before he died, and we talked about designs and materials. He had a model he wanted me to work from, made by his daughter."

"What kind of boat?"

"Wooden. Classic."

"Not McCabe's normal style of boat."

"No, I guess not."

"What did he want it for?" Holmes asked, and Dan could almost read the mind of a man who would be an

FBI agent: What good was a pretty wooden boat in the modern world of speed and efficiency?

"He wanted it for his daughter," Dan said.

Joe Holmes nodded. Dan's palms were sweating; he started working again, to keep himself occupied. He had notched the dinghy's frames, so while the breast hook's epoxy dried, he began setting the inwales flush with the frame's face and sheer, half turned away from the agent.

"Did he seem like a family man to you?" Joe asked.

"I didn't know him well," Dan said. "So I don't know."

"But commissioning a boat for his daughter would tend to tell you something, right?"

"I guess so," Dan said, concentrating on the boat to avoid getting into that question. The smell of sawdust and epoxy was strong, and Dan could hear his own heart thumping in his ears.

"Mrs. McCabe told me she's an old friend of yours."

At that, Dan looked up and nodded. *Okay, good*, he thought. *Bay has already talked to him.*

"Known each other a long time?" Holmes asked.

"We knew each other a long time ago," Dan said. "But then we both went our separate ways and didn't speak again till this summer."

"Before her husband died."

"No," he said. "After."

"And Sean McCabe knew of your friendship? Or was he, perhaps, an old friend, too?"

"I didn't know Sean well," Dan said. "He grew up at the same beach as Bay, and I remember seeing him around. But that's about it."

"Then it's quite a coincidence, isn't it, that Sean Mc-Cabe would walk in here," the agent said. "Not knowing you used to know his wife."

Dan let that pass. "The reason I called the local police," he said, "is that a woman called here asking about Sean McCabe."

Joe Holmes raised his eyebrows.

"When?"

"A few weeks ago. Late August."

"What did she say, exactly?"

"She asked me if Sean had been here; if I'd spoken to him."

"Did she say what she was looking for?"

"No. It was very brief. I thought she might call back, but she hasn't so far." His heart was pounding hard, just from being in the middle of an investigation; good thing he hadn't done anything really wrong. "What do *you* think she wanted?"

The agent stood tall, hands clasped behind his back. He was gazing at Dan, as if he wanted to read his mind. "Hard to say," he said. "The man had a lot going on."

"McCabe did know that his wife and I used to be friends," he said. "Bay told me he read some letters we wrote to each other."

"I know," Holmes said. "I have them."

"Bay gave them to you?"

"These are photocopies, and they were in Sean's possession."

Bay didn't know this, Dan was sure. She'd been worried about holding out on the FBI over something as sweet and innocent as their old letters, when Holmes knew of them the whole time.

"Do you know why Sean McCabe would have photocopied your letters?" Holmes asked.

"I can't imagine," Dan said, his heart pounding.

Dan thought back to what he'd written Bay so long ago. He hardly remembered, but he knew it had to do with their shared feelings about nature, the beach, the simple things they both loved. So different from Sean. Dan had started wondering whether Sean had mined those letters for ways to get a hook into him. But he wasn't about to volunteer that.

"You had written to his future wife, and she to you," Holmes said. "Maybe he was jealous."

"I haven't seen the letters in twenty-five years, but I remember the tone. She was just a kid, and I was just out of college, and there was nothing but friendship between us. I remember writing about the boardwalk, and a swing I made her... the moon. Some stuff about her thumb, which she had hurt helping me. Jellyfish, crabs, and sea-gulls, and all that beach stuff."

"So, if he wasn't jealous..." Holmes said.

"Then I don't know. A long time ago," Dan said, squinting with anger and impatience as he thought of Sean McCabe, realizing that he had been set up. Sean had known exactly what he was doing. "Look, I have work to do."

"I know. I'm sorry. Just a few more questions," Agent Holmes said.

Dan was sweating as he turned back to the dinghy. He had notched the inboard short frames over the seam batten, rounding their ends, and he now began screwing them in, through the planking from outboard and through the inwale from inboard. He was on autopilot, glad to have something to do with his hands.

"Did you have any accounts at Shoreline Bank?"

"Did I? No," Dan said. *Here it comes*.

"So, Sean McCabe didn't handle any of your money?"

"My wife's family had accounts and a trust at Shore-line."

"A trust?"

"For my daughter, yes."

"And are you trustee of that trust?"

"Now I am. I took over for my wife. She died just over a year ago."

"Ah," Holmes said. "I'm sorry. And who is the other trustee?"

"Mark Boland," Dan said, telling the truth. "All correspondence comes from his office."

"Do you know Ralph, or 'Red,' Benjamin?"

"He's in-house counsel for Shoreline Bank, isn't he?" Dan asked.

"Yes."

This was a big, stupid chess game, Dan thought. He just wanted to get it over, get back to work. Things that were totally innocent could be made to look questionable; his encounters with Sean had taught him that.

"How's business?" Holmes asked.

"Fine," Dan said, looking up.

"There's been a downturn in the economy. People still have money for pretty wooden boats?"

"They seem to," Dan said.

"How about twelve, thirteen months ago? How were things back then?"

Where's he going with this? Dan wondered, even as he answered, "Fine. I made it through. And as you can see, I'm still in business."

"Good. Glad to hear it," Holmes said. "Well, thanks for your time. Here's my card—call me if you think of anything else."

"I will," Dan said, glancing at the agent's card, propped up on the small boat's bow. He extended his hand, then pulled it back and shrugged apologetically—his fingers were stained with flecks of dried epoxy and varnish.

He returned to work, carefully avoiding lifting his head to watch the agent leave. His hands were shaking.

There was something about a stranger asking personal questions that made Dan really want to get into one of the boats he built and go out sailing. He was like Bay; he liked his life to be simple and private.

Finally he heard the agent's engine start up, clamshells crunching under tires as the car drove through the parking lot. After a few moments, the boatyard was silent again. Well, not silent—never silent. The sounds of power tools, boat engines, seagulls crying overhead, the train coming into New London, the bells of the crossing gates.

And his own blood, pounding in his ears. Somehow, without doing anything, he had gotten into the middle of a drama he wanted no part of.

JOE HOLMES PULLED OUT OF THE ELIZA DAY BOAT BUILDERS yard with a strange feeling in his gut. It told him to pull over and look in his rearview mirror. He stopped in front of Chirpy Chicken, on Bank Street. This was really the neighborhood. Two nights ago, cruising the boatyard for inspiration, law-enforcement style, he had been captivated by the action on Bank Street.

To call it "seedy" would not do it justice. Riot lights bathed the scene in a warm orange glow. A couple of drug transactions here, a pair of hookers on the street corner there, a store with alluringly blacked-out windows and the sign "Book and Mag" over the door.

On the other hand, the quarter had a true, undeniably maritime and literary air about it. Joe could easily imagine Eugene O'Neill soaking it all up, the absinthe and morphine, the human suffering and boundless longing of the human heart: the stuff of literature and FBI investigations.

There was the stately and solid granite Custom House, the oldest in the nation; the row of brick buildings and clapboard houses; the cozy brick bookstore/coffeehouse; the vest-pocket restaurants; the saloons—places Joe wouldn't mind raising a few—good drinking establishments called the Roadhouse and the Y-Knot.

The salt air blew off the Atlantic, through the Race— that rough, wild body of water where the Atlantic Ocean met Long Island Sound, up the Thames River. Joe could see Ledge Light, the square brick lighthouse set at the mouth of the river, and he could see Pfizer and its smokestacks and labs and offices across the river, along with Electric Boat, with its nuclear subs.

Trains plied the waterfront, arriving from and departing to Boston and New York, and ferries crossed the Sound, so that there was an almost constant cacophony of whistles and grinding machinery and horns and bells, the sounds of journey-making, a mixed message of joy and urgency and the sorrows of leave-taking.

Joe's investigations had taken him to many small cities over the years, but he'd never been so captivated as he was by New London. There was so much yearning here. These streets were soaked with blood, beer, whale oil, and desire.

The Ancient Burial Place, the Huguenot House; State Street, anchored at the bottom by Union Station, H. H. Richardson's cavernous redbrick landmark, and at the hilltop by the elegant 1784 courthouse, all wood, white clapboard, and black shutters, and immense and too graceful to have been the site of murder trials.

Joe liked New London. He liked the shoreline in general. Any place that had Tara O'Toole living on it was okay with him. The high point of this investigation had been running into Tara at Andy's Records.

He liked Bay McCabe as well. They were best friends, lucky to have each other. Tara was a character: tough cookie/protective friend on the outside; soft, loyal, vulnerable heart on the inside. Joe knew the type. Knew it all too well. He lived in Southerly, when he wasn't chasing down bank fraud in Black Hall, but he found himself envying Dan Connolly, even as he sat in his car watching in his rearview mirror.

The guy had a good life—or appeared to. On the other hand, so had Sean McCabe. They had both, at different times, enjoyed the affections of Bay. Did Dan know she'd been in love with him? Anyone reading the letters could tell.

Joe's investigation had turned up improprieties in the Shoreline trust department as well as the loan operation. The corpus of two trusts had been invaded, resulting in combined losses of over five hundred thousand dollars. While combing bank records, tracking down the theft, however, Joe had come upon another trust, the Eliza Day trust.

Established eighty years ago by Obadiah Day, it had passed first to his wife, Eliza, and then to his daughter— Dan Connolly's wife, Charlotte—and now to his granddaughter, young Eliza. The trust contained nine million dollars.

Interest was paid quarterly; until her accident, Charlotte had been one of two trustees. The other had been Sean McCabe. Connolly was right; Mark Boland was now a trustee. But he had taken over only after McCabe's death. Daniel Connolly had taken over after Charlotte's accident. Why hadn't he mentioned that Sean had been a trustee until his death in June?

What, if anything, did he have to do with the juggling of funds that had taken place thirteen months ago?

Just around the time of his wife's death.

The investigation of Sean McCabe's crime had opened a deep cavern at Shoreline Bank. Joe was looking for an UNSUB—an unidentified subject. He wasn't sure who or why or how that person had aided McCabe, or even for sure if such a person existed.

All he knew was that there had been misappropriation of funds in two departments: the loan division and the trust division.

And although the money had been quickly paid back, the Eliza Day trust had been pilfered and restored—the records proved it.

Bob Dylan's *Oh Mercy* had been playing on Joe's CD player; inspired by Dan's shirt, he popped it out and inserted Springsteen's *The Rising* in its place. He waited, and watched, feeling the music.

And then his wait became worth its while: Dan Connolly was on the move.

He exited the boat shed, pulled the heavy doors shut, and locked them. He walked across the parking lot and climbed into his truck. As Joe watched, Dan pulled out onto the street, drove straight past Joe's car, and headed west on the Shore Road.

He lived east, across the Gold Star Bridge, in Mystic, so Joe took a wild guess about Dan's destination. He didn't really have any reason for thinking Dan might want to go there; it was more of a gut feeling, an instinct. Perhaps because if he were Dan, that is where Joe would want to go.

The ride took about twenty minutes.

There was very little traffic. With summer over, the crowds had gone. Route 156 was almost empty, except for a slowdown by the grocery stores in Waterford and Silver Bay. Then a straight shot past the Lovecraft Wildlife

Refuge and Rocky Neck State Park, past the Wellsweep and the Fireside Restaurant. Connolly turned left under the train trestle—the same tracks that went to New London, past his boatyard—into Hubbard's Point.

He drove past Bay's house, then Tara's, into the beach parking lot. It was September now, and the lot was empty. Joe stopped on the side of the road, just around the corner. He got out of the car and walked through an empty yard to watch.

Dan Connolly was out of his truck, walking across the footbridge that led onto the beach. Hair blowing in the wind, he strode onto the boardwalk, as Joe had known he would.

Although he had a pair of small binoculars in his jacket pocket, Joe just watched Connolly with his naked eyes, from across the yard and sandy lot. He saw the man glance down, as if to remind himself he had built that boardwalk himself, over two decades earlier.

And then he sat down on the white bench, the long empty white bench where so many people must have taken rest and solace over the years. His head was turned slightly, looking west, directly at Bay's house. He was thinking of her, Joe was sure; and he was also listening to the sounds of the waves and gulls.

Two staples of the sea, inseparable from summers at Hubbard's Point or any other beach; a reminder of summers and youth.

And innocence gone by.

20

SEPTEMBER WAS CLEAR AND BRIGHT, FILLED WITH golden light as summer slid into autumn, and then it was October, and the air grew cooler, but the water stayed warm enough to swim, and the light turned amber. Like the actual substance of amber, having captured for eternity ancient life, leaves and bees and crickets, the October light of Hubbard's Point was forever filled with preserved memories of summer.

Bay worked hard at Augusta's, mulching, pruning, planting bulbs on Firefly Hill. And then, as if inspired by the promise of beauty in the coming spring, she'd rush home before dark and do the same thing to her own yard.

It gave her hope and comfort to know that these hard, dry bulbs inserted deep into the rocky hillside soil now would yield clouds of snowdrops, scillas, daffodils, narcissus, and tulips, come April and May.

At night, Bay and Tara often met for tea by the fire, always at Bay's, where they could keep an eye on the children doing their homework. Bay had been completely wrapped up in work for the first time since her marriage, and in helping the kids cope with returning to school after their father's death.

"October is actually my favorite time to sail," Tara said, bundled in a shawl. It was a warm evening, so the two friends were sitting outside, under the moon. "The breeze is more steady, and the water's warm, so if you capsize, it's a nice swim home."

"That would be nice," Bay said, smiling as she sipped her tea, wishing Dan were there to see the moon with her. "So nice..."

"Why don't you call and invite yourself again?"

"I can't."

"It's because you don't think it's seemly, right? How dare you go sailing again with someone who likes you?"

"It was so good, just to be out on the water with him," Bay said. "I'd forgotten it could be like that. He's so gentle."

"You deserve gentle, Bay."

"Sean was always so fast and busy, so high-gear... it was wonderful to just sail along in an old catboat, not trying to get anywhere fast."

"He's a good friend," Tara said. "I remember how much time you used to spend with him—I hardly saw you that summer. You enjoyed each other's company even then, when you were just a kid."

"I know," Bay said, glowing with the thought of that moonrise. "It really was an amazing friendship."

"And still is? Why don't you invite him over for dinner some night?"

Bay had been thinking the same thing. Annie had been hounding her to see Eliza, and Bay had said she could soon.

They stared across the marsh, to the craggy tree-covered hillside. It was dark and mysterious, silvered by moonlight, just a hint of the path leading into the woods, to Little Beach. Bay thought of the adventure, the trail of life, and wondered where it would lead them all next.

"Want to join us for dinner Saturday?" she asked Tara.

Tara smiled, shaking her head. "No, thank you. I think Andy's having a sale that starts that day. I might stop in there."

"You want to see Joe Holmes, don't you?" Bay said.

"I feel so disloyal," Tara said. "Considering he's investigating Sean."

"You really are tired of artists, aren't you?"

"Exhausted, darling," Tara said. "You have no idea."

Laughing, Bay heard a car pull into the driveway. She got up, just in time to see Alise Boland coming around the corner of the house carrying a huge pot of orange chrysanthemums.

"I know it's late," Alise said, setting the pot down on the back step. "I should have called first, but I've just finished the craziest job, and I had some leftover mums, and I wanted to give you some!"

"Thank you—that's so nice of you," Bay said. "Would you like some tea?"

"Yes, join us," Tara said.

Alise shook her head. "Thanks, I'd love to another time. But you know how it is—I've been working all day, and I just want to get home and take a shower."

"Oh," Bay said, smiling. "Then I'm especially touched you'd stop by. I didn't know you worked with flowers..."

"I don't, usually," Alise said. "I usually just do interiors, but I have one client who likes me to oversee the terraces as well, and I went a little overboard this time. Mark told me you've started gardening."

"I have," Bay said. "For Mrs. Renwick."

"Isn't she a character?" Alise asked, laughing. "Mark just loves having her as a client. He always comes home with great Augusta stories."

Bay nodded pleasantly; Alise probably didn't know that Augusta had been Sean's client, till last June ...

"Anyway," Alise said, "enjoy the flowers. You know, maybe we can work together sometime, Bay. If I get a client who's looking for a gardener, I'll keep you in mind."

"I'd appreciate that," Bay said.

It was a small thing, really, but the night made Bay feel ... normal, after all the months of desolation. To be sitting outside with Tara, having another friend stop by to give her such a lovely plant. It was enough to make her believe everything was going to get better. Bay had felt so unwanted by Sean, and then she had lost him; her grief had been doubled.

But tonight she felt good. She felt secure, to have such good friends, part of a community. To have started working at something she had a talent for, something she understood, that might be the beginning of a real future for her and the kids. To be sitting in front of the house she loved, with her children safe inside.

And to be able to watch the moon and wonder whether Danny was seeing it, too.

THE GOOD—THE GREAT—NEWS WAS THAT THEY WERE GO-ing to the McCabes' for dinner, but first Eliza would get to spend the whole day with Annie.

The not so good news was that Eliza felt the darkness coming back. She felt threatened by everything: a knocking at the door when her father wasn't home. A feeling that someone was following her. Scratching at the screen in her bedroom window one warm night last week, and a soft voice: *Eliza, Eliza, your mother wants you.*

It sounded so real!

And when she looked, the next day, she saw scratches on the metal mesh—as if someone had tried to cut through with a knife. She even showed her dad. He looked at the marks and said they were just from wear and tear, branches scraping the house during gales and nor'easters. Of course he thought it was in her mind. *Let's face it*, Eliza thought. *Even I think it's in my mind.* It was just like the boy—or girl—who cried wolf. And most of Eliza's life was just one big cry for help.

Some things helped. Annie helped. Sunny days helped. New clothes helped for a short while. But for such a short while, she had to wonder: Why spend the money at all?

Earrings helped, but the piercings helped more. A little prick of pain, another hole in the skin, letting some of the pressure out.

Starving was good. It was so real. The body was really pretty dumb, when you thought about it. It was trained to be hungry when it really didn't need food. Like, show the body a ham sandwich, and its mouth would start to water. Same thing with a chocolate bar, especially, for Eliza's body, one with almonds.

That was the crazy thing: other bodies might go wild for peanuts or coconut. Bodies were very personal in their appetites. Annie, for example, had struggled with her weight. But now, according to the most recent phone calls, the hunger was a bit under control, and her body was shrinking just slightly.

For Eliza, life was a constant struggle. She felt like a worker at a nuclear power plant: Keep the pressure up here, let it off there, let the steam build to a head, then twist the valve and let some escape.

Eliza did that with starving and cutting. Starving let her body build up pressure till her muscles were screaming for vitamins and nutrition, and cutting let the screams fly out of her organs, into the sky.

Her dad was out in the boatyard, outside, and Eliza was in the shed, after work, sitting at the desk, her favorite place in the world to do her work: her cutting.

She called it "the grandfathers' desk," because that was what it was: created by one grandfather for the other. Not exactly like Annie's story of the beloved grannies, however. This was commerce, not friendship: Her mother's family had had all the money, and her grandfather from that side, Obadiah Day, had hired her grandfather from her father's side, Michael Connolly—poor Irish immigrant that he was—to build and carve him this desk.

It was so, so beautiful, built of mahogany, carved with mermaids, scallop shells, fish, sea horses, sea monsters, and Poseidon. As a little girl, Eliza had had sweet dreams of the mermaids and sea horses. Now, as an almost-grown-up, she had nightmares about the sea monsters.

She sat at the desk, slowly, reverentially, taking her knife from its hiding place, in her sock. Her pulse went up, with excitement. And her throat began to sting with the tears she wished she could shed. Sometimes she thought that maybe, if she could cry, she wouldn't have to cut; her body could weep in a normal way.

Letting her fingers run over the desk's carved surface, she wondered whether this piece of furniture was cursed. If it hadn't been ordered, if one grandfather hadn't been hired by the other grandfather to build and adorn it, would their family have ever come into existence?

Would her mother have met her father? Would Eliza ever have been born?

She so often wished none of those things had ever happened. It was one reason she liked going to Banquo, felt it to be a sanctuary—although a locked one, with hard plastic-covered pillows and too many meds—because there were people there, other girls, who understood her life, who would not think it was one bit weird to hear strange voices outside her window in the night, calling her to join her mother, and who knew, at least a little, what it felt like to be her.

To be her.

Eliza Day Connolly.

Annie knew, a little. She had a tender heart, just like the girls at Banquo, but she also had an amazing core of strength that Eliza loved. It intrigued her the way Annie handled everything so well, and she wished she could learn from Annie.

But she lived so far away; if only Eliza lived in Hubbard's Point, where she could see Annie constantly. She thought of the haunted feeling of the place, as if ghosts of all the beloveds congregated there. She knew Annie felt it, too—and that was just one more reason she loved her.

Ghosts and worries and secrets.

Eliza's mother, for example. When would her hateful secret come out? And did her father already know? She adored him, more than he could ever know, and she would die to help him. That's why the voice at the window bothered her so much—because it reminded Eliza so much of that night her mother died.

But the voice at the window didn't know Eliza's true feelings. It didn't know the secret. That's why Eliza had checked to see if a real person was outside on her roof—because the voices in her head would have known better.

Because the voice at her window was ignorant. It didn't know that Eliza had no desire to join her mother. None at all.

Family secrets.

Banquo Hospital was in existence, if you thought about it, because of family secrets. People hurt by the people who loved them most. What other reason could there be for going crazy? Eliza couldn't really think of one. Her father, one of the best secret-keepers of them all, had better watch out, or who knew how he'd get by? He needed Eliza, just to keep him in line.

She was willing to admit this: She gave him a hard time.

Okay—she sometimes did her level best to make his life hell. To keep him on his fatherly toes and remind him that SHE was still here, SHE still needed him, SHE would never desert him. If he was busy taking care of her, he would have less time to feel tormented by what had happened to her mother.

The man was so good and fine, but he was ridiculously blind to certain truths. He thought his good sweet Charlie had left him only in death, that last night by the side of the road? Ha!

Sometimes a daughter knew so much more.

Her lungs searing now, her heart a jackhammer in her skinny chest, Eliza watched her father out the window. She knew he'd be occupied for some time . . .

Eliza closed her eyes, thought of her mother talking to Sean McCabe. Her trusted banker.

It was strange that Annie, her new and only best friend, was Sean McCabe's daughter, but what good was having Dissociative Identity Disorder if you couldn't use it to occasionally dissociate on demand when you wanted and needed to most? It kept her from seeing the maroon van in her dreams . . .

Or from remembering where she had seen it before. It tormented her, the knowledge that she had seen that van before. But where? And where had she heard that voice outside her window?

The questions were driving her crazy, so she lifted her knife.

She picked a spot on her body that her father couldn't see—the top of her forearm, just below the joint; it was fall now, and chilly, and long sleeves were in order—and Eliza began to ever so gently press the blade into her skin.

Nothing too dramatic. Just enough to free the blood, to let the blood come bubbling out. One drop of blood. Another drop of blood.

Her blood; Eliza's blood.

It shocked her anew, every time she saw it.

Oh, she wished she could cry. She felt like it, she almost could...

She watched the blood spring out of the little sixteenth-of-an-inch cut and trickle down her arm, and she felt the searing anguish in her chest, knowing that everyone was just blood and bone, and death could come so suddenly and take it all away, and love could be replaced by rage, and both could be left with nowhere to go...

And she let the red blood spill off her arm, onto the dark, rare wood of the grandfathers' desk, and she watched her blood drop down Poseidon's mahogany face, into the ocean waves curling at his feet, and with her teeth gritted but no tears in her eyes, Eliza rubbed her blood into the king's face, into the sea.

21

SATURDAY WAS A LONG, LOVELY, TERRIBLE DAY. TO Annie, it felt like going to a movie she loved and finding out that, instead of watching it, she was actually *in* it; in fact, it was her life. It was like having, on a temporary basis at least, most of her wishes come true. As well as fears she didn't know she had...

It started with Eliza being dropped off at nine-thirty. Her dad pulled his truck into the driveway, and Annie's mom went out to speak to him about returning at six-thirty, for dinner, all of them together. The reason Eliza was allowed to come so early was that they'd promised to do two hours of homework, and they decided to get it out of the way first thing.

While their parents consulted in the driveway, the girls went up to Annie's room, where Annie offered Eliza her desk.

"No, that's okay," Eliza said, plopping down. "I want your bed."

want to see beneath her sleeves, to see whether there were any new scars there. "Life with me is," Eliza concluded, "unfortunately, one big chapter out of Dickens, urchins and skullduggery and hunger and dirty streets and evil people out on the roof whispering to sleeping girls . . . so please, go ahead now: Read your French lesson to me."

"What evil people?"

"People FOLLOW me," Eliza said, baring her teeth and making claws with her fingers. "The EVIL people . . ."

"Really?" Annie said, shivering with the pleasure of such creative playing.

"Yes . . . everywhere I go, I feel them there, but then I look over my shoulder, and they're GONE. Only to return in the night . . ."

"What do they do in the night?"

"Call my name—'Eliza, your mother wants you.' "

"I wish my father would call me."

"It's not really my mother," Eliza whispered. "It's just my crazy head."

"You're not crazy."

"Sometimes I'm worried that I am." But then Eliza smiled. "It's really not too bad, though. It's a good way to be in touch with all the beloveds . . . You know, last night I had a talk with the two grannies and told them you and I are the newest best friends at Hubbard's Point. Hey, maybe it's one of them calling at my window!"

"Maybe!" Annie said, her head spinning as it often did when Eliza got going—what MUST it be like to be in Eliza's mind? So Annie read her dialogue out loud, perfecting her pronunciation a little more as she went along, thrilled to have an audience, a friend, a fellow passenger in the lifeboat.

———

A LITTLE LATER, ONE MOVIE REEL ENDED, AND THE FILM changed.

After homework, when the two girls decided to take their lunches as a picnic over to Little Beach—so Eliza could chuck hers along the way, big surprise—Eliza took note of the black car driving by.

"Ooh," she said. "Cops, right?"

"Mmm," Annie said, frowning and feeling embarrassed.

"They're digging up dirt on your dad?"

"Mmm," Annie said, her shoulders caving in a little more.

"Don't be ashamed," Eliza said, squeezing her hand. "So, your dad wasn't perfect. Who is?"

Annie couldn't quite speak at first. She watched the unmarked car cruise past, like a shark on wheels: black car, white death. "I thought my father *was* perfect," she said, her voice failing her.

"I know, Annie. I thought my mother was, too."

"When did you find out she wasn't?"

Eliza stared at Annie as they walked, as if trying to make up her mind about whether she could go the whole way and confide in her or not.

"Whatever she did, it couldn't have been as bad as my dad."

The two girls walked down the beach road, away from the boardwalk their nondead parents had built. When they got to the foot of the rocky path leading up to the pine- and cedar-studded hill, Eliza tilted her head back and looked.

"What's that?" she asked.

"The path to Little Beach," Annie said. She half expected Eliza—in her long black spandex dress and platform shoes—to protest. But instead, Eliza's eyes widened with interest.

"This looks just like a place where secrets can be told!" she exclaimed. "A hidden, enchanted path where good girls can tell each other terrible and amazing things... and where the evil people will never find them!"

"You're kidding about the evil people, right?" Annie asked nervously.

"I think so," Eliza said.

Satisfied, Annie felt a magical tingle go down her spine. The deliciousness of talking about terrible and amazing things, of not having to hide the truth, made her take Eliza's hand and help her up the steep path. The trees grew along the trailside, branches interlocking overhead, sending dappled green sunlight spilling onto their shoulders.

Once in the woods, the first thing Eliza did was to unwrap the sandwich Annie's mother had made and throw it into the bushes.

"For the birds," she explained. Then, "Oh—I should have asked if you wanted it... you could have had two."

"I only want half of mine," Annie said, removing from the plastic wrap part of her turkey sandwich, tossing it after Eliza's.

"You're losing a lot of weight," Eliza said.

"You can tell?"

"Yes. Pounds are melting from your frame. Be careful you don't tip over into the land of anorexia. Once you start, it's hard to break the addiction. Starvation is like a drug. Who needs heroin?"

"I don't do drugs," Annie said firmly.

"Me, neither... except my PRN."

"Your what?"

"At the hospital. Tranquilizers on demand. They didn't

want us getting too upset—outwardly, at least. How we felt inside was another story; they couldn't do anything about that. Being upset inside was why we were there."

"Why *were* you at the hospital?" Annie asked as they walked through the dark, twisting path, two girls in a fairy tale, on their way to the sorcerer father's cell...

"You want the whole story?"

"Yes."

"Well, it's not pretty," Eliza said. "And it's about my mother...and your father."

"MY father?" Annie asked, shocked.

"Yes. So be sure you really want to hear..."

"Tell me!"

Eliza put up her hand and motioned Annie forward. They walked in silence for another minute, and then they came out of the darkness—miraculously, like being born—into the sunlight of Little Beach. Usually this was the part of the walk where Annie relaxed, but right now every muscle in her body was tense, as if she knew she was about to meet a monster. And what was that crackle in the woods—like someone following them? She forced herself to shake off the fear; Eliza had just spooked her.

But when they'd walked about halfway down the first beach, toward the "Super Simmy" shark rock, she stopped to listen: someone *was* walking in the woods, just out of sight. She definitely heard twigs and leaves snapping under someone's feet. "Do you hear that?" she asked Eliza.

"Hmm," Eliza said, listening.

"Is it the evil people?" Annie whispered.

"Yes!" Eliza said, making her scary face. "They want to hear the story, too. Are you ready to hear?"

"I guess so," Annie said, watching the woods, but see-

ing nothing there, knowing that she was playing on the
edge of craziness with her friend.

"Your dad was my trustee," Eliza said.

Annie scrunched up her nose, trying to remember
what a trustee was. Museums had them, she knew, because her father had been one for the art museum. She
didn't want to seem dumb, but why did Eliza need one?

"See, my grandfather was very rich," Eliza said, almost
apologetically. "His father owned whaling ships, and they
used to sail the seas, killing beautiful and gentle whales.
He owned a whole fleet...and then he invested in a
shipping line...and then he diversified and invested in
power companies."

"Oh," Annie said. One of her grandfathers had sold
ice, and the other had built stone walls.

"Grandfather Day—Obadiah Day—set up a trust,
which means he put tons of money in the bank in a special account that can't be touched."

"So what good is it?"

"Oh," Eliza said. "It earns interest. We can spend the
interest all we want."

"You and your dad?"

"Um, actually, just me," Eliza said. "I say 'we,' but I
mean me. I basically pay for everything."

"You mean, you buy your own things?"

"No. I pay for everything. Our expenses, my dad's business costs...it costs a lot to be a wooden boatbuilder. In
fact, my mom used to tease him and say she was bank-
rolling his hobby."

"But...he charges a lot for the boats he makes," Annie said. "My mother told me."

"Sure, because the materials cost so much. He uses
really expensive wood. Sometimes it's rare, from Zanzibar
or Costa Rica. Do you know how much it costs to get a

load of goose teak here from Lamu? A fortune. And his labor is expensive. But because he builds each boat by hand, himself, he doesn't make a lot."

"But he's the best at what he does. My mom told me that, too."

"Sure he is," Eliza said. "I'm just saying my mother told me his job is like a hobby. And she paid for him to do it."

"Did he mind that?" Annie felt confused. In her house, her dad had been so proud about her mom not working. He liked being "the breadwinner."

Eliza shrugged. "I don't think he cared. Or cares. He's different from anyone else I know; he loves his work, he loves the sea, he loves me. He loved my mother. Certain things are important to my dad. As long as he has them, he's fine."

"You said," Annie said, swallowing, "that my dad was your trustee."

"Yes. He supervised the trust. Along with my mom."

"That's how they knew each other?"

Eliza nodded, picking up some small shells, letting them jingle in her palm. The girls continued to walk, between the huge rock and the overgrowth of poison ivy— a sorcerer's way of blocking people from passing by, but Annie showed Eliza how to go sideways, back to the rock, to avoid touching the glossy green leaves—to the second beach.

Once again, Annie thought she heard someone in the woods, just out of sight, following them along the beach. When she stopped, the rustling of leaves stopped. Could it be a deer? She shivered, leading Eliza onto the second beach.

This beach was all rocks: big granite boulders in the water, smaller egg-sized stones above the tide lines. The girls moved slowly—Annie with bare feet, Eliza because she didn't want to twist her ankle. Annie cast a glance out at the small archipelago of rocks jutting into the Sound; that was where she often saw Quinn Mayhew, scattering white flowers in the waves, gifts for the local mermaids.

"He helped her make investment decisions," Eliza said. "He was a good banker, she said."

"Did you ever meet him?" Annie asked.

"Yes. When she would take me to the bank with her."

"What did he say? What was he like?" Annie asked, her voice breaking, hungry for new details about the father she would never see again, forgetting to fear the invisible watcher in the woods, the evil people, the monster she sensed lurking behind Eliza's story.

"He was very friendly," Eliza said gently. "He treated me as if I was very important. He called me 'Miss Connolly.'"

"That was Dad," Annie breathed. "He was so nice to everyone."

"He made me trust him back then," Eliza said. "I met your dad and thought, 'No wonder they call him a 'trust officer.' Because I trust him...'"

"Why didn't you tell me this before?" Annie asked, starting to cry. "You must have known I'd want to hear. Why didn't you tell me?"

"Oh, Annie," Eliza said, her face so sad and her chin wobbling so hard it looked as if it might break off. "I don't want to tell you the rest, even now..."

"You have to, Eliza. What about my father?"

"He kissed my mother," Eliza whispered, tears rolling down her cheeks. "I've never told a soul, not even my father. But I saw them one time. They thought I was asleep in the back seat...and they kissed."

"No," Annie said, closing her eyes tight.

"He handed her some papers, she signed them, and they kissed. I hate them both for it . . . I never trusted him again. Or her. I'm so sorry to tell you."

"You had to," Annie said, holding in the sobs. It wasn't even that she was shocked by the news; she knew all about Lindsey, after all. She had already heard her mother crying herself to sleep. These tears were different, and even more awful.

It was knowing that Eliza had seen.

Annie's shame was very deep, but it had always been her own. Her very own, very private shame: guarded under lock by her own body, in her own mind. Knowing that her best friend had been a witness to her father's infidelity crushed her heart and made it hurt so much she wasn't sure it could go on beating.

But then Eliza hugged her, pulling her close in a tight embrace, and Annie knew they were together in this—sisters like Annie and Pegeen, only more so. Sisters who both had their own imaginary evil people to contend with.

Sisters with a secret.

22

WHILE THE GIRLS SPENT SATURDAY TOGETHER, BAY was busy with a transportation marathon, taking Billy to soccer in Hawthorne and Pegeen to art classes in Black Hall, and making another trip to Kelly's to buy more bulbs to plant at Firefly Hill and in her own yard. Then, retrieving her two youngest, reliving Billy's great goal-scoring moment and admiring the pastel Peggy had done, and stopping at the grocery store to buy dinner, before heading home.

Annie and Eliza were back from their walk to Little Beach, and Bay was thrilled to hear Eliza's enthusiasm, adoring the discovery of the *Secret Garden* aspect of the beach—the hidden, out-of-time feeling it gave everyone who went there.

When Dan arrived, Bay served lemonade for the kids, Mount Gay and tonic for the adults. They sat in the backyard, waiting for the grill to heat up, with Eliza going on and on about Little Beach.

"It's kind of like Brigadoon, Dad," she said. "Like you wonder if it really exists, or if it's just a figment of your imagination...and even more, it's like a totally enchanted place with elves and fairies and wicked spying trolls and magic."

"Spying trolls," Dan said, laughing. "I missed them, but I know Little Beach well, from the summer I worked here at Hubbard's Point. That's where I hung the swing for your mother, Annie."

"She showed me when I was little, I think."

Bay glanced over; as talkative as Eliza was, Annie had been unusually quiet since returning from the walk. She had been avoiding junk food, but right now she was attacking the nachos with almost desperate abandon. Asking for her help in the kitchen, Bay closed the door behind them.

"Is everything okay, honey?"

Annie nodded.

"Really? Because it doesn't seem—"

"Daddy tried to help families keep their houses, right?"

"Yes," Bay said. Of all the things she'd have expected Annie to say, that wasn't one of them.

"And he didn't want to see businesses go bankrupt, right?"

"Right, sweetheart. Why are you asking me this?"

"And that made him good, right, Mom? He wasn't all bad, right?"

"Oh, Annie—no. He wasn't. Not at all. Did Eliza say something bad about him? Is that why you're upset?"

"No, Mom...I was just wondering...Did Dad have lots of affairs?"

Bay's stomach lurched. She hated that her daughter knew about Sean's behavior, that it was still haunting her even after his death. And why was she thinking about it tonight? Did it have anything to do with Bay inviting Dan for dinner? Seeing her mother having dinner with another man?

"I don't know," Bay said. "The important thing for you to know is that he always loved you. You, Billy, and Peggy. Nothing could have changed the way he felt about you."

Annie nodded miserably, as if she didn't quite believe that but had made a silent pact to pretend she did.

"Are you okay, Annie?" Bay persisted. "Would you rather the Connollys not have dinner with us?"

But Annie just shook her head and backed away. "No, Mom. No. I'm SO glad they're here. I was just . . . thinking. For no reason—it's just been in my head. After dinner, Eliza and I are going back to Little Beach, okay?"

"It'll be dark, honey."

"I know. We'll take flashlights."

Bay nodded and smiled, relieved. Day, night, it didn't matter, the kids of Hubbard's Point found their way up that steep path and through the woods to the hidden beach whenever they could. She liked thinking of the the two girls reveling in the magic of the place, something that had thrilled Bay and Tara at their age.

When the chicken was finished on the grill, Bay and Billy assembled fajitas for everyone. October's chill was in the air, and they moved inside, to eat at the dining room table. Annie and Eliza lit every candle in the room. Bay had laid the fire earlier, and she let Billy strike the match.

But Annie and her questions lingered on Bay's mind. She told herself that this was normal, that as long as the investigation was open, the kids would be hearing all sorts of things about their father. Annie's clear pleasure in Eliza's company was reassuring. And although at one point she caught Billy staring at Eliza's wrist, where a thin bracelet of scar twisted around and around, the other kids were warming up to her, too.

Dinner was fun. Everyone wanted to hear the story of how Dan had built the boardwalk and Bay had helped.

"You know how Michelangelo has the Sistine Chapel? Well, I have the boardwalk," Dan said. "That's my masterpiece."

"It's pretty cool it's lasted all this time," Pegeen said.

"Yeah, we get some wicked storms," Billy said. "They could have washed it away."

"I'm not saying it's the greatest boardwalk in the world," Dan said. "But it's right up there. Atlantic City, Coney Island, Hubbard's Point. I think I saw it on the cover of *Boardwalk Magazine* one time. Of course, it probably wouldn't have made the cover if your mom hadn't helped me."

"How did she help?" Billy asked. He chuckled. "Dad used to tell her she had two left hands."

"True," Bay said. "He used to say that."

"'Cause you kind of do, Mom. Leave the hammering to me."

"Oooh, sexist boy!" Eliza said.

"I believe the proper saying," Pegeen said, in unconscious imitation of Tara, "is 'sexist pig.'"

Annie and Eliza laughed, and Billy turned red. He was at the age when his sisters' friends had started to intrigue him, and he wanted to look good in their eyes.

"Well, she had a pretty good right hand when I knew her," Dan said. "And the thing is, I'm trained to find the best hammerers. I had my pick of all the hammerers at the beach, way back then, and honestly, I couldn't have picked a better one than your mother."

"Are you the same age?" Peggy asked.

"No, she's a kid compared to me," Dan said. "I was already finished with college the summer I worked here; your mother was fifteen."

Bay smiled—the kids were really putting Dan through his paces. But he just rolled with it, seeming to enjoy every minute.

"So, you build boats now?" Billy asked.

"Yes."

"Fast ones?"

"Sailboats and dories, Billy—they go as fast as you can sail or row. Do you like to row?"

Billy shrugged and grinned. "I like Jet Skis," he said. *His father's son*, Bay thought.

"I don't build those," Dan said. "You ought to try rowing sometime."

"Maybe I will."

"I like rowing, Mr. Connolly," Annie said.

"That's what I hear, Annie," Dan said. "I'll bet you're good at it."

"Not that good," Annie said, blushing. "Well, if it's okay, Eliza and I are going back to Little Beach now. I'll be sure to protect her from wicked trolls."

"I'll count on that," Danny laughed.

"She's my girl," Bay said.

Billy and Peggy wanted to go down to shoot baskets under the lights, so Bay gave permission for them all to take off. She and Dan watched all four kids launch themselves out of the room, out of the house, leaving the adults alone with a lot of dirty dishes and a symphony of crickets coming through the windows.

"Would you like some coffee?" Bay asked.

"Let me help you do the dishes first," he said.

She laughed. "You don't have to."

"I want to," he said.

They cleared the table. The kitchen was cozy and bright, and they stood very close together as she rinsed the plates and he placed them in the dishwasher. It felt sweet and surreal, as unexpectedly familiar and gentle as their sail, as if they had never stopped working together, as if they were still working side by side on the boardwalk.

When they were finished, they went into the living room, where the candles had almost burned down. The fire crackled softly. Bay threw another log on, and they watched it roar to life. She glanced over at Dan. He was so tall and dark, the handsome Irishman she'd fallen in love with at fifteen. But right now she was struck by the sad turns their lives had taken since then.

"What are you thinking, Bay?" he asked.

She shook her head. "I'm not sure you want to know," she said.

"Go ahead—try me," he said.

She'd been leaning on the mantel; she brushed the splinters and bark off her hands and sat in the chair beside his. He had taken her usual chair, and she was now in Sean's.

"I was thinking," she said, "of how hard it is."

"Which part? Being a single parent?"

"Yes—and all that goes with that. The extra work, trying to be in two places at once, the financial worries... but even more, making sure the kids are okay. They're all so sad. They've taken such a blow, so young. I know they're going to be affected by everything that happened and everything that *will* happen; but how can I control the damage?"

She noticed that Dan was half smiling, but with his head down, as if he was trying to hide it.

"What?" she asked.

"Oh, just the 'control' thing. I'm trying to remember the last time I thought I could control anything."

"Really?"

"Yes. I used to think I could. You know? If I just paid attention, took care of business, kept track—"

"I have my own version of that," Bay said wistfully, thinking of the last two years. "If I was a good person, Sean would love me, our family would be happy, and the world would be good to us."

"Sounds like the same philosophy," Dan said.

"Then tell me how to make things better for Annie and the other kids. How do you do it for Eliza?"

"Eliza…" he said, the light changing in his eyes.

"What did she mean," Bay began, "that day I first met her at your boatyard, when she said you blamed her…"

"For her mother's death," Dan said, shaking his head, bowing it slightly. "She says that—I hope she doesn't really believe I feel that way. I've told her over and over that I don't, trying to convince her…so she won't have to go back to the hospital."

Bay waited. The logs crackled and shifted, sparks flying up the chimney.

"What happened, Dan?" she asked softly.

"They were driving home one night in April, a year ago. Charlie had had some business in Black Hall and Hawthorne, and she'd taken Eliza with her. Eliza is, well, high-strung…and she'd been angry with her mother. Friends who saw them getting into the car in Black Hall said that Eliza was shouting, waving her fists. I've asked her why, what the problem was, and she refuses to tell me; says I just want to blame her for getting upset and causing her mother's accident."

"Is that true?"

Dan stared at the fire, then shook his head. "No."

"Why was Eliza so upset?"

"I don't know. She never likes waiting—the tedium of errands, going to the bank, the post office, the library. She likes to move on as fast as possible. I'm sure her mother had meetings, and Eliza didn't like them dragging on. Charlie probably shouldn't have taken Eliza in the first place," Dan said, "but papers had to be signed . . ."

"Papers?"

"Eliza is the beneficiary of Charlie's family trust," Dan said. "Charlie was trustee for the trust itself, but there are a couple of small accounts that are Eliza's outright. And Charlie needed her that day, to move some money around."

"In Black Hall? Which bank? Sean's?" Bay frowned, suddenly wondering.

"Yes, as a matter of fact, it was," Dan said. "It was set up years ago, back when Obadiah Day built his ships here in Black Hall, and we never moved it to Mystic."

Bay listened. The reality shimmered between them, like a dark star that had come to earth. She had no idea what it meant, why the sudden revelation should make her throat tight; was it because Danny hadn't volunteered the information? That even now Bay had had to ask?

"Did . . . she know Sean?"

"She did," Danny said. "He was the cotrustee for Eliza's account. He had taken it on a couple of years before she died, I think from someone else at the bank who retired."

"Henry Branson," Bay said. "He was the dean of the bank; he handpicked Sean out of everyone, to take over his most important clients."

She watched sparks popping, drifting up the chimney. The mantel was covered with framed photos: Sean with the kids on the boat, at the beach, waving from the raft, holding up the fish they'd all caught. Blinking, Bay turned to Danny.

"Did he—" She couldn't put the question into words, but she bowed her head, looked up, tried again. "Did he take money from Eliza?"

"No," Danny said softly. "He didn't."

Bay nodded. Her hands were damp; she had been so afraid Danny was going to tell her something she didn't want to hear about Sean. Her eyes burned with tears and anger. Sensing her emotion, seeming disturbed himself, Danny reached across the space between their chairs and took her hand. The candles made his eyes shine, deep blue in the low light.

"Charlie was on her way home from town?" Bay asked now, wanting to hear the rest of the story.

"Yes," Danny said. "They had done errands, gone shopping. Eliza won't tell me the details, but I know they stopped on the side of Route One fifty-six, just past Morton Village. Just past the bottom of that steep hill, where the road bends around—"

"It's a bad curve," Bay said, her blood feeling cold in her veins.

"Yes," Danny said. "It is . . . Charlie got out of the car for some reason. She and Eliza had been fighting; she wanted to give Eliza time to cool off. Charlie hated upsets, and she would do anything to avoid them. Even walk away from the car, leave our daughter sitting there . . . That's what Eliza said right after the accident happened, but then she wouldn't speak at all. For a whole month afterward, she was in complete shock—"

"The poor girl," Bay whispered.

"She saw it happen," Dan said quietly. "She was sitting in the front seat of the car, watching her mother walk across the road. She was screaming, she said. Yelling at her mother, telling her to come back and not leave her alone. Charlie had her back to the car, crossing One fifty-six—there's nothing there for her to go to. No stores, no restaurants—everything is a mile back, in Silver Bay. Nothing but a field and woods, in the spot where Charlie was crossing. It all seems so aimless—just to avoid Eliza's emotions."

"Oh, Dan."

"A van hit her—heading out of Silver Bay—he never even stopped."

Bay couldn't speak; she'd driven that stretch so often in the last months, even in the last week. She thought of the blind curve, of Charlie crossing the road, of Eliza sitting in the car and witnessing the whole thing.

"Eliza had a breakdown," Dan said, his voice cracking. "She was a different girl before it happened. Always intense, but so happy and funny—just so cute and great, always wanting to joke around. In the weeks before the accident, she'd become a little reserved, maybe. As if she had something on her mind. I mentioned it to Charlie, and she said something about adolescence. But after the accident, Eliza just—went away."

"Away?"

"Away from herself. Away from me. Deep inside."

"But she told you what happened?"

"Yes—at first. She was hysterical, positive it was her fault, because she had gotten her mother upset. She saw the van, bearing down on Charlie as if he *wanted* to hit her, she said, and he just sped away..."

"Did they ever find the driver?"

"No," Dan said. "At first she said the van was dark red, but then she thought maybe it was white and covered with blood. Then she thought maybe it was dark green, or navy blue or black..."

"How terrible for Eliza," Bay said. "It's unthinkable, a child watching her mother killed. No wonder she's been so devastated."

"She feels a pull to be with her mother."

"Does she say that?"

"No. But she imagines she hears people calling her name, telling her that her mother wants her. She thinks they're coming in her bedroom window. 'The evil people,' she calls them. She's psychologically very fragile; she always has this look of panic in her eyes. Panic, and constant, helpless longing—"

"Why would she call them evil, if they want to take her to her mother?"

"Her mind is wild. I can't figure it out."

"You sent her to the hospital?"

"Yes. The first time she had to go, I thought I'd die. I know that sounds dramatic, but she's my baby. To see her starving herself, cutting her skin—it's terrible, unbelievable. That first time she went, I wanted to visit her every day. They told me to stay away, give her a chance to heal. Those were the hardest days of my life, wanting to see my daughter but knowing I had to let her get better without me."

"But you got through them."

"I did. She came home, and I thought, Thank God. This time I'll do everything right—I'll keep her spirits up, I'll stock the house with food she likes, I won't work such late hours so she won't ever feel alone..."

"But it didn't work?" Bay asked.

Dan shook his head. "No. My dream of being a perfect father was nicely dashed. I mean, forget it. The next time she went back to the hospital, I felt a little easier about leaving her. This last time, I was so relieved to take her there—I never want her to know how much."

"Only because you want her to be safe and healthy," Bay said. "You must be out of your mind with worry."

"You have no idea," he said. Danny had always had a huge capacity for love and concern, and Bay felt it almost as a palpable force between them. She clasped his hands in hers. And he pulled them both out of their chairs, so they could hold each other.

Standing in front of the fire, while the October wind blew down the chimney, swirling coals in the grate, Bay pressed herself into Dan's chest, feeling her heart beat against his. His arms were around her back, holding her so tight. He smelled like cedar and spice, and his blue cotton sweater was soft against her cheek, and she heard the smallest sound escape from her own lips:

"Help," she heard herself murmur.

If Dan heard it, he gave no sign. He just held her in his arms, rocking her by the fire. Bay closed her eyes and held on to Danny Connolly, held on to this moment. She thought of that word, "help," and how much she knew she needed it, how worried she was about the kids, especially Annie, how alone she felt every night.

Dan held her tighter, seemed to never want to let her go. He needed help as much as she did, the first love of her life, she thought. The boardwalk they had built was just down the road, on the beach, and Bay thought of the boards they had laid side by side, the nails they had driven in, the closeness they had shared so long, long ago and on the water that September night.

She felt it again, right now.

His heartbeat racing against her skin told her that Dan did, too.

UNDER THE LIGHT OF A MILLION STARS, WITH THE HELP OF
two flashlights, Annie and Eliza took the path through
the woods. Everything was different at night than it had
been during the day: The forest glowed with eyes. Deer,
raccoons...sounds in the woods—cracking sticks and
leaves: *The evil people were back*. Bats etched the air
above, darting after mosquitoes and swirling in macabre
figure eights.

"'The woods are lovely, dark and deep,'" Eliza said.

Annie looked over her shoulder, startled by the line in
her father's favorite poem, shivering from Eliza's revelation from before. "'But I have promises to keep,'" Annie
continued.

"'And miles to go before I sleep.'"

"'And miles to go before I sleep.'"

They had reached the beach clearing, and now the
thick trees gave way to a vault of stars. Overhead, the
hunter brandished a blazing sword, while storied constella-
tions danced with white and blue fire. Annie remembered
the noises she had heard that afternoon, tried to push the
fears from her mind. The girls' feet crunched on the sand,
and their flashlight beams swept the beach ahead.

"I hear them," Eliza whispered, almost inaudibly, taking Annie's hand.

"I thought maybe I was imagining it," Annie whispered back.

"No. You really hear them, too? I'm glad—I'm not being crazy."

"Maybe it's boys, like my dad and his friends used to do
to my mother and Tara."

"Do you think?" Eliza asked, breathless. "I hope so.
No—it's someone else, Annie. Real people, not imagi-
nary trolls. We've got to run back to your house. Oh,
God..."

"Can we make it?" Annie asked, frozen with terror as she heard someone whisper. The voice was very soft, and she tried to make out words, but they got lost in the sea wind and the sound of her own heart beating fast. Eliza squeezed her hand tight, starting to tug her back toward the path.

But just then a voice got louder—it seemed to swing around, come from the cove. Were they surrounded? Almost blind with terror, Annie gasped.

"Did you hear that?" she asked Eliza.

"Look—" Eliza said, hopefully, pointing overhead as a V of migrating geese flew across the sky, honking loudly.

Annie stood still, her heart racing, wanting to believe that they had made the noises she had heard. But after the geese were gone, and the beach was again silent, she knew that coming here was a bad idea.

"Come on, Eliza," she said firmly, grabbing her hand, "Let's go home."

Eliza didn't argue. As if she felt the same fear, she ran ahead down the dark path, toward home.

23

WITH RAIN SOAKING THE SHORELINE EVERY DAY for a week, Bay took advantage of the softened earth to transplant some plants and bushes at Firefly Hill. The rain pelted down as she dug up clumps of stonecrop to place in front of a huge stand of black-eyed Susans, to hide the bare lower stems, and she transplanted sweet williams to a border that needed more color. Because Augusta loved herbs, Bay focused on the concentric circles of mint and sage, cutting back the tallest plants to ensure they made it through the winter.

High winds had brought down the leaves, and Bay raked them into great piles for Augusta's lawn service to pick up. Every day her hands felt rougher, more callused. She had blisters on her palms from gripping the wooden handles of her gardening tools, and her feet were raw from being wet inside her rubber boots.

One afternoon, just before Halloween, she hauled the frame lights out from summer storage in the shed behind

Augusta's house. Head down into the driving rain, she fought the wind as she tried to cover several Cyrethea bushes.

"Need some help?"

Glancing up, feeling the wind trying to twist the frames from her grasp, she saw Dan coming across the backyard. Shocked but happily surprised, she shouted over the wind, "Sure! Can you tie that side to those stakes?"

He lashed the simple pine frame to the iron peg she'd already pounded into the wet ground. Bay did the same to her side, remembering how her grandmother had always said the roots of Cyrethea bushes needed to be protected from winter wet.

"How did you find me?" she shouted above the wind.

"Billy told me you were working," he shouted back.

"And you came by just to help me?"

"I came to take you out to dinner."

"What?"

"Come on, Galway. Dry off—you're having a burger with me."

"The kids—"

"Annie and Eliza are making pizza for Billy and Pegeen. There's really no excuse—you're not getting out of this, okay?"

Her hands were numb from the cold, her face was stinging from the rain, her clothes were soaked through, and she tingled all over with the excitement of seeing him. "Okay," she said.

She dropped her car at home, and made sure all the kids were fine—they barely spoke to her, busily decorating their pizzas to look like jack-o'-lanterns—and changed into dry jeans.

Dan drove her to the Crawford Inn in Hawthorne, an

old tavern that had been in business since before the Revolutionary War. White-shingled with green shutters and a long front porch, it had seven chimneys and a sleigh out front. Legend had it that General John Samuel Johnson had used the sleigh to sneak past the British one Christmas Eve, on his way to deliver gifts to his betrothed, Diana Field Atwood, across the iced-over river in Black Hall.

"Do you believe that story?" Bay asked, sitting across from Dan by a roaring fire, the heat in her face coming more from his closeness than the flames. "About the general and his true love?"

"Sure I do," Dan said. "Don't you?"

Bay sipped her beer, watching the piano and banjo players getting ready.

"I used to," she said. "When I was young. Back when I believed people did things like that—crossed rivers for love."

"You don't anymore?"

She shook her head slowly.

"I loved being married," she said. "At first. I thought it was so amazing. Your best friend under the same roof, always there if you wanted to tell them a good story or joke, or if you needed your back scratched...or if you were scared of the dark..."

"Going through life together," Dan said.

"Having kids—didn't that seem outrageous? You were this little unit, just the two of you, and suddenly there were three?"

"And she looked like the best of her mother..." Dan said.

"And her father," said Bay, remembering how Annie had had Sean's twinkle in her eyes.

"And you were more in love with each other," Dan

said, "because of this mysterious addition. It's like, instead of having to spread your love out more, it was actually more concentrated—for each other."

"Yes," Bay said, so eager to hear more, because Dan got it exactly; he was summing up her life.

"It must have been even more intense for you," Dan said. "Because after Annie, you had two more."

Bay nodded; some of the fizz went out of her chest, and she had another sip of beer. "Sean loved having a son," she said. "He really wanted a boy. I'd never tell Annie, but he'd wanted one right from the beginning. Did you?"

Dan shook his head. "I wanted Eliza. Just Eliza. Whatever she was would've been fine."

"That's what my dad used to say," Bay said. "My mother said he'd always get so mad if someone asked if he wished I'd been a boy. But Sean . . ."

"Yes?"

"Sean was very happy to have Annie, even happier when Billy was born. He thought our family was perfect then—a girl and a boy. He wanted to stop."

"But you had Pegeen."

Bay nodded. She flexed her fingers. They had been so cold, they were just starting to get back to normal. "Yes, I had Pegeen. We weren't expecting her, and . . ."

Dan waited.

Bay couldn't bring herself to tell him that Sean hadn't wanted a third baby. He hadn't at all, and it had been the source of many fights, the turning point in their relationship: the minute it, literally, went from bad to worse.

"Sean was always very weight-conscious—for me, thank you very much! He thought the third pregnancy was . . . a mistake. That it might be 'bad for my health.'"

"Was it?" Dan asked.

Bay laughed. "No. I had lost the weight so easily after

Annie, but it was really hard after Billy. You know, two kids, and Sean's career taking off at the bank, and, well, it was a lot harder to get out there and go swimming or running. And then I had Pegeen, and I gained more weight with her than with either of the other two. Did Charlie gain a lot with Eliza?"

"Sixty pounds, I think," Dan said. "I kept giving her ice cream. She liked butternut ice cream."

"It's easier to lose after the first one," Bay said, repeating herself, remembering how terrible things had been after Pegeen's birth. How Sean had made her feel fat and ugly, how he had stopped wanting to make love to her. "I tried, though."

"What difference does it make?" Dan asked. "It's all for the good of the baby, right? It comes off eventually. The point is, you had your family."

Bay nodded. She finished her beer as the banjo began to play "When the Saints Come Marching In." It was loud and raucous, and everyone in the tavern was singing along except for her and Dan. She really wanted to join in their spirit, but she was remembering that awful year after Pegeen was born.

"Her name," Dan said, "is so pretty."

Bay nodded, smiling now. "I played Pegeen in *Playboy of the Western World* in college. It's a wonderful play. Do you know it?"

Dan nodded. "Synge. Getting in touch with my Irish roots, I went to the Aran Isles once."

"I remember," Bay said. She'd been thrilled when he sent her a letter from there.

"Right after my summer at Hubbard's Point," he continued, "I decided to travel for six months before getting down to real life. Have you ever been?"

"No," Bay said. "I've always thought I'd like to go."

"Why did you name your daughter after that character?" Dan asked. "As pretty a name as it is, why that one? And not Margaret, or Maggie, or another 'Peg' type name?"

Bay didn't reply. The music got louder, more good-time and raucous. The waitress brought their food, and Dan ordered two more beers. The burgers were rare and delicious, and because the music was so loud, Bay just ate her food and didn't even try to talk. Neither did Dan. It was enough to be sitting there, together.

When the banjo player broke a string and had to replace it, Dan said, "The Aran Isles are in Galway Bay, you know."

"They are?" Bay asked, her neck tingling.

"I spent most of my time on Inishmore," Dan said. "Got the ferry from a dock in Galway town."

"Was it beautiful there?"

"It reminded me of Hubbard's Point," he said. "With a lot of rocks, and clear cold water, and pine and oak trees. Riding that ferry, I thought of the Connecticut shore. I thought of you."

"Me?" she asked.

"Yeah," he said. "Because it was Galway Bay."

Bay looked down at the table. It was highly varnished, glowing in the firelight. Her heart was beating fast, and suddenly she was afraid to look up. She gripped her hands in her lap, and she remembered how he had held her, shocked by how much she wanted it again.

"I've sometimes wondered whether that's the reason I went to Inishmore," he said. "So I'd have the chance to sail through Galway Bay. With all the rest of Ireland to visit, and my relatives coming from Dublin and Kerry . . . I wanted you to have a letter from Ireland . . . from *that* part of Ireland."

"You were pulled to the Aran Isles, by the ghost of John Millington Synge," Bay said.

"Not because I wanted to visit your bay, Galway?"

She shook her head, her pulse racing.

"No," she said. "Synge persuaded you."

"Did he persuade you to name your youngest child 'Pegeen'?"

Suddenly Bay felt hot, light-headed. The fire was too strong, or they were sitting too close. The music was too loud, the crowd too boisterous. She wanted to get some air, and Dan knew. He called for the check, put cash down on the table. The band struck up "Won't You Come Home, Bill Bailey?" as Bay and Dan left the room.

"What's wrong?" Dan asked, walking her to his truck.

Emotion filled her chest. She and Sean had gone to the Crawford Tavern all the time when they were young. They had loved the music and beer, the free popcorn, the sleigh outside. Once, Sean had pulled her into the sleigh, pulled his coat over both of them, and kissed her passionately while people walked up and down Hawthorne's Main Street.

"I don't believe that sleigh crossed any frozen river," she said suddenly as they walked past. "I don't believe it's even very old, or that there was any great love affair between General Johnson and Diana whatever-her-name-was."

"You don't?"

"No. I don't believe anyone ever loved someone that much—to take the risk of going right past the enemy camp just to deliver Christmas presents."

Dan was silent. He opened his truck door and let her in. She watched him come around the truck, and she shivered in the damp cold. Rain slicked the streets, and fallen wet leaves blew down the curb.

"He did," Dan said quietly, starting up his truck.

"How do you know?"

"Because Diana whatever-her-name-was was Eliza's great-great-grandmother," Dan said. "And their child, the first Eliza, married the first Obadiah Day."

"Really? Charlie came from that kind of family?"

"Yes," Dan said. "As blueblood as you can get."

"And the story is true? The general risked his life to bring her a Christmas present?"

"Yes," Dan said. "A silver cup, made by one of the top silversmiths in New England. A man by the name of Paul Revere. Commissioned just for her."

"What happened to the cup?" Bay asked.

"It belongs to Eliza," Dan said. "It should be in a museum, and I keep thinking we should donate it to one."

"I can't believe it's true," Bay whispered. Her heart felt so precarious, as if she was standing right at the edge of a very steep cliff and with one false move she might fall off. She looked away from Danny, pressing her forehead against the cold glass. If love like that between the general and the first Eliza was possible, what had happened to her and Sean?

"Tell me about Pegeen's name," Danny said, and suddenly she felt him take her hand, hold it from across the seat.

"It's Irish," she whispered.

"It means something to you," he said. "Annie and Billy—Anne and William. Those names are good and strong, but they're one way, and Pegeen is another. Tell me, Bay."

"It was because of how I felt inside," she said, needing that cold glass against her skin, just to keep her grounded and still, to keep her from flying apart. "Everything had changed with Sean after I got pregnant that third time and I needed a powerful name for my new baby.... Billy was born...he had his son, and he loved him so much, but it was as if he didn't need me anymore."

"But he did, he had to..."

Bay shook her head, still not looking at Danny. The memories were so deep and eviscerating.

"He stopped wanting me," she said. "He needed me to mother the kids, but he didn't want me. He thought I was fat, boring, as if my only interests were milk and diapers. When he wanted to have fun he'd go looking for a friend. The guys at first, kids we'd grown up with, who had kids of their own. Sean would grab one of them, and they'd go out for a boat ride..."

"While you were pregnant?"

"Yes. I told myself it was because I was so huge. After the baby was born, I told myself I'd lose weight. I'd take it all off, get my body back to the way it used to be, never gain weight again. I'd see the way he'd turn away when I got undressed; how he wouldn't sleep near me in bed." The details were so painfully intimate, but the rain thrummed on Dan's truck roof, and Bay couldn't have stopped the words if she'd wanted to. They needed to come out, and she let them.

"He had an—it wasn't even really an affair. A 'thing.' Got drunk and went home with some girl at the bank Christmas party. I found out because she called him at home."

"That's terrible, Bay," Dan said.

"You wouldn't have done that to Charlie, right?" Bay asked, trying to get some laughter into her voice, to make it all a little light. What was the point now, anyway? Sean was dead and gone.

"No, I wouldn't," Dan said, not laughing at all. "I'd never have done that to her."

"Well, Sean did it then, and he did it again on Saint Patrick's Day. Same girl . . . that time Tara saw them at the Tumbledown Café. I was going to kick him out. But he promised. He swore."

"You were still pregnant?"

"Yes," Bay said, and she touched her stomach in the dark of the truck, so no one, not even Dan, could see, just to remind herself that three children had come out of her belly, that she had carried them all and carried them with love. She thought back to her last month carrying Pegeen, when Sean would come home every night—not because he wanted to be there, but out of a sense of duty, personal responsibility, as if he had sworn to himself that he'd be faithful, that he'd be a good husband, that he'd be the father he'd been before.

Bay could picture Sean in his chair by the fire, staring at the TV. Focused on the screen, on basketball games and sitcoms, on anything but Bay. She'd try to talk to him about the kids, about being a week overdue with the baby, about his job at the bank and how great it was that he kept getting promoted.

She had tried to talk to him about the garden, how she wanted to plant a garden for each child, how the new one felt so light and buoyant that for it she wanted to have beautiful, airy, feather flowers like anemones and violets and larkspur.

And she had tried to talk to him about how lucky they were to have known each other forever, to be bound by history and family and Irishness, to have Hubbard's Point as the place they had met and where their kids would spend all their summers and maybe meet the loves of *their* lives . . .

And Sean had nodded and acted polite and stared at the TV, especially the thin, beautiful, large-breasted, not-pregnant basketball team cheerleaders on the screen with such interest and lust that Bay had longed to smash that TV—with a poker, a bat, her garden rake, or even Sean's stupid, selfish head.

She had gone into her bedroom and mourned alone. Her grief was deep and total; she had created a family with a man who could not care less for her. With their third baby on the way, he didn't know a thing about her. She felt as if they were two ships sailing in different directions, completely unconnected, an unbridgeable gulf between them.

Those hours were the darkest moments of her life—worse, even, than finding out about his affairs. Bay was filled with deep despair as she faced the truth about her life, her marriage.

And in that moment, the air had shimmered with a very particularly Irish magic. Bay recalled looking out the window, seeing the marsh sparkling under starlight.

And Bay had taken a swift emotional journey, down the marsh and into Long Island Sound, where salt water and the Connecticut River met in the estuary. History unfolded, backward and forward—all the way into the future, when her children would be grown, playing on the beach with children of their own. And with silt swirling, Bay had thought of her own name . . . Bay.

And she had thought of all the great bays, the powerful bays of the world, the bays that spawned shellfish and finned fish, the bays that provided dockage for great shipping lines: Hudson Bay, San Francisco Bay, the Bay of Fundy, the Baie des Anges, Biscayne Bay, Galway Bay, and of course, Hubbard's Point Bay . . .

"In a way you were there," she said to Danny now, her voice and hands shaking as she turned to look at him across the front seat of his truck. "The night I named Pegeen."

"I was?"

They sat there in the parked truck, looking deeply into each other's eyes. Bay remembered the end of that night: how, after Sean had gone to bed and she had known for sure her baby was Pegeen, she had called Tara and they had unplugged the bosom-laden TV set. Tara had muscled it barefoot through the nettles—telling Bay that being a week overdue entitled her to merely watch—and thrown it with a resounding and satisfying *splash-kerplunk* into the salt creek.

"You were," Bay said.

"How?"

"Because it went through my mind, as I was christening my daughter 'Pegeen,' that John Synge had been sent across Galway Bay to the Aran Isles by the greatest poet in Ireland, and how I had been given *my* other name, 'Galway,' by you. So somehow, I'm not sure whether you can follow my logic in the same way I did that night and still do, but somehow you were there."

"I don't have to follow," Dan said, reaching across the seat as Bay did what she'd wanted to do for so many years: slid closer, right into his arms.

"You don't?" she whispered, forgetting to be nervous as she tilted her head back to kiss the only other man besides her husband she'd ever loved.

"No," he whispered back. "I don't have to follow, because I'm right here with you."

He's Irish all right, she thought, admiring Danny Connolly as a poet just two seconds before he lowered his face to hers, kissed her with such fire and passion that she felt it all through her body, all the way down to her toes, erasing every year and memory and event and sorrow that had ever happened in her life.

They kissed each other, the independent woman who had once played Synge's Pegeen and the Irish poet wooden-boat-and-boardwalk builder, the widow and the widower, who touched and tugged and moaned and needed so much more than they could get in a truck parked under a streetlight in Hawthorne.

Bay pushed her hands up under his barn jacket, touching a button of his chamois shirt, just touching that button, thinking what it might be like to undo it, feeling his arms come inside the sleeves of her jacket, pushing up the left cuff of her sweater, trying to do the same with the right, getting stuck on the lining, his hands so rough with calluses and so warm on her cold skin...

Skin that hadn't been touched in so long, a heart that hadn't been touched in even longer. His mouth was hot on hers, and his beard scratched her cheeks and chin. She wanted to kiss him forever, to feel her smooth face scrape on his beard shadow. Feeling his lips on hers, turning her inside out, making her live again! That's what this was—nothing less than *magic*, being touched where she'd thought she was dead, being brought back to life...

They kissed, so unexpectedly, and as frantic as she felt inside, she wanted to be conscious of taking this slow—it wasn't at all slow inside, but they had kids and kids and kids and kids to worry about. There were the kids.

The kids.

What could a kiss have to do with those kids?

Bay didn't want to know, but of course she had to know. The heater blew hot air into the steamy, cold truck, and Dan's hands were so slow and hot inside her jacket but outside her sweater, and the instant he felt—

zzzt—the electricity change, the thoughts of the kids stopping her in her tracks, mid-kiss...

She stopped herself by thinking of that sleigh, of Eliza's ancestor dashing through the snow with his precious silver cup for his true love...snow falling, the river frozen, Christmas angels singing above, the redcoats sleeping in their fort...Diana—the first Eliza's mother—not knowing whether her beloved general would make it to her alive...

Oh, there was love like that, she thought.

It allowed her to slow down, to not take everything she wanted from the kiss right then. It made her believe in something truer than she had felt in so long, so so long, in years.

She hadn't believed in love, that kind of love, for such a long time.

Probably not, as hard as she had tried, for the whole duration of her youngest daughter's life, for Pegeen's life.

"Are you okay?" Dan asked, pressing his rugged hand against her cool cheek, pushing the hair out of her eyes.

"So okay," she said, knowing that her eyes were shining, seeing them reflected in his.

"I shouldn't have kissed you," he said, shaking his head.

She laughed; she wished he hadn't said that, wished he felt just as incredible and miraculously alive as she did. "Why?" she asked.

"Because..."

The expression in his eyes took her aback. He was wrapped up, in his mind, with something bad. *He didn't want to kiss me, didn't want me, I started it*, she thought, suddenly confused, ashamed.

"I've wanted it so badly, for so long," Dan said, reaching for her again, but visibly holding himself back. "I had to kiss you, but I should have waited—"

"Till what?" Bay asked.

Dan looked not just thoughtful but tormented, touching her hair, trying to make up his mind about something. "To tell you about Sean. He came to me, to build a boat, but that wasn't the only reason."

"What was?" she asked.

"It's complicated," he said.

"I need to know," she said, feeling suddenly afraid.

"I wish none of these intervening years had happened," he said, holding her face between his hands. "I wish I'd trusted what I knew deep down twenty-five years ago, that you were the one. That I'd waited for you to grow up..."

"So do I," she said. "Everything but the kids—"

"I've made a big mistake," Danny said. "You know what you used to say, about Sean flying too close to the sun?"

"Yes," she said, feeling afraid.

"I was tempted to do that myself."

"In what way?"

"My wife was very rich," Danny said. "And your husband oversaw her trust. He—I think he wanted me to come in with him on something illegal."

"Don't tell me this," she said, bowing her head, not bearing to think of him this way.

"Bay, please listen. Nothing happened. I was tempted, though. I heard him out, thought it over, and told him I wasn't interested."

Bay was silent, her heart pounding in her chest.

"Bay?"

"Drive me home, Danny," she whispered. "Okay?"

But she never heard the answer, because instead of driving her anywhere, Danny Connolly just leaned over to pull her into his arms, to kiss her again. And in spite of all the questions and doubts raging through her mind, she could only kiss him back.

24

"T ara," called augusta from her dressing room.
She was tangled up in blue, swaths of midnight blue, almost black, really, chiffon—or was it taffeta; she could
never get them straight—and she couldn't extricate her
arms. "Tara, dear! Can you come help me?"

"Augusta, what happened?" Tara asked, running in
from the bathroom, smelling of lemon-scented cleaning
fluid.

"I'm attempting to decide what I should wear to the
Pumpkin Ball," Augusta said, "and I have this marvelous
bolt of witchy-blue taffeta—or is it chiffon?—that Hugh
brought me back from Venice on one of his painting
jaunts, and I thought to myself, Augusta old dear, it's now
or never. Since the theme this year is 'Witchcraft,' what
better color than night-sky blue? Thank you, darling,"
she said, as Tara unwound her like thread from a spindle.

"Steady there," Tara said, supporting her as she finished untangling the cloth. Augusta felt as dizzy as a child

who had been spun around too many times in Pin-the-Tail-on-the-Donkey.

"My Lord," Augusta said, plopping down onto the faded chintz chaise longue in the corner of her dressing room. "I loathe the feeling of being trapped...a prisoner..."

"In blue taffeta," Tara said, a smile in her voice.

Augusta sighed. Her children had always thought her frivolous—constantly getting ready for the next party, preparing a costume for another ball, needlepointing yet more throw pillows—and now Tara was conveying the same emotion.

"Life isn't all costume parties," Augusta said. "I do try to do good works."

"You gave Bay a chance," Tara said. "And she loves her job."

"Well, she is enormously gifted. I watch her out the window, you know," Augusta said. "She handles the soil and plants in such a way...the earth is her canvas. Believe me, I know an artist when I see one. I adore watching artists at work, when they are in their element and in touch with their muse. I can't wait to see her canvas come to life, into bloom, next spring."

Tara nodded, pleased and proud of her friend.

"How is Bay faring?" Augusta asked, after a moment. "Emotionally and financially?"

"She's strong," Tara said. And that was all she said.

Augusta admired her restraint. Loyalty to friends was paramount; she had always taught that to her daughters. Loyalty and love.

Augusta had learned so much about love over the years. She had once thought that it belonged only between a man and a woman, that romantic love was the real love, that all else was secondary. She had hated deeply, as well. The women who had slept with her husband, the man who had invaded her kitchen so many years ago with his gun and a desire to kill.

Her children, her brilliant and wonderful daughters, had taught her to forgive. To forgive everyone, and to love them. Wasn't that the point of life? To transcend your own suffering and try to love and give to others?

Augusta sighed. Such deep thoughts exhausted her. She must be making progress as a human being, though. Thinking of Bay and her family instead of her Pumpkin Ball costume.

But all good, saintly things had to come to an end, so Augusta took a deep breath and stood. Again, she began draping herself with the fabric. With the theme "Witchcraft" and her stature as Hugh Renwick's widow, Augusta planned to dress as a witch in a famous painting.

Should it be from "Witches Flying," by Francisco Goya? Or "Four Witches" by Albrecht Dürer—a particular favorite, hanging at the Met in New York, and it might be such fun to raise eyebrows by going nude! Or—and for shock value and fun, Augusta was leaning in this direction—"The Obscene Kiss" from *Compendium Maleficarum* by Fra Francisco Maria Guazzo of Milan?

"Tara, what are *you* wearing to the Pumpkin Ball?"

"I'm not sure I'm going," Tara said, diligently refolding Augusta's cashmere sweaters in her sweater drawer.

"Perhaps you should invite Agent Holmes." At Tara's look of surprise, she said, "Oh, yes. I've picked up on your feelings. He *is* one to turn a woman's head."

"He's turned mine, but I'm not turning his."

"Darling, I'm sure you are. But he's worried about conflicts of interest. Or the appearance of impropriety. Why not just come out and tell him that the Pumpkin Ball will be a grand place to encounter all Black Hall's white-collar criminals? You can be his Mata Hari and help him to go undercover."

"I'll think about it."

"Well, you must attend the ball even without him," Augusta said. "You are young, vibrant, and single. And you should take Bay with you. There's a lot of pressure in this town to become a professional widow—believe me, I know. But she should go anyway."

"Sean's only been dead for five months," Tara said. "I don't think she'll want to."

Again, Augusta sighed. If only she could impart to these young women that life was terribly attenuated. Too short, too short. One never knew whether another Pumpkin Ball would even come to pass. It always took place on the night of the November Full Moon, just before Thanksgiving, and while it was often devastatingly romantic, the point had always been to celebrate life's harvest.

"She should attend," Augusta said firmly. "And you should get her there."

Tara laughed, dusting Augusta's shoes. "The last time I tried to meddle in her well-being, I nearly lost her friendship. And yours."

"Well. Look how it all turned out: She's happy, I'm happy. My garden is going to be an earthly delight. Oh!" Augusta said, shocked by the brilliance of her own subconscious.

"What is it, Augusta?"

"That's it! Hieronymus Bosch—'The Garden of Earthly Delights.' One of the wickedest paintings ever done. A triptych of creation, heaven, and hell . . . a depiction of the world, with the progression of sin. Sinful pleasures! It will be marvelous! I'm ancient now, but darling, there's no one in this town who's partaken of more sinful pleasures than I. I'll wear a midnight-blue cape, and as a prop, I'll carry a magic cup. Which reminds me!"

"What's that, Augusta?" Tara asked.

"Have you found my Florizar cup yet?"

"The silver cup..."

"I still can't put my hands on it! I've looked high and low. It would be the perfect addition to my costume. What good is a witch without a magic potion?"

"I'll pay extra attention today, Augusta," Tara said. "It can't have gone far."

"The last time I recall using it—and this is rather haunting—was when Sean McCabe stopped by the week before his disappearance. To bilk me, as it turns out, but at the time, I thought it was just that he wanted me to sign checks moving money from one place to another. We toasted the success of my yield..."

"Oh, Sean," Tara said under her breath.

"He can't possibly have taken my Florizar cup," Augusta said, rejecting the idea. "He wasn't a kleptomaniac, after all. White-collar confidence men don't get their hands dirty with actual *stealing*..."

The words were suspended in air, in time, as Augusta and Tara pondered the notion of stealing—the act of one person taking from another, whether from bank accounts or trust funds or from a wallet or a pocket or from the wall of a museum or the vault of a jeweler—and whether in the Piazza San Marco, the Place Vendôme, or Firefly Hill. The "hows" and "wheres" didn't matter, and neither, ultimately, did the "whys."

"Stealing is the true sin," Augusta said. "Not earthly pleasures."

"I know."

Augusta took a long breath in, and then let it go. "I

have too many things," she said. "Accumulation is a fact of life...and not a good fact. When I get to heaven, Saint Peter won't let me carry in Hugh's paintings, my photos of the girls, my black pearls, my Florizar cup."

"No, I suppose he won't," Tara said.

"Just as I'm certain he didn't admit Sean with all that stolen money."

"If he admitted Sean at all," Tara said sadly.

JOE HOLMES THOUGHT BLACK HALL WAS PROBABLY A FINE place to be if you lived here—nice houses, views, stores, schools, restaurants, music shops—but as a place for temporary assignment, it was pretty lonely, geared toward couples or families.

He sat at his desk, drinking yet another cup of coffee from the place next door, doing what FBI agents did best: paperwork.

One of Joe's recent girlfriends had always answered the door with expectation in her eyes, as if she was expecting him to be James Bond. Or at least Tommy Lee Jones. When she realized that what he did was more in line with geek accountants than glamorous movie spies, she left him for a lawyer.

Joe's father had taught him that lawyers were much more likely to have Aston Martins than FBI agents. Also, much more likely to get sent on sexy missions that included good hotels with pools and fancy sheets and expensive drinks at sleek bars. If FBI agents wanted to track a suspect around the country—even staying in airport Radissons—getting a supervisor to sign off on the expense requisition would be as thrilling as actually solving the case.

"You're not doing it for the glamour," his father had

said to Joe one time when Joe complained about life on the road. "You're doing it to catch bad guys."

"I know, Dad," Joe had said. "Just like you."

"You make me proud, son," his father had said.

That had really been enough to make up for the crummy motels and the fast food.

Now, outside, the rain beat down. Perfect for Joe's mood as, again, he went through the Shoreline Bank documents. One confusing aspect was the discovery that Sean had paid back ten thousand dollars from one of the accounts he had starred.

Had he been intending to move it somewhere else, convert it to cash later on? Joe wasn't sure. In another case, last May, Sean had stolen six hundred dollars from one account on Friday, put it back the next Monday. What had caused his change of heart? Joe pored over the account statements, looking for answers. Could it have had something to do with the mystery woman—"the girl"? Or with "Ed"?

There still wasn't any clear-cut "Ed." Ralph Edward Benjamin's nickname was "Red," a contraction of the two names as much as a reference to his childhood hair color. There were also Eduardo Valenti and Edwin Taylor, neither of whom seemed very promising. Valenti had been at Columbia until May, and Taylor's record seemed spotless.

Joe stretched, listening to the rain fall. At least he didn't have to slave in a wet garden, like Bay McCabe. He'd driven by Firefly Hill twice that week, and both times he'd seen her laboring outside.

That second time, he'd seen Tara O'Toole running across the wide expanse of lawn, toward her friend. The image endured in Joe's mind: She looked like a young girl, wild with abandon, oblivious to the driving rain. Her long legs, slender arms, black hair . . .

And last night he had dreamed about her.

About them, really. These two best friends, right at the center of Joe's investigation. In his dream, they were all in a boat on the Sound. Joe was someone's husband—a novel idea in itself. He was at the helm, steering over the waves. Shards of memory, long buried, of being on the deck of his father's fishing boat, came up and took hold. The joy of being at sea, running with the wind.

And the two women were there. Bay leaning against the coaming, Tara with her arm slung around Joe's neck. The wind ruffled his hair, tickled his ear. No, it was a kiss. The sensation was so intense, her kiss even stronger than the breeze itself, moving him even as the wind moved their boat.

"Joe," she whispered in his ear. "You don't have to steer anymore. Just take your hands off the wheel...go ahead..."

But Joe's hands couldn't relax their grip; he had to hold tight, keep the boat on course. She caressed his neck, his back; all he wanted to do was grab her in his arms and take her down below, rip off all her clothes, make love to her, his wife.

Tara O'Toole Holmes. She seemed to spend a lot of time in Andy's. Yesterday she had been talking to the clerk about something called "the Pumpkin Ball," pointedly, it had seemed to Joe. What did she have in mind? That Joe walk over from the "Over the Hill" rack to ask her if he could have the pleasure of taking her? Sad to say, dating someone in the investigation was against Bureau policy.

Nothing so tormenting in his dreams, though...

Joe had wakened, smiling, content, but then, right away, the sense of connection was broken. He had held his motel-room pillow close to his chest, as if it was Tara, as if he had rolled over to actually find her in his bed.

He wondered what it would be like to spend time with Tara, to go with her to Bay's house on a fine fall evening. He had seen them sitting there together often enough, just the two of them together in the midst of Bay's kids. Two lifelong friends with such beautiful smiles and spirit, riding through the garbage Sean McCabe had left behind for them. Joe would never do that to a woman he loved.

He just wouldn't. On the other hand, he couldn't figure out why a good guy like himself had had so little luck finding a girl like Tara to love. He had high standards. His parents had loved each other so much, he knew he couldn't settle for anything less than that. And he knew he needed someone like his mother, who understood the crazy life of an FBI agent and wasn't scared off by a guy who wore a 10mm gun out to pick up a quart of milk.

He wondered whether the granddaughter of the number-one pistol shot in the country would be able to handle that. Maybe he should start by shocking the hell out of Tara O'Toole, showing up at this Pumpkin Ball to ask her to dance.

He shoved his paperwork aside and reached into the lockbox.

He had had decent success, tracking Sean's offshore account to a bank in Costa Rica—where the chances of getting access were next to zero. Especially because the code required an additional access number that Joe didn't have. He had started the process to open that account, and it would either happen or it wouldn't. Bureaucracy, nothing more.

Maybe he should go down to Costa Rica himself. He could take Tara. She'd appreciate what a trip that place was. A tropical paradise, magnet for vacationers: located between the Pacific and the Caribbean, great beaches, fishing, hotels, romantic moonlight walks on the beach together.

Stop it.

It was also a mecca for con men. Con men loved Costa Rica.

They didn't get extradited, they had secure banking, they had cheap help and favorable exchange rates, so a million U.S. dollars could buy a luxurious life on the lam. The beach bars were packed with white-collar criminals who'd packed up their families and cash and made the big break—run away from prosecution, or from prison. They'd sit at the bars all day, under the palm trees in the warm sea breezes, talking endlessly about how they'd done it, the fine arts of embezzlement, of conning, of fleecing the people who trusted them most.

Half of them believed their own stories, their own gigs—that they hadn't meant to take anyone's money, if only the victims hadn't gotten impatient they would have paid it back. The other half knew they were lying, thieving scum, but didn't really care because they hadn't gotten caught. Or had, but managed to get away.

Joe thought the first half were actually the most dangerous.

Con men who conned themselves were doubly bad. Because they justified every single move they made. Every theft, every lie.

Sean McCabe had been one of those. Joe knew the type so well. The guy had so much invested in what everyone thought of him; the irony of his crime was that he had probably wanted more money, more toys, to win more friends.

More golf buddies, more women to admire his taste and acumen.

When the idiot bastard had already had paradise in his own house. What a fool...

Joe turned his attention to Daniel Connolly's letters to Bay, Sean's wife.

The letters had had significance to Sean, and Joe was beginning to get an idea of why. Reading through, Joe realized that Dan Connolly was as different from Sean as one could get. Dan had something Sean had wanted, and Joe thought Sean had studied the letters to get into Dan's mind, to figure out what he needed to say to manipulate him. How much of his motive had to do with jealousy—that Dan and Bay had once, obviously, connected on a fundamental level?

Joe wasn't sure; and he wasn't sure how much the manipulation had worked. He turned to the silver cup, and stared at it.

Joe knew it needed much more analysis. He had sent photographs to the art lab, hoping they could make sense of the three marks stamped into the rim. If he could trace the cup...

Sean McCabe's safety-deposit box had been his equivalent of a serial killer's trophy room. Joe wasn't sure what each of the three items signified, but he knew that the symbolism was probably more important than their actual worth. He wondered whether there was more silver elsewhere: Fiona's silver bowl, for example.

Perhaps the keeping of trophies was a connection to Sean's partner, if he had one; perhaps it had been Sean's insurance policy, against betrayal. Or maybe it had been their way of showing off, one-upping each other.

The number, the letters, and the cup...

Joe almost had the connection—it was so close—he was positive he almost had it. But it proved as elusive as holding on to Tara in last night's dream. Now he took out the manila folder he had found on the boat.

He stared at Sean's tortured notations on the cover and in the margins—when had he made them? The girl . . . and Ed. Inside, the accounts he had begun to pay back. Thumbing through, Joe calculated the dates.

What if Sean had started feeling guilty about his crimes? What if he had been determined to make restitution, instead of continuing to steal? Hadn't Bay told Joe, in one of their first interviews, that Sean had promised her he would change? From the dates in the folder, it seemed that Sean had started to do just that not long before he died, late last spring.

What if Sean had actually tried to change—and someone hadn't liked it?

Joe's heart beat faster, and he knew he was on the right track. What if "the girl" wasn't one of Sean's conquests at all—but someone Sean knew to be in danger?

Bay, for example?

Or one of their daughters?

He stared at the truck, and let his mind drift. What role did a truck play in this case? Nothing much, unless you counted the hit-and-run of Charlotte Connolly. Hadn't she been killed by a truck?

He thumbed through the file—there it was: a van. She'd been killed by a dark red van. Now Joe looked back at Sean's drawing. Maybe a van, maybe a panel truck. Too much hood to be clearly a van. A boatyard truck? Still, it was all he had, so he closed up the folder and decided to take a drive east.

25

K ELLY'S LANDSCAPERS WAS BRIGHT WITH PUMP-kins, haystacks, and apples. Filling the back of her station wagon with mulch and lime, Bay couldn't concentrate on next summer's flowers.

She couldn't get Dan out of her mind. The feel of his arms around her. His rough skin against hers. Their closeness. The thing he had started to tell her at the end . . .

She headed for New London. Driving down to the waterfront, she pulled into the parking lot of Eliza Day Boat Builders, parked beside Dan's truck, and walked inside.

She stood inside the vast shed, looking at the various boats under construction. Two were old, in the midst of restoration. A new sailboat appeared ready to be painted. And a new dinghy was being built. A radio was playing, the music echoing through the space. Following the sound, she found Dan standing on a ladder on the far side of a beautiful old boat. Her heart caught as she saw him:

his wide shoulders and strong arms, his blue eyes, the lips that had kissed hers.

"Hello," she said.

"Bay," he said, eyes registering joy. He wore jeans and a sweatshirt, both smeared with varnish, and he climbed down the ladder two rungs at a time. Their gazes locked as he stood before her, but he picked up on her tension and didn't come any further.

"She's pretty," Bay said, pointing at the boat, to put an end to the awkwardness of not hugging.

"She's a six-meter," he said. "Beautiful, graceful boat. She's an old plank-on-frame, filled with dry rot."

"What's this wood?" Bay asked, running her hand over the rich, fine-grained timber.

"Honduran mahogany," Dan said, breaking into a big smile. "You've still got a good eye."

"Thanks," she said, but she found she couldn't smile back. Her skin hurt, and her heart was solid, heavy in her chest. Even her breath made her ribs ache. Everything had taken such a toll lately. "Can we talk, Danny?"

He nodded, leading her into his office. Again, she admired the magnificent carved desk—it seemed to tell a story, with all of its sea creatures of legend. Taking a chair opposite the desk from Dan, she drew in a deep breath.

"I'm glad you came," he said.

"Me, too..."

"If you hadn't come, I'd have gone to find you."

She nodded. They stared at each other, unspoken words hanging between them. She wondered whether he felt the same conflicts she did. She had steeled herself for this moment, and she knew she couldn't go forward with Danny until she knew everything.

"Tell me the rest of what you wanted to say. What did

Sean want?" she asked quietly. "I'm confused about all of it."

"I know." He picked up a brass tool from his desktop, frowned at it, put it back. "It's been driving me crazy. Trying to figure out what he had in mind, and why he came to me. I haven't said anything about it—wanting it to go away, I guess."

"I want to understand what happened," Bay said, staring directly into his eyes. "I—there's been so little to trust lately, Danny. I always thought you were the one person who, unconditionally—" she stammered. "It's probably not fair, the way I idolized you. No one could have lived up to that. But I have to ask you this: Did you help Sean?"

"Help him?"

"Are you . . . is the investigation focusing on you?"

"No, Bay. Not that I know of," Danny said.

Bay let her head drop in relief. "When the police first told me, at the beginning of the summer, that Sean stole from his bank clients, I thought the world had ended," Bay said, remembering the cold shock of those days. "I really did. And then you were there, and I thought it was such a gift, to have you back in my life, as a friend . . ."

"I'm still your friend, but I'm human," he said quietly. His forehead was lined, worried. He gazed at her, his blue eyes dark with exhaustion and upset. "Will you let me tell you what happened?"

She nodded, pulling her jacket tighter, wrapping her arms around herself.

"I'd like you to start by telling me why you lied to me, about not having seen Sean until recently. When I first came to you, you said you hadn't seen him before he came here wanting you to build a boat for Annie."

"That was true, Bay."

"But if he was trustee for your daughter's trust—"

"Charlie handled that," Dan said. "The money came from her family, and there was a lot of it. I never cared about that. I know that sounds disingenuous—and maybe, in a way, it is. I mean, I liked not having to worry about the mortgage, the way other people do. But I have pretty simple tastes—I wasn't into flying off to the Bahamas, or buying BMWs and Rolexes."

Bay nodded. The Dan Connolly she had known had cared about the wind, the stars, the sea, fine wood, good tools, friendship. In that way, he had been so different from Sean, to whom material things meant success, prestige—things that had gained dramatically in importance every year they were married.

"Even Charlie wasn't that impressed with money, or what it could do. I think that's how it is for people who've had it their whole lives: they just take it for granted, and there's no reason to flaunt it. I've had that old truck out there forever; Charlie drove a ten-year-old Ford."

Bay nodded, listening.

"She . . . Eliza . . . the money was all theirs. I never wanted anything to do with it, and I was proud about not needing it. I come from a working-class Irish family, always pulled our own way. My grandfather was a builder, and he carved this desk . . ."

"For her grandfather . . ." Bay had been struck by the bond.

"We were two kids from opposite sides of town. Her family owned the mansion, my family worked in it. They were landowners, we were tradesfolk."

"Then why—"

"Why did we get married?" Danny asked. His gaze shot sideways, taking in the pictures on his bookshelf. Charlie looked out from one, blond and confident, elegant but now—to Bay—cold; a woman who walked away, instead of dealing with her daughter's emotions. "Opposites attract, right?"

"That's for sure," Bay said, thinking of herself and Sean; night and day.

Danny nodded. "I was this big, gawky working-class hero with a tool belt, and Charlie was a finishing-school debutante who always knew which fork to use."

"You were more than that," Bay said, in spite of herself.

Dan shrugged. "There were always obstacles. I'm Irish Catholic, she's a WASP. Caused a few problems, on religious holidays, and when Eliza was born. But mainly, we got through them. We learned how to fight: Never do it. Charlie could never stand anyone raising their voices. So the easiest way to be, for me, was to let Charlie win."

"You gave in?"

"Pretty much," Dan said. "'When she's right, she's right; and when she's wrong, she's right,' as the song goes. Maybe I was just afraid that we were too different, didn't really belong together—so I didn't want to make waves."

Bay caught a glimpse of herself, reflected in the glass of a picture. Her wild red hair and freckles left no mystery about her origins; she was from Irish working-class stock, like Dan, and like Sean. But while she had felt proud of her roots, Sean had spent his adulthood trying to scour his life of any history of toil, any reminders of the fact that the McCabes hadn't always belonged to the yacht club, hadn't always had a membership at Hawthorne Links.

"I thought you were very happy," Bay said. "The way you said her name that first day."

Dan nodded. "I know. I do that. Trying to convince myself, maybe. Because I loved her so much . . . we were happy at first, and for a long time. But about a year before she died, something shifted. I don't know what it was, but I know the day it happened. I came home from work one day, and she wasn't there. Eliza was home alone, upset because her mother was gone."

"I know how that feels," Bay said, hugging herself tighter, thinking of her children's faces on nights when Sean didn't come home.

"Charlie came home about an hour later, and she was happy and excited, talking on and on about a movie she'd seen. I forget which one—but she'd gone with a friend. She said..."

"Did you think—?"

Dan shook his head. "I thought she'd gone with a friend. Period. To this day, I still do."

But he didn't really—Bay could tell. He was lying to himself as hard as he could.

"After that, her eyes were different. Before, they'd always light up when I came home. But that year, I began to wonder whether she was thinking of leaving. I'd ask her—I'd even beg her to tell me. Charlie didn't like begging, didn't like strong emotions...I guess it's the way she grew up. Keep your feelings totally inside, don't let anyone see you hurt."

"Eliza seems able to express them," Bay said.

"I want her to," Dan said. "It's harder for her than it sometimes seems. She strikes out, then shuts down totally. Nothing gets in or out. But anyway—going back to that last year with Charlie, my work really slipped."

Again, Bay knew what he was talking about. She thought of her own intense level of distraction, trying to help the kids with their homework, keeping things normal, inwardly frantic with anxiety...

"I worried I was losing her, and I stopped caring as much about work. I mean, wooden boats are beautiful, and for me they've been a labor of love, but they're nothing compared to my family."

"But your business kept running—"

"Yes," he said. "My heart wasn't in it, though. This is all sounding like a big excuse, I know—and it isn't. I don't mean it to be. I just want to tell you the whole story. See, Charlie invested in my company."

"This one?"

"Yes. It's not a huge moneymaker, to put it mildly. In fact, people say boating is so expensive and basically uncomfortable, it's cheaper to just stand in a cold shower ripping up hundred-dollar bills. Well, building wooden boats is a lot like that. Hanging out in this basically unheated shed all winter is pretty crazy. Some years I'll clear a small profit, but usually if I break even on the boats I build, I'm lucky."

"So, Charlie helped you out."

"Yes. She bankrolled me. I never thought it bothered her—in fact, I thought she liked it. She'd say it was romantic. Knowing my grandfather built this desk, and that I had basically followed in his footsteps, working with wood...making classic boats from scratch with my hands. She has mariners in her ancestry. But that's looking into the past; maybe we forgot to look forward."

"Or be in the present."

"Maybe. Anyway, she began making comments. Who needed another classic gem of a ketch, anyway? She got really into the finances of Eliza's trust, wanting to understand the mechanics of it—talked about getting an MBA. Suddenly I think it seemed to her that I was just another laborer with a hammer."

Bay thought of Sean, of his superior attitude regarding workmen. He really looked down on them, thought they were a lower class of people. Even though his own father had been a railroad worker.

"So, that year I really screwed up. Took too many commissions, and did a lousy job on some of them. Then I went the other way—stopped taking orders at all. The money I did make went away fast. So I had to ask Charlie for more from the trust, just to cover my overhead, the bills I had outstanding. It all snowballed."

"Was she upset?"

Dan stared at his desk, as if straight into the eyes of Poseidon. "That's almost the worst part," he said. "She didn't seem upset at all. She seemed amused."

"Oh . . ."

"As if it wasn't to be taken seriously; that my work had always been just a hobby, and now I needed more money to keep it going. She seemed to be getting so much more from the people she was meeting at the bank, the lawyers' office—in 'getting up to speed,' as she called it, regarding Eliza's trust."

"Sean?" Bay asked. "Was he one of the people?"

Dan nodded. "Yeah. I remembered him from the beach. I hadn't liked him then. I never knew you two had married. I hadn't seen him in all those years, but she talked about him a lot. How helpful he was, how sharp with money, how much he encouraged her to educate herself about the trust, how willing he was to help her."

Bay had seen Sean in action; it had, at one time, seemed attractive. He had the gift of gab, and he was great at convincing people they were so smart, that he could learn from them, that if they joined forces with him they would form a formidable team. The quality had made him a superb businessman. But with Charlie . . . she was so pretty, and so upper-class, and so everything-Sean-wanted-to-be ... perhaps with her he had actually meant the words he said.

"I think your husband wanted to sleep with my wife," Dan said.

"Do you think he actually did?"

Dan shook his head. "No. I swear, I'd have known that. I knew Charlie so well. I could read her like a book. I knew she was turned on by everything he knew, how smart he was in the financial world—all that stuff was diverting her. And I think he flattered her, and I think she liked that."

Bay cringed at the image, but she believed it totally.

"Long before I met the guy again," Dan said, "I wanted to kill him. I thought he was after Charlie, and even though I didn't really expect her to fall for it, I didn't like what it was doing to our family."

"I'm sorry."

"Not your fault, Bay. Okay—that's all the background. Now here's the rest."

Bay steeled herself, watching Dan's face. He was grave, holding her eyes with his.

"Charlie died. I won't even go into what that was like—for me and for Eliza. My business had been on the brink for about a year, but after that, it was heading straight to hell. I took over as trustee from Charlie—the potential was there for me to use Eliza's money. One day, I called Sean, to see about borrowing a few thousand from the trust—above what they paid me—to cover a check. He showed up here the next morning."

"Oh," Bay said. Sean had seen an opportunity.

"He was all sympathetic and kind of easygoing friendly ... looked around, admired the boats."

"Even though wooden boats weren't his thing," Bay said.

"You'd never have known it," Dan said. "I started to think maybe I'd been wrong about him. Suddenly I had a new best friend."

"You really felt that way?" Bay asked skeptically. Yet she wanted to believe it: that someone had seen something good and true in Sean.

He shook his head almost sadly, not wanting to let her down. "No. I knew he was after something. I was being played—I could feel it. But I was pretty desperate myself—Eliza was having such a hard time. I felt that I was on the verge of going down the drain, losing everything, if I didn't figure something out."

"The trust..."

Dan nodded. "'There's all that money just sitting in the bank,' Sean said."

"What did you do?"

"I thought about it overnight," Dan said. "Because he really didn't suggest anything, or make it sound illegal, I thought he meant there was a way to juggle things, so that I could use the money—borrow it from the trust— and pay it back. But the next day, I called him."

"Sean?"

"Yes. And I told him to forget the loan. I didn't want the money—even a few thousand. Next day, he showed up again."

"Here?"

Dan nodded.

"He said he wanted to hire me to build a boat for his daughter..."

"At least he did that," Bay said.

But Dan shook his head. "No, Bay. I think it was a front—a reason for him to come here. He said Annie liked boats, but that she wasn't very active—that she probably wouldn't put the boat to much use."

"That bastard!" Bay cried.

"I know. Both of us," Dan said. "Hearing him say that, I really knew that he wanted something wrong. He was trying to feel me out—see how much money I needed, how far I'd be willing to go. He was using his daughter, and I'd be using mine."

"But you didn't—"

"No." He shook his head. "I shouldn't have even considered it in the first place. But I was going through rocky times, and I was so afraid of losing this place, losing my livelihood. My daughter has all the money she'll ever need, but I think of myself as providing for her. I want her to be proud of me, of what I do."

"What did Sean want you to do?"

"He said that as trustees, we could arrange for the business to use cash from Eliza's trust. I started thinking: Maybe I could do it one time, essentially taking a loan against the principal. He was throwing around numbers—fifty, a hundred thousand."

Bay folded her arms, hating Sean for trying to get Dan to take money from his own daughter.

"I thought, what if I did it for a year? Maybe six months. I'd get aggressive and start selling boats. I'd cut back on my materials, maybe use cheaper wood. My customers tend to be wealthy yachting types, and they don't blink at big bills. I'd get better at accounting, collect some back debts—I'd gotten sloppy in all that."

Bay just listened, wishing Dan had never even thought about it.

"Sean said that, compared to what was in the body of the trust, it was nothing."

"What did he want in return?"

"Looking back, I think he wanted to use the trust as a holding company. He asked how I would feel if there were some unfamiliar deposits and withdrawals, as long as they didn't affect the long-term value of the trust. I said I wasn't interested."

"Just like that?"

Dan nodded. "As soon as he asked the question, I knew he was after something wrong. I don't know banking, but I knew the look in his eyes. He covered it right away—talking to me about building that boat."

"That creep," Bay said. "She *made* that boat."

"I know," Dan said. "I told him I didn't need to keep it—that if he just showed me, I could calculate the dimensions on a larger scale, build Annie something really pretty."

"And you think the whole thing was a front for him to—what? Launder money?" Bay asked, the strange, law-breaking expression sounding bizarre even as she said it.

"I don't have any proof," Dan said. "That's just how it seems to me now, as I try to piece it all together."

"Why didn't you tell the police?"

"Because I'm Eliza's trustee. And I felt bad for even entertaining it with him, even briefly. I just wanted the whole thing to disappear."

Bay was shaking inside. Her husband had been busy plotting all this, working it, all the time, and she hadn't even seen it? She stared at Dan, thinking of how in love with him she had been as a young woman, and how right she had felt in his arms the other day. She had wanted to see him as her hero . . . the incorruptible man . . . Standing up, she began to pace.

"Why you?" Bay asked. "Of all the trust funds at Shoreline, why Eliza's?"

Dan cleared his throat, tucked his chin down slightly, staring Bay right in the eyes. "I think," he said, "because of you. Or, maybe I should say, us."

"What?"

"Those letters of ours," Dan said.

"He showed them to you?"

"No," Dan said, shaking his head. "No. But he knew a lot about me. He knew that I had always worked with my hands, that I didn't much care about bank accounts and money—things I had written to you about. Even though that was so long ago, people don't really change, in important ways. And I guess a lifetime of not caring about stuff like that makes me a bad bet as a dad with a kid who has a trust fund."

"Sean picked you," Bay said, breathless, "because you weren't paying attention."

"It's a great feeling," Dan said, "to know that you were singled out for being a total dupe, a jerk just asking to have the wool pulled over his eyes."

Bay blinked, nodding. She couldn't say anything to console him, because she knew how he felt. Exactly.

"Bay," he said, rising, walking around the desk. As he approached, she felt a primal urge to be held, to hold him again, but instead she took a step back.

"No..." she said, shaking, moving toward the door. "Even if you didn't take the money, I hate that you thought about it. I can't stand that Sean tried to use your daughter."

"Bay, please—"

"You know what the worst part is?" Bay asked, tears in her eyes. "Annie's boat. Do you know what that little model boat meant to her? She made it for him. And he was willing to use it as just another prop in his rotten con jobs."

"You know what the irony is?" Danny asked, eyes pained. "I think, in the end, he really wanted me to build Annie the boat. Because why else would he have come back to leave me the model? That was long after I'd told him I wasn't interested in helping him."

"That detail almost doesn't matter," Bay said.

"I know."

"Good-bye, Danny," Bay said, trembling inside and out. "I have to think about all this."

Out in the parking lot, she fumbled with the car keys, slamming the car door behind her. The shame of what Sean had done, sleazing around, trying to get into a young girl's trust fund, all for money, made her sick. How could she not have known? Had she been living in another world?

She tried to track the time: Sean had changed after Mark Boland was made president. He'd become angrier, more competitive. Had he suddenly thought more money would make up for his career disappointment? Had he somehow imagined that plundering his clients' money would make him feel like a bigger man? And what about that lie, his promise to Bay that he would change?

"You're pathetic!" Bay screamed, alone in her own car. "How could you have done it?"

Her husband's crimes suddenly became real. Until this minute, she'd known in the abstract—with cops and agents asking questions, the papers reporting vague details. Even Augusta hadn't brought it all home to her so searingly. But Danny had just made it real. Now Bay had the picture of her husband trying to get Danny to let him use Eliza's trust, trying to recruit another father to be a slimeball.

"I hate you, Sean," Bay sobbed. She knew she didn't want to see Dan again, didn't want to face the man who'd seen Sean in action, or be reminded of who her husband really was. She hated Sean for his crimes, for throwing away everything they had, their home together, their beautiful children. And she hated him for tainting something that had been clean and precious that had been hers alone. Driving away, she nearly hit Joe Holmes entering the parking lot.

26

S AW MRS. McCABE PULLING OUT OF HERE IN A
hurry," Joe said, carefully watching Dan Connolly's face.
His eyes looked uneasy, and they kept flicking toward
the door, as if Bay McCabe might walk back in at any
minute.

"Yep," Connolly said.

Joe nodded, waiting for him to offer more, but he didn't.

"Listen," Joe said. "I have a few more questions for
you. About your wife's death."

"Okay," Connolly said, tensing his jaw. "Go ahead."

"I've read the police reports, and all the follow-ups,"
Joe said. "And everything I've found indicates that Charlotte was hit by a red van. Not a truck. Is that right?"

"A dark red van," Dan corrected. "At least, that's what
Eliza thought at first."

Joe nodded. "Yes. The police report stated that she
was—" he paused, wanting to be sensitive, "—traumatized

by the event. That she was unable to be questioned much, because of her mental state."

"She was wrecked by it," Dan said.

"So there's no—no doubt about her memory, about what she saw? Is it possible it was a truck, but she thought it was a van? Do you think she knows the difference?"

Dan gestured toward the parking lot. "I run a boat-yard," he said. "She's grown up around lots of both. She knows the difference. On the other hand, she's a young girl, who saw her mother killed. Her memories of that night are confused."

"Would you mind if I talked to Eliza?" Joe asked. "Just to confirm what she saw—"

"Is this about Eliza?" Connolly asked sharply. "Or about me?"

Surprised but not showing it, Joe took a breath. "Why don't you tell me," he asked slowly, "what you have in mind?"

Dan shook his head, then rested his forehead in his hands. Joe sat back, giving him time. He knew that Dan had something to say, and he'd held the story inside as long as he could. It was eating him up: Joe knew the signs.

"I'm glad you're here," Dan finally said. "I was going to call you. There's something I have to tell you. It's about Sean McCabe and my daughter's trust fund...the Eliza Day trust."

BACK AT THE OFFICE, JOE HOLMES CALLED HIS CHIEF, NICK Nicholson, to report that he now had confirmation that McCabe had wanted to use the Eliza Day trust to "park" funds embezzled from other accounts.

"Was Dan Connolly involved?" the chief asked.

"No. I'm sure of it. But it's weird—I went to ask Connolly questions about his wife's death, and he winds up answering questions about McCabe."

"You had already noticed irregularities in the trust."

"Yes. Which Connolly didn't even know about. The wrongdoing occurred before his wife's death. He was unaware."

"So, if McCabe was already parking money in the Eliza Day trust, why would he need Connolly's participation?"

"McCabe was all over him, the minute he figured out that Connolly's business was in trouble."

"Business in trouble?" Nick asked skeptically.

"I know, I know," Joe said. Usually that was a red flag for financial misdeeds, but his gut told him that this time it wasn't. "Look, I might be wrong, but I think McCabe and the UNSUB were just waiting Connolly out."

"Waiting him out?"

"Yeah. He was ripe for the picking. After his wife's death, he had some difficulty holding it together. The business, his daughter...everything was falling apart around his ears, and he was running as fast as he could to hold on.

"Anyway, here's my theory. McCabe had been using the trust already; he wanted Connolly's go-ahead to start actually taking money—not just parking it. If Dan Connolly was broke or desperate enough, Sean could look like a hero, sending funds his way while skimming for himself."

"So, Sean was trying to recruit someone new."

"Yes."

"The way he'd recruited people before. Because he didn't do this alone."

"Right," Joe said. McCabe was kiting checks, money orders; he would deposit small amounts into his Anchor account. The big money would be parked in large accounts, like the Eliza Day trust.

Joe examined the trust statements spread across his desk. "Eventually funds were moved offshore. But that came later. I think he used other trusts as well—as a trustee, he could write checks, retrieve the money when needed."

"He probably preyed on people who had had recent losses, deaths—people like Connolly who weren't interested in the financial details."

"Right," Joe said. "But then it gets interesting. About a month before he died, McCabe starts paying people back. It's subtle, in just a couple of cases—but I think if I keep digging, I'll find a pattern there."

"You're saying he found a conscience? That's rare—he's been successfully stealing from his clients for how long? And he suddenly decides to go clean?"

What happened to you, Joe wondered, staring at the balance sheets. *What changed your mind?*

"I'm staring at that first big deposit, sixty-two thousand dollars, going into the Eliza Day trust just over a year and a half ago," Joe said quietly, running his finger down the column.

"Before Mrs. Connolly died."

"She *did* know," Joe said, reviewing the papers.

"Was she part of the thing?" Nick asked.

"Or did it get her killed?" Joe asked, staring at the numbers, and then at the notations and drawing on the manila folder. "Could she be 'the girl'?"

"Doesn't track. The timing's off."

"True. It couldn't be Charlie getting killed—that was a full year before he started making restitution on the accounts. So, what happened to Sean?"

"Maybe the UNSUB threatened his family. Keep going along, or he'd hurt his wife. Or one of their daughters."

"Run her down with a truck?" A *dark red van?* Joe wondered.

"Hasn't happened yet—maybe Sean took the bullet for whoever it was. He followed through on his plan to get out, and his buddy killed him. Why bother with his family now?"

"And have you noticed all the trouble started after Boland got to Shoreline? The UNSUB has to be Boland," Joe said.

"Can't be Boland," Nick said. "He was clean at Anchor Trust. There was never a complaint, never even a hint of wrongdoing on his watch. What, he goes over to a new bank and suddenly goes bad? Doesn't work that way. No, he walked into the den of thieves and shook everything up."

"So you think the partner is someone who was working with Sean before Boland arrived? Someone Sean enticed to join him?"

"What about Fiona Mills, on that trip to Denver—"

"Fiona Mills," Joe said. "You know, during my last interview with her, she told me she was missing a silver trophy."

"Oh—that reminds me. Got a fax to send you; stand by." Joe heard the sounds of paper rustling, the line dialing. His fax began to whir. He carried the phone across the office, to see what was coming through.

"It's the results on that silver cup," Nick said. "The one McCabe had in the safety-deposit box. Mickey sent the silversmith markings down to Quantico, and they farmed them out to some scholar at Penn. Turns out, from the markings, the cup's not that old—made in 1945."

Tucking the phone under his chin, Joe opened the

safe, removed the cup. He stared at its handsome design, its long stem, the leaves and vines entwined at its base, and then scanned the report:

The silvermaker's mark is that of Giovanni Armori, who worked in Florence, Italy, from 1930–1945. This chalice was the last he ever made, and it was produced for the parents of Anne-Marie Vezeley of Paris, for the occasion of a Catholic mass celebrating her wedding to the art dealer Jean-Paul Laurent.

Armori was killed by the Germans on the same day he completed this commission; a courier for the Vezeley family escaped with the chalice, but he reported Armori's death. Many of the silvermaker's records were burned at the same time—just two weeks before the Americans arrived to liberate the region, in April, 1945.

The chalice, a gift to the young couple from Anne-Marie's parents, remained in the Vezeley-Laurent family for twenty-five years. During that time, Jean-Paul Laurent, who specialized in prints, became known for selling prints by the most influential artists of the day, both in Paris and abroad. He and his wife enjoyed an exalted social life, and during the sixties, there were reports of Laurent smuggling works of art stolen by the Nazis out of Paris.

This activity placed him within our field of interest. During the early 1970's, surveillance of the family apartment on the Avenue Montaigne in Paris's Eighth Arrondissement revealed that Madame Laurent entertained artists while her husband traveled on business. She was the lover of, among others, Pablo Picasso and Hugh Renwick.

Agents reported a vicious fight one night, following Renwick's arrival at the apartment, direct from his flight into Orly, to discover Picasso on the balcony in his underwear. Shouting ensued, and a fight of such violence that police were called to break it up. It was during this altercation that Renwick sustained his famous scar. Although it came at the hand—and knife—of Picasso, Madame Laurent paid the police to keep it secret.

As a way of mollifying Renwick, and perhaps buying his silence as well, Madame Laurent made a gift to him of the Armori chalice.

The Armori chalice then crossed the Atlantic, smuggled in the luggage—the painting case—of Hugh Renwick, and has been assumed to be at his family home, Firefly Hill in Black Hall, Connecticut, ever since.

"So," Joe said, as he read, "this cup belongs to Augusta Renwick."

"The rich really *are* different," Nick said. "But we knew that."

"The question is, did she give the chalice to McCabe or did he take it?"

"Maybe she's our UNSUB," Nick said.

"Augusta Renwick?" Joe laughed. "I don't think so. You'd have to meet her to appreciate how wrong you are."

"Think about it," Nick said. "She's old, she's rich, she's bored. She has some young—well, young to her—studly banker managing her affairs. They get to talking. She tells him about the artistic shenanigans of her husband Hugh, a little smuggling here, a little beating up Picasso there—next thing you know, they're Bonnie and Clyde."

"I'll remember that when I go question her."

"Good luck," Nick said. "Quite a town you've stumbled into."

"Yeah. Black Hall. Garden spot of the East Coast. Just don't bank your money here," Joe said, checking his watch. Andy's had closed while he'd been talking to Nick, reviewing the information about the cup.

So, no running into Tara tonight.

On the other hand, it felt good to have solved one part of the three-part safety-deposit box mystery. That left two to go. And the chance to drop in on the inimitable Mrs. Renwick.

27

Y OU FOUND IT," AUGUSTA RENWICK SAID BREATHILY, clutching the silver chalice to her heart. "My Florizar cup!"

"Florizar cup?" Joe Holmes asked, frowning.

"Yes," Augusta said. "That's the name of my favorite drink—shall I fix us one?"

"I'm on duty, Mrs. Renwick," Joe said. "And I'll have to have that cup back, for evidence."

"Well, I'm not on duty, and you'll get it back after we discuss a few things. Come out with me to the flower room, and tell me what the Federal Bureau of Investigation is doing with my Florizar cup."

Firefly Hill, her home, was truly incredible, filled with Hugh Renwick's paintings, statues of the Buddha and Hindu deities carved from rare jade and exotic woods, a totem pole, a cabinet of what looked like Fabergé eggs, and about a million pictures of the Renwick sisters, their husbands, and their children. The flower room had a stainless steel sink and counter, and Augusta explained that, although it doubled as a bar now, it had traditionally been used all summer for arranging flowers.

"Firefly Hill used to have magnificent gardens and now, thanks to Bay McCabe, will again. How is that case coming, by the way? Have you retrieved any of my money?"

"No, but we retrieved your cup," he said, watching her carefully as she stood on tiptoes, reaching for a bottle.

"What does that have to do with the case?" she asked, indicating that she would like him to get the bottle down.

"First, tell me what you know about the cup, Mrs. Renwick. Why did you call it 'Florizar'?"

She laughed, clinking ice cubes into the silver cup and also into a tall glass. "A joke," she said. "A private joke. You see, I used to tell myself that I always came in second... with my own husband. While he was out romancing the wives of other men, I was home with our beautiful girls. I was like the second-place finisher."

Joe nodded, waiting. At eighty or so, the woman was still charming and beautiful. Cold air blew through the flower room's uninsulated walls, but as if untouched by the chill, she happily cut slices of lime and ginger.

"You see, Mr. Holmes," she said. "Florizar ran second in the 1900 Kentucky Derby, after Lieutenant Gibson." She filled the glass with Diet Coke, dropped in some lime and ginger, and handed it to him. "I prevailed, however. I married Hugh, and we loved each other until he died; in our own fashion, of course."

"The man was very fortunate," Joe said.

"Indeed. A true Florizar has some lovely Russian vodka in it—are you *sure* you wouldn't like some?"

"I'm on duty, ma'am," he reminded her.

She peered at him, raising her glass to toast. "Someday, when you are not on duty, it would be a true pleasure to drink with you."

"I agree," he said, smiling.

"Now, dear, tell me," Augusta said. "Where did you find the cup?"

"It was in a safety-deposit box rented by Sean McCabe."

"I knew it!" she gasped. "I told Tara I thought he had taken it."

"Mrs. Renwick," Joe said, jolted by the mention of Tara's name, "what did you tell her? What made you *think* McCabe would have taken it?"

Mrs. Renwick opened her mouth to speak, but then a strange thing happened. She took a long, thoughtful drink from her Florizar, and her violet eyes sparkled.

"You know, dear," she said, the faintest of Mona Lisa smiles playing on her lips, "I can't remember. Suddenly, I can't seem to remember at all. You'll have to ask Tara."

THE NEXT MORNING, FROST COATED THE MARSH. IT SHIMmered white in the early light, over the brown flats and grasses, right down to the edge of the tidal creek. Yesterday Tara had cut the last roses, and she gazed at them now, beautiful in a vase for a few more days. They would have died in today's frost.

Things change, everything passes, Tara thought, sipping her morning coffee. She heard a thump on the front porch. Thinking it must be the morning paper, she yanked open the door and came face-to-face with Joe Holmes.

"Agent Holmes!" she said, jumping back with her hand on her heart. "You scared me!"

"I'm sorry. Good morning, Tara," he said, seeming all business, yet also a little embarrassed. He was already bureaued to the max: dark suit, white shirt, blue tie, shined shoes. She noticed him staring at her intently, and she cursed herself for not having answered the door in a peignoir, with her hair done. She wore the bottoms of some blue-and-white star flannel pajamas, a Black Hall Elementary T-shirt, and Billy's Black Watch tartan bathrobe that had somehow wound up in her laundry.

"Rat's nest city," she said apologetically, touching her mad-looking black mane.

"You look lovely," he said sternly, in an FBI tone of voice.

"What brings you here at the crack of dawn?" she asked.

"Looking for you, actually," he said.

Tara's eyes widened. He might just as well have swept her off her feet. She touched the doorjamb, cold to her fingertips, just to make sure she was actually awake. "Really? Your detective work is stunning. Come on in. Want some coffee?" She had seen him haunting the Roasters, emerging with super-grandes. In the kitchen, she pulled down a mug for him. "How do you take it?"

"Black," he said.

"Same here," she said, beaming at him. "So, how may I help you?"

"In a couple of ways," he said, as she led him into the living room to sit by the now roaring fire. She remembered the blueberry muffins she had baking and ran to take them out of the oven, returning with several on a plate.

"You bake blueberry muffins at dawn?" he asked.

"Why not?" she said, smiling, omitting the part about removing them from the package in their ready-to-bake pan. "Go ahead, have one."

"Thanks. So. I saw Mrs. Renwick yesterday, and she mentioned something that I need to ask you about."

"Okay," Tara said.

"The silver cup," he said.

"The one you told me you had in your office?" she asked.

"Yes," he said. "It belongs to Mrs. Renwick. She told me that she had told you she thought Sean McCabe might have taken it."

"She *did* say that!" Tara said, smacking her own head. "Augusta has a tendency to misplace things. And she does use the goblet to drink Florizars. After a few of those, she could misplace anything."

"She couldn't quite remember the connection and told me to ask you what she said, what she might have thought in terms of McCabe taking it."

Tara closed her eyes, trying to remember. "I think she said that the last time she'd seen it, or recalled seeing it, Sean had been there with papers to sign. It didn't occur to her at the time, but only in retrospect, that he might have taken it. But—"

Joe was listening intently; she saw his blue eyes drinking her in, and if the whole matter weren't so dire and criminal, she'd have leaned into his strong arms and given him the kiss of his life.

"But why?" she asked. "That's what we couldn't figure out. Why would Sean risk getting caught taking a silver cup? When he was obviously after so much more, in terms of money and assets?"

"I don't know. Anyway, Tara, I need to ask you a favor."

"Of course, Joe."

"It's about this event, the Pumpkin Ball."

"Yes, I know about it," Tara said.

"It's a fund-raiser, as I understand it . . ."

"It is. Sponsored by a few Black Hall companies. They always say it's to 'give thanks for the harvest,' but really it's to raise money for local charities. After-school programs, the visiting nurse . . ."

"Shoreline Bank is one of the lead organizers," he said.

"Yes. Traditionally, they have been. Bay and Sean hosted it one year. This year it's Mark Boland."

"The point is this. I need to get inside. I've questioned everyone at Shoreline—every single bank employee. They're reasonably confident that we're about to close the case, so I don't want to tip anyone . . ."

"So, you need an invitation?" Tara asked. "You can buy tickets at any branch office. You just pay your own way, and go."

"That's not what I mean. I understand that. But I need to go with someone who knows everyone, who can make my presence there seem a little . . . smoother."

Tara's heart kicked over. "You mean *me?*"

"Yes. Would you come with me? To the Pumpkin Ball?"

"Is this, um . . . am I being deputized?" she asked.

"Not officially," he said. "But yes. In the spirit of law enforcement, I'd like you to accompany me."

"Wow. Sure. I'll be your cover," she said. "Anything, especially if it helps solve the case. It would help Bay, I think—give her closure."

"Let's see, the ball starts at eight. How about I pick you up at seven-thirty?"

"Excellent. I'll be dressed and ready. By the way, the theme is witches. So don't be shocked when you see me in my black hat."

"That won't shock me, Tara," he said gravely.

"Bet it takes a lot to shock the FBI," she said tenderly.

28

J ACK-O'-LANTERNS GRINNED AND LEERED FROM THE
porch of the large Victorian house, smoke wafting from
their pumpkin heads, blue wispy smoke...candles lit
and burning inside, the old way, the traditional way, because this was New England, and a witches' ball needed
fire. The house, painted pale gray with darker gray gin-
gerbread, gleaming black shutters and doors, old leaded
windows, and a spooky and majestic cupola on the
mansard roof, looked just the part.

Cars were arriving in a constant stream, parked up and
down Lovecraft Road. Tara wished life were different, that
Bay could be here with Danny. But Bay was so closed off
now, upset by her last visit with him, by the inescapable
truth of what Sean had done. Glancing over at Joe, Tara
felt her heart beating like the wings of a flying swan.

"Yeats wrote this great poem," she said, feeling her
own mad heartbeat, "about 'clamorous wings.' It's called
'The Wild Swans at Coole.'"

"Yeats?" Joe asked, cruising up the narrow street, taking note of all the cars.

"The greatest poet ever to write in the English language. Irish, of course."

"Hmm," Joe said, slowing down and focusing on a black minivan.

"Don't you like poetry?"

"Poetry?" he asked, typing what seemed to be a license number into what looked like a tiny computer.

"Yes. You know . . . words, sometimes rhyming, sometimes not? The language of the soul?"

Joe glanced over at her from across the seat. "I don't get to read too much of that."

Tara smiled. Any man who didn't delve into poetry on occasion needed help; and she was ready and willing to offer it. She sank back into the seat, leaning against his car door. She made a rather sexy witch, and she knew it. She had dressed herself like a *House of the Seven Gables* version of a James Bond girl, in a short black cocktail dress, a French demibra that emphasized her plunging neckline, and a beaded silk scarf given to her by Bay last St. Patrick's Day, in a hundred iridescent and mysterious shades of green; the highest heels she owned, a pair of Manolo Blahnik slingbacks, and a black cashmere beret to pull low over one heavily kohled-and-lined eye.

"Agent Holmes," she said, smiling a bit wider. "If you're living life without poetry . . . something is wrong."

"My job doesn't leave much room for reading," he said. "Except for law enforcement publications."

"As interesting as I know those must be, and I'd like to read a few myself," she said, "you really need some Yeats in your life."

"Hmm," he said again. He checked out another minivan, this one dark green, and a maroon pickup truck, and he pulled into a parking spot almost a quarter mile past the house.

"'The Wild Swans at Coole,' you said? What's it about?" he asked.

"It's about growing old," Tara said.

Joe turned off the engine, and walked around to open Tara's door. "Do swans grow old alone?" he asked, his words billowing white clouds into the frozen November air.

Tara had been smiling, enjoying her Mata Hari role, her costume as a seductive spy-witch—but suddenly her temptress smile dissolved.

"No," Tara said gently, not feeling like a spy-witch at all in that moment, gazing straight into Joe's eyes. "They mate for life."

Joe, the real spy, couldn't seem to find words to respond to that. He just nodded, his eyes thoughtful instead of stern. And, taking Tara's arm—as part of the brilliant cover he'd planned for this night's operation—in the frosty air he walked her along the line of expensive cars, all of their owners potential suspects, and into the Bolands' house.

"What are we supposed to be looking for?" Tara whispered, once they were inside.

"Anyone who seems particularly nervous to see me," he whispered back.

They walked through the crowd, a compendium of witches from the annals of art—"The Incantation," by Goya; "Witch with Demonic Spirits," by Ryckaert; "The Love Potion," by Evelyn de Morgan; "Circe Offering the Cup to Ulysses," by John Waterhouse; "The Three Witches," by John Henry Fuseli.

Slinky, slithery, voluptuous, elegant, and mysterious: the witches came in all sorts of packages. Some men wore black tie, others black jeans. Augusta stood with several bank executives, swathed in her Venetian blue; she gave a knowing nod as Tara and Joe passed by.

"That Mrs. Renwick," Joe chuckled.

"I'm sure she's doing her best detective work," Tara said.

"Can I tell you, I hope you're kidding?" Joe asked.

"You don't know Augusta," Tara said. "If she senses injustice—especially when it's been directed at her or her family—she's all over it."

"Great," he said wryly. "I just hope she doesn't get herself in trouble. Here come our hosts. Hold my hand and pretend I've just asked you to dance."

Tara felt excited, as if he actually *had*. The band was playing "Cat Samba," but the dance would have to wait, because Mark and Alise Boland edged their way through the crowd to greet Tara and Joe.

"Welcome to the Pumpkin Ball," Mark said. "Tara, so glad to see you. And Joe—nice to see you off duty for a change." He laughed. "At least I *hope* it's off duty . . ."

"You bet," Joe said. "I finally got Miss O'Toole to say yes to a date with me."

"Well, after all those nasty questions I've heard you've been asking all over town, I think it's the least you can do," said Alise. "Right, Tara?"

"Right," Tara said. "Looks like you have a full house, Alise."

"Well, it's a good cause, and we want everyone to have a good time."

"Everything looks spectacular," Tara said. "The Pumpkin Ball is flourishing in the hands of a professional decorator."

"Thank you," Alise said. "We didn't want to be as kitschy as Halloween, but somehow do more pagan, about the harvest—that's what all the pumpkins are supposed to mean."

"I'll bet a lot of people came because they wanted to see inside this house," Tara said. "It's such a landmark. The other biggest house in town, along with Firefly Hill."

"It is a great place," Joe said, looking around at the architectural details: the cornices and crown moldings, the handsome walnut bookcases, and a single shelf that ran the length of one wall, about eighteen inches down from the high ceiling. Tara could see that the shelf was filled with trophies.

"Back from Mark's college days," Alise said, following their gaze. "He was the captain of *everything*. I couldn't resist him."

Mark laughed, hugging his wife. "Excuse us, will you? I see some new arrivals. Make yourselves at home—there's food in the next room."

"Thanks," Joe said, glancing back over his shoulder at something. Tara watched the Bolands walk away. Mark continued straight, on to the door, to greet people. But Alise swerved a bit and paused subtly, by Frank Allingham. Although they seemed not to speak at all, Tara was sure they'd exchanged a few words.

Tara opened her mouth to say something, but she saw that Joe had been watching the same thing. This was probably child's play to him: observing suspects, noting behavior. But to Tara it was brand-new, and exciting. She was following in her grandfather's law enforcement footsteps.

"Want to dance?" Joe whispered into her ear, sliding his arm around her.

"Sure," she said, thrilled. "But I thought we were working."

"We are," he said, leading her onto the dance floor. He clasped one hand, slid his arm around her waist, and began to glide her around. His step was sure and confident, and his arms felt so powerful, as if she were being held by tensile steel. After a lifetime of sensitive artist-types, Tara nearly swooned. "We've got to make our cover look good," he continued, with a slight smile.

"Do you think we're succeeding?"

"Maybe just a little closer," he said. His arm was around her, and she felt the electricity in her own body, as they danced together.

"Like that?" she asked.

"Yes," he said. "Very good. You're a natural, Tara."

"I want my grandfather to be proud of me," she said into his neck. "He and my granny were swans, you know."

"They were together a long time?"

"Yes," she said. "For life."

"My parents, too," Joe said. They kept dancing, and Tara didn't think she had ever, in her entire life, felt so happy. "I wonder if they read Yeats."

"They must have," Tara said, looking over his shoulder. "Oops—watch out. Mark and Alise are dancing past."

She and Joe fell silent as he wheeled her around the dance floor, away from the Bolands. Tara watched them in each other's arms, and thought of Bay and Sean. She shook her head.

"I can feel you disapproving of something," Joe said, mouth against her hair.

"Sean was so jealous of Mark when he took over as bank president," Tara said. "But they really have so much in common."

"What do you mean?"

Tara glanced up at the shelf of sports plaques and stat-ues: basketball, football, baseball, golf. "They're both jocks. They played against each other in high school."

Joe followed her gaze.

"Only it's too bad..." she said.

"In what way?"

"Well, that Mark learned sportsmanship, and Sean learned how to cheat. All he cared about was winning; he should have known it was supposed to be about how he played the game."

Joe stopped her, right there in the middle of the dance floor. With all the other witches dancing around them, she looked up in his eyes and saw him grinning.

"Tara O'Toole," he said. "The captain *would* be proud of you."

"The captain?"

"Seamus O'Toole, your grandfather."

"Why?" she asked, as he wrapped his arms around her, brought his face down to hers.

"Because you just solved my case," he whispered, just as he kissed her lips.

29

THERE HAD BEEN A FEW SLEEPLESS NIGHTS. LYING IN bed, thinking of what he'd said and how he could have said it differently. The local papers were full of ads and stories about the Pumpkin Ball, and the morning after—following another night of lying awake—Dan wondered whether maybe Bay had gone, whether she had dressed up like a witch and tried to forget the stuff he had laid at her feet.

He worked all day, dividing his time between two boats he was trying to finish. The clock ticked by—should he call her? He could say he just wanted to see how she was doing. Or he could try to explain a little more.

Pride was a weird thing. Almost as bad as being taken by a con was knowing how close he had come, and not just by anyone: by the husband of a woman he was falling in love with. Telling the FBI the whole story really stuck in his throat.

Joe had listened, taking notes; at one point, he asked

Dan if he wanted to have a lawyer present. Dan had stayed calm, kept a poker face. But he'd been shaking inside.

"You withheld information," Joe said. "This could have helped us sooner, to know that Sean had wanted to use your daughter's trust fund. It might have helped explain that anonymous call you got last summer."

"How?" Dan asked.

"Someone knows your connection to Sean. The call might have been an attempt to learn if you wanted 'in' on a continuing operation. Or it could have been a subtle threat—maybe you know too much. Why didn't you come forward?"

"This is new to me," Dan said roughly. "Living in the middle of an investigation. I have a very sensitive daughter. Anything regarding her mother needs to be handled carefully. I don't want her around this. What do you mean, 'threat'?"

"It's your daughter's trust McCabe was going after," Joe said. "Didn't you think that should come to light? And don't you think his partners would still want it?"

"Look, I protected it from him—I'm sure he told his 'partners,' whoever they are. I did my part, and now I want it over. We live private lives around here—I don't like being studied, or feeling as if I have to report in to you or anyone else. Okay?"

Dan was really sick of guys in suits and the half-truths they lived by; it made him even sicker that for ten seconds he had been tempted to join them. That was the only real threat he could think of. Money was bizarre. He had become a boatbuilder because it was pure, something true, and because it was far from the rat race. But it came with expenses, just like anything else.

Eliza should be home from school, or would be soon.

He'd call her in a little while, ask what she'd like for dinner.

But he had a bit of time before he needed to be home. Having unburdened himself to Joe, feeling free, he couldn't wait any longer to see Bay. He climbed into his truck and started it up, and with his foot heavy on the gas, headed westward, toward Hubbard's Point.

ELIZA HAD LINED UP HER PEAS: TWELVE OF THEM.

They had been frozen, and she had defrosted them. Cooking them would remove too much of their flavor and crunch. Even too much of their nutrition. Eliza wanted to want to be healthy. She was a step or so removed from actuality and realization, but she really *was* trying to improve her eating habits.

She poured a tall glass of water.

Then she put on her favorite Andrea Boccelli CD and lit a candle. If she made eating seem special, maybe she'd want to do it more. She looked out the window, wondering when her father would be home.

Sitting down, she ate the first pea, chewing it thoroughly. Her gaze roamed the kitchen. The knot in her stomach wasn't as bad as it used to be as she thought about her mother: how she used to fix Eliza's dinner. Until Eliza had seen her kissing Mr. McCabe, her eating had been mostly normal. The anorexia had kicked in right afterward.

It felt so good to have told Annie. In fact, the relief of divulging the truth to someone had made her want to tell even more of it: to her father. As they said at Banquo, "You're only as sick as your secrets." Perhaps that was truer than Eliza ever would have believed.

Midway through chewing her third pea, she decided to

do something even more special for herself: drink her water on ice, from her silver cup. Now, this was progress. This was fighting the demons, moving through the illness, taking a step toward healing.

Her mother had given the cup to her. It had come through the line of ancestors, all the way back to the general: the most romantic military figure in the history of the United States, or maybe anywhere in the world. General John Samuel Johnson had had the cup struck by Paul Revere himself, as a gift for his beloved, Diana Field Atwood. And he had delivered it to her across the frozen river.

As a baby, Eliza had drunk her milk from the cup.

Her mother used to tease her, saying she might be the only little girl in America to be drinking her milk from a cup made by Paul Revere. She had taught Eliza to recite the first part of the Longfellow poem the way other little children learned nursery rhymes:

> Listen, my children, and you shall hear
> Of the midnight ride of Paul Revere,
> On the eighteenth of April, in Seventy-five;
> Hardly a man is now alive
> Who remembers that famous day and year.

Although Eliza had long ago outgrown drinking milk from a baby cup, a *quart militaire*, even one as precious as hers, she had always loved knowing that it was right here in her house, for her to see and hold whenever she felt like it. And this was the first time since the accident that Eliza had felt like it.

Padding into the dining room she opened the cupboard. There was her doll china—tiny monogrammed cups and saucers. But behind them . . . it was empty! Eliza reached in and felt around: it couldn't be true. She gasped, on her knees now, peering inside. It was gone! Her special, priceless Revolutionary War heirloom, made by Paul Revere, gone...

Inherited from her mother, who had inherited it from her mother, who had inherited it from HER mother, all the way back to Diana, who had received it from the general! It had been in a special little cabinet her father had built for her—a miniature version of the desk in his office, carved of Honduran mahogany with mermaids and scallop shells, to hold her doll dishes and the silver cup—but the silver cup wasn't there now!

Frantic, Eliza tore through the room, searching through the sideboard, on the bookshelves, even under the chairs. Where could it be? The cup was priceless—putting it mildly. Not only was it part of a legend, but it had been her mother's most precious gift to her.

And no matter what her mother might have done, she was Eliza's one and only mother, and she loved her, and when she was a little girl her mother had let her drink her milk from that cup and it had been their special time. What other mother would let her child drink milk from a priceless antique!

"Oh, God, oh, God," Eliza cried and prayed as she searched the house. Eliza sobbed, circling the room, wringing her hands. She felt paralyzed. A robber had obviously stolen it! Her father wouldn't have moved her cup...She had to call Annie; Annie would help her know what to do. Grabbing the phone, she dialed Annie's phone number.

"Annie, Annie," she said out loud, waiting for her friend to answer.

Just then, there was a knock on the door.

Eliza jerked her head toward the sound and then

looked back at the phone. What should she do? She wasn't really supposed to answer the door...But she was very upset, and she needed to see who was there.

Peeking out the window, she felt at first puzzled, but then relieved.

"Mr. Boland!" she said, opening the door. "I was just about to call the police! Someone took my cup, my silver Revolutionary War cup."

"They did? Are you sure?"

"Positive. It's gone."

And suddenly it felt a little strange, to be seeing Mr. Boland at her house. Previously, Eliza and her mother had seen him only at the bank, with Annie's father, and that had been enough—Eliza had found those banking excursions to be so incredibly dull. But now, seeing him just brought back sadness; she'd gladly endure a boring day at the bank to have her mother back.

"Um, excuse me, but I have to call the police now."

"Well, I'm just glad you haven't done that yet."

"Why?" Eliza asked, thinking she had heard his voice much more recently than at the bank...

Eliza, Eliza, your mother wants you...

And, then, watching a small yellow sponge emerge, her heart racing with fear she felt but didn't understand, she tried to back away. "What are you doing here, anyway?"

She smelled something sweeter than a garden of flowers, and sank heavily to the floor.

THE PHONE HAD RUNG, BUT BY THE TIME ANNIE FOUND the portable, the person had hung up. She held the receiver, listening to the dial tone for a minute. She hoped it was Eliza, and that she would call back; Annie had something huge to do, and she needed moral support.

She could check caller ID—the box was on the table. But just then she heard her mother's car in the driveway, and she knew she'd have to do it without Eliza's help.

"Mommy," Annie said. "Can I talk to you?"

Just inside the door, her mother's eyes looked faraway and awfully sad, the way they used to all the time when her father was still alive, out at night instead of home. Annie's stomach dropped, and she almost lost her nerve, because she didn't want to add to her mother's pain, just when she had started seeming happy again sometimes.

"Of course, honey," her mother said.

Billy and Peggy were each in their own rooms, reading or doing homework. Annie had been watching through the window, in the gathering twilight, for her mother's headlights, but now that she was actually here, Annie wasn't at all sure about this. How could she be the one to break her mother's heart? Perhaps she should wait, talk to Eliza first . . .

"Would you like some tea?" her mother asked. "It's getting so cold out."

"No, that's okay," Annie said, forcing herself to be brave. "Can we talk in my room?"

Together they went upstairs, and her mother stopped to check the thermostat in the hallway. It had been so cold, they'd turned the furnace on early this year. But Annie knew her mother was very worried about money, conscious of keeping the heat down as much as they could. She dialed it down another notch.

"I can't believe it's November," Annie said.

"Seems like summer was just yesterday," her mother answered.

"Summer . . ." Annie said, looking out her bedroom window at the bare trees scratching the darkening sky. Summer seemed so out of reach, impossibly far away.

"It will come back, honey." Her mother smiled a little, as if she could read her mind. "Summer will be here again before we know it."

"It doesn't feel that way," Annie said, her voice breaking. "It feels as if winter will last forever, and it's not even here yet."

"Oh, Annie..."

"Mom, Dad kissed Eliza's mother," Annie blurted out.

Her mother flinched, as if she had been slapped. She just stood there, her mouth slightly open, trying to make sense of what Annie had said. Was she picturing it in her mind, as Annie had done a hundred times? Did the image of her father kissing another woman hurt her mother as much as it did Annie?

"Sweetheart, who told you that?"

"Eliza," Annie said.

"Hmm," her mother said. She hugged herself, as if she was suddenly cold, and she turned away from Annie. Taking a deep breath, Annie could almost read her mind: She was trying to find a way to make this better for Annie. To say, *Honey, your father wouldn't do that*. Or, *I'm sure Eliza was mistaken*. *Don't say those things*, Annie silently begged now.

And her mother didn't.

"Did she say how she knows?" she asked instead.

"She saw them. She said her mother had business with Daddy at the bank," Annie said, and the relief of spilling the truth was so great, she began to let go inside, to feel tears in her throat and her eyes. "They used to go to the bank, Eliza and her mother, and Daddy was their banker."

"I know," her mother said.

"They have a trust," Annie said. "It means they have a lot of money. But they don't seem that way, do they? They seem so normal."

"They do," her mother said. Her voice was steady and calm, but her face was very pale. "Did Eliza say anything else?"

"No. Just that they were in the car one time, and they thought she was asleep, and they kissed."

"I'm sorry Eliza had to see that," her mother said. "And I'm so sorry that you've had to learn about it. Have you kept this inside for a long time?"

"Since the night they came for dinner," Annie said, her forehead wrinkling with worry. "She told me over at Little Beach. I felt someone watching us—Eliza talks about 'evil people' who want her. I thought I heard them walking in the woods, following us down the beach. Do you think it was real? Or my imagination?"

"I don't know, Annie; Eliza is very sensitive and fragile. Maybe she conjured it in her imagination, and it began to seem real to both of you," her mother said, but Annie could tell she was totally distracted by the other revelation.

"I'm sorry I didn't tell you sooner, but I didn't want to upset you."

"So you protected me," Bay said, trying to smile. Annie nodded and went over to hug her, and she and her mother stood there for a long time. Annie didn't want to let go.

"Why did Daddy do it?" Annie asked.

"Kiss Eliza's mother? Honey, I don't know—"

"No, I mean, why did he kiss *any* of them? And why did he take that money? Did he really take drugs? Was he going to run away? Why didn't he just want to stay home, and be our dad?"

"It had nothing to do with you," her mother said forcefully, taking Annie's shoulders and giving them a gentle shake. "Don't think that. Ever, okay?"

"I can't help it," Annie said, feeling the tears well up again, a sob filling her chest. "If I had been better...I know he thought I was ugly, that I couldn't control myself. He always talked about my weight. If I hadn't eaten so much, he would have stayed home. Or if I'd played field hockey, or basketball—"

"That had nothing to do with why your father did the things he did. He was unhappy inside, Annie. We don't know why, but he was."

"So we should feel sorry for him?" Annie wept, wanting that to be true. It was so much easier to have pity for her father than to feel anger at the things he'd done.

"We could," her mother said, "feel sorry for him. But we can feel a whole range of other things for him, too, including incredibly angry. They're all okay, Annie."

"I wish...I wish...Eliza hadn't seen him doing that. I don't want her to know."

Her mother just held her, listening.

"She's my best friend; I don't want her to think of Daddy that way. She said he was so nice to her at the bank, and then she saw him doing that. I like that he was nice to her...I wish the rest had never happened!"

"So do I, Annie," her mother said into her hair.

"I'm glad I told you," Annie said after a long minute. "That I *could* tell you. Eliza doesn't want her dad to know. He idolizes her mom, and she's afraid of destroying what he thinks."

"Parents know a lot more than their kids give them credit for," Bay said. "Eliza might be surprised by what her father really thinks."

"Really?"

Her mother nodded.

Annie let that sink in, but she found herself thinking of her father again. She wished he could see her getting thinner. If only he was right here right now. He would know how much he'd hurt her, but how much she still loved him.

And then, as she watched, her mother walked across the room, to take Annie's model boat off the bookshelf. Annie ached, just to remember how much love she had put into it. Her father had appreciated it so much, too. He had held it for so long, examining every board, every line, the color of the paint.

"He promised me he'd keep it with him always," Annie whispered.

"I know he did," her mother said, with surprising bitterness in her voice and eyes.

"It was a symbol of my love," Annie said. "And it still is."

"I know, honey. It always will be."

"Do you think Daddy knows? Wherever he is right now?"

"I hope so," her mother said, her face flushed, her voice cracking. "I really, really hope he does."

Just then, Tara's voice came calling up from downstairs. Annie's mother set the boat down on the desk, and kissed her. "Let's talk more after dinner, sweetheart," she said as she left the room. Annie picked up her little boat again and heard something rattle. Maybe a piece of wood had come loose. She couldn't see anything wrong, and started to look more closely. But first she had to check to see if the call had been Eliza. She bet it was...

As she headed downstairs to check caller ID, she heard voices coming from the den.

Best friends, Annie thought, scrolling through caller ID. That's what best friends were for: to talk, to listen...

She found the last call—yes, it had been Eliza. There

was the by-now-familiar Mystic number . . . and the time: 4:45 P.M.

A record of the exact moment Annie's mother had come home and walked into the terrible, hard truth about another woman in her dad's life. And Eliza, just by making that call, had somehow been with Annie, giving her strength, offering her blessing.

Annie dialed the number, and it was busy.

Okay, she thought. Try again. Still busy.

Seven more tries. She looked at the clock: now it was 5:50. She tried ten more times, once a minute, until six o'clock.

With every call, Annie's emotions changed. She started out being neutral, fine. Then she felt a little jealous: Whom could Eliza be talking to? Did she have another close friend? Then momentarily relief: Maybe she was on the phone with her dad. But that idea went out the window as the time ticked by: NO ONE talked on the phone with their parents more than a minute or two. Finally, at six, her strongest and growing emotion was worry.

Her mother and Tara walked into the kitchen. Their faces brightened up at the sight of Annie.

"Hi, Annie," Tara said. "How are you?"

"I'm worried about Eliza."

"Why?" her mother asked.

"Because she called earlier, just before you came home, and I've been trying to call her back, and I keep getting a busy signal."

"Maybe she's talking to someone else," her mother said.

Annie shrugged. "I know it's possible, but I just have this feeling . . . this awful feeling. I can't explain it."

Her mother and Tara exchanged glances. "You don't have to," her mother said. "We get it."

"Call the operator and tell her you want the line checked," Tara said.

"How do you do that?"

"Dial 'O' and give her Eliza's number. Say you want to know whether there's conversation on the line, and ask her to break through. Tell her it's an emergency."

"But what if it's not?"

"Then you'll say you're sorry." Tara smiled.

"Go ahead, honey," her mother said. "If you're worried..."

"Your mother and I do it to each other all the time," Tara urged. "It's a very best-friend thing to do."

Annie felt very grown up and efficient as she gave the operator Eliza's phone number and waited, just knowing she'd be mortified when Eliza came on and Annie told her she had the operator break in just because the line had been busy for fifteen minutes...

But then the operator came back on to thank Annie, telling her that there was no conversation, that the line appeared to be out of order, and thank you for reporting it.

"Well?" Tara asked.

"Honey?"

"Something's wrong," Annie said, her heart starting to race. "The phone is out of order at her house. Something's happened to Eliza—I can feel it!"

BAY UNDERSTOOD THAT FEELING SO, SO WELL: THE GUT feeling that harm has befallen someone you love. She had felt it about Sean so many times, over the years, when she didn't know where he was. When she saw the panic in Annie's eyes, heard it in her voice, she began to churn inside, too.

"What can we do, Mom?" Annie begged.

Bay took a breath. "We can call her father at the boat-yard," she said.

"Or I could call Joe," Tara said slowly. "She's probably fine. She probably just knocked the phone off the hook and didn't realize it..."

"No, but, we don't *know*," Annie said. "It could be something *awful*."

Bay nodded at Annie, trying to pass on a sense of calmness. She knew the moment had less to do with any danger Eliza might be in than with giving Annie a feeling that she was doing something, not just stewing with worry. "I'll call Danny," she said.

"Looks like you might not have to," Tara said, pulling back the curtain and looking into the driveway. Bay's pulse skipped a few beats as Tara said, "It's him."

"Mr. Connolly? Why is he here?" Annie asked.

"Come on, Annie," Tara said. "Let's let your mother have a word with him."

"But I have to tell him about Eliza!"

"Your mother will. Won't you, Bay?" Tara asked, tugging Annie's hand.

"Yes. I promise."

Bay watched them as they left the kitchen, Annie reluctantly following Tara down the hall. Her palms felt sticky, her heart sore, as she stood by the door, waiting for him to knock. She heard his feet on the steps, and then a long pause, as if he was getting up his nerve. Bay stood very still, holding the doorknob, conscious of the fact that he was doing the same thing outside.

He knocked; she pulled the door open.

"Bay—"

"Why did you come?" she asked. "Didn't we say everything at your office?"

"No," he said. He stood out in the cold, cheeks

flushed, eyes intense. She could read so many things in his face: He was tense, and he was sorry, and he wanted to take it all back and make things right between them again—when they weren't his to make right.

"This is about me and Sean," she whispered, and that was really all she had to say.

"I'm so sorry," he said. "You don't know how much—"

"It doesn't matter," she said. "None of it is your fault."

"But I care about you!" he said, his voice rising. He reached out to clasp her hand, but she pulled it away. In the split second that their fingers touched, she felt a jolt straight to her heart.

"I've spent my life loving you," she said. "I didn't even know, until I saw you at the beginning of the summer . . . I thought I had you in perspective, and I thought that perspective was about a beautiful memory. Of someone who cared about me, who took time with me, who took care of me when I hurt myself. Someone who was different."

"All those things are still true," he said. "You have to believe me, Bay."

She looked up into his dark blue eyes, gazing directly into hers with a challenge and just a glimmer of humor in them.

"Because I'm an idiot," she said. "I see what I want to see—that's what happened with Sean. I was shocked when you told me what he wanted you to do."

He shook his head, hands in his front pockets. A cold November wind blew off the Sound, across the marsh.

"I know," he said.

"I wish you had told me sooner," she said. "That first week, when I first showed up at your office. I don't like that you kept it from me."

"You don't believe in forgiving a friend?"

That stopped her short.

"I believe in it," she said quietly, riveted by his eyes. She thought of the men who ran away from talking, from trying to make things better, and she knew, by the sincerity in his voice, in his eyes, that he was serious, but that she had no idea how to do this. This man gave everything of himself. He deserved no less. But she was empty, hollow.

Life with Sean had taught her nothing about working things out in a relationship; he had worn her down. She felt unutterably raw, just thinking about it now. It was all she could do to keep it together for Annie and Billy and Pegeen. She had nothing left for Dan. Not now. Not for a long time, if ever.

"I told Agent Holmes everything I told you," he said.

"You did?" she asked.

"Yes. Whatever help it can be. I told myself I wanted to keep Eliza out of this whole mess."

"Eliza!" Bay said, remembering.

"Yes... what about her?"

"Annie was worried," Bay said. "I don't think it's anything, but she's been trying to call Eliza, and the phone is off the hook."

"Our phone?" Dan asked, frowning.

"Yes. And she had the operator verify the line—there's no conversation."

"God, Eliza," Dan said, seeming to turn pale before Bay's eyes. Suddenly, thinking of Eliza's self-harm, cutting, thoughts of suicide, Bay's stomach dropped and she berated herself for not saying something immediately.

"Go," Bay said, touching his shoulder. "Do you want to call a neighbor from here? To have them check on her?"

"I have a cell phone," he said, fumbling in his pocket.

"I'll call from the truck. Bay—" he began. "Bay, will you..."

"I'll come with you, Danny," she said.

And then she ran in to tell Tara and Annie that she was going with him, that she'd be back soon, that they should keep trying Eliza's line to see if they could reach her.

30

S HE WAS ON A SHIP.

Rocking on the waves.

Tossed back and forth like a piece of cargo in the hold.

Everything dark red, the color of wine, the color of blood.

A sweet taste, marzipan, rising up inside, filling her nostrils, a memory of the yellow sponge.

And she smelled gasoline, exhaust. Sick to her stomach, tape over her mouth, a blindfold over her eyes. Seasick, carsick. And scared...starting to cry because she was on a boat and she didn't like boats and because she was going to throw up. Making the sounds of getting sick, wriggling around on her side, her hands and feet tied.

"Oh, God." The angry voice. "Pull over!"

The tape pulled off her mouth as the ship—no, not a ship at all, but a car, a vehicle—swerved to the side of the road for Eliza to stumble out, to bend over, throwing up what little she had in her stomach all over the road and her shoes.

And no one to hold her head or stroke her hair, because she hated vomiting; she was scared of how violent it always felt; she had always felt so sorry for all the bulimics at Banquo. So, crying now, wanting her mommy and daddy, she gulped in fresh air and, because they had stood back to let her vomit, she tried to run.

Feet tied, hands tied, she tried—and fell to the ground, facedown, hard. The sound of a crack—bone against tar. The worst dizziness she had ever felt, head spinning, salt in her mouth—no, blood. Her tongue, her lip split, running her hurt tongue around inside, sharp surfaces in front—her two front teeth broken.

Spitting out blood, crying harder, a hand on her arm, helping her up.

"Don't touch me!" Eliza's voice high, shrill, surprisingly loud in her own ears—a revelation. She couldn't run, but she could scream.

"Help me, help me, help!"

Hand over her mouth, trying to grab her from behind, to control her, biting and kicking and flailing—the other slamming the door, rushing over to subdue her, the blindfold slipping from her eyes—nighttime, dark, a streetlight shining just enough...

"Oh, God!"

"Get it out, hurry—" to the other person.

"Oh, God!" Eliza shrieking at the sight, not of the sweet-soaked yellow sponge that was coming back her way, but the car she'd been riding in that wasn't a car at all—

It was a maroon van.

She had seen it before, but not for a long time, not for more than a year, not since the worst day of her life, not since she had seen it strike her mother on a lonely country road...

Not since she had seen it kill her mother.

EVEN IN THE DARKNESS, BAY COULD SEE WHAT A BEAUTIful house the Connollys had. It was an old sea captain's home on Granite Street, directly across the Mystic River from the Seaport. A white Federal with a broad porch and Doric columns, gleaming black shutters, brass ship's lanterns—unlit—on either side of the wide door.

The view made Bay feel that she had stepped into another era: the dark river, and on the other side, the ghostly spars of old whaling ships. The Seaport buildings silent at night, but wind in the ships' rigging clanging with tuneless but eerily affecting music.

"The lights are out," Dan said, parking in the driveway, getting out of the car. "She always puts them on for me."

Bay took a breath, followed him up the brick sidewalk, up the wide granite steps to the front door. As soon as he put his hand on the knob, she knew something was wrong—the door swung open.

"She always keeps it locked," he said, rushing inside.

Bay went in behind him. She had the impression of faded gentility, beautifully burnished furniture passed down through generations: an ebony chest, a Newport desk, Hitchcock chairs, paintings of ships and the Seaport, brass lamps, a Tabriz rug.

Through the dining room, where, from the light of one candlestick lamp, Bay noticed a cabinet door wide open, into the kitchen. The lights were on here—bright overhead lights, illuminating Eliza's dinner.

"Eliza!" Dan yelled, running through the house. "Eliza!"

"Oh, God," Bay whispered, staring at the huge dinner plate with Eliza's dinner on it: nine shriveled peas. The poor girl, the poor baby, Bay thought, thinking also of Annie.

"She's not here," Dan said, tearing into the kitchen. "What did she do to herself?"

"Dan," Bay began.

"She's been suicidal before," he said, raking his hand through his hair, pacing the room. "She's cut herself, talked about drowning herself..."

"Dan, I don't think she's hurt herself," Bay said. She took his arm, led him to the table, showed him Eliza's plate. "She was trying to eat."

He stared at the peas, and Bay knew that only the parent of a child with eating disorders would understand, would comprehend the good news on that plate.

"She was," he agreed, eyes closing with momentary relief, then blinking open. "You're right, Bay. But where could she be?"

They wandered through the first floor, through rooms that Bay found beautiful, impeccable, but somehow cold. Where were the pictures of Eliza? Where were her school drawings and wall hangings? The plaster-of-paris molds of her hands? The shells and rocks she would have picked up and painted?

There, over the mantel, a portrait of a young woman. Bay stood still, staring into her amber eyes. It was an exquisite portrait of Charlotte Day as a debutante: white satin dress, long white gloves, soft brown pageboy, perfect bow lips, but a smile that didn't quite touch her eyes.

The woman who had kissed Bay's husband.

Gazing at the picture, Bay felt a visceral, churning dislike for Charlie Connolly—for her perfect, impersonal house, for the way she had lied to her husband, for the fact she had kissed Sean in front of her daughter, sleeping or not.

"That's Charlie," Dan said, pausing, standing beside Bay to regard the painting.

"I figured."

"It was done by Wadsworth Howe—one of Renwick's contemporaries. Her parents commissioned it for her eighteenth birthday, after her coming-out party. I've thought I should have one done of Eliza..."

Bay shook her head, never looking away from Charlie's cold stare. "It would never do Eliza justice," she said. "A portrait like that could NEVER capture Eliza's sweetness and spirit. Never."

Dan noticed her tone, and it took him aback. He stared down at Bay, shocked, and she came very close to telling him that she didn't like his wife, that she considered Charlie to be the perfect candidate for pristine entombment in a debutante portrait, but they still had to find Eliza, so she held her tongue.

"Come on," Bay said. "It's late, it's dark, she hasn't eaten. We have to find her."

"But where? Where could she be?"

"Something at her school?"

Dan shook his head. "I wish. Eliza's a self-proclaimed hermit. She says she's practicing for joining the convent."

"And this is her cloister," Bay said sadly, thinking of a young girl walled up—by choice—in her own home, her father working too hard to keep ahead of his bills, and the memory of a dead mother who had kissed another man.

Thinking of the four wounded children, her three and Eliza, Bay accompanied Dan back the way they'd come, looking for something they missed. In the dining room, Bay again noticed the open cabinet door.

"What's that?" she asked.

"A cupboard I made for Eliza's tea set," Dan said. "She loved her grandfather's desk so much, I tried to carve some of the same things into the door."

Bay crouched down, to see the shells, fish, mermaid, sea monster, and Poseidon. She reached inside, took out one of the blue cups and saucers—tiny, monogrammed with Eliza's initials—and imagined Eliza serving tea to her dolls.

"Oh," Dan said, standing above Bay, brushing her shoulder with his hand as he opened the door a little wider. "The general's cup is in there. Remember the one I told you about?"

"The one that proves there's true love?" Bay asked, as his hand lingered just slightly on her shoulder.

"Yes," he said.

Bay peered inside. The cupboard was filled with shadow, and Dan moved the candlestick lamp closer, to illuminate the interior. Two stacks of doll-sized plates, cups, and saucers were inside, as well as a teapot, pitcher, and sugar bowl.

"I don't see it," she said.

Dan crouched down beside her. "Neither do I," he said.

"Could she have it with her? It must mean a great deal to her."

"It does," Dan said. "But not because it's worth a fortune—because she used to drink her milk out of it, with her mother. She'd never take it out of this house."

"Dan," Bay said, growing cold inside, suddenly feeling an overwhelming rush of dread. "I think you need to call the police."

"I know," he said, already moving for the phone.

NOW ELIZA WAS COLD. SICK TO HER STOMACH AGAIN, BUT mostly cold. She felt the wind, and she smelled the sea. The salty tang chilly in her mouth and nose, her lungs—but refreshing her, getting rid of that sickly sweet smell and taste.

She made her body as limp as a rolled carpet, lying on the hard floor as they bumped along. The blindfold had been pulled back down over her face, and they had replaced the duct tape over her mouth; she could barely breathe.

Their voices were low, and she tried to tell how many they were—men, women? A man, just one, or two? And someone else, a woman sounding anxious, afraid...

And then, suddenly, she remembered Mr. Boland!

The memory hazy, swimming back to her from the predrugged past...Mr. Boland coming to her door at home, just as she'd been about to call the police. Maybe Mr. Boland had seen these people take her, maybe, even now, help—her father, the police—was on the way...

Unless—no...it couldn't be...she refused to believe, even though the voices sounded so familiar, so incredibly familiar...It was him...no—how could it be? Someone who knew her? Who had always been so nice to her?

"Maybe I shouldn't have listened to you at all. Maybe I shouldn't listen to you now," Mr. Boland said.

Just let me go, Eliza begged silently. *Let me go home*...

"I know your thoughts on the matter, so please keep them to yourself. We already have two to answer for—you know that, don't you? Have you counted lately?"

Two? Eliza wondered. What did that mean? Her heart was beating so hard, she prayed Mr. Boland and the woman wouldn't hear it. She strained her ears, wanting to hear the voices one more time, inwardly begging for mercy, and terrified that she'd hear that familiar voice again—yet, at the same time, hoping—

"Then what will we do?"

"We'll drive around, and then we'll go to the bridge."

"The bridge? The same one as ... McCabe?"

"Isn't that what we decided? The tide is fast there—"

"I know, but—"

"Don't lose your nerve. Stay cool here. She's the only one who has seen anything. As long as we keep our heads and don't let them divide us, we'll be fine. She's still the only witness, right?"

Eliza lay still. Her eyes filled with tears.

She shivered, trying to block out their words. The least they could have done was covered her up with a blanket. You didn't just lay a sleeping person on a cold van floor without placing a blanket over her. Even if she hadn't heard their words, if she were better able to push them from her mind, she would know that they cared so little about her that they were going to kill her.

Mr. Boland had called her in the dark, through her own window, had tried to get her to climb outside, saying her mother wanted her ...

Eliza squeezed her eyes tight and gulped on her tears, knowing that she was lying in a maroon van, the blood-colored van; she knew now that it was dark red and not dark blue or dark green, and she knew she had seen it somewhere before, somewhere before that she couldn't remember, and she shuddered to think that she was riding in the same dark red van that had killed her mother.

With the people who had whispered in the night that her mother wanted her ...

THE POLICE CAR DROVE UP GRANITE STREET, STROBE lights reflected in the flat, black calm of the Mystic River. Followed by an unmarked sedan it glided into the Connollys' driveway, its presence a stark contrast to the sea captain's architecture and a reminder that no house is so gracious that it can't be touched by trouble.

Bay sat in the living room, remembering how just six months ago the police had entered her peaceful life one hot summer day and changed everything forever. The memories raced through her mind as she sat beside Dan and tried to help him get through this.

Two detectives, Ana Rivera and Martha Keller, sat opposite them, watching Dan intently as Rivera asked questions. Bay had an uneasy feeling in her stomach: Missing children always made police suspect the fathers. Bay inched closer to him on the sofa.

"Tell me her name and age," Detective Rivera said.

"Eliza Day Connolly," Dan answered. "She's almost thirteen."

"And you came home from work at your regular time, and she wasn't here?"

"No," Dan said. "I was actually a little late. I had stopped by Bay's house—"

"Bay?"

"That's me," Bay said. "Bay McCabe. I live in Black Hall. The Hubbard's Point area."

The look of recognition was unmistakable. Both detectives registered the name; realizing that "McCabe" was probably notorious to law enforcement agencies from Black Hall to Westerly and beyond, Bay felt herself blush.

"My daughter is Eliza's friend, and she told us that Eliza had tried to call her at about four forty-five. When Annie picked up, the phone was dead, but caller ID registered this number. That worried Annie, and she told us—"

"Why would that specifically 'worry' Annie?" Detective Rivera asked. "Maybe Eliza changed her mind; maybe something came on TV that she wanted to see, or—"

"But she wasn't here, when we arrived," Dan said, a thread of panic beneath his trying-to-be-patient demeanor. "That's the point. No matter what distracted her, she's not here."

"What I'm asking," the detective said calmly, "is there a reason that her friend would instantly worry? Something about Eliza that would put her at risk?"

Dan took a breath, exhaling long and hard, and Bay knew how devastatingly hard this was for him, to lay Eliza's life and history out for these strangers to see.

"She's very sensitive," he said. "Her mother died last year, and Eliza has had a very hard time with it."

The detectives were silent, waiting. Bay could see him trying to gather his thoughts, not wanting to betray his daughter by revealing anything too private. But Bay saw compassion in their eyes.

"We know this is difficult, Mr. Connolly," Detective Keller said. "Please tell us what you can."

"Tell them, Danny," Bay said, encouraging him, staring into his eyes as he turned to look at her. "So they can find Eliza."

"She's been hospitalized," Dan said. "At Banquo, in Massachusetts. It's a psychiatric hospital ..."

"Yes, a very good one," Detective Rivera said kindly.

"She witnessed her mother's accident," Dan said. "And she was traumatized. She's been diagnosed with P.T.S.D. and D.I.D."

"Dissociative Identity Disorder," Detective Keller said. "Does she have multiple personalities?"

"No. But she dissociates. Just shuts down and goes inside ... She's very imaginative. Once she thought—"

he stopped, looking toward the stairs, then at Bay. "Once in October she thought she heard strangers—'evil people,' she called them—at her window. Saying that her mother wanted her. I checked—"

"What did you find?"

Danny shook his head. "Nothing. Scratches on the window screen—but they were made by tree branches."

"Which window?" Detective Rivera asked.

"Her bedroom," he said. "Upstairs, on the left. The window just beside her bed."

The detective gestured for one of the uniformed officers to go up and check.

"Has she ever run away before?"

Dan shook his head. "The opposite. She's very cautious about going out. She talks about wanting to live in a cloister. Home is her favorite place to be, except for going to Hubbard's Point to see Annie."

"Is it possible she is on her way over there now?"

"No, she would need a ride."

"Might she have decided she needs to go back to the hospital?" Detective Keller asked. "And made her way up there?"

"No. She would have told me," Dan said.

"Kids have secrets from their parents," Detective Rivera said. "It's nothing personal, it's just a fact of life. Could she be seeing someone you don't want her to see? Or could there be drugs?"

"No," Dan said. "To both. Eliza is very . . . very special. She's fragile; she doesn't go out after school. Getting her to even *go* to school is hard. That's one reason," he glanced at Bay, "I've been so grateful for her friendship with Annie."

"Drugs?" Keller asked again.

"No," he said.

"I hate to ask you this," Rivera said. "Because I know it will cause you pain to hear it, but—has Eliza ever talked about or attempted suicide?"

At that, Bay saw Dan clasp his hands, staring down at them for a long time. Bay pictured the scars she had seen on Eliza's wrists, and she knew there were many more she hadn't seen.

"She has," Dan said, his voice strangled. "She began to talk about it after her mother's death."

"So it's possible," Detective Rivera said gently, but with urgency, "that she might be thinking of it now."

"I don't know," Dan said. "I . . . It's possible."

Detective Rivera nodded, and she stood up and walked into the hall, where Bay heard her talking to the two police officers. Detective Keller leaned forward. "Has she ever mentioned ways she would do it?"

Dan shook his head. "She cuts herself," he said quietly.

"Oh . . . I'm sorry."

"I told her if she did it again, I'd send her back to the hospital," he said, and his eyes filled with tears. "She's so beautiful. She has such incredible beauty, inside and out, and she wants to mutilate herself. She thinks she's ugly . . . and her mother's death left her so full of pain, she has to let it out."

"We'll find her," Detective Keller said.

But it was as if her words meant nothing, carried no weight. As Bay watched Dan hold in the silent sobs, she felt him thinking that his daughter had already been lost, or taken from him, in so many important ways; that her grief was so heavy, that it was dragging her down somewhere he could never reach. Bay reached for his hand and held it.

When Detective Rivera walked back into the room, she had a different look on her face: sharp, edgy, and galvanized. Joe Holmes accompanied her. Detective Keller looked up, alert to his presence and Rivera's change of attitude. Police radios crackled in the hallway.

"I got the word," Joe said.

"If someone came to the door, would Eliza open it?" Detective Rivera asked.

"I hope not; I don't think so," Dan said. "Unless she knew them. Why?"

"Have you had any plumbing repairs recently? Any heating system breakdowns?"

"No," Dan said, standing up, catching the sense of something new in the room. Bay heard the police in the hallway calling for the forensics squad. "What are you talking about?"

"The officers found duct tape outside, in the bushes. Do you know how it could have gotten there?"

"No, I don't."

"Do you own any?" Joe asked.

"At the shop, in New London," he said. "Not here."

"Exactly what did you find when you walked into your house," Detective Rivera asked sharply, "that was different, unexpected?"

"The door was unlocked," Dan said. "The phone was off the hook. Eliza had started eating, but not finished."

"And the cup, Dan," Bay reminded him.

"Right—and her silver cup is missing."

"Her silver cup?"

"It's priceless, almost. Paul Revere made it; it plays a part in a state legend, almost like the Charter Oak. It belongs in a museum, but her mother gave it to her, and Eliza won't let it leave the house."

"And the cup was here when you left for work this morning?"

Dan shrugged. "I don't know. I assume so. It reminded

both me and Eliza so much of Charlie—her mother—
that we've left it in the cupboard all this time. I haven't
even looked at it—Eliza either, as far as I know—since
just before Charlie died."

"Describe the cup," Detective Rivera said, writing it
down.

"You think someone took it?" Dan asked, growing agitated. "That's what happened?"

"We're not sure," the detective replied. "But the duct
tape makes us think someone might have taken your
daughter."

TARA HELD DOWN THE FORT WITH THE KIDS, WHILE BAY
stayed with Dan Connolly and tried to help him from going crazy. Tara could only imagine. A lifetime, so far—
and, at a little past forty, looking like forever—of not
having kids left her wondering what true parenthood
must be like. She experienced the blessings of faux parenthood . . . even faux aunthood . . . through her relationship with Bay and her kids.

Tara had loved Annie, Billy, and Pegeen (but secretly,
especially, her goddaughter Annie) since their births.
She had helped Bay nurse them through colic, chicken
pox, poison ivy, jellyfish stings. Many nights, baby-
sitting, she would rock them back to sleep after nightmares.

But at the end of the day—or night—she always got to
go home. Kiss the children good-bye, close the door behind her, and enter her own single paradise of solitude,
pedicures, and a secret passion for reruns of *I Dream of
Jeannie*.

But that didn't keep her from empathizing to the point
of heartache with Danny right now. She loved Bay's kids

so much, it was as if she had children herself. She couldn't imagine what he was going through, and she was so glad he had Bay there with him.

It made her long for Joe. But with Eliza missing, and the hours ticking by without word, she knew he was right where he belonged: at Dan Connolly's house in Mystic.

And she was really glad she'd been the one to call him in.

31

IT WAS PROBABLY ALMOST MIDNIGHT NOW.

Although there were no windows or clocks in the back of the van, although she hadn't worn a watch, Eliza could feel the time passing and sensed that it was very late, and that they had stopped moving.

Why were they keeping her alive?

Her face felt sore and swollen, from where she had fallen, and she couldn't stop touching her broken front teeth with her tongue. She nearly cried every time she thought of her chipped teeth, but her mouth was covered with duct tape, and crying made her gag, so she held back the tears. She knew she was lucky to still be alive.

She prayed all night long. Deep in the darkness, she had felt her mother with her, in the van that had killed her, wrapping Eliza in her arms, in her angel wings, to keep her warm. She was sure that if her mother hadn't come, she would already be dead. Her mother was keeping the murderers from killing her.

Her mother was saving her life, and from that Eliza discovered within herself a huge, overriding desire to live. Now that she was faced with terror, she knew she had to get out of it alive. She would do *anything* to survive this and see them all brought to justice.

Suddenly, the thought of suicide seemed terrible, self-ish, and frivolous—as alien to her spirit as anything she could imagine. Eliza wanted to live, and she prayed to God that she could make it.

DAN CONNOLLY HAD EXPERIENCED HEARTACHE, GRIEF, and terror before. His parents had been good, kind people, and they had both died too young. Charlie's death had left him feeling like a specter, a lost soul. And he had been desperately worried about Eliza since then. But nothing compared to what he felt now, as if he had been ripped apart, limbs torn off his body by wild animals. He thought he understood the idea of shark attack, in slow motion.

Eliza was his baby. She was part of him and he was part of her. He had held her in the moment of her birth—first Charlie, then him. From the instant he'd seen her face, looked into her eyes, Dan had been locked into the kind of love that never quit, that had him for life, that regardless of the responsibility and intensity, he wouldn't change for anything.

The police came and went: Detectives Rivera and Keller, members of their squad, and forensics experts, as well as Joe Holmes. Throughout the night, various bits of information came through: the duct tape had been part of a lot sold to the maintenance department at Shoreline Bank.

No unknown fingerprints had turned up on the

house's doorknob or porch railings, but Joe seemed to believe that the scratches on Eliza's screen hadn't been made by branches at all, but by a knife trying to pry apart the frame. He thought the tree had been used to get up on the roof, and the police were combing the area for any clue that might still be left behind.

Bay stayed right by Dan's side.

"You must want to get home," he said, checking his watch at eleven-thirty.

"I'm not leaving," she said.

Their eyes met and held. He saw in hers all the care and affection she'd had for him all those years ago, but clouded now with pain. She put her arms around him and he buried his head in her shoulder, feeling that he was holding on to her for dear life.

"Think of this, Dan—how strong she is. How much she's been through already. And how much you love her—she knows that."

"Do you think she does?"

"I know she does," Bay said, still holding him. "You're the most important person in her world."

"Her mother used to be," Dan said. As he said those words, he imagined yet again Eliza seeing Charlie get hit by that van, and he flinched. The trauma had nearly killed his little girl—how could he expect her to withstand whatever she was going through right now?

Bay didn't respond, but kept her arms around him, gently stroking the back of his head.

"She loved Charlie so much," Dan said. "Her mother never let her down. God, I can't help thinking that this wouldn't be happening if I had been more together myself these past few years. Charlie was so steady—she never stepped off the path, did anything wrong. She was just so upstanding, with such integrity. And Eliza saw her that way. She never—"

"Eliza *didn't* see her that way," Bay said, releasing Dan, stepping back. Her voice was angry, her eyes filled with tears.

"What do you mean? Yes, she did. She—"

"NO, Dan," Bay said, a sob ripping from her chest. "She didn't! She didn't see her mother that way at ALL!"

The police were all over the first floor, so Dan took Bay's hand and led her upstairs into his bedroom, the room he'd shared with Charlie. He led her to the edge of the bed, and they sat down together, Bay crying heavily. Now it was Dan's turn to hold her, his right arm around her slender shoulders, his left hand trying to tilt her chin up, to get her to look him in the eyes.

"Tell me, Bay. Please."

"I'm sorry, Dan," she cried. "I shouldn't have said anything. Not tonight, at least . . ."

"Well, it's too late for that. You might as well finish what you started. What were you trying to say about Eliza and her mother?"

"Eliza didn't idolize Charlie. She didn't see her as someone with integrity at all."

"Bay, she did."

"NO, Dan. She didn't. She saw her mother kissing Sean!"

"What?"

"She saw Charlie kissing my husband. They thought she was asleep in the back seat of the car."

"Eliza told you this?" Dan asked. He felt numb, cold inside.

"No. She told Annie."

"And Annie told you."

"Yes. That's supposed to be how it works. The child

turns to the parent for love and comfort—not deception and betrayal! I'm sorry, Dan, but I hate her. I hate her for kissing Sean, for letting Eliza see, for making you—" She stopped short.

"Tell me," he whispered, holding Bay even tighter now, his mouth against her hair. "Please tell me what you were going to say."

"For making you feel you were doing something wrong," she said, with such wrenching sobs her whole body shook. "For making you feel you weren't enough. That you weren't making her happy. That if only you found that magical combination, if only you could guess the words she wanted to hear, the place she wanted to go ... if only you touched her the way she wanted to be touched ..."

Dan knew that Bay was talking about herself and her own husband, but he related to every word, took it in and processed it through his heart and soul, and knew that she and he had been in the same place, at least during that last year, and not even known it.

"I'm sorry he did that to you," Dan said. "Sean ..."

"And I'm sorry Charlie did it to you."

"How did I not figure it out? Why didn't Eliza say something?"

"You didn't figure it out," Bay said, her voice raw, "because you trust. You love with your whole heart and mind."

"I do," he said, looking down at the top of her head, at her golden red hair glinting in the cold November light, wishing she'd look up into his eyes.

"And Eliza didn't say anything because she didn't want you to be hurt more than you already were. The kids have protected me more than I can stand to know."

"Do you know when it happened?"

Bay shook her head. "Not long before Charlie died, is the impression I have. You can ask Eliza."

What if he never had the chance?

Bay saw the pain in his eyes and shook her head. "Don't think that," she said, and with tears streaking her face and mouth, she reached up to touch the side of his face, slid her hand around the back of his neck, and kissed him on the lips.

The kiss was wild and alive, life-giving and miraculous. Dan clutched Bay with every ounce of strength he had, feeling her hands on his back, sliding up under his sweater as if she had to touch his skin, had to get as close as possible to his heart and blood and bones.

When they walked back downstairs, they found Joe Holmes in the dining room. As he heard them enter the room, he pointed at the wooden china cupboard. "Is this where Eliza's silver cup was stored?" he asked.

"Yes," Dan said. "I told Detective Rivera—the cup was made by Paul Revere. It belongs in a museum. Is that why they, whoever, took Eliza?"

"It could have been bought at Walmart," Joe said grimly. "The value had nothing to do with who made it, how old it is."

"What do you mean?" Dan asked. "Of course it does. Why else risk, justify, taking a child? What else could explain—"

Joe shook his head; he seemed impatient, but his eyes were bright.

"The cup is connected to her disappearance," he said. "It's connected. But it's incidental."

"How is it connected?"

"We've known since the night of the Pumpkin Ball who we were after," he said, staring at Bay. "Tara helped me figure it out. We were at the Bolands' house, looking at all his trophies, and she said that he and Sean might well have played sports against each other."

"They grew up in different parts of the state," Bay said. "Mark lived here on the shoreline; Sean only summered here. He grew up in New Britain. The schools were in different leagues."

"Yes," Joe said. "Except for the state championships."

"The time it counts most," Dan said.

"Basketball, their senior year," Joe said. "Their teams made it to the state finals, Gampel Pavilion at UConn. Mark Boland and Sean McCabe, head to head on the court. We went back and read the old clippings."

"Is Mark the other inside man?" Bay cried. "Did Sean talk him into embezzling from clients, too?"

Joe shook his head. "It was the other way around," he said. "Boland had been doing it for years at Anchor Trust, and he'd never gotten caught. Never left any hint of a paper trail. Not one complaint, not even a suspicion. He was very, very good at covering his tracks—the forensic accountants are just starting to uncover them now. He arrived at Shoreline, and turned the whole thing into a game."

"With Sean?" Bay asked, looking shocked.

Joe nodded. "A big competition. Like the state finals, all over again."

Bay thought of all the years she'd watched Sean playing basketball, football, baseball, fighting to the death just to win the game. Why hadn't Sean told her about him and Mark being rivals? Because his anger over the promotion had been too great, she supposed.

"To see who could make the most money," Danny said.

"Who could conquer the most accounts," Joe said. "And every time one of them succeeded, there had to be a prize..."

"The silver cups," Bay said.

"Yes, but there was an even bigger prize," Joe said, reaching into the cupboard, taking out one of Eliza's little blue teacups.

"I don't get it," Danny said, frowning.

"The accounts," Joe said. "All the money they stole. There was just one witness who could put them away. Ed."

"Ed?" Bay asked, remembering the notations on Sean's manila folder, his doodles of the truck and . . .

"I assumed 'Ed' was a man," Joe said. "A banker, or maybe a client. I never thought—"

"Eliza," Bay gasped, her eyes falling on the monogram, so delicately painted on the teacups and teapot: *ED.* "Eliza Day!"

WHO WOULD HAVE EXPECTED THAT THE VALUE OF ONE OF the trophies would have exceeded some of the other spoils? The Eliza Day trust had come with quite a nice prize: a silver cup forged by Paul Revere. The day Sean had started using the trust as a way to hide and move money, he had taken the cup from the Connolly home. Alise Boland thought again how stupid he had been, as they waited for the tide to rise.

Who knows how he had talked his way in—that was Sean. Perhaps he had seduced Charlotte; or perhaps she thought she was seducing him. And although Charlotte Connolly hadn't caught the shifting of funds in the family trust, she had most certainly noticed that Sean McCabe had stolen her daughter's silver cup.

Ironic, to have an icon from someone so connected with freedom. Because that was what the whole thing had started off to be: a way to get free, to have more, to rise

above the rest of the world's worker bees. To take what
people wouldn't even miss... and hadn't, for so long.

But then Charlotte had threatened to call the police,
and just as all that was finally dying down, Fiona had
caught Sean's slip with the Ephraim account. Things
were falling apart.

If only people had been more careful. No one would
have had to die. There could have been ways to avoid
this entire nightmare. When everything was considered,
a lot of the blame had to go to Fiona. She had never fit in,
could never have been invited to join. In fact, wouldn't
she be surprised to know that Mark had taken money
from her very own money market fund?

That had rated the taking of her horse show trophy.

Sean had laughed at that—been amazed by Mark's au-
dacity. That was more Sean's style. But Sean's daring extended only to sports and money. When he learned that
the child had witnessed her mother's murder, was the *only*
witness, he folded.

His soul-searching had started with Charlotte's death,
and led to a few foolish attempts to pay back some of his
smaller raids on various accounts. But it wasn't until the
problem of what to do about the girl began to grow...
until she emerged from the hospital... that Sean had
really begun to fall apart.

He swore he'd protect her if they tried... well, if they
tried this.

And that had been his downfall. Mark required absolute commitment; there was too much riding on this.
He demanded total loyalty, and when Sean was adamant,
they all knew it was only a matter of time. Mark knew
that no witness could be overlooked; Sean should have
known that, too.

This night had been a long time coming. First Sean

had gotten in the way, and had had to be killed. It was too bad, but unavoidable. Alise herself had tried to get Dan Connolly into the circle, tie him in as a way of assuring his daughter's silence, by phoning him, floating Sean's name out there—if Connolly had had any second thoughts about the money he was passing up, he would have taken the bait. But he didn't—signing his own daughter's death warrant.

Mark and Sean had insisted on considering it a game. But Alise knew that that was just their way of making themselves feel better. They wanted the boyhood lie: If they were playing for trophies, it really didn't count. They stole from their richest clients, the ones who would never notice. Sean, at his most exuberant, had called Mark "Robin Hood."

But in the end, what was it all for? Why had Charlotte had to be killed, and why had Sean himself ultimately had to be stopped, and why was Eliza Day Connolly about to die?

Wealth.

That's all.

Wealth—the pursuit of it, the protection of it. Big houses cost money, and so did antiques and artworks, and fine cars, and precious jewels. Not everyone was born with such things. And not everyone wanted them, as hard as that was to believe. Mark had taken such good care until now; he could be excused his boyish need to reward himself and his "teammates" with silver. Now, as the tide rose and the time arrived to drown the girl, it was time to protect the gold.

IT WAS SO LATE, AND HER MOTHER WAS STILL AT MR. CON-nolly's. Annie felt so afraid for Eliza. Whatever was happening, she knew it was bad, and no matter how much Aunt Tara stroked her hair and sang lullabies, Annie couldn't fall asleep.

"Where could she be?" she asked Tara.

"I don't know, honey. Everyone's looking for her, though. Joe, the police..."

"What if they don't find her?"

"We have to believe they will. We have to send her our love, so she can grab on to it and come home to us."

"Love," Annie said, as if it was the first time she'd ever said the word.

"It's the most there is," Tara said. "Eliza knows that. Wherever she is, she'll be able to feel our love for her."

"But I still don't see how that can help."

"Do you believe in guardian angels, Annie?"

Annie shrugged, not wanting to hurt Tara's feelings. Angels seemed like nice creatures in stories.

"I think you do, Annie. I know your mom does. And so do I. Our grandmothers told us about them."

"But what can they do?" Annie asked, her voice high and thin. Outside the window, all the stars were out. The moon was new and the sky was very dark. Owls migrating through Hubbard's Point, as they did every November, flew out from the oaks, calling on the hunt. "What can spirits do, when we're right here on earth? We're here; we should be able to save the people we love!"

Tara held her, as if she knew that Annie was crying about her father, about her worst nightmare coming true with the news of his death.

"We can do a lot," Tara said, "and we can turn to them for help."

"Do you really believe that?" Annie asked.

"I really believe that. And it helps to know that Joe and the police are looking, too," Tara said. "Eliza is a survivor, Annie. She has a light inside her. We've all seen it, and we love her for it."

"We do," Annie whispered.

Then an owl called again, from the top of the tallest pine, and that seemed like a signal that something was about to happen. Tara kissed her, and Annie tried to breathe. She thought of Eliza out there in the night, somewhere on this rocky coastline of coves and bays, cold ground covered with fallen leaves and pine needles, out there in the starlit darkness.

Annie's small wooden boat was on the bedside table; she stared at it now, thinking of how she had given it to her father, so he would know who to row home to. She closed her eyes and thought of Eliza and the light within.

And then, she wasn't sure why, she reached for her small wooden boat and gave it a little shake. That rattle was still there.

AT HOME, DAN SAT ON THE SOFA, HIS ARM AROUND BAY, who slept with her head on his shoulder. It was so late, and Eliza was out in the night. He stared at the phone, as if he could will it to ring. Joe had told him to stay home, by the phone, but every muscle in his body ached to be out searching for his daughter.

His thoughts, in the silence, were cacophonous. He was the Monday-morning quarterback of his own life, trying to figure out what he could have done differently. Holding Bay, he stared at Charlie's portrait, the painting of his unhappy wife. They were Eliza's parents, keeping vigil together.

Charlie . . . She had grown up so very privileged. Charlie knew she was an aristocrat. Her family had had money for generations; they gave away more in a year than some people make in a lifetime. She had an unassailable sense of superiority—never overtly snobby, but very reserved. Isolated.

That's how Dan had seen her when they'd first gotten to know each other, the year after he had worked at Hubbard's Point. Her uncle had hired him to restore a beautiful old wooden yacht, a Concordia yawl. All work was to be done at a yard in Stonington, just across the harbor from Charlie's house. Mansion, really. It was a huge white Colonial with outbuildings and a dock. Dan had started noticing her every day: always alone, always self-contained.

One day, on his lunch hour, he pulled a dinghy down to the water and rowed across. He'd started viewing her as a poor little rich girl, and he thought he'd give her a treat: take her for a boat ride.

He still remembered pulling up to the dock, calling across the broad green lawn, asking her if he could take her for a row. And he could picture her carefully laying her book on the garden bench, smoothing her slacks, and walking down to the water. He had offered her his hand, to help her into the boat, but she didn't take it.

Almost amused, she climbed in herself. And she let him row her to the end of the harbor and back. The day was bright and clear, with fish jumping in the cove and swans swimming around the moorings. He still remembered the day perfectly; and he recalled the sense that Charlie considered that she was giving him the pleasure of her company.

That feeling never really left him.

He had married her—maybe he'd been her chance at limited rebellion. Don't marry the boatyard owner; marry the employee and give him a boatyard to run. What better way to own a person?

He had never given up loving her, trying to make her

happy. And deep down, wanting her to love him more than she did, to accept him as her equal. But Charlie had never really had any equals. Everywhere she went, people knew her as the heir to Day Consolidated. If they didn't, five minutes in her presence made them realize that she was somebody different. Somebody who epitomized the expression "born with a silver spoon in her mouth." And it had been Dan's role as her husband, and as her employee, to protect her. To take care of his poor little rich girl.

Dan had wondered what it meant that last year, that Charlie had suddenly, for the first time in their marriage, gotten very interested in something outside herself, outside her home. She had become intrigued with the bank and banking. She began to talk about going back to school for an MBA.

So many days in a row, she had gone to Shoreline Bank, to ask in-depth questions about her accounts, about her and Eliza's trust. After so many years of letting others manage her life—her fortune—Charlie had started taking charge.

While Dan had felt happy to see her truly animated by something, he had also felt her pulling away. It had confused and hurt him in small ways—sometimes he'd come home and find her talking on the phone, pad and pen ready, taking more notes. Or had the learning and studying been just a smokescreen? Had his wife been covering up an affair with Sean McCabe?

Knowing that they had kissed made Dan think it was a little of both. At the boatyard, he dealt with the absolutes of marine architecture: center of gravity, length overall, beam, draft. In love, in marriage, there were no such things. It was all a gray area, like sailing in the fog.

But sailing in the fog can be beautiful, he thought, holding Bay. *You sense your way home; you smell the pines on-shore, listen for the bell buoys, feel the wind shift and drop as you near land.*

If only he and Charlie had done more of that with each other. Maybe if they'd had a better marriage, Charlie would still be alive, and Eliza would still be home.

But that made him hold Bay even tighter. She was so straightforward and real, and she seemed to need—with the same imperative that she needed to breathe—to tell the truth about what was in her heart.

Dan prayed for the chance to do more of that—with Bay, with Eliza. He wanted the chance to be the best father on earth to his daughter. He wanted to help her get stronger, to help her see how wonderful she was. To never want to hurt herself again.

Thinking of her out there somewhere, his guts twisted. He had the sense of time draining away, of Eliza in horrible danger. The clock was ticking in his head. The world, even the shoreline, was such a big place to search. If only he had some idea where to start . . .

32

DID THEY THINK SHE WAS ASLEEP? OR HAD THEY
just decided to stop thinking about her at all?

The people in the front were just driving quietly
along, waiting for something. But what? So many questions, and Eliza was haunted by all of them. She lay still,
her ear folded over on itself, aching under her head. Vi-
sions of a maroon van filled her mind. She saw it hit her
mother, her mother's blood on the road.

And then she saw the van again, in a flash, just a
whoosh as it visited her memory. Where had she seen it
before?

The memory came in pieces. Eliza, her mother, shopping on a Saturday. They had had lunch at the Sail Loft
Café, then gone to Hawthorne. Eliza had loved poking
around in the boutiques, trying on a bright yellow
sweater, getting a new pair of shoes. Her mother had
wanted to look at house things...

Shiny copper pans and cast-iron skillets in one store,

embroidered pillows and fancy lampshades in another, and then, in the last place, squares of tile and swatches of fabric...a designer's studio...a place people went to have their houses designed and decorated.

Eliza blinked under the blindfold. She could see her mother, hear the surprise in her voice. "Oh, I didn't know that this was your business!"

And the designer—so petite and stylish, dressed in a black suit, with pretty blond hair and gold earrings— smiling to see them, letting Mom look through some fabric samples, asking Eliza what she thought of a certain wall sconce.

"Do you like this one?" the woman had asked, holding up a brass lantern, then lowering it and raising up a pewter candlestick with a black shade, "or this one?"

"I like the lantern," Eliza said.

"So do I!" the woman had said, smiling brightly. "What excellent taste you have! Charlie, you have a charming daughter."

Eliza's mother had nodded, smiled, and said "Thank you," as she'd continued looking at the squares of material. The shop had seemed so cozy and feminine, fun and creative, and the woman had looked so dainty; and right now Eliza was remembering how her mother had said, "I've been spending so much time at the bank; both Mark and Sean have been so helpful. I've imagined going back to school, somehow getting into finance...but then I come in here, and I think how great it would be to do *this...*"

And Eliza had felt curious, hearing that her mother wanted to change the things in her life—not scared, not worried, but just curious, because she had never heard her mother say anything like that before.

"This?" The woman had smiled.

"Yes—surrounded by such pretty things, so much beauty."

The woman had made a muscle with one arm and pointed out the window with her other hand. "That's what the job is really about," she said. "Lugging things around. Sample books, bolts of fabric, antique armoires, paintings—I'm really just a workhorse."

And Eliza and her mother had leaned over, to look out the window, to see what the woman was pointing at, and there it was, sitting in the driveway behind her shop, in front of a red barn.

A maroon van.

Eliza moaned as she remembered.

"Did you hear that?" the man's voice asked. "How much longer are we going to wait? Christ, Alise."

"I know, I know," the woman's voice replied.

"We should have just done it right away. Like the others."

"The others were different," she said. "The others we didn't have to take from their houses."

"So, what—you're losing your nerve?"

"Aren't you?"

Be human, Eliza begged silently. *Lose your nerve.* Now that she could see the woman's face, her blond hair, her shop with its pretty colors and fabrics and objects, now that Eliza could hear the woman talking to her mother, telling her how charming Eliza was, now that Eliza remembered her name, *Alise*, and the name of her business, *Boland Design*, it was all so different.

"Yes, I am," Mark said.

"Well, you can't afford to," Alise said. "And neither can I."

"The longer we wait—" Mark said.

"I know," Alise snapped. "I know, I know. Don't talk about it."

"That will make it go away? Make the problem disappear?"

I'm not a problem, I'm a girl, Eliza thought, struggling behind the duct tape. Knowing if she could talk to them, make her hear them, she could get them to see this was a mistake. She wouldn't tell; they wouldn't have to go to jail.

"Nothing can make this problem go away," Alise said. "That's what we're dealing with. We started something that used to be so simple. It was all paper till Sean screwed up!"

"She's not paper," Mark said.

"I know that. Jesus! That's what's making this so—impossible."

Eliza heard someone shifting in the front seat; turning around to look at her as the van kept moving. Couldn't they see that she was a real live person, her father's daughter? She raised her bound feet, let them clang to the van floor.

"Christ, I can't take this anymore," Mark said.

"What's the alternative?" Alise asked sharply. "Just pull yourself together. We'll do it now, okay? We're almost there; the tide is high enough."

"This isn't like Sean," Mark said. "She's not bleeding to death—"

"That part was an accident," Alise said. "Who could have expected him to fight like that?"

"We should have just left him on the boat," Mark said bitterly. "He would have died there, and no one would have thought it was anything."

"Except maybe he wouldn't have. Remember the facts, okay? He was strong, he was still conscious. He was talking about this one here—" Eliza could almost feel herself being pointed at.

"She's a kid," Mark said, lowering his voice.

"Now you're sounding like Sean. Do you want to end up in prison?"

"No."

"Then..."

Eliza had been holding herself back, afraid of annoying them, but suddenly the logic and reason part of her brain shut off, and the panic and terror part took over and she began kicking and thrashing, screaming behind the sticky slimy patch of duct tape.

"Put an end to this," Mark said. "Jesus, I can't take this anymore."

"Clear your head," Alise said, and she must have opened her window, because suddenly Eliza felt a blast of cold air, a wonderful, icy, refreshing gust of fresh air swirling through the closed-in horrible maroon death van as it kept moving, but slowly, slowly.

ANNIE WENT DOWNSTAIRS, TO THE KITCHEN TABLE. SHE had made the model right here; there was a cabinet filled with scissors, glue, paper, paint—craft things to keep the family busy on rainy days.

She shook her small model dory, and it rattled again. But she had built the boat herself, entirely of wood and glue; there were no nails or any other moving parts.

She examined the boat, and all was exactly as she had built it: not a seam, not a frame, not a board was out of place.

The clock read twelve-twelve. Twelve minutes past midnight.

She tipped the boat to port, heard something roll and

hit the left side; then she tipped it to starboard, heard the same something hit the right side.

She had built the model with strips of balsa glued to fine frames, and she had inserted a cutout bottom, carefully made to fit directly inside the boat itself and provide a sturdy deck. Now, examining it under the bright kitchen light, she saw little scratches in the paint—as if someone, at one time, had tried to pry the bottom up.

"What are you doing there?" Tara asked, coming into the kitchen.

"Just trying to figure something out," Annie said, concentrating. Tara watched for a few seconds, then went to the stove and put the kettle on.

"Want some tea?" Tara asked.

"No, thanks," Annie said, although she felt comforted by the question.

She reached into the craft cabinet for the long tweezers Billy used to use during the two months—more like two minutes—that he was a stamp collector. He'd gotten a starter kit for Christmas one year, and he was bound and determined to become a philatelist. Annie almost laughed now, remembering how he couldn't even pronounce the word, but how he had saved every stamp on every letter that came to the house.

His long tweezers came in handy now, though. Annie used them to loosen the tiny seats, to remove them, and to pry up the boat's deck. She was afraid the piece of balsa, just eight inches long and pointed at one end, flat at the other, would break, so she worked very slowly and carefully.

But she did it. She lifted the deck out of the boat, and looking at what was hidden beneath, gasped. Tears filled her eyes at the sight of the small gray-blue periwinkle shell, at the folded note in her father's handwriting.

"What is it?" Tara asked, leaning over to see.

"Something from Daddy," Annie whispered.

"Do you want me to read it for you?" Tara asked, as Annie unfolded the paper.

But Annie, seeing the first words, shook her head. "No," she said. "It's to me. I'll read it." And she did, out loud.

"*Dear Annie,*

You know that bankers write a lot of letters, but this is the hardest letter I've ever written in my life. Maybe because I'm writing it to one of the people I love the most—there are four of you: you, Billy, Peggy, and your mom. No man ever had a better family. And no man ever screwed it up more. Maybe I can still fix things, make them right.

I have a lot on my mind, and you're the one I'm going to tell it to. Annie, I hope you never have to read this letter. Because if you're reading it, it means I'm gone. I can't imagine what you and everyone must be thinking. But I hope what I have to say here will help you understand—and help the others, too. I'm putting this letter into your boat, and leaving it with Dan Connolly. I'm looking at this boat you made me, knowing how much I love you. I'm going to leave it somewhere safe, with someone who will give it back to you.

The reason I'm writing to you is that you're my oldest daughter, and right now I'm thinking about someone else's daughter. Her name is Eliza. She's the daughter of an old friend of your mother's, and she's on my mind all the time now. She's the girl in all my thoughts and fears because she's in danger. Something I did put her there.

I did some things I'm not proud of. I got tempted at
the bank, made some very bad choices. People trusted
me, including my own family, and I destroyed that
trust. I was greedy, Annie, and I'm not blaming
anyone but myself for that.

Other things, however . . . Mark and Alise Boland
murdered Eliza's mother, Charlotte Connolly. I had
nothing to do with that, Annie—I want you to know
that. But I stayed silent, because I knew that my part
in the embezzlement would come out, and silence is
another way of being involved. Of looking the other
way, making it possible. What I won't make possible is
them hurting Eliza. They want to kill her, because she
witnessed the hit-and-run of her mother. I'm going to
go to the police, to turn them in and—also, myself.
For what I've done at the bank.

There's a cove, down the road from the marina. I'm
sitting there now, in my car. In fact, I walked down to
the edge of the water and found this shell for you. The
blue reminds me of your mother's eyes.

The name of the spot, and you can see it on the
chart, is Alewife Cove. It's an inlet between the Gill
River and the Sound. I'm telling you because it's a
place I love to come and sit. I showed it to the Bolands
once, when we went down to make plans, and they
said it would be a good place to take Eliza. That's
when I knew they were serious.

I'm writing this to you, Annie, hoping that you can
forgive me. When I finish this letter, I'm driving over
to Eliza's father's boatyard, to hide this in your model
boat. That way you won't get it too soon—and maybe
I'll have the chance to make everything right. You
deserve a real rowboat as pretty as the model you made
for me. I finally figured out that I'm the luckiest

*man—father—in the world. I just hope I have the
chance to prove it to you and the others. I love you.*

Love, Dad"

Annie had started out reading the letter out loud, but
midway through she had become choked up with tears,
and by the end she couldn't speak or even read at all, so
Tara had taken over.

Now, sobbing silently, Annie reached out her hand,
and Tara gently put the letter in her fingers. Tara's arms
came around Annie's shoulders, and although Annie was
talking to her dad, she didn't mind that Tara could hear
the words: "We love you, Daddy. We love you, too."

Now Tara left Annie sitting there, holding the letter
and the shell. She took another piece of paper that had
been hidden in the boat—beneath the deck, along with
his note—and went to the phone.

Annie stared at the tiny periwinkle shell, turning it
over and over in her hand.

"Bay?" Tara said. "Is Joe there? He left? Listen to me.
Annie just found a letter from Sean ... Yes, I'm serious ...
she found it in the bottom of her boat, her model boat ...
He had wedged it under the floorboards ... Bay, it's part
confession part something else ... He says they wanted to
kill Eliza ... there, at Alewife Cove ... Do you think—?"

Annie was silent, listening, and so, apparently, was
Tara.

"Go, then," Tara said hurriedly. "I'll get ahold of Joe."

33

AND THEY WEREN'T SURE; AND THEY DIDN'T know, but how could they not check? How could they not get into Dan's truck and, just in case, drive to the Gill River? Bay had called the police; she knew that Tara was calling Joe Holmes.

Dan drove crazily, down the middle of the road, as if his truck was a missile, shooting straight for the Alewife Cove and prepared to take out anything in his way.

"What would they be doing there?" Bay asked, holding on to the door handle. "Why would they have taken Eliza to the same place?"

"Because that's where they killed Sean," Dan said, swerving to pass a car. "Because they know they can do it there."

"They killed Sean," Bay whispered, in shock over the revelation, the confirmation that her husband had been murdered by people they thought were friends. But more intense, immediate, was a growing terror for Eliza's life.

"You know the waters over here better than I do," Dan said, referring to the creeks and coves across the Thames, meandering through the towns west to the Connecticut River. "So you have to tell me where to go."

Bay directed him off the highway at Silver Bay, told him to turn right, toward Black Hall. Her heart was shimmering; it felt hot in her chest and sore, almost skinned, with the unbearable news propelling them forward. She touched her chest, felt pain under her fingertips, thought of Eliza, thought of Annie reading her father's letter, thought of Sean and bowed her head.

"Now where?" Dan asked, his voice a little loud, frantic. He was keeping it together, but just barely.

"Along the river, a quarter mile," she said as she saw the Connecticut gleaming darkly across the narrow strip of land, the river full and black under the starlit sky. "Then left here," she said, "and right just past that boulder..."

Water gave life to water. The Connecticut River was the parent of tributaries, and Long Island Sound provided an inflow to hidden coves. The river was tidal here. It was brackish, the water neither quite fresh nor all salt, but still home to saltwater species—bluefish, weakfish, flounder, fluke. And in winter, seals were sighted, seeking rocks and good fishing.

Bay leaned forward, watching the road, trying to find the right turnoff. She had come down here alone this summer, just once, to see the spot where her husband's life had ended.

"There," she said, pointing at the narrow lane.

Dan turned the truck, and they bounced over a series of potholes. It was quiet, untraveled, back here. In the summer, people sometimes came down for picnics and fishing, and during very cold winters, kids sometimes looked for ice thick enough to skate on. But right now, in the dead of November, there was no one here.

Or maybe there was.

Up ahead, blending into the darkness, was a wine-red van. It was camouflaged by night, but the headlights of Dan's truck picked it out as they came around the corner. Beside the van, like two deer caught in the headlights, were two people, their faces white in the light.

"Where is she?" Dan shouted before he even parked the truck. "Where's Eliza?"

Bay fumbled with the door, shocked despite everything she now knew to see the Bolands here in this tangle of white pines at the edge of this salty cove, in this place where they had already killed her husband.

"Eliza!" Bay screamed.

Alise and Mark ran for the van; Alise jumped inside, and Bay heard the engine start up at the same second she heard Dan's fist smash Mark's jaw.

"Where's Eliza?" Dan shouted, and his punches landed again and again. "Where's my daughter?" The van rumbled to life, the headlights firing on, hanging in the air for a split second as Mark clung to the passenger door, trying to shake free of Dan, crashing onto his face as Alise threw the van into reverse, swung onto the rutted road, and drove away, plunging them into darkness.

But not before—for one brief, God-given second—Bay saw Eliza's face, chalk white, like a shorebird, her ferocious eyes raking the sky, begging the angels to come down from heaven, those eyes reflected in the white headlights of the maroon van, and then the red taillights, before sinking into the dark and brackish cove.

Bay ran for the water. She kicked off her shoes and dropped her jacket on the ground. She didn't think twice. The first jolt was the worst—icy cold frigid water on her toes and then her body and then in her mouth. Her clothes turned into dead weight instantly, anchoring her body, dragging her down into the cove.

Gulping water, spinning then swimming downward, hands flailing around because her eyes were of no use whatsoever; her only vision was coming from somewhere else, either deep inside or high above. It was the vision of the heart—Bay's own, but also Charlie's and Sean's, guiding her, sending her plunging to the very bottom of the cove, this inlet of the Sound and tributary of Gill River, down down down as she used her hands to feel and see, the way lobsters use their antennae.

And she heard silence in her ears, huge, thunderous silence, underwater silence…she had never imagined drowning before, but she was experiencing it now, all but the last breaths of seawater…a few wrong seconds, a desperate drawing in, and it would happen, and it would be all over. She would drown…and Eliza would drown…in this water, salt mixed with fresh mixed with Sean's blood. Her husband had bled into this cove; his car had driven straight to the bottom, his last stop on this earth. The minerals of Sean McCabe's blood had joined these molecules of water.

He was dead and Charlie was dead, but Bay and Dan were alive, and they were both in the water now. And Bay felt moved by the spirits of Charlie and Sean, parents who had tried to live and tried to love as well as they could, and had made so many mistakes, and whose journeys had ended far too soon; and Bay saw this as their last chance to make things right, to save what they had nearly, themselves, killed.

And Bay's fingers touched wood, a drowned log at the

bottom of the cove, and they brushed weed, swaying in the current, only Bay knew: It wasn't wood, and it wasn't weed. Her lungs burning, she tangled her fingers in the hair, and she gathered the body into her arms, and with her legs kicking, a mother swan moving her cygnet through a patch of dangerous water, Bay brought Eliza to the surface.

Dan was beside her as they broke the surface, as Bay sputtered and passed his daughter into his arms. They emerged from the icy water to find a theater of blue light, strobes blinking from the forest. Crawling in the mud, Bay choked and spit out water and dead leaves. Her hand so numb she couldn't even feel her fingers, she reached over to Eliza's mouth and pulled off the silver tape.

Eliza's eyes were shut, her face blue, her lips white.

Danny heaved himself up from the mud, holding the young girl he'd brought into this world, and watching him Bay thought of Annie's birth, how Sean had taken their baby into his arms and held her while she cried for the first time. She watched as Dan slapped her back, trying to get her to spit the water out. He tilted back her head, shook her hard, kissing her face, frantically lowering her to the ground.

"Eliza," he said, as if he was just waking her up for school. Then he took a breath and blew it into his daughter's mouth. Then another, then another.

"Come back," Bay said, her voice cracking, and she could have sworn she heard the wings of angels fluttering in the air, of Sean and Charlie themselves hovering over Eliza.

But the words, whoever had spoken them, were filled with power. And so was Dan's will to save Eliza, and so, especially, was Eliza's need to survive.

Because she coughed. She coughed very hard, and she rolled over, to throw up seawater. She retched for a long time. And when she stopped, she looked up into her father's face, right into his eyes, and she said, "Daddy," and she threw her arms around his neck and started to cry.

34

THE WINTER SEEMED VERY LONG, LONGER THAN IT
ever had.

Christmas came and went, and for the first time in her
life, and as much as she had to be grateful for, Bay was
glad when it was over. The moons passed, some in a clear
sky, others obscured by fog, by clouds, by driving snow.
Bay kept an internal clock of the lunar cycles, always ac-
knowledging the power and brutality of nature—in the
sky, in the garden, in her own life.

So much in life seemed new, unfamiliar. She watched
the news, read the papers, had to ask herself whether she
had been sleeping through her life, surrounded by people
she thought she knew, she thought were friends. People
she had never known at all.

Mark and Alise Boland were charged with murder, attempted murder, kidnapping, bank fraud, conspiracy, and
embezzlement. Frank Allingham had been involved, too,
and was charged with bank fraud, conspiracy, and embez-

zlement. Sean's role had come to light: He had embezzled from his clients, but at the end he had died because he'd been opposed to killing Eliza.

"How stupid could I have been? How could I have missed it all?" she asked Tara one night in March.

"You missed it because you have trust," Tara said. They were bundled up in pajamas and robes, listening to a fierce gale roar off the Sound. "Because you loved Sean. Because you looked at Alise and Mark and saw them as friends."

"I thought they were friends," she said. "And so did Sean. And they killed him."

"I know," Tara said. "And they killed Eliza's mother."

"And they almost killed Eliza. Oh, Tara . . . what were we living with? In the midst, on the edge of all that, and I didn't know . . ."

March was just too soon for any understanding to emerge. The darkness that had finally almost engulfed them that November night, when Eliza had nearly died, was taking a long time to chase away. All of the children had nightmares. Eliza was, of course, the most affected. But Bay's kids were cut to the bone by everything that had happened. The crimes their father had committed, the one he had tried to prevent, the letter he had written to them through Annie.

Danny spent many nights and most weekends in Massachusetts, where Eliza had been readmitted to Banquo Hospital. Bay drove Annie up for a few visits, and as the girls' friendship deepened, and as Eliza made good progress, Bay and Dan found themselves so firmly entrenched in their parental roles, they rarely had any time alone.

It was probably for the best, Bay thought. Her kids needed her so much, wanted her home every second, and that's where she wanted to be. She immersed herself completely in them, as together they all felt their way through the dark months. Billy and Peggy were full of questions about their father, and what he had done, and how he had tried to help Eliza. Bay sensed them needing to turn their father into a hero, and she was surprised to hear Annie speaking to them one day.

"He wasn't a bad man, was he?" Peggy asked.

"No, he wasn't—it's right there in the letter," Billy said. "He wasn't going to let anything happen to Eliza."

"He loved us," Annie said. "We know that for sure. And the dad we knew wasn't a bad man."

"But is it still okay to love him?" Peggy asked, starting to cry. "If he did those things?"

"It's fine to love him," Bay said. "And it's also fine to be mad at him. You can feel both ways."

"The thing I'm maddest about," Billy said, "is that he's not here anymore. That's what SUCKS. I almost hate him for it."

Bay hugged her kids, and tried not to talk them into or out of any one feeling. She remembered a poem from long ago, about "the dark unknowability" of another person. What did that mean? She had been young, she had grown up in the Connecticut suburbs, the sun was shining. Or, if it wasn't one day, it would be the next. Good things happened to good people.

She had married Sean McCabe, a boy she'd known her whole life. His pictures, all through their house, showed the open, smiling, friendly face of the most popular kid at the beach, in school. A man his friends and clients had loved, had trusted with their money.

A crook.

In the end, though, Sean had turned back into Sean the good man, full of fire, who would put someone else's well-being, her life, above his own selfish desires. Bay had read Sean's letter to Annie over and over; she was pretty sure, from everything he said, that he had been prepared to go to jail to save Eliza's life.

Sometimes she wanted to call Danny, to talk it all over with him. But there was no getting past the fact that her husband had been involved with the people who had killed his wife and tried to kill Eliza. And right now, his daughter needed all of his attention.

As Bay's kids needed hers. Still, every crescent moon, she would look out the window, and wonder whether Danny could see the moon from wherever he was, and her heart would go out to him and Eliza.

Tara was always there for the family. Now that the case was over, she had started spending time with Joe Holmes. Since Bay was going to be a witness in the trial against the Bolands, he couldn't really get to know Tara's best friend yet—a fact that riled Tara no end.

"How can I know what I truly feel about him," Tara asked, "if I can't get you to check him out?"

"I think you already know what you truly feel about him." Bay smiled, watching Tara blush.

"It's the most amazing thing," Tara said. "Who would have thought, in the midst of the worst time of our lives, that I'd find myself falling in love with the man investigating my best friend's husband? Oh, Bay—will you always have bad feelings and memories when you see me with Joe?"

Bay shook her head, smiling. "Not if he's making you happy," she said, hugging Tara.

"I want you to be happy, too," Tara said, hugging her back. "I want you to make it through the rest of this awful winter, Bay. I want you to feel the sunlight again. I promise it's coming..."

"I'll hold you to that," Bay said, looking out at the brown garden and gray skies.

So she buried herself in seed catalogues, planning her own and Augusta's gardens for the spring, reading, taking care of her children, waiting for the sunlight Tara had promised.

When Eliza returned home from Banquo, she and Annie resumed their visits to each other. Bay picked Eliza up and dropped her off. She, Annie, and Tara were the first people Eliza wanted to see the day she got her new front teeth, to cap the ones that had been broken during her kidnapping.

All the silver, even the Paul Revere cup, was being held as evidence, but at least it had been recovered. Eliza was thrilled it had been found, and couldn't wait to have it back, for the memories it held. "The best things in life aren't things," she said, one day when Bay was driving her home. "One thing I learned in the hospital is that I still love my mother, no matter what."

"Can I tell you something?" Bay asked.

"Sure."

"You know, that night..."

"Yes," Eliza said. Her voice dropped. The memory of that night was still so traumatic for her, Bay wanted to tread very lightly.

"I felt your mother right there," Bay said.

Eliza looked across the seat.

"You did?"

Bay nodded. She remembered that feeling of extra strength, knowing that it had come from Sean and Charlie. "I did," Bay said. "Your mother was with me... with you. She was a strong woman, Eliza. Just like her daughter."

"I survived," Eliza said. "Thanks to you."

"Thanks to *you*," Bay said, knowing that one could

never remind one's own daughter, or one's own self, too often of the power she had within.

THE CASE WAS OVER, OFFICIALLY CLOSED, AND JOE HOLMES was proving to be not only tough and valiant at crime solving, but ineffably tender and gentle as a boyfriend. He held Tara's hand whenever they went walking together, and on nights when she thought of all that had happened, of how close her best friend had come to drowning in an almost-frozen cove, she would sometimes call Joe and he would drive right down Route Nine, to hold her till the sun came up.

One day he took her to the range, to teach her how to shoot his gun.

"I don't believe in guns, you know," she said.

"What do you think your grandfather would say about that?"

"Well, I believe in them for cops, but not for me," she said.

"I want you to have protection," Joe said. "I'm worried about you in that isolated spot all by yourself."

"Bay's right across the water. And the kids..."

"There are bad people out there, too, Tara," he said. "I can't stand to think of anything happening to you. To any of you."

"The Bolands turned out to be pretty bad," she said.

"Yes. The worst."

"What made them do it?" she asked.

"Greed," he said. "And competition. In some ways, it was a game to them."

"All that silver they stole," Tara said. "Just to have trophies...a way for Sean and Mark to one-up each other."

Joe nodded silently, his brown eyes dark and grave, listening as Tara proved his point.

The Bolands had driven each other, their illicit thrills fueling their marriage. The couple had liked material things, and their tastes had become more expensive with every payday. Mark had worked alone at Anchor Trust, but when he arrived at Shoreline Bank and came to know Sean, his old rival, better, he'd seen a wild man, with a need for casinos and other women.

Sean had also been more careless, and when he let one money order sneak through to Fiona Mills, the operation was all over. Sean had also taken Charlotte Connolly's silver cup; once she discovered that theft, she became suspicious of all the attention he'd paid to her. She had opened her books, run the numbers, and realized the fraud. Confronting Mark Boland with it had been her undoing.

And the killing began.

Giving Sean drugs had been Alise's idea. And he was so easy to seduce—she'd gotten him high aboard the *Aldebaran*—set him up for Mark. After the fight with Mark, they'd taken him down that deserted coast road, and he'd been too drugged-up, too badly hurt and bleeding—losing consciousness, unable to perceive the situation—to stop Mark from leaning in to shove the car into gear. They had been so careful about some things, but Alise had dropped the perfume bottle that had held her cocaine. Small details, compared with murder.

The bridge had been Sean's spot to stop and think— he'd showed it to them, met with them there—but the Bolands adopted it as their killing cove, the place to which they'd brought Eliza. If they had killed with the tide too low, her body might have stuck in the reeds.

They'd been waiting for the tide to rise and turn; to sweep Eliza's body out to sea.

"They almost got away with it," Tara said.

"No, they didn't," Joe said. "They didn't almost get away with it; they maintained their cover for a relatively long time, but there was never a chance we wouldn't have caught them. They were greedy and stupid, Tara. Good does triumph over evil. Thanks to you finding the slip of paper with the account number in Annie's model boat, the money from all their offshore accounts is coming back this week—we'll try to redistribute it to the people they stole it from."

"Then why do I need to learn how to shoot?"

"So you can triumph over evil," he said, laughing, holding her from behind as he helped her grip the 10mm, as he helped her straighten her arms and raise them, aiming for the target.

"I'll tell you what," Tara said. "I'll do this, just to prove that I have my grandfather's genes...that I can hit the target. But then that's the end of it."

"End of what?"

"End of my shooting career."

"On one condition," Joe said, his mouth against her ear as she raised the gun and squinted toward the target.

"What's that?"

"You let me take you dancing this weekend, to make up for the Pumpkin Ball."

"What was wrong with the Pumpkin Ball?" Tara asked. "I had a wonderful time."

"So did I," Joe said, kissing her neck. "But we were both working that night."

Tara aimed, cocked, and shot. She hit the bull's-eye, felt the recoil in her arms and shoulders, and handed Joe back his gun. He holstered it, never taking his eyes off her.

"Well," she said, stepping into his arms. "You might have been working, but I had the time of my life. The *best* time of my life."

"Don't tell the FBI," Joe said. "But so did I."

And he folded her into those steel arms and kissed her, and as Tara stood on tiptoes to kiss him back, she thought how she was forty-one and he was forty-seven, and how finally, after four whole decades and one extra year, she knew how it felt to be falling in love.

It felt wonderful.

THE VERNAL EQUINOX CAME, AND SUDDENLY IT WAS spring. All the bulbs that Bay had planted last fall came shooting out of the earth. She thought of the words from the liturgy: "faith in that which is seen and unseen."

Daffodils, jonquils, narcissus, hyacinths, and tulips were everywhere. Bay and Tara called a springtime meeting of the Irish Sisterhood, and inducted Annie and Eliza as members of the new generation. They brewed a pot of tea, put out Granny O'Toole's linen napkins and Granny Clarke's silver spoons. Lighting a candle, they invoked the spirits of the beloveds.

Putting their hands together in the middle of the circle, Bay and Tara locked eyes. They had been together forever, as had their grandmothers before them. Now came Annie and Eliza, so excited but solemn, clasping hands beneath theirs, part of the unending and unbroken circle of Irish sisterhood.

"Thick and thin," Tara said.

"*Faugh a ballagh*," Bay said, invoking the grannies' Gaelic battle cry.

"Fog-on-baylick," Annie said, repeating slowly.

"What does it mean?" Eliza asked.

" 'Clear the way!' " Tara translated.

"Because we're coming?" Annie said.

"Exactly," Bay said, overwhelmed with love for her daughter and Eliza. "Because we're forces to be reckoned with."

"The sisterhood," Eliza said. "I've never had real sisters before!"

"None of us has," Bay said, "except Annie."

"Some sisters," Tara said, "are truer than blood."

"That's how it already seems to me," Eliza said.

Annie nodded happily, looking around from Eliza to Tara and, finally, to her mother. "When Pegeen turns twelve, we'll have to induct her, too."

"We'll be waiting for her," Bay said, smiling back.

ONE SATURDAY MORNING, BAY WAS HANGING WASH OUT-side; Eliza had slept over the night before, and Joe and Tara had taken all the kids mini-golfing at Pirate's Cove. The sunlight had burst forth, as Tara had promised. It warmed Bay's head and bare arms as she soaked it up, savoring the delight of late spring, slowly shaking out the wet clothes and pinning them to the line.

She felt almost like a flower herself, coming back to life after a long winter underground. The clothes felt cool to her fingertips; the wooden clothespins clacked as she fixed them to the line. All of her senses were wide awake. Nearly a year had passed since the day Sean disappeared; she had been hanging out wash that day, too. She had felt happy that day—or had she? She remembered loving the summer weather, trying to love her life.

But there had been so much she didn't know. So many secrets covered up with layers and layers of lies. Bay felt so much wiser now. She had spent this past winter healing, helping her children, promising herself to live with her eyes wide open from now on. And it was working, because she felt herself starting to feel joy.

She heard soft splashing in the inlet behind her house. She turned around, and there, coming through the marsh from out in the Sound, she saw a beautiful, classic dory moving through the reeds and the calm, still water.

Dropping the basket of clothes, she ran down to the water's edge, her bare feet sinking into the warm silty mud. Grabbing hold of the bow, she pulled the boat up onto the shore.

"Dan," she said.

"I had to see you . . . I rowed over from the boatyard."

"All that way?" she asked, scanning the sparkling horizon.

"I left early," he said, pulling the oars into the boat, gazing into Bay's eyes. "May I come up for a minute?"

She nodded and he climbed out of the lovely boat. Bay touched her sides, feeling the smooth beauty of the wood, the superb fairing, the finished brightwork. Then she looked up at Dan: He wore jeans and a T-shirt, a sweater tied around his waist, and he looked rugged and tan, with blue eyes so incredibly vulnerable that Bay couldn't stand it.

"Why did you come?" she asked.

"How could I stay away?" he asked, stepping forward.

Bay inched back. Her heart was pounding, and her mouth was dry. The warm sun beat down on her head, and she felt her eyes fill with tears.

"Bay, what's wrong?" he asked.

"I never thought I'd make it through this winter," she said.

"Neither did I."

"The whole time, I've wanted to call you," she said. "I've wanted to."

"You have?" he asked, his eyes bright.

"So much! But we've been pulling together, just the four of us till now—well, five, with Tara. But getting ourselves back on solid ground."

"Just like me with Eliza," he said, nodding.

"And are you there?" she asked. "On solid ground?"

"I think so—better than we've ever been. She's doing so well, and I know a lot of it has been Annie. And you. She loves coming over here. I've wanted to join her."

"I've wanted you to," Bay said.

"But I didn't want to confuse the kids," Danny said, taking a step closer. "Because I knew that once I got here...things would start to change."

"I knew that, too," Bay said, feeling the heat shimmer between them, rising from the earth and sparkling in the air. They took a step closer.

"I hope it's okay I'm here now," he said. "Because I really couldn't wait any longer."

"We've made it through a lot, Danny," Bay said. "We made it through a very long winter."

"We did," Dan said, taking her into his arms.

He held her then, kissing her in the sun, with the summer in and around them, pulling them together. She felt herself unfolding, like a blade of green grass, as new and delicate as the ones springing out of the earth. And she felt Dan's kiss, like the sun, warming her and making her want to come to life again.

They held hands, and Bay found herself leading Dan down to the beach, onto the path up the hill and into the woods. About halfway to Little Beach, they took a right and headed into deeper trees, until they came to a clearing.

"This is where I put the swing," Dan said, with delight

and wonder, looking all around. Black walnut and oak trees grew in thick groves, but in the middle was a soft sandy rise covered with salt hay. Nestled into the grass was the weathered piece of driftwood, carved by the sea into a crescent moon.

Dan picked it up, running his hands over the wood, feeling the two rusted bolts and eyes, where he had tied the ropes to hang it. Looking overhead, he saw the two frayed rope ends, wafting in the breeze.

"It didn't last," he said.

"It lasted many years," Bay said. "The sun beats down, and the wind comes off the beach and marsh . . . it lasted many years. I'd swing on it every summer after you were gone, and think of you. And I brought Annie over here, when she was little . . . I'd ask her if she wanted to swing on the moon, and she'd know exactly where we were going. When the ropes broke, we were so sad."

"Couldn't you have asked someone to fix them for you?"

Bay thought of Sean, of how she had asked him, how he had said, "Sure, I will. As soon as I finish . . ." whatever it was. When she didn't respond, Dan took a step forward and put his arms around her.

"I would have come," he said. "If you had ever called me."

Then he began to kiss her. He slid his arm behind her back, supporting her as he very slowly lowered her onto the sandy ground. He untied the sweater from around his waist and spread it out; she noticed the way he smoothed it down, and the way he gently eased her till she was lying back upon it.

Here in the clearing of the crescent moon, she felt his lips so tenderly kissing hers, his rough hands stroking her face, her hair, his face buried in the side of her neck. She tasted his skin, salty and warm with sweat and salt spray from his long row. His hands moved gently, but their surfaces were rough, and she moaned, liking the feel of the friction.

It all seemed new, in every way, as if it was the very first time for everything: making love outdoors, being touched with such hunger and tenderness, both at once, by the man she had always loved. She wanted to pay attention to every detail, so she would have this moment with her forever: the way the sun struck Danny's hair, and how the leaves threw dappled shadows on the ground, and how his mouth felt so hot on hers, and how engrossed and in love was the look in his eyes.

But then something happened, and Bay was separated from thought. Her senses took over, and she was taken by the sun, and their skin, by the hard and the wet, the slide of their bodies and the solidity of the ground, the heat in his kiss and the passion in hers, his strong arms holding her and the feeling that although making love to Dan Connolly was brand-new to her, it was also ancient and familiar, and something she had wanted for her whole life.

When it was over, they lay still in each other's arms, far from words. The sun moved above the branches, writing time on the sandy ground. Bay must have dozed, because she woke with a start, with Dan holding her.

"I'm right here," he whispered, and Bay opened her eyes and knew that his words were true and always would be.

"So am I," she said.

After a winter longer than this last season, than the last few months—years of winter, of feelings being frozen and buried inside herself—Bay felt the summer inside her skin.

Summer meant the garden. It meant roses, hollyhocks, larkspur, geraniums. It meant birds. It meant long days and starry nights. Summer was hot sand and blue water. It was the season of pleasure, of holding on to every joy and blessing for as long as possible, before letting it go, to welcome the next and the next.

They pulled each other up, brushing off sand and dry grass, feeling like teenagers, only better—teenagers were too young to know how swiftly moved the current, how powerful was the tide. When you found something worth keeping, you picked it up—because you never knew when the sea might rise and wash it away.

Dan pulled the driftwood moon from the sand, dusted it off, tucked it under his arm—to make it new again, she knew. To hang it in the sky for her. His movements were slow, the aftermath of their lovemaking, and when Bay took his hand, she felt it trembling. Or perhaps hers was. She wanted to tell him what she was thinking—that she loved him. That she always had.

But instead, she just looked up into his face, squinting in the bright sunlight, and felt grateful that he had come back. That after all this time her first love was here again. It was spring now, with all of summer still to come. There would be time to find the right words.

So they walked back through the path, past the turnoff to the Indian Grave and the one to Little Beach, back down the hill to the main beach, and along the sandy road to Bay's house.

The children had returned from playing mini golf. Tara and Joe sat on the porch, swinging back and forth on the glider. Billy and Pegeen were having a catch in the side yard, the thwack of the baseball hitting their gloves hard and rhythmic.

"Dad, I didn't know you were coming over!" Eliza called.

"Yep, I did. I had to."

At his words, Bay blushed, but didn't react.

"It's a really pretty boat," Annie said. "Did you make it?"

"I did," Dan said.

"My father builds the best boats around," Eliza said.

"It reminds me of the boat I made for Daddy," Annie said. "My little green dory. The one where he hid the shell...and the letter."

"The letter that saved my life," Eliza said.

"I know," Dan said. He reached into the boat and pulled out the oars—they were brightly varnished, gleaming in the sun. "It's supposed to remind you of that boat."

"Why?" Annie asked, frowning, still not understanding.

"Because it's for you, Annie," Dan said.

"Me?"

"Your father wanted you to have it."

Bay held back tears as she watched her daughter's face. Annie's eyes widened with shock, then a dawning realization. "But I thought—" she said.

"Yes. I think your mom told you that he came to see me last summer, to talk to me about building you a boat just like your dory."

"I know," she whispered, her eyes flooding. "Mom told me. But I thought he died before that could happen."

"No," Dan said. "He told me exactly what he wanted. He brought me the model you'd made, to show me. He was very proud of it...and you, Annie."

"He said that?" Annie asked.

Danny nodded, handing her the oars. "We talked about you a lot. He said you're wonderful and talented, and he wanted to make sure the boat I'd build you could live up to the model you'd made for him."

"Thank you, Mr. Connolly," Annie said, crying for a minute, hugging the oars to her chest.

"Can you take me for a row?" Eliza asked after a moment, bumping Annie gently on the arm.

Annie looked at her mother, to ask if it was okay. Bay still couldn't quite speak, but she also couldn't quite stop smiling. She nodded, and holding the bow steady on the sand, Danny helped the girls climb in.

Bay watched Annie, thinking of how brave people had to be, to accept the wonder of life—the gift of a new boat, the chance to be with friends on the water and forget the fears that had held them down before, the kiss of the sun, the fact that no one, not even your own father, was perfect, but knowing, somehow, that love was integral to it all, inherent in every moment.

And so, Bay took a step forward, into the clear water of the shallow cove, and helped Dan give the boat a gentle push. It floated like a stick on the current, hovering still for a moment, and then Annie got the oars settled into the oarlocks.

She dipped one oar into the water, and then the other. The dory weaved back and forth, with both girls laughing, with Tara and Joe calling encouragement from the porch, with Peggy and Billy looking on and razzing their big sister. Bay took Danny's hand; if the kids saw, that was okay with her.

Suddenly Annie got the rhythm, dipping both oars at once, pulling the handles into her chest... The boat began to move in a straight line, the water behind rippling in a V. And as she did, Bay could see that Dan had painted the boat's name on the transom—the same name Annie had put on her model boat, to remind her father who he should row home to:

ANNIE

"I'm doing it," she called. "I've got it!"
"You do, Annie," Bay called out. "You do."

"*Faugh a ballagh*," Tara shouted the sisterhood's battle cry from the porch: *Clear the way* . . .

Dan squeezed Bay's hand, and once again it was all she could do to keep from saying the words out loud: I love you. They were right there, in the air. They were shimmering like quince blossoms on a branch, like morning glories on a vine, just waiting to be picked for a beautiful bouquet.

But Bay McCabe was a gardener, and a mother, and a woman in love, and this year she had learned that there was a season for everything. Every single thing. There was time, plenty of time.

They had the whole summer ahead of them, and like that sweet season so many years ago, it was going to be perfect.

About the Author

LUANNE RICE is the author of twenty-seven novels, most recently *The Geometry of Sisters, Last Kiss, Light of the Moon, What Matters Most, The Edge of Winter, Sandcastles, Summer of Roses, Summer's Child,* and *Silver Bells*. She lives in New York City and Old Lyme, Connecticut.